The Foxtrot's Easy

D1438437

ANDREA RUSSELL

Published by Howard Publishing

A CIP catalogue record for this book is available from the British Library.

ISBN 978-1-7390852-0-9

Book layout and cover design by Clare Brayshaw

Prepared and printed by:

York Publishing Services Ltd
64 Hallfield Road
Layerthorpe
York YO31 7ZQ

Tel: 01904 431213

Website: www.yps-publishing.co.uk

The Foxtrot's Easy

Foreword

As many people do, at a certain point in my life, I longed to get away from my career as a journalist and write the novel that had been brewing in me for some time. But where? My next-door neighbour suggested England and, more precisely, York. 'It's a lovely city – not too big, nor too small. It has a beautiful cathedral and a fine university, where my brother-in-law, Graeme, is a professor in Politics. I'm sure he'd be happy to show you around.'

I followed her advice and I've never looked back. Two years later Graeme and I married.

He was several years older than I, and a built-up shoe and metal brace supported the right leg that had never fully recovered from a childhood attack of polio. But it wasn't only his courage, grace and sense of humour that won my heart – Graeme was devilishly good looking, too. I fell for him, hook, line and sinker.

The Foxtrot's Easy is his story. Much of it is true. As he told me about his life, before and after polio, he was glad that I planned to write a book about the extraordinary boarding school that changed his life – Maiden Erlegh School for Boys. We ended up with several hours of memories, all recorded on audio cassettes. He also managed to find some fellow classmates on the social networking site, Friends Reunited; later, I visited them and recorded their memories, as well.

Sadly, the fabulous house of Maiden Erlegh, once owned by the wealthy diamond magnate, Solly Joel, no longer exists, but some of its land and lake are now a nature reserve, overseen by Grahame Hawker, Park Ranger of the property. He and his wife, Lesley have been a tremendous help in getting *The Foxtrot's Easy* published.

Graeme died ten years after we married, and I continue to thank my lucky stars I met him.

Chapter 1

Crying was always shameful, but at night it was dangerous. Crying might wake Father, Dundee's most famous eye doctor and Scotland's Royal Eye Surgeon. If King George V was relaxing at Balmoral and out of the blue, something hurt his eye, they'd send for Father. And if Father hadn't had a good night's sleep, he might blind the King and it would be Alastair's and my fault. He was six, I was four.

Our beds stood side by side on the top floor above our parents' room. Luckily, I was born a light sleeper, so the second Alastair woke me with his groanings, I knew what to do. One of his horrible earaches had struck. My job was to fetch Berry, our nanny, before the pain got so bad, he woke Father.

Berry was a lighter sleeper than even me. Up she'd pop like a jack-in-the-box, snatch the olive oil from her bedside table and fill a hot water bottle at her sink. Later, if Alastair wouldn't settle, she'd carry me to her bed and sleep in mine.

Mother tried several nannies before hiring Berry. Some we hated, some we liked, but if they were sound sleepers, out they'd go. We thought Nanny McGregor was perfect, till Mother found her one night in the back garden with her young man.

'Imagine,' Mother said, 'a vixen like that sleeping under our roof.'

Then came Berry, who truly was perfect. She could spot a four-leaf clover just by looking down. 'There's one,' she'd say, and pinching it off, took it home to Mother, who believed in such things.

But nothing could fix Alastair. Pus was chewing away the bone behind his ear, and a surgeon in hospital would have to cut the rotten bit out. It was a serious operation, but he wouldn't die. 'Do you promise?' I asked Father.

'I promise you Dr Hickling is the finest surgeon I know. Now, let's go find your mother.'

Nights were the worst for missing Alastair, for that was the time he and I made up stories as we lay in bed, him telling a little, me a little, till we had a great adventure. I couldn't do it alone. Berry found me staring at his empty bed and asked if I were all right. 'Of course,' I said, but she took to sleeping in his spot, just in case. In case what, she didn't say.

* * *

Alastair was gone six weeks and came home a strange and pitiful thing. We didn't know what to say until, as we were getting ready for bed, he asked me what his scar looked like. 'Purple railroad tracks,' I said, which pleased him and our splendid stories returned.

Spring came, but Alastair was still scrawny and frail. The dreich Dundee air was hopeless for recovery, Father declared and, of all the cruellest, unfair things in the world, Alastair got sent cruising round the Mediterranean Sea! With Berry!

'Why can't I go?' I raged, stamping my foot.

'You're not ill, that's why,' Mother said. 'Be glad you're sturdy and strong.'

'I wish I weren't.'

'Don't you ever say that! The Devil might hear you.' She rushed to get her coat and helped me on with mine.

'Where are we going?'

'Shush,' was all she said. Outside, she showed me how to cross my fingers tight, and keep them crossed until we touched iron. 'There!' she said, breathing hard. 'That's how to undo bad luck.'

This time, Alastair disappeared for a month. The good part was that Mother went on one of her golfing trips to Carnoustie, and Father took me to Craigisla, the big estate where Mother grew up. Here, he taught me how to run round the inside of the dry fountain, faster and faster, till I was nearly sideways; and when he held out his arms, I hurled myself into them. 'Oof!' he grunted and laughed. 'I see a future in rugby for you, son. You've got the fast Moodie legs!'

'I do?'

'Yes! You might follow in my footsteps.'

These were the finest words I'd ever heard. Everyone knew that, before turning to eyes, Father played on Scotland's National Rugby Team. Photographs on our sitting room walls proved it, though he looked quite different then.

I loved that trip, just him and me. What a shame he had to spend so much time on people's eyes. I said this to him and he said eyes were his business, like some people worked in the marmalade trade or in linen. We weren't rich, the way Mother's family was.

'Our house is a sensible sandstone, just right for a working doctor.'

He could be right. I liked hearing the trains below our bedroom, as they chugged along the shore of the River Tay, carrying goods to the fine cities of Great Britain and beyond.

When Alastair came back in good health at last, he was due to start proper school that autumn. The law said children of seven had to, no matter what. The only one near us taught children from the Dundee docks. Some were dark-skinned and poor; others were just the usual Dundee poor. But they all carried diseases. Mother didn't even like it when Father took us to watch them unloading jute from the mile-high ships lined up in the harbour, their black smokestacks pluming out clouds. 'Alastair's just got well, and he's not about to sit cheek by jowl beside filthy bairns with nits and cholera.'

A doctor-friend of Father's suggested Miss Kidd, who ran a little school in her flat for other doctors' children. Mother was satisfied and so was the School Board.

Alastair was happy at Miss Kidd's. Sometimes at night, instead of telling stories, he taught me what he'd learned: how to add numbers and the sounds of the alphabet. He made an 'a' sound, and I'd say, 'map' or 'apple.' I thought this was great, another kind of game.

'Watch what Graeme can do,' Alastair announced to our parents one night when we gathered as always in the sitting room before our bedtime and their dinner. I was sitting in front of the fire, tracing my finger along the deer and birds in the carpet. Father had set up the card table to start a jigsaw puzzle. 'Spell "dog," Graeme,' and I did, hopping around like one myself. Map – certainly. Tree – easy-peasy. Taking a pencil and paper from the table, he wrote: '3+2' and I got it right.

'Oh,' Mother said, 'you really are marvellous.'

And because I was so very marvellous, I went off to Miss Kidd's too, even though I was only five.

So began my secret name, Marvellous Me. In one of Alastair's comic books, I'd seen a boy, his chest puffed out, eyes closed and thumbs tucked into his braces. He looked so happy and proud, I decided to become that boy, though I never said the name out loud.

I wasn't sure if Alastair was happy about me joining him at Miss Kidd's. I could be a pain, he said. I got so excited about everything.

We were different, him and me. He didn't smile much and didn't like looking at people. He found that hard. 'Look people in the eye when you greet them,' Father told him. 'Hold out your hand, not a fish! Watch how Graeme does it.' Alastair was fine with family, but with strangers, he looked away as if they were fools. Perhaps there was something wrong with me for being so happy and friendly.

Anyway, I liked Miss Kidd's.

There were never more than six of us sitting at small desks near windows or curled on a sofa reading. One thing distracted me though. Miss Kidd had an affliction. I wished my parents had warned me. Inside her collar, which went down into a V, were what could only be her lungs, but on the outside of her body instead of inside, where ladies' lungs usually were. A dark line separated them. I had the sense not to ask Miss Kidd about them. Don't make personal remarks, my parents said, and this might be one.

I'd be safe asking them, however. Surely.

They were sitting in their usual chairs before the fireplace, Mother with her G and T, Father with his whisky. 'There's something I've been thinking about,' I said in a wondering voice.

'And what's that?' Mother asked.

'Are there many people with lungs on their outsides?'

'I'm – not sure,' she said slowly. 'I wouldn't think so.'

'That's what I thought,' I said, 'but Miss Kidd's are. I can see them.'

No one said anything for the longest time, and I knew I shouldn't have brought up the subject of lungs. Mother stood and walked to the hearth. 'Oh my. Alex, save me,' she said. But my father had his eyes closed. He was shaking, which meant he was about to have a laughing fit. Luckily, this didn't happen often because, when he did, the man exploded.

He began with a low rumble, then threw his head up toward the ceiling. Huge shouts shot from his mouth. Tears poured from his eyes, and I knew why – he was laughing at me.

I looked to Mother for help, but she was holding on to chairs as if her legs couldn't hold her up anymore.

The worst thing in the world was when parents laughed at you. They said they were laughing *with* you, but that made no difference. My tears came, too. Here I was explaining something scientific and they thought it was the funniest thing in the world.

Now I had noticed that when things got too much to bear, my legs had a life of their own. Without my even knowing, they'd march me out of the room. This time, I found myself in the front hall.

Alastair followed, no laughter from him. 'They're not lungs. They're her bosoms. Women have bosoms. You know that.'

'Of course I know that.' I hissed. 'Do you think I'm an idiot?' All women had bosoms, even my mother, but you couldn't see hers, thank the Lord. 'Bosoms' was one of those faraway, adult words one never said. 'Bosom' if you had to. 'Bosoms' – never.

* * *

Despite these dangers, I continued to learn, and by the following year I could do basic sums, read, write and speak a few words of French. Alastair also made good progress.

One evening Father announced, 'Come autumn, Alastair will be going to Bannerman School for Boys. Not more than thirty students, so one won't get lost. From all reports, it's a grand place. Right by the sea, grounds all around, and a golf course next door. Sounds like a holiday, eh?'

'I'll be going, too, won't I?' I asked.

'Oh, no, you're far too young. You've got another year with Miss Kidd. Maybe two.'

He might as well have said, 'Don't worry, lad, we're going to cut off your head, but you'll still be able to walk around and go places. You won't notice a thing.'

Over the next week I begged and wept. In my life of nearly seven years, I had spent every minute with Alastair – except during his operation. We slept, ate and played together; he was by my side at school, helping me not make mistakes over lungs and things.

But my parents held firm. No matter how I pleaded, they would not let me go to Bannerman. So I thought some more.

When you were young, parents ran your life; you could only fight back so far. They could kill you if they wanted but they didn't want to go to prison. And they did love you, there was that. And you loved them – usually. It was an agreement of sorts.

So I took a big chance coming downstairs with my satchel going bangetty-bang all the way, to say farewell in my most reasonable style. 'If I can't go to Bannerman with Alastair, I will not live in this house any longer. I'm sorry to do this to you, but I'm leaving.'

Mother looked at Father. And he said, 'Well, my son, we can't have that, can we? We'd be terribly lonely without you. It just so happens that your mother has been on the phone with your Aunt Herald, and they've come up with a plan. Since you and your cousin Jack are the same age, we've decided to send you both to Bannerman, along with Alastair. That way, you can keep each other company. Stave off the barbarians.'

I didn't know what barbarians were, and I wasn't so keen on going with Jack – he was as thick as two planks – but I did hear him say that I was going to Bannerman. I was glad. I didn't want to live on the streets of Dundee, but I would have.

Chapter 2

Mother and Father drove us to Bannerman on the first of October, stopping at St Andrews to pick up Jack, then heading to the Kirkcaldy Road. We sat in the back wearing our new uniforms – grey jackets piped in red. They were nervous, I could tell, but not me. I'd be with Alastair, so what could go wrong? Father did his best to jolly them along with 'I Spy' and funny songs, but only I joined in. Mother kept looking out of the window and smoking. 'How much longer, for Heaven's sake?' I asked.

We got to Largoward, a wee village with just a couple of stone cottages and a shop, and turned left toward the sea. Then came a crossroads with big stone pillars on the other side. 'Well, boys,' Father said, 'this is it.'

We stared at the heavy grey stones. 'Impressive,' Mother said.

Father drove through the entrance, saying, '*Iacta alea est*,' which, he told us, Caesar said as he crossed the Rubicon river. It meant, 'The die is cast,' but not like when a worker threw dye into a vat of linen. A 'die' meant one dice – the kind you roll in a game. And the whole thing meant – no going back.

I liked the strange Latin phrase, with all those ya-ya sounds. But there was something fearsome about it, too. If you were wrong, too late. Your goose was cooked.

We continued, dark trees arching on either side. At last, as the sky opened up to blue, about a cricket field away was a big stone house with a fine tower on the right corner. 'There she is, lads.'

We piled out, Father leaving the car in a gravelled area where others were parked. I could see boys, all big, gathered in a courtyard, shoving each other, staggering about, laughing. As a man walked toward us, they stopped, and Father introduced us to the headmaster, Mr Moffet. A hard ball stuck out in the middle of his skinny neck.

Like a fox grabbed a rabbit – I nearly yelled it hurt so much – he snatched my hand; then sweet as you please, turned to my parents to chitter-chatter about the lovely summer, a good year for whisky, ho-ho.

'Rotheringham!' Mr Moffet shouted out of nowhere. A boy ran up, panting and smoothing his yellow hair. Mr Moffet turned back to my parents. 'Long farewells are not advised,' he said.

'But I thought we were staying for lunch.' Mother looked panicky, but Father stuck out his hand for us to shake, and after a bumbling hug from Mother, they left.

'Right,' said Mr Moffet, 'let's get you sorted.' He looked at his clipboard. 'Alastair Reid Moodie, or, as you will be called from now on, Moodie One. Age nine?'

'Yes, sir.'

'You're in Hood House. Best all-round last year. You'll have to work hard not to let them down.' He looked at Jack and me. 'And you two, which is which? You look the same.'

'My name is Graeme Cochrane Moodie, sir,' I said in my best, firm fashion.

'No need for the middle bit, young man.' My face went hot. 'You're Moodie Two now. How old are you?'

'Seven, sir, two weeks ago.'

'Small for your age, aren't you? He looked at Jack, still half-hiding behind me. 'And you must be Hunter.'

'Yes, sir. I was seven four weeks ago. I'm older.'

'Nelson House. Both of you. Room Six. Rotheringham will show you the ropes, eh, boy?'

'I'd be pleased, sir,' he said, snapping his heels together like a soldier.

'You'll find there are a great number of ropes to learn at Bannerman.' Away he went, studying his board, to another group of names.

Rotheringham jerked a pretend-rope from his neck, crossed his eyes and stuck out his tongue like a dead man. 'Let's go, fellows,' he said. 'See if you can last three days.'

We hobbled after him into an enormous hall, where paintings of old people in wigs watched Rotheringham dash up the staircase two steps at a time. A dim stained-glass window hung in the clammy landing.

Our room had six beds, Jack's and mine side by side. A gigantic mistake! I should be with Alastair, in Hood House!

A woman in a nurse's headdress announced she was called Matron. When I asked about being with Alastair, she smiled as if I were a silly creature. 'That could never be, my dear. Ages are kept strictly together. Now, these first days are very important. Most boys already have their friends, so you'll have to impress them. Just laugh at their tricks. You'll get along, and whatever you do, don't cry. You'll be ruined if you do.'

The next few days were nothing but rules. They threw them at us like stones. Wake at seven. Wash. Dress. Run a mile to the pond. Run back. Breakfast. Prayers. Classes. Dinner. Games. More class. Prep. Tea. More prep. More prayers. Lights out. If you were good, you got a star. If you were the tiniest bit bad, you got a stripe and one stripe undid two stars.

Nothing was how I imagined! I saw myself, sitting on a bench, sun all around. A boy sits down and says, 'Hello, my name is Rory,' and he likes me right away because I'm clever and fun. Why wouldn't he? I'm Marvellous Me.

* * *

About the third day, everyone was called into the gymnasium, empty except for a table in the middle. Boys lined along the walls, muttering, heads down. I did the same. The others knew what was coming; I did not. A wild, frightened feeling held us. Mr Moffet came in holding a long, thin yellow stick, which he slapped against his leg. I'd never heard so many people make so little noise.

'Would Turnbull step forward,' he said, and a boy, older than Alastair, twelve, maybe, stepped forward. 'Turnbull, here, has committed a grievous offence, made more grievous on two accounts. One, he disobeyed a rule, which is loathsome. But even more despicable, a fault I cannot abide, he will not confess to his crime, even though we have two witnesses. In short, he is a liar.

'Therefore, I am compelled to mete out punishment. I ask that Reid, one of our senior boys, an exemplary lad and strapping fellow,' and he made 'strapping' loud and important, 'will carry out the deed. Reid!' And out stepped, yes, a strapping fellow, wide and strong with bushy eyebrows and a piggy nose. 'Cane him. I'll tell you when to stop.'

I'd seen this in cartoons, when Henty got into trouble at school, but never in real life. I looked at the normal, steady faces. No one was shocked. Across the room, Alastair had his grey, sleepy look. Jack looked the way I felt – terrified – and put half his body behind me, leaning against my back. I leant backwards against him, giving both of us comfort.

Our parents weren't hurting parents. Alastair got the slipper sometimes for being rude, and Mother sometimes gave me a whack on my bottom to hurry me along, but that didn't count. Mr Moffet handed his cane to Reid, while Turnbull, white-faced and shaking, bent over the table, hands together in a prayer.

A singing, whipping sound cut the air. 'Harder, please,' Mr Moffet said. And so it went. Swish, whack, swish, whack. Turnbull made no sound at first, then gave out a shivering humming that turned into a fast in-and-out breath, then louder gasps that became high, little calls of 'oh, oh,' until he cried out, 'stop!' and I knew he was broken, truly broken. Reid looked to Mr Moffet, but the man shook his head. And each time Turnbull shouted 'stop' it was like another hunk of him broke off and landed on the floor.

'I did it, I did it!' Turnbull cried into his hands, begging for mercy from Mr Moffet, who at last gave a signal to stop. I felt sorry for Reid, being dragged into such wickedness. Blood ran down the back of Turnbull's legs.

Then we went to dinner.

I couldn't sleep for the longest time. Yellow cane cutting, the many different sounds. I didn't even know Turnbull's crime. What would I have to do to be hauled up and caned till I bled? The dormitory was quiet, all six of us. I whispered, 'Jack?' to the bed next to me, but he just sighed in and out. I had to get away. And getting out was impossible. I'd cooked my own goose. *Iacta alea est.*

* * *

Ten weeks to go.

Next morning, at breakfast, Jack puked on the bench where we were sitting. Everyone laughed. He cried and a kitchen maid took him away to Matron. At first I was glad; I'd wanted to get away from Jack to show the other boys I was a topping fellow. Whistling, I went to the dormitory to fetch my books for the first class.

Older boys passed, ignoring me as they headed down the corridor with long, sure strides. I was a scurrying little thing, tiny-stepped, trying to please.

I watched them saunter toward the light from the window on the landing. Nothing for it. Get going, Moodie Two. But the oddest thing – I could not take another step. My legs wouldn't move. Before me stretched the hall to Mr Cubbage's class. Behind was the dormitory. I hated both.

'Eeh, lad – what's the matter?' From a room ahead came a housemaid, carrying a bucket and mop. She waited for me to speak, and when I didn't, put her hand on my shoulder. 'This won't do, you standing there, still as a statue. You forget something?' She had a blue kerchief tied behind her ears. Tears pushed up from under my cheeks. 'Ah, don't cry, sweetheart. You're new, aren't you? It's hard at first. It'll be all right in time. Tell me your name.'

'Moo-moo-d.' She pulled a handkerchief from her pinny pocket.

'There, there. Take a few deep breaths. Like me.' She sucked in air, lifting her shoulders toward her ears. 'Pretend you're a bellows.'

The two of us puffed away, and eventually I got out my name. Even the 'Two' part.

'Moodie Two? Oh, I don't like those names. What's your real name?'

'Graeme.'

'Ah, that's a fine name. Do you spell it with an 'H'?'

'No. I spell it "G-R-A-E-M-E." The Scottish way.'

'Ah.' And she said it so kindly, I longed to wrap my arms around her pinny and stay like that for the rest of my life. 'My name's Aileen,' she whispered. 'Do you ken where you're going?'

I nodded. 'Mr Cubbage. Downstairs.'

'Then you'd best be off. It won't get any better, standing here like a lost soul.'

'No,' I said, still not moving.

'I've got an idea. I'll watch you go down the stairs. What do you say?' I nodded. 'Let's go. On the count of three.' She leant her bucket and mop against the heavy dark panelling, held out her right leg. I matched her, and 'One-two-three,' we were off. The tricky part came when we got to the first step, but I had got myself going and I didn't want to stop.

The air outside Mr Cubbage's classroom closed my throat. Inside, the faces were sharp as knives. I heard Mr Cubbage explaining how to borrow numbers, something I already knew from Miss Kidd. I wanted to show how clever I was, but his wobbly cheeks and the way he twiddled with his watch chain froze my legs again.

'Hey!' shouted Walker. 'I see Moodie Two!' The class looked up, a few stood and pointed. I had my hand on the knob when Mr Cubbage's face appeared in the window and the door swung open, knocking me backward against Aileen. Dear God save me.

'What's going on?' he barked, looking down at me.

Trying to be helpful, Aileen said, 'Nothing, sir. I found the laddie upstairs, feeling a wee bit shoogly.' She put her hand on my shoulder. 'I think he'd lost his way. I was just helping him find the right place.' She bobbed a little curtsey.

Mr Cubbage yanked me into the classroom. To tell the truth, I don't think I could have made it by myself. He stood me in front of the eight boys. My eyes closed, for they weren't ready for being in the room. Mr Cubbage's voice came at my ear. 'Good of you to join us, Moodie Two. Care to open your eyes? These boys are an ugly lot, but they can't be that bad.' Tears burned my cheeks. 'Oh dear, Moodie Two is crying. Poor wee soulie. What do we say about crying?'

A great shout went up. 'Only cowards cry!'

* * *

Eight weeks to go.

I never ever saw Alastair – the only reason I wanted to go to this bowfing hell-hole was to be with him. He might as well have been on the moon. Had our parents known we'd be kept apart? They must have, which meant they lied.

Autumn slowly drove the leaves from the trees. Gardeners raked them into big piles that the junior boys played in at free-time. My shadow, Jack, and I did, too, pretending to be merry.

I hated free time. It wasn't like afternoon games, when everything was organised. Free time showed who your friends were, and I had none. Only Jack. So he and I jumped in leaf piles and picked up acorns but we didn't really see them because we were dying of loneliness. When a fat boy named McDonald asked to join us, Jack said yes, the eejit. People called McDonald 'Specky' because he wore glasses and worse, he was said to be wet, which meant he cried and weed in his pants. I planned my escape to a worthier group.

A fellow named Baillie was the leader of the Year Twos. If I could get in with him, I'd be moving toward Marvellous Me again. The next day, after lunch, I grabbed my chance. Sneakily, I followed him out the side door instead of the front door where Jack always waited for me. Baillie was leaning against an oak, surveying the world. Swallowing hard, I sauntered up, smooth as butter, my chest sticking out with a rolled-up *Beano* comic inside my jumper. Father had ordered me a subscription. The best comics came out of Dundee. It was still in its wrapper.

'Hey, Baillie, look at what I've got.' I pulled the comic from my jumper. 'I happen to have here, hot off the press,' (my father's expression), 'the newest *Beano*. Baillie half closed his eyes, but his neck stretched toward me.

'Want to see it?' I paused; then added, 'when I'm done?'

He shrugged. 'Maybe.' But before I could react, he swooped the Beano away, like a bloody hawk. 'Oh,' he said, turning. 'Thanks.'

'Wait!'

'What?'

'"When I'm done!"' I said.

'But I don't want it then. I want it now.' I never thought so much meanness could come from one person. He bounced it back and forth as if it were burning his hands. 'Ooh, ooh, boys, look out! Hot off the press!' In a flash, three or four thugs ran up. 'Look what Muddy Two gave me. Wasn't that nice?'

'Topping!'

'Hey, can I see it after you?' Rotheringham asked.

'Hmmm. Let's see.' He put his hand on his chin. 'Yes. Then Palmer.' He pointed. 'Then Hargreaves, then, oh, I don't care, Muddy, I suppose. Don't worry, Mud, you'll get it back by Christmas. That all right?'

* * *

Six weeks to go.

Every Sunday we had to write a letter home. We lined up outside the dining room and handed them to Mr Moffet, so he could check that we covered both sides of the sheet.

What we wrote was supposed to be good news. 'Bannerman was founded on the principle of turning you into fine British officers and gentlemen. That's why your parents sent you. And I trust you will make them proud. No whingeing. Possible topics for your letters are the jolly games we play, what themes you wrote, if you've won any stars, who your favourite teacher is, all your new friends. Use your imagination.'

Imagination was right.

I was too young for rugby but we did practice cricket, and my Moodie legs ran like the wind. But last week, I tried to catch a ball when I was facing the sun. The ball whacked me right in the eye. My eyebrow bled so I couldn't see. Mr Burns sent me off to Matron, who pressed a bandage on it till it stopped. 'You're a fine, brave lad, aren't you? You'll have a nasty black eye. It's getting swollen already. Come back tomorrow and let me see it.'

I was proud. Even Baillie came to have a look after breakfast.

On Sunday, I wrote to Mother and Father, like a true Lathallian, 'Guess what? I got a cricket ball in the eye, but I'm all right now. Don't worry. It didn't hurt much, and I didn't cry.' And then I went on with the usual rubbish.

Next day, who should I see but Mr Moffet, standing outside Mr Cubbage's class. 'I'd like a word, Moodie Two. Over here.'

'Yes sir.' His tall body curved over mine as I leant against the wall. I forced my face upward and stared at the lump on his neck.

'You can't get a cricket ball *in* the eye. It's much too big.' He poked a finger into my chest. 'Accuracy is all, my boy. Be careful what you say.'

That dirty bugger had read my letter. Read them all, I found out later.

* * *

Four weeks to go.

They put our marks on the notice board, first to last. The prize for being the highest was sitting in the back row nearest the door; the lowest in the front row, nearest the teacher. It was a hilarious reward – to be allowed to sit as far as possible from the smelly things.

I knew I was clever, but loneliness was making me stupid. I couldn't keep my mind on work. All I wanted was to be a jolly chap, win races and stroll the way they did, as if on invisible wheels. By half term, I found myself two seats from Mr Cubbage's desk! This was beyond horror.

I sat on my bed, thinking. By some terrible misfortune I found myself here. I – who was not big, nor did I look like I rolled on wheels – but I was certainly not *stupid*. Moodie Two – if there's one thing you can do, you can get to the back-row desk, and never have to smell Mr Cubbage or any other bloody teacher again.

Two weeks later, with only a little effort, I won the prized desk, nearest the door. The air was sweet as roses.

* * *

Two pissing weeks left.

Mother had our school jackets made in Dundee, at Reuben Brothers Tailors. They were the best, she said, and made Father's suits as well. So I was proud of the label stitched just under the inside pocket. In early December, on an unusually warm day after lunch, Jack, Specky and I were playing hard at football. I took off my jacket and folded it carefully, as I was told to do, under an oak. When they rang the bell I found my jacket lying in a heap under the tree. Oh well, someone being mean again.

As we stood in line to go in, Baillie, behind me, said, 'I see you got your jacket at one of those horrible little Jewish tailors. My mother says their glasses are so thick they can't sew straight.'

* * *

During the last week I dreaded seeing my parents in case I cried. From his throne at the head table, Mr Moffet told us again and again the importance of not doing that. 'Now lads, I hope that you have a joyous holiday. I know that for some of you – the junior boys in particular – this term has seemed long. So when you greet your parents, show them that their money has not been wasted. You have become proper gentlemen.

'Shake your father's hand with vigour. Look him squarely in the eye. As for your mother, one of the weaker sex, she may want to kiss your cheek. Receive it with grace, but do not fling your arms about her like some jungle bunny and above all, under any circumstances, do not disgrace your school by weeping.'

That final morning, we sat in the dining room, waiting to be fetched. Alastair and I, together at last. Jack had already left with Aunt Herald. We'd watched him tear out onto the lawn to greet them, as if he'd never heard about gentlemanly behaviour. From my satchel I took a comic to read. After all this time apart, once again Alastair and I had forgotten how to talk to one another.

'It's snowing,' Alastair said. 'Wait! I think I see them. He jerked in his chair. 'Is it them? Graeme, for God's sake, look!'

I'd gone numb reading my comic. How Dennis the Menace stole his sweets back from a nasty gang was nicer than seeing my lying parents walk across a brown lawn. 'Graeme, it's them. They're here.' He elbowed my ribs. I sighed and lifted my heavy head. Someone, possibly Father, held the brim of his hat against the wind. The woman I didn't recognise. Brown hair puffed around her face and a red hat with a jiggly feather stuck to one side of her head. My mother had long hair pulled back in a knot at the back of her neck. They got closer, and yes, it was them – just Mother with a hairdo change and Father, when he took off his hat, just Father. Alastair, usually the calm one, dashed to the door to greet them.

Such a fuss, such a fuss. Mother cried when I pulled away and offered my hand to shake.

'Let's get out of here,' Father said. Off we drove, like nothing had changed. Mother lit a cigarette and Father said, 'We've got a surprise for you at home. Guess what it is, boys?'

I wasn't having it, but Alastair, being nine, played along. He hadn't suffered as much. He could become his old self. Well, let him.

'A new bicycle?'

Father shook his head.

'Is it something that I wanted for Christmas?'

'No. It's for both of you.'

'A trip?'

'Good guess, but wrong. What about you, Graeme? What do you think it is?'

'Don't know.' And then I did. Something from a letter he wrote. The answer came to me, perfectly, and I knew I was right. 'I do know. But I'm not telling.'

'Ho-ho! You do, eh? What is it?'

'I'm not telling,' I repeated.

Signs of Dundee greeted us at last, its battered farms, warehouses, factories – but best of all, The Law – an enormous peaked hill that used to be a volcano. My heart sped even though I told it not to. We skirted round the dank rows of workers' houses, headed north, and there it was – 166 Nethergate. Home. Leafless creeper vines curled hairy fingers up the grey stone walls; the front door stood shiny black. Father's keys clattered, which gave me the old safe feeling. He opened the door.

Don't get excited.

The smell of home made me dizzy. 'Where's the surprise?' asked Alastair. He roamed about the wide, square hall, a Christmas tree, still undecorated, stood beside the stairs. Do not be fooled. Stay stony or you'll be sorry.

Father, putting a friendly arm round my shoulders, gave me a little shake. 'Maybe you'll have to find it, eh? Go on a hunt. Graeme, you still think you know what it is?'

'Yes,' I said, dull and flat.

'Well?'

I sighed. 'It's a wireless. For the schoolroom.'

His lovely smile told me I was wrong. 'Good guess. But Graeme, me lad, I'm sorry to tell you, it's not a schoolroom wireless. You'd best look in the kitchen.'

'The kitchen? I don't want anything from a kitchen.'

'You never know...' I almost felt sorry for him, he was trying so hard to please. So I walked through the dark dining room, opening the kitchen door that always brought light because of the windows.

It was the shock that broke me. Mr Moffet had prepared us so well – to stand tall, punish weakness, tell our lies in nice, long sentences. But not for this.

On the floor was a small, reddy-brown, baby dachshund, staring up at me, scared because he didn't know me. But maybe since I was small, he must have known I was safe; he shot all over the place, like a party balloon when you let the air out. Yapping and whining and snorting in circles, rolling over on his back, his pretty red coat shining, his clumsy big paws with little black nails hurting my legs as he jumped up.

'We'd thought we'd give you something to come home to,' Father said, 'since you're so grown up and don't need us anymore. Besides, we were lonely, your mother and I. We needed some noise about the place.' He knelt, sitting back on his heels, and tried to pet the little dog, but he wouldn't keep still. 'You've missed us, haven't you? I bet it felt like a lifetime, eh, Rufus? Rufus, meet Graeme.'

I felt so tall next to the little thing that I sat, cross-legged. And what did Rufus do but climb on Father's lap and wee – right on his trousers! 'Thank you very much,' he said and took his handkerchief from his breast pocket to mop up, going 'tsk-tsk' in a pretending-to-be-angry way. 'At least you could have waited and weed on Graeme.' He gave me a wink. Part of me laughed, but part of me couldn't. Then he put Rufus in my lap. I bent, and he licked my face, finding the tears that leaked from my eyes.

In that minute, we got mixed up. I became Rufus, and he became me, and it broke me. I just – fell over – and lay on that shiny painted floor and cried as if I'd never stop. I thought the entire kitchen might flood and they'd have to phone a plumber; that did make me laugh. Then Rufus climbed over me, and weed on me, too.

Everything was the same in our room, and in our side-by-side beds, Alastair and I talked at last. Bannerman was christened 'Lousy Old Hole' and we invented terrible punishments for those we hated. Exhausted and lulled by the hazy rumble of trains along the harbour, we fell asleep.

After a while, though, we didn't want to poison our room by even mentioning LOH. And day by day, I got softer and more forgetful of Bannerman.

Chapter 3

Scottish people didn't think much of Christmas. The very word was suspicious. It meant 'Christ Mass', and anything to do with Masses was Catholic, which was like being a friend of the Devil. Father thought that was nonsense, but even so, Hogmanay – Scottish for New Year – was our big celebration and we always spent it at Craigisla, Mother's family home.

Still, we boys were allowed a tree with coloured lights and glass balls, and on Christmas morning I got the Meccano set I wanted and Alastair got a sheath knife because he was nine. At midday we had Christmas dinner at Grandma Moodie's house, on the other side of Dundee. Unfortunately, it was boring because she was deaf.

But Hogmanay at Craigisla – nothing boring about that.

We set out after breakfast, the car packed with luggage, a thick rug over our legs and the lovely smells of petrol and Father's pipe floating backwards. Rufus took turns on Alastair's and my laps. It was a journey of perfect length, not too long to get sick, but long enough to know one was going somewhere exciting. We took the Alyth Road all the way, past ploughed fields and soft green hills sleeping till spring. No snow had come yet.

Mother took out her list of spelling words for Alastair and me to practise. Because Granny Cochrane was a stickler for spelling, Mother had arranged a spelling contest as part of the Hogmanay entertainment the next night. She wanted to show us off. She and Aunt Herald were always warring for Granny's attention, and Mother knew I was a better speller than Jack.

Two hours later we got to Alyth, a pretty town, just on the border between Fife and Perthshire. Almost there. Butterflies began leaping in my belly. A new honour awaited Jack and me. For the very first time, having both reached the grand age of seven, we'd be allowed to stay up for the Hogmanay entertainment. We'd be part of the great noise that had rattled our ears when we were little, lying in bed.

Father coaxed the car up the final steep hill – and there was Craigisla in all its glory. A long time ago it had been just a farmhouse, but as Mr Cochrane got richer and richer, he added on this and that, till its many pointed roofs shot up like mountain tops. But then he died, just when he began to enjoy himself, leaving behind that beautiful house, with its white-pebbled walls and pink stone hugging round the windows.

Craigisla had everything required for a happy life – tennis courts, a croquet lawn, a walled garden, and a veranda with long wicker chairs made for napping. Granny's land stretched for miles. Beyond her lawns and gardens were farms she rented to families who raised sheep and cows or grew barley and such.

My favourite thing was The Den – a long path that curved round a woodland hill, up and up, till one came upon an amazing waterfall. You could feel its magic sparking around your feet as soon as you set up the path. Along the way, nooks and crannies welcomed you to sit and catch your breath. A bench might be inside, beside a half-hidden statue of a rabbit or a wild little forest spirit with hooves. By and by, just when your legs were worn-out with trudging, you saw ahead a giant pine, blocking out the light, and heard a faint rushing sound. Beware: this was the spot where children could go no further without a grownup. For around the bend lay the great Reekie Linn, largest waterfall in Scotland and it lived on Granny Cochrane's land.

Father honked his car horn, and out came a crowd to welcome us – Mother's three brothers, the cousins, the servants we knew – all making a fuss. Mrs Galbraith, the cook, shook her head at Alastair and me because we were so tall and thin, particularly Alastair. 'I'll have to get busy and fatten you up. You'll leave here sleek and fat as otters!' Then, after all the hugging and handshakes, from the front door, fine as a queen, strolled Granny Cochrane. She must have waited, just so everyone would notice her and not us.

Granny wasn't tall and she was rather round, but she carried herself like an ocean liner easing into harbour. In her hand was a shiny black walking stick and she looked this way and that, as if anyone who saw her would be overjoyed to catch a glimpse of her majesty.

Granny C had worn black ever since I was born, because her husband Andrew Cochrane died the same day, 27 August, 1924. Mother said it was God's way of being kind, so that losing Mr Cochrane wasn't such a terrible sorrow.

He was the reason they were rich. When he was young, he opened a grocery in Glasgow, and because the city was growing so fast, he soon had a hundred shops. Now rich as a king, he bought Craigisla, famous for its healthy air, far from Glasgow's dirt and coal smoke.

All to no avail. The poor man took ill with a burst appendix. They didn't even have time to take him to Dundee Hospital, where I was busy being born. He died in his bedroom.

I loved Granny Cochrane. She had crinkly blue eyes that always suspected mischief but wouldn't mind if she found it. And the doers of the mischief were Mother's brothers – James, Alexander and Charles. Feckless, Father said – the lot of them.

Now Granny aimed those merry Cochrane eyes at Alastair and me. 'Look at my two tall grandsons. Aren't they becoming handsome lads? Have you learned all there is to know yet? Come inside, you'll catch a chill.'

The crowd lumbered into the hall, which was enormous and dark because the veranda blocked the light from the windows. A bright fire burned inside a big stone inglenook, making the wood-panelling glow like honey. Boughs of prickly holly lay across the mantle to keep out bad fairies, with bunches of mistletoe tucked here and there to ward off sickness in the New Year. Granny Cochrane was ten times more superstitious than Mother, and both ladies did their best to pass their notions on to Alastair and me. It drove Father mad.

Mrs Galbraith led us upstairs to our room, past Grandfather Cochrane's bedroom. I didn't look in. Once I made that mistake. Curtains covered the windows, blocking the light except for a thin sliver in the middle, so I could see his ivory brushes and combs lying on the dresser. Black evening clothes lay across the bed, as if waiting for the ghost of my grandfather to put them on. A smell of mothballs and something sweet and flowery floated toward me. I ran and never looked in again.

Like magic, tea awaited us in our room – with fat scones wrapped in a linen nest to keep them warm. We sat on a window seat, safe from outside, where twigs jiggled and scratched against the panes. Mrs Galbraith unpacked for us – like we were princes! – brushing our kilts and hanging them in a wardrobe. And all the while we talked.

'Be ye ready for Hogmanay?' she asked. 'Ye paid off all your debts? It's bad luck to start a new year with money owing, you know.'

'I know,' Alastair said, 'Except we don't have enough money to have any debts.'

'Not me, neither. But I know this house is clean, that's for sure. Mrs. Cochrane worries the year will go bad for her if the brass isn't shining, the chimney clean as a whistle, and every stick of furniture waxed. It took two men two days just to polish the panelling in the hall. Of course, I don't do any o' that. I'm the cook and nothing else,' she added with pride. 'Except when I'm greeting me boys.'

She kissed our foreheads, saying, 'Now you two get off to sleep. Your mother will wake you for dinner.'

We did sleep, digging deep under silky quilts and pulling them around our necks. The sun was going down and we got fooled into thinking it was night-time. I didn't have a wisp of a notion of where I was when Mother shook my shoulder and called my name. She turned on a lamp and watched us blink and struggle to sit. 'Lads! People are gathering downstairs, already. Hurry yourselves!'

She helped dress us in our best suits – the kilts were kept for Hogmanay – pulling and yanking us, combing our hair flat and licking her fingers to wet it. 'Don't put your spit on me,' Alastair said, jerking away.

'Don't be so crabbit,' she snapped. 'You lived inside me for nine months, you know. There, you'll do, I suppose.' She stood back from us and sighed. 'I wanted to go over the spelling words again.'

'Oh Mother, it's not till tomorrow night. And we know them anyway.'

'You better.'

Coming down the grand staircase, I heard shouts and laughing that could only come from my uncles. I scuttled down the steps fast.

They were the jolliest people – James, Alexander and Charles. Mother said Granny C had spoiled them rotten, but she was just jealous. Whenever her sons were around, Granny was cheerful as a girl, but she watched her daughters like a hawk.

The oldest, Uncle James, was tall and skinny and ran the Cochrane grocery stores. He would have preferred to be an actor, but even Granny C said no to that. Uncle Charles, the youngest and shortest, would join the business one day, but until then he collected cars and raced the fastest ones. Uncle Sandy – short for Alexander – was in the middle and perfect in every way. Neither too short nor too tall, he had the friendliest smile you ever saw; and when he aimed it at me, I felt I was getting a sunbath. He could play the violin and make coins disappear.

Sure enough, the front hall was roaring with uncles. They stood in a rough circle near the fireplace, short whisky glasses in their hands, a great fire roaring, too, jumping and crackling and sending out arrows of light.

Right away I walked up to Uncle Sandy and tapped his elbow. In a flash I was high in his arms; he held me out to get a good look. 'Graeme, me darling,

I've been waiting to see you all afternoon. Come, I want you to meet a friend of mine.' He plopped me onto the crook of his arm as he carried me to a lady in a red dress talking to Mother.

'Queenie, my love, may I interrupt?' ('Queenie' was Mother's Craigisla-name, from when she used to survey the world from her pram like a queen, her nanny had said.) 'I want Miss Marshall to meet Graeme.'

He set me down and put a hand on my shoulder, another on the lady's. 'Doreen, this is the young lad I was telling you about. Smart as a whip and twice as handsome. Graeme, meet Miss Marshall.' We shook hands.

Mother's eyes looked back and forth between us, not trusting something; probably the varnish on Miss Marshall's nails. 'But you've nothing to drink,' Uncle Sandy said. 'Let's find a wee dram of what you fancy.' He gave a wink to Miss Marshall and said, 'I'll be right back,' and he held up his finger to show how quick he'd be.

Behind a long table stood Edward, pouring drinks. He'd been at Craigisla forever. 'Ah, Master Graeme,' he said, reaching under the table and bringing out my own pewter goblet, 'GCM' engraved on the side, 'what's your pleasure this evening?'

'I'll have a ginger ale, please, Edward.'

'Well?' Sandy asked me. 'What do you think?'

'About what?' I took a long drink and collected several fat pieces of cheese from a silver platter.

'Miss Marshall, you goose. Isn't she the bonniest lass you ever saw?' He whispered in my ear, 'She's my sweetheart.' The way he said it, I could tell this was important.

I whispered back, 'I see,' and gave my best cagey nod.

I hadn't given a thought to whether she was bonnie or not. Wavy yellow hair, red lips, bosoms bigger than Mother's, but smaller than Miss Kidd's, peeking out at the top of her dress. All I saw was a grown-up lady. She was chatting with Alastair now, who looked bored. We joined them and I rescued Alastair by saying, 'Let's go find the cousins.'

They were playing cards on the library floor: Jack, his bossy, older brother, Tam, and his sister, Isla, who could play the piano better than was natural for her age. Aunt Herald showed her off whenever she could, which made Mother cross. 'That Isla is bewitched,' she said.

Seeing Jack reminded me of Bannerman, how we'd clung to one another. Now he ignored me and I was glad. Neither of us wanted give LOH a thought. Cousin Irene was also there, Uncle Jim's daughter. I knew her least. She was older – twelve – something like that. Mother said she didn't have a brain in her head.

At last, Aunt Herald bustled in to say dinner was served, but as we filed in she gave us her terrifying warnings. 'Do not touch your grandmother's lovely violet wallpaper. Sit up straight, no elbows on the table, don't talk with your mouth full and keep your fork upside down at all times.'

Father said grace, which took longer than at home. We six cousins were at the other end.

Little by little the noise increased, as toasts and courses came and went – soup, fish, game, cheese, dessert. We could hardly hear ourselves; the laughter was so ferocious. Uncle James was holding forth with a story, while Father called out, 'stop, stop,' as he wiped away tears.

Alastair built a tower of sugar cubes and flicked another one at it to knock it over.

'Alastair, you'll get into trouble,' I said.

'Nonsense. They won't notice. They're drunk.'

'They are?'

'Don't look so surprised. Hogmanay's tomorrow. Everyone goes wild.'

I joined his game of football with sugar cubes. Tam and Isla played too; then Jack took out some little cars and we zoomed them through roads marked by silver cutlery and crystal.

Perhaps it was the candlelight or the crystal glasses ringing, or just laughing, but I fancied I felt drunk, too – if drunk was the word for how everyone was behaving. I gave a toast, wishing Mr Moffet would fall through the ice, and Isla, who was sitting across the table, laughed her head off. I'd never been so clever.

Isla had the Cochrane look – the far-apart eyes that went up on the outside edges. A bit squinty, as if she was always laughing and smiling, which she was. Her yellow curls tumbled from the knot at the back of her head and her foxy blue eyes made me think of mischief, perhaps coming up behind her while she was playing the piano and tickling her. Something.

It was Aunt Herald who eventually remembered we were there and sent us up to bed.

* * *

Next morning, when Alastair and I tiptoed down to the breakfast room, it was 8:00 and only beginning to get light. All the places were still set. We took ours, at the children's end, and Mrs Galbraith brought us sausage and egg and warm toast standing in a rack.

We stepped out onto the veranda. The wind was strong, colder than yesterday. We went back for our overcoats and caps with the earflaps down. Alastair brought a tennis ball so we could play catch and slipped his sheath knife onto his belt. We decided to head for one of the walled gardens where it might be warmer.

It was, but the empty flowerbeds looked sad with no flowers, just a few barely dressed statues, looking to die of cold. We tossed the tennis ball over the head of a chap standing on one foot. Little wings grew out of his hat and heels. 'He's one of the Greek gods,' Alastair said. 'I forget his name, but he's about to fly off, delivering a message I think.' I looked at him standing there, on one foot, forever. He was stuck. Like me at Bannerman.

'This is boring,' I said. 'Let's do something else.'

'Race down the path?'

'No. You always win.'

'I won't always win. You'll beat me someday.'

'No, I won't.'

'You will.' His voice was flat and certain. 'I'm not good at sports, you see.'

'Who says?'

'You know.'

He meant Bannerman.

'I've an idea,' he said, a little sunshine coming into his face. 'Let's carve our initials on this tree. He took out his sheath knife. 'But we'd better be careful. Granny C might not like it.'

'How would she know it was us?'

The slow way he turned his head toward me, a hand covering one eye meant I'd said something unbelievably stupid.

A loud creaking saved me. 'Look out! Someone's coming! Put your knife back!'

Ahead, a blue-painted door in a brick wall opened and in came Uncle Sandy and Miss Marshall; they were so busy noticing each other, they didn't see us. We watched them head down a frosty brick path. She had a scarf tied round her head and was cuddled up against his shoulder, while he said something close in her ear. They stopped. Next thing I knew, they were kissing. And it went on so long! Was it fun sticking lips together like that? I would have been the first to laugh.

Then they did something stranger. They started dancing! I could hear Uncle Sandy humming as they bobbed, perfectly together. His arms held her – like she was a nest that might fall – and they turned this way and that – jerky then smooth – jerky then smooth – swaying and dipping as if they were one beautiful toy – moving by the power of Sandy's hum.

Seeing us, they stopped. Alastair waved, calling, 'Windy, eh?' We trotted round the fountain to where they stood, pink in the face.

'Oh aye,' Sandy said.

'We need to foxtrot to keep warm,' Miss Marshall said, a bit puffed. 'Scotland's so much colder than London.' Her scarf had slid from her head and her hair was blowing. She pulled the curls from her eyes. 'Come on, who wants to dance with me?'

We looked down. Alastair said, 'We don't know how.'

'Ah,' she said. 'The foxtrot's easy. I'll teach you.'

Alastair shook his head.

How could anyone say no to that? 'I'll have a go.'

We stood in a line, me in the middle, and they taught me – the slow, quick, quick. Slow, quick, quick. Tricky at first, but once I got the knack of it I was off. Sandy hummed his tune; Miss Marshall put my left hand into hers and my right one hugging her waist, and away we sailed – doing that beautiful dance known as the foxtrot.

Uncle S took a silver flask from an inside pocket and, unscrewing the top said, 'I was thinking of taking Miss Marshall to Reekie Linn. Now, Doreen, not to see it would be a sin. Never mind the other thing.'

'That rhymes!' I said.

'What does?' he asked.

'Reekie Linn. Not to see it would be a sin. Do you see?'

'I do, indeed. How about that, Doreen?' She looked down, trying not to smile.

'Then I suppose I had better see Reekie Linn,' she said. 'As I don't approve of sinning.'

'Understood.' He gave a soft swish of his finger across her hot cheek. 'You lads want to come?'

'Oh, yes please,' we both said at once. Alastair thought that we should let Mother know, so while he ran off to find her, I did some more foxtrotting with Miss Marshall.

'Will you dance with me tonight?' She looked down at me, pulling away a little, and I saw, as if for the first time, how her cheeks were glowing soft and pink. I felt fluttery and strange. Was this what Sandy meant about her being bonnie? 'Say yes, Graeme? There'll be a band playing. Promise you'll foxtrot with me, won't you?'

'Yes,' I managed to say. 'If you want.'

'That's the ticket!' Uncle Sandy clapped me on the back and took another swig. 'You've learned an important lesson today, me lad. Dancing gets the girls. Dinna forget it!'

As soon as Alastair returned, we were off, him and me kicking the bark chips that paved the way up the Den's path. As we got higher, the wind grew stronger, making the bushes swish and rattle. I was surprised how out of breath my Sandy was. 'I'm fair puckled,' he said, sitting on a bench and mopping his face with a handkerchief.

One could not see Reekie Linn yet, but we knew it was near. Ahead of us loomed the great warning pine. The smell of damp was everywhere.

And then we could hear it, a white rushing, not loud yet, but steady and strong. One could feel the might of it. We went on, round a bend of bushes, the sound getting louder and more terrifying – and there it was – raging and tumbling like thunder.

Eighty feet it fell – not all at once, but in great chunks and I knew why. A giant (or so they said) had stamped up the river, angry because the giant-lady he wanted to marry wouldn't have him. What was left were the stairs of Reekie Linn. The giant was supposed to be still down there, fuming away, luring curious children to get a closer look until they fell, joining the water that broke into a million pieces in the pool below.

Oh my, she kept saying, pointing out things right and left – thick ice blankets that covered the rocks along the falling water. Trunks of trees were covered, too, and their broad crowns arched over our heads, blooming with flowery frost. 'I don't think I've ever seen anything so amazing,' she said.

Uncle Sandy explained that Reekie meant 'smoky' and a linn could mean either a waterfall or a pool. Our Reekie Linn was all three. Then he told the tale of the giant-lady who wouldn't marry the giant. He pointed to his steps that climbed the falls, the left-right footprints so clearly there. We watched the white water pouring out over the rocks, down that beautiful staircase.

'That may be,' said Miss Marshall. 'But I'm sure she took him in the end, for that's her bridal veil laid out upon the rocks. Don't you see? It's made of silk, and you can see through it, it's so fine.'

'Yes, you can. The sun's coming out, that's why. A good omen, eh?' He tipped up her chin, Alastair and me forgotten.

'Yes,' Miss Marshall said in a whispery, wee voice.

'I want to carve my initials somewhere,' Alastair said, jolting us out of whatever magic was going on. 'And Graeme's, too. I've brought my sheath knife. I got it for Christmas because I'm nine.'

'My, that is an achievement,' Uncle Sandy said with a slow, deep breath. 'Let's have a look.' Alastair took it out and handed it to him. 'That's a beauty, for sure.' He turned it over a couple of times and touched its tip with his finger. 'Nice and heavy, but not too much. Your father chose well. Let's find you a tree.' He found a pine, safely away from the falls. 'Just to be sure you don't fall in.'

'Can I carve my own?' I asked.

Alastair shook his head. 'I daren't let you. Father made me promise.'

'No arguing, then,' Uncle Sandy said.

As it was, Alastair had trouble himself. 'It's harder than it looks.'

'It is,' Uncle S said. He showed him how to hold it with both hands, one on the handle, the other at the foot of the blade. 'Give little sliding jabs, like this.' We watched his strong hands work the knife, the pale sun on the blade, the reddish hair on his knuckles. Alastair took over, his nine-year-old fingers looking a bit scrawny after Uncle Sandy's. He managed, though. 'ARM' for Alastair Reid Moodie.

'Woof, my fingers ache,' he said, shaking them; so Uncle Sandy carved mine, 'GCM,' and added the date. 31.12.31.

'The day is the same as the year,' Alastair said.

Miss Marshall set her hand on his shoulder. 'So it is. Tomorrow will be 1932. How strange it sounds.' I loved the way she found everything amazing.

Chapter 4

Mother was waiting on the veranda, all worked up. 'Thank heavens you're back. Your Aunt Herald's been up to her tricks. She's talked Mother into having the children recite poetry instead of spelling. All except Isla. She'll be playing the piano, of course.' She shook her fists. 'What a snake that Herald is. I bet she had this planned all along.'

'Don't worry, don't worry,' Alastair said, just like Father. 'Graeme and I know lots of poems.' True, enough. LOH had made us memorise a poem every week.

'Thank Heaven,' she said and took us upstairs to hear our poems. Alastair chose, 'My Heart's in the Highlands' because he loved it, and I chose 'Daffodils' because it was short.

* * *

I must have dropped off, for the next thing I knew Catherine was calling out in a gentle whisper, 'Mr Alastair, Mr Graeme, time to rise. I've brought you tea and those scones you like from Mrs Galbraith.' That got us up. We could hear the wind howling. 'A mighty storm a-coming.' Dinna worry. We're safe inside.'

A little later, Mother hurried in. Out came the Robertson tartan kilts, matching neckties, and our tan leather sporrans. Our socks were made of fine white silk, and our shoes had big brass buckles. In fun, Alastair and I kept pushing each other from the stand-up mirror, to get a better view of ourselves, we looked so bonnie.

Downstairs, the men were just as handsome, in short, silver-buttoned jackets, cascades of lace falling from their necks, and magnificent white seal sporrans. The women looked fine in their long silky dresses, but nothing Scottish.

I'd just fetched my ginger ale when I heard Father's voice booming above everyone else's. 'Cochranes and their connections! Your attention, please.' He stood on a big wooden platform, newly assembled for the evening's entertainment, his head high above the crowd, which included the cream of Alyth gentry. 'Gather round, everyone. Our fine hostess wishes to say a few words.'

He stepped aside to make room for tiny Granny C and taking her hand, helped her onto a podium.

'Good evening and welcome,' she said in her slow, grand way. 'As some of you may know, I am acquainted with the Duchess of York, the former Lady Elizabeth Bowes-Lyon of Glamis Castle. Years ago, she showed me a poem, one of her favourites. I have since recited every year at Hogmanay: "God Knows" by Minnie Louise Haskins.'

And I said to the man who stood at the gate of the year:
'Give me a light that I may tread safely into the unknown.'
And he replied:
'Go out into the darkness and put your hand into the Hand of God.
That shall be to you better than light and safer than a known way.'
So I went forth, and finding the Hand of God, trod gladly into the night.
And He led me towards the hills and the breaking of day in the lone East.

When she'd finished reciting, a low drone started – a sound I adored – as a fine, fat-faced piper in full Scots dress appeared at the top of the stairs. The din was tremendous, shuddering through my bones as we formed a line and followed him into the dining room. How lucky I was to be Scottish. How lucky to be safe in that great hall, about to begin my first true Hogmanay, when I'd dance the foxtrot with Miss Marshall.

* * *

After a 400-year-long dinner, sitting next to Alyth's Presbyterian Minister, I was overjoyed to be back in the hall.

Up stepped Father onto the platform, banging a fancy stick on the floor. A piano stood nearby – for Isla, I guessed. We gathered in a big circle on chairs and benches, as he said this and that about the War and how we were looking forward to a bright future. He opened his mouth again to speak but Uncle Sandy leapt onto the platform, and pushing him away, began playing his fiddle! How rude! I felt sorry for Father – till I heard everyone laughing as he chased Uncle Sandy around with his stick.

Then Uncle Sandy took off his jacket and *really* played, some wild and fiery Scottish tune, so when he stopped, the room went wild, too – stomping and shouting. My hands burned from clapping so hard.

Uncle Sandy stuck out a hand and someone put a glass of whisky in it. By now I knew this was planned. The din died down as he held up his glass and began the toast everyone knew, even me. We joined him, like in a prayer:

Here's tae us
Wha's like us
Damn few,
And they're a' deid
Mair's the pity!

Father's turn to leap up and shove Uncle Sandy away. 'Off with ye, Alexander Cochrane! Time for the children's entertainment!' More applause. 'To open our grand show, may I present the famous Miss Isla Hunter, Craigisla's very own child prodigy.'

Pale as a ghost, the poor thing walked to the piano and turned toward us as if we were a firing squad. 'Fur Elise,' her voice trembled, 'by Ludwig van Beethoven.' Sighing, she scraped the piano bench noisily, setting her fingers above the keys – and damned if she didn't take off like a rocket! Down she bent, inches from the keys, and woof, back went her head, playing without looking at the keys! She wasn't showing off – she couldn't help herself. I decided she was bewitched, like Mother said, but in a nice way, maybe like a blessing.

Wild applause. Hooray for Isla! I could see her relief melting away like snow. She gave the sweetest curtsey, ran off and buried her face in Aunt Herald's shoulder.

Her worry, though, flew to me; the poetry reciting was next.

Father called us by age, which meant Tam was first. I'd be last.

Tam clomped his big feet to the middle of the stage. '"The Rainbow" by William Wordsworth.'

My heart leaps up when I behold
A rainbow in the sky:
So was it when my life began;
So is it now I am a man;

I didn't think much of it. Him, a man? Not bloody likely. His voice hadn't even changed.

Next came Irene, dolled up in ringlets. I'd heard Mother whispering to Father that because Uncle James wasn't allowed to be an actor, he had hopes for Irene becoming the next Shirley Temple. Ugh. Irene's recitation of 'Pippa's Son,' sorry to say, brought another ugh from me.

Alastair followed. As if he didn't mind in the least, he strolled to the performing spot, and in a proud, strong voice began his favourite poem.

My heart's in the Highlands, my heart is not here;
My heart's in the Highlands a-chasing the deer;
Chasing the wild deer, and following the roe,
My heart's in the Highlands, wherever I go.

After all the verses, everyone stood and applauded. He'd done such a beautiful job, reciting so boldly in his fine Scottish accent, I was shocked. 'How did you manage it?' I asked, clapping him on the back when he came off. 'That was pure dead brilliant!'

'Ah dinnae ken,' he said. 'I thought of my poem. That's all. Rabbie Burns did the rest.'

Part of me wished he hadn't been quite so good. I might not do as well.

Eejit Jack came next. He could make a dog's breakfast of anything. Batting his eyes and doing a silly formal bow to the crowd, he began: 'Dafferdils, by William Wordsworth.'

What? Did he mean 'Daffodils'? *My* 'Daffodils'? Yes. Gazing at the ceiling, smiling like a dunderheid, Jack began:

I wander'd lonely as a cloud
That floats on high o'er vales and hills,
When all at once I saw a crowd,
A host of golden daffodils.

On and on he went, hand gestures and all. Pardon me while I boke.

I was next. Now I understood how Isla felt. The strangest whacking banged against my ribcage, as if Mr Moffet was inside, having a go with his cane.

My shoes squeaked as I walked to the centre of the platform. I filled my lungs with air to begin. Someone laughed. Doomed.

But moving from my shoes up into my chest was a prickly anger that drove out the fear. No one would laugh at me. Think of your poem, laddie. And as if some Scottish highlander had ridden up behind me and flung the words into my mouth, I declared, '"Reekie Linn," by Graeme Cochrane Moodie.'

Reekie-reekie-reekie Linn,
Not to see it would be a sin!
Just make sure ya dinna fa' in
Ta Reekie-reekie-reekie Linn!

As I finished my poem, I pointed my finger, making the 'R's of 'Reekie' go on and on.

Total silence. Was it over already? As quickly as my highlander came upon me, he galloped away, leaving Graeme Moodie feeling a fool. What was I thinking of? Was I mad? My shoulders shrugged, and with a feeble smile, I walked away.

But then, as if I were Rabbie Burns himself, the audience exploded. Maybe, just then, I was.

They shouted something. Father ran to me, saying, '"Encore" means do it again!' He pushed me back on. 'Go on, they love you!' So I encored; then encored again. By the third time, they shouted it out with me. The 'R's were so long, each 'Reekie' became a line of its own.

Uncle Sandy went mad about my poem. 'Ye don't mind, do ya' if I claim a wee bit o' credit? About the sinning and all?' He poured a bit of whisky into my ginger ale, as we stood near the bar. Just like that he'd taken a bottle out of Edward's hand and gave himself some more too.

'Don't forget,' said Miss Marshall, looking grand and pink as usual, 'I get the first dance. Remember you promised to foxtrot with me.'

'Oh, is the foxtrot next?' I was trying to sound calm, but inside I was leaping like a hare.

'Not quite. Just one more part of the entertainment,' Uncle Sandy said.

'Aw, no,' I groaned.

'Eh, don't pull such a face. You're going to love this, Graeme. It's the greatest poem in the world by our own Rabbie Burns, and your uncle Jim's reciting it. I'll tell you the story; I've already filled Doreen in, but you'll have no trouble with the Scots dialect. Here's all you need to know: a man named Tam O'Shanter, is drinking in a pub with all his friends. It's getting late and he must ride his horse all the way home. Oh, and ye need to ken that a "cutty sark" is a short skirty thing. I must go and sit with Doreen, in case she needs help with the words. Ah, it's starting. Here goes!'

Someone turned off all the brass chandeliers hanging from the ceiling, leaving just candlelight here and there, and the light from the fire glowing red and hot. All went quiet as we sat in chairs placed around the hall. With everyone still, we could hear the mighty wind hammering the house.

From the top of the staircase hurled a loud, drunken hiccup. People smiled and wriggled in their seats, cosily looking forward to what was coming.

Down came Uncle Jim, but not looking like himself at all. He wore an old, battered kilt, a leather waistcoat, rough socks and heavy brown shoes. He'd messed his hair and, on his head, tilted a big blue shanter. In one hand, an enormous tankard swayed. He set it on a table, wiped his lips and began.

I copied the others, smiling as Uncle Jim recited all about Tam drinking in the pub, his cross wife, Kate, waiting at home; the storm building, and Tam putting off leaving, but at last sets off on his trusty steed, Meg.

The speedy gleams the darkness swallow'd
Loud, deep, and lang, the thunder bellow'd:
That night, a child might understand,
The Deil had business on his hand.

I knew that 'Deil' was Scottish for Devil, a creature real and terrifying to Mother, and now to me. 'Speak o' the Deil and he'll appear.' Torrents of fear tumbled from my heart down to my feet. The walls thinned; sharp shadows stabbed the browning light. Had the Devil heard his name? I looked round. Everyone looked happy as Larry, but I wasn't soothed. What was wrong with them? Or wrong with me?

Jim continued, la-de-da. Tam must travel through a haunted forest where unspeakable things had happened – a baby murdered! A man smothered by snow – and with each horror, Jim rushed up to one of us, inches away, eyes popping, spit flying in the candlelight.

Please don't come to me. I can't take it. He did, of course, yanking a pretend-rope round his neck, just like Rotheringham had done on my first day at Bannerman.

Things only got worse. Tam comes upon the ruins of a church, Kirk Alloway, roofless and blazing with hellish light, where:

Coffins stood round, like open presses,
That showed the dead in their last dresses

On the altar lay wee, unchristened bairns. Rotten corpses creep out of coffins. Tongues of lawyers turn inside out; priests' hearts lie rotting and stinking; a bloody knife with hairs still on it. Please let this be over soon.

But no. Haggy, old witches dance to squealing bagpipes, played by the Devil himself. And when the ladies get hot, they throw off their dresses! A terrible sight, but Tam notices one witch, young and pretty, who dances in her cutty sark better than anyone else. He goes wild with watching her, so wild he forgets where he is and shouts: 'Well done, Cutty Sark!'

Cutty Sark is furious at Tam for watching and chases after him, but just in time, he makes it over the bridge, for a witch cannot cross over water. Tam is safe, but Cutty Sark manages to snatch poor Meg's tail. The end. Thank God.

But everyone loved it! You'd think they'd been hearing Little Bo Peep. At least, the dancing was coming up next. I had to get the terror out of my heart.

'Quick, now,' Mother said, her arms out, ready to sweep us away. 'Off to bed with ye. It's nearly eleven.'

'But what about the dancing?' I protested.

'No, no, no, no. Don't be silly.' She made a move to pick me up.

'I'm not leaving.'

'Oh yes, you are.'

'I'm going to do the foxtrot.' Father tried to pick me up, too, and I gave him the hardest push I could. 'Get away, I'm not a baby.'

'Well, you're acting like one,' Father said. 'I've never seen such behaviour. Obviously, you're very, very tired.'

'Graeme, darling,' Uncle Sandy said, going down on a knee beside me. 'This is my fault. Everything has taken far too long. You have years to do the foxtrot. Don't worry.' I put my arms around his neck and he carried me off to bed. I didn't care if I was being a baby. I'd had enough.

* * *

It was the pressure on my willy that woke me. I had to go to the lavatory a hundred miles down the corridor. I tried to ignore the have-to feeling. Impossible. Was there a pot in the room? No. I'd have to go past Grandfather's room, where he died the night I was born. He might want my soul so he could live again. The wind battered twigs against our window. 'Alastair?' I called softly.

In the cold moonlight, I saw his sheath knife gleaming on the table between us. With that, I'd stand a chance of making it. Alastair would never know.

I took the knife, dragged it out of its sheath. How long it was, curving to a sharp point. I got out of bed, remembering Father's instructions to always point it downward, and began my trek. No sounds came from any room. First footing had come and gone. Just the hateful wind that would never stop. Steadily I walked, not racing, eyes ahead, slippers patting softly. Ice-cold death was with me all the way. Do not look into Grandfather's room.

Made it. I put the knife on the floor, slid the brass bar across the doorjamb as quickly as I could. Safe for the moment. Weed the longest wee in the universe. Phew. Done. I'd been told not to pull the chain, not to wake the others. Now, all I had to do was get back.

Someone turned the doorknob. Sweet Jesus, protect me. Slowly, I picked up the knife, but the footsteps went away, faint and light – like a ghost.

A few minutes later, footsteps came again. Door rattling. A voice, so small, I could barely hear it whisper, 'Is anybody there?' I said nothing, but shaking, lost my footing and banged softly against the wall. I had never, ever, been so frightened. 'Please, is anybody there? Is anyone hurt in there? Open the door, if you can, and I'll help you.'

It sounded like a woman, possibly a child, but Granny was the only woman on this floor and she had her own bathroom. All the guests were upstairs. Who was out there? Could it be Cutty Sark, called forth by Uncle Jim's poem? Anything was possible. 'Please,' she whispered again.

She sounded afraid herself, so I said in a faint, trembly voice, 'Who is it?'

'It's Doreen Marshall,' she finally said.

'Miss Marshall?'

'Is that Graeme?'

'Yes.'

'Open the door, for God's sake. What's wrong? Are you ill?' I opened the door, so glad to see her, I almost wept. She saw my knife. 'What's happening here?'

'I was afraid,' I said. 'Of Cutty Sark.' We were both still whispering, and she closed the door quickly, took the knife and hugged me with her other arm. I held on to her. 'The story frightened me so, so I took Alastair's knife to protect myself...'

'From what?'

'From the ghosts.' I was starting to cry.

'Oh dear, I told Sandy it was too much. You poor thing.'

'I'm afraid to go back. They'll chase me all the way. I know they will, as soon as my back is turned. They'll grab my shoulder...'

'Shhh... I'll take you back.'

'We mustn't wake Alastair. He mustn't know.'

'Of course not.'

'Why are you here? There's a lavatory upstairs.'

'Oh. Is there?' she asked vaguely.

Again the door rattled, this time loudly, and Uncle Sandy's voice rasped out in a loud whisper, 'Hello? Who's in there?'

'It's Doreen.'

'Are you all right?'

'Yes.'

'Well, come back to bed. You must be freezing.'

It was true. Poor Miss Marshall was in a little white – sark. A cutty sark. She and I looked at each other. She pointed at me. I nodded and she said, 'Sandy, Graeme's here with me.' She opened the door. We all looked at one another, trying to understand why we were meeting up in a lavatory in the middle of the night, with Miss Marshall holding a sheath knife, on the first day of 1932.

Doreen explained to Uncle Sandy what had happened and he looked at me, smiling and shaking his head. 'Poor fellow.' Then he laughed, but kept his voice down. 'We all need a drink. You, specially, Graeme. Miss Marshall and I were...' His voice trailed off. 'Let's just go.'

His room had a roaring fire. The wind was dying, and the air in the room was loose and warm. So was the whisky and water, which I found I quite liked and had no trouble getting down. We sat on chairs close by the fire for a long time after, covered by blankets taken from the bed. We didn't talk much, but we did make an agreement – clinking glasses to seal it properly – never to tell each other's secret: that Miss Marshall had spent the night in Uncle Sandy's room and I had taken Alastair's sheath knife to protect myself from ghosts. And before I went to sleep, Miss Marshall and I did the foxtrot while Uncle Sandy hummed.

Chapter 5

It started as a cut on my knee.

Right knee. U-shaped. Like a frown or a smile, Father said, depending on which way you looked. From falling, stupid falling, just as I had overtaken Alastair. Alastair who always won. Alastair who was eleven. Two years older. That's why he won, not because he was better.

But I fell.

It wasn't a bad cut. It didn't need stitches and I hadn't even cried.

The screams came later.

* * *

'Come on, Graeme,' Alastair said, at the beginning of all this, 'Let's have a race.'

'Don't want to,' I said, and to show I meant it, I kicked a sharp white rock, bright among the pine needles in the road. 'Too tired.'

'I'll race you to the church. No – I'll race you all the way home!'

Home that summer was Lossiemouth, where our parents had rented a big house in the village sharing it with Aunt Herald, Jack and Isla, who still had to practise the piano every afternoon. Pity.

Alastair and I had had another year at Bannerman. I still hated every minute but after two years of hell and now nine, I'd learned to survive. How to cheat to get more stars – like taking out library books I had no intention of reading, and jamming stuff under the covers when they inspected the room, that kind of thing.

We'd spent the afternoon on our bikes with Cousin Jack, riding along the sandy path that curved in a wide rim round the sea, stopping for scallop shells, dead fish or the slimy seaweed that was fun to pop.

At three o'clock we headed home, but Mother told us tea would not be served for an hour. We should get out from under her feet till then. Jack, still the double of me, but with half the brains, went for a nap, and Alastair said in that way he had of deciding everything, 'Come on, G, let's see what we can find.'

Lossiemouth was a family treat. We boys had done well at Bannerman; Father was exhausted, operating on eyeballs; and Mother, well, Mother loved the sea, and she was the one organising the holiday. Still, it was the perfect choice, everyone agreed – except me, who could have done without Cousin Jack tagging along.

Our grey stone house had belonged to a rich vicar when Lossiemouth was a famous fishing village, but now had more holiday makers coming up from the south. Away from the long rows of fishing cottages that lined the cove, our house stood close to the Presbyterian church where our family went every Sunday morning, as regularly as a trip to the lavatory. Church was what one did, but Father put more faith in science and logic and Mother swore by her old Scottish superstitions – full moons and new moons, or things viewed in mirrors. The only times their religions joined was in the matter of Mother's warts. Every now and then, she'd get a cluster on her right hand. The only cure was Father's healing touch.

'Rubbish,' he said, but nicely.

'It most certainly is not,' she said. 'You've proven it again and again.'

'Very well,' he said, smiling as if he knew it were true and she'd somehow guessed his secret, 'sit down.' He lifted his long legs from the leather footstool where he'd been doing the crossword and patted where his feet had been. Let's have a look.' Down she sat, like a child, placing the hand with warts in his lap. His long-fingered hands, that held magic, we knew, moved over hers.

'There,' he said after a minute, and while Mother's eyes were still closed, he gave us a wink as if to say, you and I know what a lot of nonsense this all is. But Mother was right. In a few days, the warts disappeared.

Alastair and I spent the hour before tea in that lazy, do-nothing way that was rather pleasant. Then he said the thing about racing, and I said I didn't want to.

What he said next changed everything. 'You might win, you know. You're getting faster all the time.'

Hope blew against my back and into my legs. I might win.

'Very well,' I said, imitating his slow, calm voice, so not to let on the trembly way my heart was stuttering. 'I'll draw a starting line. It must be fair.' I found a stick and pulled a line across the sandy road.

'Ready, steady,' – we bent, examining each other's toe tips with eagle eyes. A magnifying glass would do no better.

'Go!'

I dashed for the inside lane along the curving road, where crowds of white-barked birches cheered me on, their leaves waving like flags. Alastair came up easily alongside me, his long, cricket legs taking their time. He could do one for my three. I heard his thudding feet, clunkety-clunk. He looked clumsy, my brother, my kind, fair, reasonable brother – foolish, even. And from somewhere, came all the strength in the world. My machine gun legs rattled toward victory.

I didn't see the bend to the right. Thick tree trunks blocked the view and, before I knew, I was in the outside lane. Alastair was ahead! My chest floundered to catch up. I ran across the widening road, treacherous with rocks and sand. I tore up behind him, knocking against dusty nettles and brambles. He stepped to the left a bit, a mistake; I pushed more power into my legs. Side by side, we reached the church. At last I moved ahead a couple of inches, and I knew I would win. I saw home. The home we called home that summer. The first time I beat Alastair.

Something grabbed my foot or caught my toe, something, and my whole flying self pitched forward. Pain rolled through me as I tumbled, dragging sand and grit and shells, till I stopped.

'I'm all right!' I shouted to make it true, and it was true. No whacks or jabs had been too bad. But Alastair had tripped me! He'd made me fall. Spluttering with fury, I got up.

'What happened?' he said, worried and blotchy-faced.

'You tripped me! That's what happened!'

As if I'd thrown poison at him, he stepped back. 'What?'

'I felt it!'

'You most certainly did not.' He stood straight, and put his hands on his bony hips. 'You were running too fast. You fell. That's all.' He was breathing hard, too, but his voice was calm, taking charge.

I stared hard at him, but I knew he was right. 'I'm sorry.'

'Right,' he said, forgiving me with a nod. 'Let's go find Father. Your knee needs attention.' I hobbled along with my arm round Alastair's shoulder.

'Superficial wounds,' Father declared. I sat on his desk blotter, looking at his steady face, so much like Alastair's. Even on holiday, he wore a suit and waistcoat, a gold watchchain looped into a pocket. 'You'll be pretty banged up for a couple of days, but right as rain. You've got a mess of shrapnel in there, eh, soldier? I'll have to pick it out, but I know you'll be brave. You'll have a scar to show people for the rest of your life. A funny-looking curve. Like an upside-down U.'

'Like a frown.'

'Or a smile, if you happened to be an ant sitting on your shoe gazing up.'

This silliness pleased me. 'How can I be an ant and me at the same time?' I asked, and we laughed.

'You want a piece of leather to bite on, like the soldiers did in the War?'

'What?' I asked. Was this still part of a joke? I had an uneasy feeling it wasn't.

Mother rushed in, the smells of lavender and cigarette smoke fluffing about her. 'What's happened? Dear God, what happened to Graeme?'

'It's all right, Ann. He's had a tumble, that's all.'

I must have looked pretty beat up, because her arms flew around my neck. My bottom lip shook. Get yourself together, lad.

I twisted away. 'I'll be all right.'

'You heard the boy,' Father said. 'He can tell you chapter and verse about his adventures over tea.'

He gave me the piece of leather, which tasted salty. 'First I'll do the shrapnel. Ready?'

I nodded and squeezed my eyes as hard as I could. And strange, it wasn't too bad. Maybe the leather worked.

But then came those drops of orange fire and nothing helped. Not the leather, not Father's healing hands. Nothing. It was the worst hurt I'd ever felt. Still, I didn't cry.

'Like a real soldier, you kept your screams inside,' said Father. Alastair watched, saying nothing.

* * *

Next day, I ached everywhere, as Father predicted. I couldn't bend my knee, but because the weather was fine, Mother decided we'd go to the seashore. She had great faith in the healing powers of salt water. So even though making our way involved a great carry-on of towels, wicker baskets and blankets, we went. She had help: Bridget the cook, Aunt Herald, and a new person, Dorothy Tindall – an old friend of Mother's who was as poor as a church mouse, I overheard Mother telling Father. I'd had hopes that Miss Marshall and Uncle Sandy would come, but they'd gone to Monte Carlo. Oh well.

Father drove us and Rufus down to the shore in two trips, but he didn't stay. When he wasn't looking at eyes, he was writing about them.

We had a little changing hut that stood on stilts, along the upper edge of the shore, away from high tide. We took turns getting into our bathing costumes. Mother helped me with my navy vest and shorts, but she banged my knee.

'My cut's bleeding again,' I said, as we went down the rickety stairs. 'I don't think I should go in the water.' I was already chilly and the morning sun had given way to clouds.

'Nonsense. Even more reason. Nothing is as clean as sea salt.'

The others were already settled on wide brown towels. Aunt Herald took Jack's hand and held out her other for me. Alastair had headed to a group of rocks that made a pool where he could float his boat.

'I'm not going,' I said. I moved off the blanket and folded my arms. 'Rufus and I are going to dig a hole.'

'Don't you want your shivery bite?' Mother asked. Shivery bites were yesterday's scones, heavy with butter and raspberry jam. They were the only reason we went in the water, for the second we came out, shivery bites were rammed in our teeth-chattering mouths, and their delicious sogginess stopped us shaking.

'Graeme Moodie, take your boat down and play with Alastair. You don't have to go all the way in.' I didn't move. 'You won't get a shivery bite.'

'I'm not hungry,' I said and realised it was true.

'Oh, Queenie,' Dorothy said in a sweet voice to Mother, 'Do you think Graeme could take me in the sea? I'm a bit afraid of water, you see, and I need someone to hold my hand. Would you hold my hand, sweetheart?' She unwrapped the red-striped towel from her shoulders, she wore a red swimming costume with a thin white belt underneath. 'Nice, isn't it? Your mother gave it to me for my birthday, which isn't till next week, but I couldn't resist putting it on.' She did a little twirl.

So I said yes, and taking a hand not much bigger than mine, guided us into the sea where we called out, 'One-two-three!' and put our heads under the waves at the same time. The bloody water still made me feel like I'd been turned inside out.

Over the next few days, my knee improved and I forgot about it, but then one evening, I got a fever, puked up Bridget's fish pie and was sent to bed early.

* * *

Somehow during the night my legs got wrapped in bicycle chains.

Alastair controlled them with gears and I was lying on a table. The chains turned into saws and Alastair didn't care. He gave me a piece of leather to bite and kept tightening the gears. I screamed for him to stop, but all he said was, 'You're a soldier. Bite the leather.' He didn't care when the chains cut into my bones. I screamed again. And again.

Father shook me, calling my name. I saw his frightened face and I stopped screaming. He held on to me, and me to him but the pain in my legs kept on.

The rest I didn't remember, only cloths and heat and cold. Every time I woke, he was there, watching from a chair beside my bed. Sometimes I felt a sharp nudge. 'Graeme? Keep breathing, damn it. Keep breathing.' Strange, hearing him swear.

Early morning. Same room. I'd slept a long time surely. Days? Jack's bed lay beside me, but no Jack. Father had gone.

Afternoon. Wide floorboards, still with knots and cracks. Pink-flowered wallpaper, not right for a boy. Wait. Look. Dorothy Tindall was sleeping in an armchair at the foot of my bed, her head back, jaw hanging, not nice. I turned toward the window, which was a little open. A fly crawled in, drawn by a tray of food on a table by the sill. A blue chamber pot lay next to it, covered by a towel.

The others must be at the seaside. I was glad to be in my bed, warm and soft, quiet, nothing shaking me to make my legs ache. The thing to do was to sleep and hold my body in a floating position. No reason to go anywhere, nothing required but sleep.

I would have been happy to stay there forever, but I heard a shiver of a drum whirring. Drumsticks rolling on skin stretched tight. Then the beautiful wail of bagpipes – getting closer. A pipe band was marching down the street. Father must have arranged it. He knew I loved pipe bands, adored pipe bands, would rush to see any pipe band.

It was my father's way of celebration. I had been ill, but I was well.

Louder and louder. I would watch them from the window, salute them as they marched, and they'd look up and salute back. I threw back the covers. I twisted to get out of bed.

Something was wrong. I could not make my legs work. I tried again. Nothing.

I rolled my shoulders out of bed and fell all in a piece to the floor. Somehow, my elbows and hands dragged the rest of me onto my knees. I moved a bit.

Collapsed out flat. Up on my knees. Collapsed again. My legs were sandbags, but I kept going, crying, so afraid the pipes would pass before I got there.

I made it to the window just in time, pulling my body up to the sill with every bit of strength.

'That's a strange way to get to a window, sweetheart.' Dorothy said in a low voice behind me.

Chapter 6

No one told me what was wrong with me. I was ill. I would get better. Be patient, Graeme.

Inside my prison of pink-flowered walls – I knew every bud and curling leaf – came people, faking calm, with soft voices and gentle touches. Below me in the sitting room, Mother cried and Father yammered on the phone in an angry voice. Then in they'd come, normal and cheerful, but a hand might shake as it passed me a glass of water, or a voice would tremble, and I could see fear in their shiny grins.

I felt all right. It was just my bloody legs. For fun, I pretended I had a mermaid's tail under the covers. Instead of my strong, jumped-on legs, my tearing-up-the-stairs-legs – how had I done it? – lay this shimmery tail I would soon master. Come on, Moodie, you can do it. Furious, I pulled the sheets and blankets away, and there they were, same stumpy toes, bony ankles, bunged-up knee.

Worst was the bedpan. Thank God, Mother had hired a nurse who did that. Best have a stranger, so that when I got better, I'd never have to see the face of the person who wiped my bottom.

During the week I lay ill in Lossiemouth, only Alastair had an explanation. 'Mother thinks it had to do with the sea,' he said from the doorway, for he wasn't allowed any further. 'The water was so cold; it froze the nerves. But Father says nerves don't work like that. He spoke to someone who said the sea isn't as clean as it used to be. A gigantic new paper mill has opened further up the coast.'

'What are nerves?'

'Long stringy things that make you move. Don't worry. You'll get better. You've mystified everybody. You're famous. Father's phoned experts in Glasgow and Edinburgh, even a doctor-friend in London.'

'As far away as London?' My voice was faint, babyish.

'Yes, imagine! Well, I'd better go. I told Jack I'd go cycling with him.' He rolled his eyes to show he'd rather be with me than Jack, but he left without a wave. Stingy tears crept from behind my eyes where they should have stayed. Stop it, Graeme, I hissed in a voice like Mother's.

Oh yes, I was special all right. Favourite foods like boiled egg with soldier toasts, rice pudding and plenty of ice cream. More boys' magazines than I'd see in a year, and Mother read to me so much, it was too much. I wished she'd bugger off.

Most of the time I lay there, asleep, awake, hearing life come and go. Not even Rufus could visit. Early morning brought grey light, birdsong and rattling milk vans, the bottles shaking as horses galumphed on stony roads; fishing boats puttered out to sea; birds sang, happy to see the day break. Then came the lonely daytime sounds I couldn't join – shouts of children playing, big dogs, little dogs barking, old men on a nearby bench, telling tales with great ups and downs in their voices. I never heard a pipe band again. Rarely I'd hear an aeroplane, a low buzz as it moved across the sky. Night time brought faraway trains taking families home from holiday or grain to a big city. Rain could come at any time, but I only noticed it at night when everyone else was sleeping, when loneliness swelled my heart. But then, a miracle, I'd hear someone walking around downstairs, unable to sleep, and I felt comforted and slept myself.

Next morning, the whole thing started again. Grey light. Milk vans. Birds.

Mother and Father were like bad dreams – looking the same, but different. Father's whiskers were sharp on his cheeks, and Mother's hair all raggedy. They'd changed, like my legs, into something else.

It was the nasty odours on them that got me most. Usually Father had an appley smell from his pipe, his wool suits brought the cedar closet, and his big, dry hands were piney because he washed them so much. A cloud of roses came with Mother, but on cook's night out her hands might smell of onions, which I loved.

Now the roses and soap were gone, as old ashtrays and yesterday's whisky took their place. Clothes looked slept in; food marks dotted Father's shirts. They'd grown old and weak, as if their science and magic spells could no longer protect me.

Father pulled a wooden chair over beside me and picked up my hand so I knew trouble was coming. But instead he said, 'Tomorrow morning, you'll be taken by ambulance to a hospital in Elgin, where you'll get very good care and we'll come and visit you as much as possible.'

'For how long?'

'Oh, only about a month. Not that long.'

Like a pinprick from Heaven, I had a thought. 'But what about Bannerman?'

'Oh son, I'm afraid you won't be going this year. Bannerman's out of the question now.' He gave my hand a squeeze, and to my astonishment, he squinted and gathered his tears with his thumb and fingers, and drew them to the bridge of his nose.

I heard the words. They didn't mean much. Exciting perhaps: a hospital where I'd remain the centre of attention, getting lovely food and books, and visits from the family as I got better and better until I'd be running around again like a steam engine.

What made me almost faint with joy, however, was that Bannerman was out of the question.

'Don't worry, Father,' I said with a tremble in my voice as I patted his arm. 'I'll be all right.'

I didn't mind lying in bed by the sea, listening to a world without Bannerman. When I was well, they might send me back, but that was later. Some saving grace would come. I was born lucky.

It wasn't so bad, now that the terrible pain was gone – food brought to me as if I were a king, enough comics to make a skyscraper, a zippy little car to zoom through the sheets, no school worries, no trying to be as good as Alastair. When this stupid illness was over, I'd be back to my old self.

One day, something did happen. An ambulance came. Up the stairs tromped two men in white clothes, carrying a long, narrow stretcher, followed by Father giving instructions they ignored. Quick as a wink, like I was a fly and they spiders, they wrapped my legs in a sheet and whipped straps around me. Then they lifted me – one, two, three – careful now, steadily – onto the stretcher, tied me tight to the sides, and took me hanging on for dear life. As they loaded me into the back of the ambulance, I saw Mother and the others standing a bit apart, looking afraid. I waved like the King from his carriage.

Father climbed in and sat with me on a folded-down chair bolted to the floor. The stretcher was then strapped to a bolted-down table beside him. Cleverly done, I thought. I admired their speedy fingers. No one was frightened – only me a little – but I was eased by their dull faces. Father put a blanket over me, saying, 'There you are, snug as a bug in a rug,' which was silly, we knew. Nursery talk didn't fit.

We lurched off. 'Aren't they putting the siren on?'

'That won't be necessary.'

'Why not?'

He smiled and patted my hands, peeping over the blanket. 'They only do that if it's a matter of life and death. And you're going to be fine. There's no hurry.'

Hours later I was in a hospital room, alone again. I hoped I wouldn't have to find my way around because they wheeled me for miles.

Soon after Father left, they set on me. 'We're going to do a lumbar puncture to see if we can find out what's wrong with you,' said a cheerful voice, but I could see no smiles because everyone was wearing white masks.

They rolled me over on my side, pulled my knees up near my chest and told me to put my head down as far as I could. A pain pushed into my spine, swelling and swelling, till a grenade went off as they pulled my backbone out. I screamed for Father, hoping he might hear. My once trusty legs didn't budge. I tried to push with my hands, but other hands, cruel and nasty, grabbed tighter. 'Don't move!' And a kinder voice, 'Almost all done, almost all done. There. All done.' And it was over. 'Stay perfectly still, boy, till we tell you. Or you'll get the worst headache you've ever had in your life.'

I didn't move, except for some shaking I couldn't help. And as I lay there, fear stalked me, from my feet to my heart. This was not an exciting adventure but a great space of – something else – I didn't know. I drew down the blinds in my mind, a trick I'd learned at Bannerman.

I stayed in Elgin for a week, even though I was no longer in what Father called the acute phase. I'd only get better. Pretty soon I could go home.

Only it still wasn't home. I'd be going to a hospital in Dundee, called Forte House. 'But just for a while,' Father explained, 'till you're a bit stronger. I have to get back to work, you see, and at Forte House you'll get better care.' I didn't see, but I didn't put up a fight. I just kept my blinds down.

The day before the move, Alastair came to see me, but he wore a mask and stood at the door. We agreed that the only good to come out of my illness was not going to Bannerman. 'I wouldn't mind missing the whole bloody year,' I said.

'You probably will, with what you've got.'

'What have I got?'

'"Infantile paralysis," Father told me.'

'Then it must be true. That's a strange name for a sickness. Say it again?'

After he left, I said it a couple of times. I hated the sound of it. 'Infantile' wasn't a nice word. It meant babyish. 'Don't be infantile.' Silly, daft, whiny. And 'paralysis' – I knew what that meant.

Next day, more fuss and bother, people flapping around as they got me ready for the journey to Forte House. They didn't want my legs to move, so a couple of men encased me in warm wet plaster from the waist down. They made jokes about me being a mummy, but I refused to play their stupid game. Next day, the cast hard as a door – I knocked on it and didn't feel a thing – more men heaved me into another ambulance and off I went to Dundee. Father promised there would be no more lumbar things.

Finally I was settled, this time with other boys.

Soon a man with a big saw and bigger smile greeted me, calling himself Dr Auchter-Campbell. Curtains swished round my bed and he started sawing away at my cast. Things were all right till he hit my leg and I hollered.

'What are you shouting for?'

'You're sawing into my leg!'

'I'm not. I've hit the metal strip, that's all.'

He started up again, and again I hollered.

'Now stop that,' he growled, and went back to his work. I really screamed this time. 'What is going on?' He was furious and I was screaming, wild with terror.

'Stop, you bloody bastard!' That got his attention. 'You're sawing me in two!' Thank the Lord. He opened his eyes wide and began poking his cold, sweaty fingers inside the cast. He waggled them down further and further.

'Good God! Where are the metal strips? There are no metal strips! And as if I'd taught him how to swear, he swung the curtain open and shouted, 'Who's made a balls-up of this cast? Who's the bloody idiot who did this?' He was so angry I thought he'd throw a fit, but at least he'd stopped killing me. Somehow, with hot packs, a hammer and painstaking unwrapping, he managed to get the cast off without destroying me. And little by little he decided we were friends. When he saw that I only had what he called 'superficial scratches' he thought it funny. 'Good thing we both have quick reactions, eh lad?' I did my best to smile, relieved to see there wasn't blood sprayed all over. Whenever a nurse peeked through the curtains, he'd tell her how he nearly sawed his patient in two. Har-har.

* * *

Other senses took over. My hearing grew excellent. Nurses made more noise than doctors, but some had shoes with rubber soles that squished. Others were silent and snuck in like robbers to take away the soft, grey food, or shove a bedpan under my bottom, whether I had to go or not. Seeing was different, because my eyes weren't where they were supposed to be; they only stared up, from a pillow. Ceiling cracks became important, and a heavy hanging light I hoped wouldn't fall on me. From a little window I glimpsed the sky, the great and many clouds, yellow tree tops going thin and brown. People were towers, with wobbly flesh under their chins – then wham! – in they'd zoomed – a kiss from Mother or a tray from a nurse – their heads went huge.

Mother brought a stack of letters from my classmates at Bannerman. Evidently Mr Moffet had got them all to write – things like: So sorry to hear you're ill; What bad luck; I know you'll be brave. The worst was from JA MacDonald, that sad little creep who tried to be my friend because no one else would. He signed his letter, 'Your little pal, Specky.'

'Oh, that's the sweetest thing. What a nice boy. Who's Specky? Isn't that adorable? Graeme, what do you say to that?'

'I say Pukems. I hate them all. The whole bloody lot of them.'

'Graeme! I will not have you using language like that. It doesn't matter if you…'

'If I what? If I am paralysed? That's what I am, isn't it? Alastair told me. Go on, say it, say what I have. Can't you even say it? I can. Infantile paralysis. A paralysed baby. That's me.'

Fat tears slid down her cheeks and dripped onto her hands like candle wax. I was frightened, because she had nothing to say. I turned my head away; I couldn't turn the rest of me.

* * *

Next stop – 166 Nethergate. Home. But I was so tired of life, who cared? I'd been in a bed for over two months. A bed was a bed. And people nothing more than pin-heads viewed from a pillow.

Two men carried me on a stretcher to the schoolroom, known before as the nursery. Special glass had been put in the windows to let the healing sunrays in. Father had contacted his old army friend from his Great War days in Macedonia and Salonika. 'He's the leading orthopaedic surgeon in London now, isn't that a lucky coincidence? He's coming all the way up here to take a look at you. I haven't seen him for fifteen years. Good old Tom Fairbank. You'll be getting the best care in the world.'

The schoolroom looked grand. Rufus had a bed so he could take naps with me during the day. The windows had big panes of glass instead of little ones.

A brand-new radio was by my bed on a table, along with a bell I could ring. Best, Berry, who had taken care of Alastair after his mastoid operation, was going to be my nurse. A bed was made for her on the opposite wall.

Poor Alastair was at Bannerman by himself. Our worlds were separate, and I wondered whose was better.

Berry was just as perfect as I remembered. She read to me, using different voices for the characters. She knew what I wanted before I did and was always cheerful. Even her name was cheerful – Berry, like merry. One day she was thumbing through my magazines, sitting in her chair nearby, but not too close. She was smart that way. The trouble with Mother was she was always too close or too far. When I was little, at Bannerman, I missed her so much I thought I'd die. Now she got on my nerves, wanting to kiss me all the time.

'Look, Graeme,' Berry said. 'Here's a competition for you.' She brought the magazine to me. '"In twenty-five words or less, tell us why you like Rowntree's Chocolate Crisp more than any other chocolate bar. The winner will go on an exciting, all-expenses paid two-week cruise of the lovely Mediterranean Sea with one parent. Only children eight to twelve eligible." Just think of that. Why don't you try?'

A trembly happiness flickered in my ribs. Chocolate Crisp was my favourite chocolate bar. Surely I could come up with the winning entry. Then I remembered how Berry had gone on a Mediterranean cruise with Alastair when he was seven to help him get his strength back after the mastoid operation. Here I was – nine. It was my turn. But I'd go for free!

'I'll do it. I know I can win. I'm good at things like that. And I will be all better by then. But Berry, you must go with me! You're the one who found the contest. It's only fair. Father and Mother are too busy. I want you to go. Just like you did with Alastair.'

'Well,' and she looked down, pleased and turning pink. 'We'll cross that bridge when we come to it.'

Thus began my goal – winning that competition. Having nothing to write on, I dictated to Berry, until Father rigged up a writing board. I must have sharpened pencils and thrown away wads of paper a hundred times.

Mr Fairbank came and went and I couldn't see what all the fuss was about. He did take a good look, turning me over like a pancake, examining my back, bone by bone. He kept calling me Timothy, even though Father said my name a couple of times before leaving us alone. I didn't think much of a man who couldn't keep his names straight.

The upshot of his visit was that after Christmas I'd be sent somewhere else again! I cried, but Father said it was for my own good. 'Morland Hall is just the place for you. Tom Fairbank will see to you himself.'

'How long will I be there? I want to be able to go on the cruise.'

'Oh Graeme, don't set your heart on that.'

'Why not?'

'Well,' and he waited before answering. 'There'll be so many entries, you never can tell.'

'You never know, though.'

'That's true. You never know.' He paused, thinking about something. 'You really will get the best care in the world. Lots of fresh air and sunshine. A man named Sir Henry Gauvain started his private clinic about ten years ago for people with tuberculosis.'

'Tuberculosis? I don't want to get tuberculosis! Are you crazy?' Tuberculosis was far worse than infantile whatever. All I needed was to walk again, get my muscles going, but these stupid people wouldn't let me get out of bed.

Father looked at me sharp. 'No, I am not crazy, and don't talk to me like that. Do you, at nine years old, think you know more than I do about medical matters?'

I knew I'd overstepped. All I could safely do was cry, which I did, turning my head into my pillow and sobbing.

I heard him sigh. 'Graeme, you must trust me. No one goes to Morland Hall until they are past the contagious stage. You won't get tuberculosis.'

I turned back, so he could see my miserable face. 'Are you sure?'

'I promise.'

'Can't I stay here and you be my doctor?'

'Afraid not. I wish you could. But doctors have their own special area of expertise, you see. Mine is eyes. Mr Fairbank knows about people who have trouble walking. People get tuberculosis in their limbs, you know, not just in their lungs.'

'How long will I be there?'

'Hmm. Hard to say.'

'I need to be walking again by spring.'

'Why's that?'

'Because of the cruise!' I reminded him again. 'Like Alastair's trip. Berry and I are planning on going together.'

'That settles it. Your best chance of going on that cruise is Morland Hall.'

Chapter 7

Mother considered the number thirteen to be good luck, in her case, and therefore mine, so we left for Morland Hall on the 13th of January 1934. An ambulance drove us to Dundee station for the 9 pm train. The driver I recognised, for he'd taken me from Elgin to Dundee. His name was Nick and I liked him.

When we arrived at the station, he lowered me into my wheelchair because my stretcher wouldn't fit on the carriage. A porter in a tight blue overcoat with brass buttons and big cap led our sad parade and carried our luggage. Mother went next.

As Nick wheeled me along the track, the sounds and steamy smells of the trains cheered me up. Even if it were only to a tuberculosis hospital, this was still a journey, and an overnight journey too. I'd never done that before.

'We have arrived,' the porter announced, stopping at a long wooden carriage, gleaming golden in the lamplight. On the side, in widely spaced black letters, shone the words, 'S L E E P I N G C A R R I A G E.'

'That must be you, lad,' Nick said in a jaunty voice. 'In we go.' Up a ramp he pushed me, following Mother and the oh-so-grand porter, who turned to the right, into a corridor that ran the length of the carriage along the outside windows. 'Madam is in the first two,' he said as he swung open a narrow door. We followed inside, where a long, narrow bed with two fluffy pillows stretched out on my left. A curved sink tucked into the right corner, with white towels hanging above, along silver rails mounted on the polished wood walls. Everything was small, but so neat and tidy, I couldn't help admiring it. Then, begging our pardon, because the four of us were quite a tight fit, the porter opened a door that led to the bedroom beside us. 'And of course, Madam has communicating accommodations.'

He swept out his arm toward Mother, as if inviting Queen Mary into his house, Nick and I just excess baggage. I peeked through the door and saw the same room but laid out the opposite way. 'Which room would Madam prefer?'

'I believe I'll take this one, seeing as I'm already in it.'

He gave a stiff nod and looked at the two suitcases at his feet. 'And which is Madam's suitcase?'

I could see this fellow was getting on Nick's nerves, because before the porter could move a muscle, Nick yanked my suitcase and set it on the shelf above the foot of my bed. With a rolling-eyed look of disgust toward the twit next door, he gently helped me off with my dressing gown and set me on my bed, legs hanging over the side. 'Now then,' he said, taking a folded blue blanket and tucking me in nice and tight. No one could have done better. He shook my hand and gave my cheek a cuff. 'I'll be off, then,' he called, and left, without waiting for a tip.

Through the connecting door, I watched the porter wait, his hand forward, while Mother dug out some coins from her handbag. Satisfied, he hurried past me, just sitting there, and gave me a look I'd never seen before. What was it? Fear, disgust? He hurried down the few stairs and banged shut the door. The train chugged off.

Mother joined me, sitting on my bed. 'This is an adventure, isn't it? I think everything will turn out all right. I feel it, don't you?' That annoyed me. How could she be so cocksure?

Someone knocked and brought in cocoa for me and gin and tonic for mother. 'First things first,' she said, 'Let's get you sorted. Turning me round so that my feet pointed toward the end of the bed, she gave me a strong, steady pull toward the head, plumping the two pillows with a couple of fist blows. I was surprised; she did it so well. 'Ah,' she said, sighing, 'this takes me back.'

'Tell you what. I'm going to get ready for bed. Then we'll both be cosy. I'll be right back.'

When she returned, she plopped comfortably at the foot of my bed. She lifted her knees and hugged them – something Cousin Isla might do. Not Mother. 'Takes you back to what?' I asked.

'Why, to my nursing days. Do you mind if I use this rug? Are you warm enough?'

I nodded. 'What nursing days?'

'During the War. You knew that.'

'No, I didn't.' Or if I did, it was something that happened so long ago; it didn't matter. My mother a nurse, like all the ones I'd seen during past months? My mother, who never kept still – fussing about her weight, hair, whether people enjoyed themselves at her parties.

'My goodness.' She looked stunned. 'I've never shown you my autograph book? With the officers' and soldiers' messages to me?'

'No.' I tried to imagine her in one of those big, white head-things.

'What an oversight! You must see it. I can't fathom that you didn't know about my war experience. My greatest moments. Maybe it's because people don't like to talk about the War. Even your father. So many injured.'

'Like me?'

She smiled a little. 'Yes, like you.' But then her face twisted into a squint, and she shook her head in a shudder. 'But oh, so much worse. You can't imagine.' But I wanted to imagine. What could be worse than what I had gone through? I wanted to know. I wanted to hear about injuries and suffering and pain.

'Tell me.'

'Well. Strangely enough, I enjoyed it. Do you mind if I put the blind up? I love looking out the window.' She turned out the overhead lights from a panel of switches, leaving on a small light beneath my bed. 'Now we can watch the world go by.' I couldn't see much, only a few starry lights on hillsides and the moon, far away. 'I need a dividend,' she said, which meant more gin, and went next door.

'Now, Caird Rest,' she said cuddling up where she was before, but her eyes fixed steadily on the nothing out the window. 'That's where I worked. The big Ogilvie house, on the Dundee Road. Wait – I need to go back a bit: When I was twelve, my mother gave me an autograph book for my birthday. They were all the rage. We would pass them around to our friends and we'd each write a poem or draw a picture on one of the pages and sign our names. The more the better; it showed how popular you were.'

'I bet you had a lot.'

'I had quite a few. But I always worried that people didn't like me.'

'I'm the same.'

'You? Oh, you're like your father. Everyone likes you.'

'They do?' It used to be true, but at Bannerman, my only friends were Jack and Specky, no matter what I did.

'Anyway, I stopped using my autograph book after a while, the way one does, until I went to Caird Rest and looked after the soldiers. I had the idea to ask them to sign it, if they could, or dictate something for me, so I could remember them. And just like the girls before them, they drew the prettiest pictures or wrote a kind message. That made me so happy. And when a soldier died, I wrote R.I.P. at the top of the page.'

'Tell me about being a nurse. What did you love about it? Tell me.'

She kept looking out the window through the dark, as if she was searching for something. 'I was doing something – important. Something useful. And I was good at it. I didn't mind, and some of them were so terribly wounded.'

'Like how?'

'I don't know. Arms missing. Legs. Some were blinded. One had his jawbone shot away.' She finished her dividend. 'I'll be back,' she said, and disappeared into her room again. Jawbone! I put my hand on mine, the part I ate and talked with – shot away! I moved mine up and down, chomping, and in a clear and terrible instant, understood its gone-ness. Forever never coming back. I didn't want to hear more.

Mother, though, was set free. She told me more and more, not about wounds, thankfully, but friends, meeting Father, the work that never ended, her fingers cracked and raw, the cups of tea late at night, when they put their feet up and found something to laugh about. 'We were doing our best. We were our best, and that's a wonderful feeling.'

But I was beginning to get a full-bladder feeling, not wonderful at all. I'd have to wee in my bottle, which was in my suitcase. Being metal, it hid whatever was inside, which was a relief; I would die if Mother saw my yellow pee swishing around. As for the other, Berry had given me an enema before I left, 'to avoid any problems on the train. But for your bottle, just ask her. She's your mother. She won't mind'.

'What shall I call it?'

'Call it what you always call it. Your bottle.'

'Will she know what I mean? She might not know what kind of bottle. She might think I mean a bottle of Orange Squash.'

I gathered my courage. 'Did you bring the men food, all their meals and everything? Even breakfast?'

'Of course! That's what I'm telling you. We did everything. We worked. You name it. I did it.' She looked at her watch and stood. 'We'd better get some sleep. I've been talking your ear off.' Without another word, she took my suitcase from the shelf, set it by my feet. Snap-snap, she opened it. I didn't say anything. She took out the shiny metal bottle, flat on one side, and curving up at the mouth where my willy went in. The moment had arrived. What if she pulled the covers back and tried to stick my willy in herself? Unthinkable horror.

Smooth as a swan, she set it down beside me against the wall and said, 'I'll be back when you're finished. The soldiers used to say, "Ready, nurse." How about you say, "Ready, Mother," and I'll come?'

'Good idea.'

* * *

I slept, but the train was so jostley, with lurches that made my heart lurch too. Then the train stopped for ages and I worried we'd broken down till I remembered Mother warning me this would happen, so that it wouldn't arrive into London in the middle of the night. As it was, we were due in at 7:20.

I was getting used to the train's comfortable rocking – it sounded like 'sugar-sugar-sugar' to me – when Mother's voice stabbed me. 'Graeme? Time to wake up. Come on. Graeme!'

'What time is it?' I felt murky and confused. Surely this was the middle of the night, but there she was, standing over me, holding my breakfast tray, already dressed.

'Six fifteen.' She lifted a silver dome from my plate and sniffed. 'Mmm. Smells delicious. Come on, sweetheart.'

Sleep pulled me back with warm, soft arms. 'Ten minutes more.'

'I'm afraid not. Look. I've got a nice, hot facecloth ready.' No use struggling. She helped me up with that firm, strong, nurse's pull. The facecloth did feel good, pressed on my cheeks. I breathed in the steam. Less pleasant, I cleaned my teeth, spitting into the water as it slapped back and forth in the bowl. A little spilled, but not much.

'Now you've earned your breakfast,' she said, placing the tray on my lap as if it were a prize. She lifted the dome again. 'Don't you love the china pattern? The little pink roses and green leaves around the rim?'

I wasn't loving anything, especially the smell of kippers. I tried to get down what I could, but she ended up finishing my kippers.

As we approached London, she raised the blind, but it was still dark, the day just beginning. Unpleasant lights from factories and long buildings shone back at us. Several tunnels made my ears hurt, 'a sign we're almost there,' Mother said.

Chapter 8

King's Cross Station, London. Steam clouds gushed toward us from the engine. People rushed from the train as if their lives depended on it, thousands of hats and coats and trolleys laden with baggage leant toward the station. Not us. We took our time. Mother helped me with my dressing gown. A lonely feeling soaked me through. How different we were from these people with important places to go. We couldn't move till Collyer came. How weak to sit and wait for rescue.

Collyer was from Daimler Hire. He was a legend in the family – the most dependable, knowledgeable, kindest chauffeur. Granny Cochrane discovered him years ago on a London trip and now the family requested him whenever anyone went someplace special. He'd even driven Granny and her sons to Monte Carlo.

Mother looked happier once we heard his jolly, loud rap at our door. He was tall, with wide strong shoulders in his grey chauffeur's uniform. I could see what Mother meant. I was a feather, the way he swooped me up and carried me onto the platform where a wheelchair waited. Soon we were seated in the finest ambulance I'd seen (and I'd seen a few). A beautiful leather divan for me, on one side, and a matching seat for mother on the other. Smoked glass allowed us to see out, with no one seeing in, and when Collyer pushed a button, we could hear him. Another button raised my head up and down. I almost perked up till Mother said, 'Stop playing with it or you'll break it.' So when Collyer began pointing out the great Houses of Parliament, the palaces, the statues honouring this or that battle, I lowered the bed, closed my eyes and disappeared.

* * *

'Nearly there, Graeme.' Mother said, tapping my shoulder. Through grey glass I peered at greyer barns, stone houses, dirty sheep. We came to Alton, 'such a pretty town, don't you think? Jane Austen lived here.' Her cheeriness made me sick.

'Where's Morland Hall?'

'There,' Collyer said. We stared. It looked a mess. Mother said it had once been a rich man's house, but some doctor had stuck glass porches all over the brick. 'A bit higgledy – piggledy,' she said, worried.

A bustle of people greeted us, smiling, welcoming, matter-of-fact. Danger. Watch out. This was how Bannerman started.

'How are you, Graeme,' one said.

I wanted to say – terrified. They never knew the old self – the clever, adventurous one. 'Fine,' but slow tears betrayed me.

A nurse took us to a big room with about eight other boys, all lying in beds. She pushed my wheelchair next to one of them, where a tubby, round face stared down at me. 'Say hello to Derek, Graeme. He's going to be your roommate.' I kept my head down.

'He hardly slept on the train,' Mother said. 'I do apologise.'

'That's all right,' a nurse said. 'Everything can be a bit much at first. It might be better if he gets adjusted on his own. It's usually the way.'

'I understand. Well, darling,' she looked at her watch, 'I suppose I should get back to London. I don't want to keep your uncle waiting.'

'My uncles? Why? What are you doing with them?'

'Oh.' She bit her lip, afraid. She'd made a mistake. 'Er, your Uncle Sandy and I have tickets to the panto.'

This was the bloody end. I gathered all the hate I could muster into narrowed eyes, lips tight over bared teeth. 'Have fun.'

'Oh, Graeme,' she said, covering her eyes, head down. Was she crying? I hoped so.

A nurse took her elbow and led her out. 'As soon as you're gone,' I heard her say, 'he'll be fine.' Oh no, I won't.

Dinner on trays came after – some reasonable muck I couldn't help finishing, but when a trolley laden with dishes of half-melted ice cream rolled in, I was ambushed! The doctor in Dundee had said I must never, ever, eat ice cream!

Well, out tumbled a Reekie Linn of tears. I didn't care if everyone thought I was a baby. I didn't care if I died and I would keep crying until I did.

I think I frightened them. They kept lifting the ice cream bowl to my mouth, but my crying hiccups made it impossible to speak. Finally I got out – 'I'm n-n-ot all-l-lowed i-i-ce cream.'

One nurse said, 'Not allowed ice cream? Whoever said such a thing.'

'M-m-y d-d-octor in D-d-d-undee.'

'Well, the doctor in Alton happens to be Sir Henry Gauvain,' she nearly shouted his name, 'Is your doctor a Knight of the Realm?' I shook my head. 'I didn't think so. You tell that doctor in Dundee that Sir Henry says any child who has appetite for ice cream is allowed ice cream.' She peeped up under my face. 'Do you have an appetite for ice cream?'

I nodded.

'Where's your handkerchief, then?' From my pyjama pocket I fumbled for the one Mother had placed there. The world could end, as far as she was concerned, but if a gentleman didn't have a freshly ironed handkerchief in a pocket, he might as well give up living. Quickly I placed it over my face, gathering the flood of tears and snot, and life began again. But as I spooned down the ice cream, I could feel the boys' eyes sneaking disdainful looks. I was glad when Derek and I were wheeled off to our room. I knew it would take a long time to live down such a complete collapse.

Derek was six months younger than me, but as we chatted, it felt more like six years. Nevertheless, I learned, people came to Morland Hall for three things. Tuberculosis, Derek said, was out of style – like short skirts or big hats – so they took stomach glands and neck glands, instead. He was in for stomach glands and would be going home in a month. He'd never heard of infantile paralysis. But then he told me, as if this was great news, that his father sold cars in Colchester, Essex.

Next morning, they asked if I would like a Marmite sandwich for tea. I didn't know what it was, but said yes, not wanting to cause trouble after the ice cream outburst. One bite told me I'd made a mistake. It looked like dog poo and tasted worse. Finishing it was impossible, so I wrapped it in comic paper and set it on the frame under my mattress.

Life moved slowly at Morland Hall. I had never encountered such kindness or low expectations; it was different from home or Bannerman. Here, wiggling toes was exciting. At occupational therapy, I learned to darn a sock and embroider a rose on a round wood frame.

Yet outside this warm circle the nurses provided were boxes of rules set by the almighty doctors. It was January and freezing, but everyone was wheeled out all day onto tin-roofed balconies. Some were there day and night. Sir

Henry had the idea that if fresh air and sunshine were good for tuberculosis, they were good for everything. 'Don't worry, when it warms up a little and you're fatter and stronger, you can join the others.'

And whenever a doctor arrived? What a turnabout. You'd think God was coming to call.

Mr Fairbank made his first of many grand appearances about a week after my arrival. He did all the flipping and poking he'd done before, asked a few questions, which I had to answer twice because he was going deaf. Evidently the curvature of my spine, which had begun at Forte House, was worse. A bed splint was ordered for me to lie in, night and day, except when I sat up for meals. He ordered a splint for my right foot, so it would stay pointing up, with a cage to fit over it, so the bed covers wouldn't get too heavy. Who heard of bedclothes getting too heavy? I was nervous. None of this had to do with walking but had a great deal to do with lying in bed for a long time. 'We don't want you crooked, do we, Timothy?'

'No sir. I've got a cruise to go on.'

* * *

Passing the time was the problem. Derek had boxes of comics and a wireless, which was nice, but no books. I was keen on the Henty books and the William ones, and anything to do with the Wild West. Then I remembered how Alastair and I made up stories, taking turns adding a bit. I gave it a go with Derek but we struggled to understand each other – me with my Scottish accent and he with God knew what. Rs didn't exist and a strange little grunt replaced a T. 'Wuh' he'd say for 'what.' And 'Bwi-ish Empa' for 'British Empire.' Still these were desperate times, so I decided to work with what I had.

'I'll start,' I said. 'Show you how it works. I tell a little, then pass it over to you, like a rugby ball.'

'Uh don play rugby.'

I began my tale: 'Dangerous Dan was the best rifle shot in the whole of the Wild West. He could shoot the Ace of Spades right out of a card's middle. His father had taught him. But then his father died, and Dan...'

'Dangerous Dan.'

'He wasn't called Dangerous Dan then. That came when he grew up... Dan had to fend for himself.'

'Wuh's "fend"?'

'Fend. Take care of. Look after himself.'

'Wuh abow 'is Muva?'

'She died, too. Shh, you're mixing me up. Listen, and don't interrupt. So, he got on his trusty horse, Meg' – Meg! – and I thought of Tam O'Shanter so long ago, at Craigisla. True, my story was in the Wild West, but surely they had ghosts there, too. I would tell the gruesome story of Tam O'Shanter to Derek, and with luck, scare the pants off him. 'So pretty soon, Dan's getting hungry, and he rides his trusty nag, Meg, into town.'

'Wuh town?'

'I don't know – town. It's getting dark as night, and the wind is starting to come up something fierce, so he goes into the saloon and orders a tankard of ale and whisky mixed together. All the men start telling ghost stories, and remembering when they last saw demons and witches...'

'Wenzit my turn?'

'Shh. Soon. Longer if you keep interrupting! After a couple of hours, it's getting late and he has to head for home.' Hold on a minute! I just remembered Dan had left home for good. I was stuck. Where could he go? Ah, I had it. Sometimes I was so clever I couldn't stand it.

'So he asks the barman, "Would there be a hotel or an inn nearby where I could spend the night?"'

'"Oh yes, there's one about three miles away. Only trouble is, you just have to go through a forest to get there, where a baby was murdered and some lady hanged herself. Further on, there's an old church, but it's haunted with witches and dead bodies who climb out of their coffins and dance about in the candlelight, but never mind." All right, Derek. It's your turn now.'

'It's about time. All right. So Dan says to the bloke, "Say, you don't have a barn I could sleep in, do ya?" "Why, sure as shootin' I do," the man says. "But it will cost ya' a quid."'

'They don't have quids in America. They use dollars!' What an idiot.

'Shh. So the barman says, "Sure as shooting I do, and what's more – it won't cost you a penny. It's free!"' Derek was pleased as punch with himself. 'He wakes, it's a sunny day and he thinks, I sure am glad I ain't slept in no hotel. I saved money, and what's more, I didn't have to go through no stupid haunted forest." And he rides off on his horse and gets rich. And that's the end of the story.'

Unbelievable. The dolt didn't know the first thing about spinning a tale. 'He has to go through the forest, you dummy, and see the witches dancing!'

'No he doesn't.'

Derek was even more stupid about the radio.

We used to listen to *Storytime* during rest after lunch, but one day, he said, 'I've got an idea,' he whispered across the bed to me, excited. 'Let's tune into the BBC News instead.'

'What do you want to do that for?'

'Because Mr Martin likes to listen to the news.' Mr Martin had the room next door and snored like a hog. 'Silly, don't you see?'

'No.'

'Well, if we tune into his station before he does, he won't be able to listen to it. Isn't that a splendid trick?'

'What are you talking about? You think only one person can listen to a radio station at a time?'

'That's the way they work... isn't it?'

'No, it isn't! Two people can't listen to two different stations on the same radio at the same time, but thousands of people, millions of people, can listen to the same station on different radios, all over the country.'

'Oh.' I laughed my head off. I couldn't wait to write Alastair and Father.

Derek got his laugh on me a few days after that, however, when some nurses came in to change the beds. 'What's that smell,' one said as she came close to me. She sniffed and made a bad face. 'There's something rather – untoward.'

'I don't smell anything,' I said.

'Have either of you had an accident?'

Derek and I both said, 'No!' in shocked voices.

'Hmph,' the other one said, sniffing, 'I see what you mean.' She walked to Derek's bed, then back to mine. 'Phew, it's definitely coming from your bed, Graeme. Have you been storing anything like cheese? She bent toward the wooden frame under my mattress, which was standing on legs above it. 'Oh dear,' she said, peeking further underneath. 'What's this?'

I knew what it was. For the past couple of weeks I'd been stashing the Marmite sandwiches on the frame. I didn't know what else to do with them.

'I'm afraid it's my Marmite sandwiches, sister. I don't care for them.' It took a few moments for them to understand what had happened. They laughed as if they'd never stop. They had to sit, and Derek started roaring too.

'Graeme, dear,' one of them gasped, 'you don't have to eat Marmite sandwiches. There's a choice, you silly goose. Whatever you like. Cheese. Egg mayonnaise. Whatever.'

After they staggered out, no doubt looking for people to tell, Derek kept laughing. 'Didn't you know the Marmite would go bad?'

'I didn't think about it.' I tried to sound haughty.

'I may not be as clever as you about Wild West stories but putting old Marmite sandwiches under the bed is the stupidest thing I've ever heard of.'

About a month later, after Derek had gone home, Mr Fairbank paid another visit. Pretty soon, I'd be joining a larger group, and after the usual once-over, he said, 'Well, Timothy, my lad, the back splint is doing you a world of good. You're straightening out like a young sapling. I think it's time to fit you with callipers.'

'What's that?' All I could think of was caterpillars.

'Callipers. You don't know what a calliper is? Goodness. The nurses should tell you these things.' He looked up at Sister Southall, who was known as Auntie. I liked her because she read to me. 'It's a metal apparatus that will help you walk. In time, your left leg could be fine, but your right one needs help.'

'I see,' I said, as cheerfully as I could. 'When can I start?'

'I'll take measurements today. You should have it in a month.'

'A month!'

'Sometimes less.'

'I need to be walking by May.'

'Why May, pray tell?' He looked over his glasses, bald head shining.

'The cruise starts!' And copying his voice, I added, 'The nurses should tell you these things.'

He glared at me. 'And what cruise would that be, pray tell?'

'The Mediterranean cruise!' I managed not to add, 'You jackass.'

'I think that's a bit prrre-mat-ure, Timothy,' he said, trilling the 'r's extra-long. 'You won't be walking until Christmas, at the earliest.'

'Christmas?' I asked faintly.

'That's the usual time. Let's take a look at your legs, shall we?' Sister Southall lifted the covers. There they lay – scrawny, white horrible things – the right one especially. The foot looked like a dead bird. My left leg was thicker, pinker. It would wiggle when I wanted. I could imagine running on its muscles, strong again. 'Cock your left leg for me.' I did. 'Good. Now wiggle your toes.' The left leg passed the tests.

'Now, bend your bad leg.' I had never heard 'bad leg' before, as if it were a misbehaving child. 'Try that movement you did last time. You had a little function, as I remember.' With concentration, I managed the tiniest movement of my toes. 'That's all? What if I tickle your leg...' and he took from his bag a battered white feather and stroked my thigh.

'Stop!' I yelled. The bloody bastard was torturing me! My left knee jerked in outrage, but my right leg could do nothing! Hideous, horrible.

'Just as I thought.' He put the bugger – I never wanted to see a feather again – in to his bag. Looked at me in what might have been a smile. 'Your left one will be right as rain one day.'

'And my right?' I asked shakily, not wanting the answer. 'How long will I need the caterpillar?'

More teeth showed. 'For the rest of your life, my boy.' His eyes went to the floor. Even he couldn't face me. 'It's been six months since you fell ill. If your leg hasn't regained mobility, it never will. What you see today is as good as it will ever be. No one's told you this?'

'No.' I could hardly hear my voice. Sister Southall put her hand on my shoulder.

'Well, you've one good leg. Treat it well; it will serve you well. Sister, hold this end of the tape measure, will you?' The two of them took several readings, then he measured my left leg. 'As I suspected. The left one is already longer. The right will require a built-up shoe in time.' He nodded for Sister Southall to put the covers back. 'I'll try to get the calliper ready in a couple of weeks.' He rested his hand on my knee and left.

'I've got to follow Mr Fairbank,' Nurse Southall said. 'Are you all right?' I gave one nod. 'I'll send someone along to be with you.' She squeezed my arm and went too.

How long I lay alone I couldn't guess. Smells of meat, clattering of metal lids and trolleys wandered into my room. Before dinnertime was always busy, I knew. I reached for a comic on my table, but it fell to the floor. I rang the little bell that had been beside it. I rang it again; then again; then finally dropped it on the floor, on purpose. I enjoyed the sound of its landing and rolling about till it stopped.

A heavy twist at the bottom of my gut grew tighter. Time to ring for the bedpan. But no bell. Should I shout? Here I was, just told I'd have to lug around my bad leg the rest of my life, in a bunch of iron and leather and a built-up shoe. And all I can do is call for a bedpan. How fitting. My shitting. Oh, it rhymed. Splendid. Oh yes, that's me! Marvellous Me, the poet.

Pressure on my bottom made me squeeze again. 'Hello,' I called, and waited. And again, but some rage inside my belly screamed. I won't wait. Here. This is for you. Here's what I think of all of you – and your bloody lies. I pushed out as hard as I could and the hatred felt like victory.

Chapter 9

No one said a word about my 'accident', but they moved me to a bigger ward with about eight boys, mostly younger, to give me company. It must be lonely all by yourself, they said. True, but it was the doing nothing that was the worst. One day I even found myself thinking fondly of Bannerman, the way the day was organised into hour-long sections – English – French – Break – Maths – Dinner – Latin – Games – and I knew I had hit the bottom of the bottom. Wishing I were back at the loneliest place in the world. Yet, these days with no shape were even worse, with the room widening out, the pale green walls and high hanging lamps moving further and further away from me, till I lay in such a hugeness that I grew afraid and rang for nurse.

The thought of the cruise died away, too, as spring threatened its arrival. Like when one is reading a book by a window and it's getting later and darker, but one doesn't notice till the sun sets at last and one suddenly can't see. How did that happen? Why did I not notice the light fading?

Ten days later, my calliper arrived. Mr Fairbank had worked a bloody miracle, getting it here so soon. A new doctor, lower-down and younger, brought it. With a handshake I mistrusted, he introduced himself as Dr Webb. He held the contraption out toward me, flat, in both arms. It looked like a long gun, a weapon of some kind, maybe a small canon. Two metal bars, long as my leg and as wide apart, were wrapped with several leather belts buckling round it. 'It's heavy,' he said. 'You try.'

I held out my arms to take the weight of it, and they collapsed onto the bed. 'Don't worry. You'll get used to it.' I looked down at the foreign, gleaming thing. 'Try again. You can lift it. It's a surprise at first, but pretty soon, you won't even notice it.' I managed the second time, and got a whiff of new leather, a smell I loved.

'Excellent.' He put his hand on my shoulder and took the calliper away, leant it up against the wall. 'Let's get started. Now,' he said, taking hold of my covers, 'May I?'

'May you what?'

'Take a look at your legs. We could get started if you like.' I stared at him. This doctor-man, what was his name, was asking my permission.

'You may,' I said, but his question sounded so odd and I was so grateful, I started to cry.

'There, there,' he said, and sitting down, held my head onto his chest. 'The world is a terrible place, sometimes. That's why we need …' I waited for his answer. But none came.

So I said, 'Callipers.'

'Exactly so,' he said, and we began.

He touched the very top of my right thigh where it joined my body. 'These muscles here, these are your hip flexors. Lucky for you, you'll be using them to walk. Everything below is gone, but these will see you through. We'll have to build them up gradually. This tiny little muscle is the key to your success. Only it isn't so tiny.' He held his hand on the crease of my thigh. He pushed my hand against it.

'Don't tickle me!' I screamed.

'Never. If I do, hit me. Give me a black eye. Now. Seeing this muscle is so important, we should call it by its right name – the iliopsoas. You put your hand on it. Close your eyes. Good. Now, can you feel my hand on yours?' I nodded. Try lifting your leg against your hand.'

I hadn't a clue what to do. 'Never mind. It's a long muscle that starts at the back of your spine and has the possibility to be very strong.' He drew a picture on a bit of folded paper he took from his side pocket. 'These are your ribs from the back, and this long thing like an eel, connects all the way from your spine to the front of your leg. Imagine that. So, we'll develop a programme for you. Five minutes a day will be enough.'

'That's all?'

'We'll increase it, bit by bit. Your iliopsoas will be like Hercules. You'll see. The first thing is for you to find the muscle.' From another pocket, he took a toy tin soldier, a simple Tommy in Mufti, and placed it on the spot. 'See if you can get him to move. Make him jump. That's all. I'll be back tomorrow.'

* * *

I was sitting up in the solarium, writing a letter home, when I noticed a man nearby in a wheelchair watching me. He had a stiff pad of paper on his knees. 'I'm sorry,' he said. 'I'm trying to figure out what kind of animal you are.'

'I beg your pardon?' I said politely, but beginning to worry.

'Perhaps I should introduce myself. My name is Harold Obken, and I am an artist. I am a permanent resident. So far we have not had the pleasure of introduction. And what might your name be, sir?'

'Graeme Moodie,' but I didn't feel happy about giving out this information.

'Graeme Moodie. Scottish, eh? I like the way you give that little burr on the "Gr." I love Scotland. Beautiful country.' He looked out the windows. 'I like to look at a person,' he went on, 'get to know him, then I paint him – watercolour is my preferred medium – as the animal that suits him best.'

Excellent. Not only was I stuck at Morland Hall, I was stuck in the same room with a lunatic who might have a knife under his drawing pad. Luckily, he was stuck in a wheelchair – unless he was faking and might leap up and stab me through the heart.

'A number of my works are on the wall here. Have you noticed? But you've only just arrived. When was that?'

'January the fifteenth.' An eternity to me.

'1934?'

'Well, of course.'

'I was one of the first inhabitants. I've been here since 1927. I don't have to be here, but I prefer it.'

'You've been here seven years? Since I was two?'

'Seven, exactly. Hold on! You worked that out. Ah, a clever lad. You know how I tell?' I didn't have to say anything. This was what Father called a one-sided conversation. 'The eyes – the eyes reveal everything. Don't worry, I'll figure out what kind of animal you are, but I have to get to know you better first. Toodle-oo. Time for my bath. *à bientôt! Auf wiedersehen.*' He wheeled himself away. At least I had something to write to my parents about.

* * *

The hardest thing was sitting on the edge of the bed. I needed a nurse on either side or I'd fall over like an axed tree and onto the floor. I got to know the nurses well, Nurse Savage (but she wasn't) and Nurse Hogg (but she wasn't, either).

'Here come the Savage Hoggs!' one of them would call out, peeping round the corner of the ward door and every time it made me laugh.

Each day, they sat a little further away, and only occasionally called out 'Timber!' as I crashed sideways and they pushed me up straight again. Eventually they trusted me to put my hands on the mattress to hold my own self up.

After I'd mastered this amazing feat, I needed to swing my legs over the bedside. But before I could attempt this, I had to work with pulleys to build up my arms and 'good' leg.

The exercise room was splendid because it used to be a ballroom with a beautiful crystal chandelier in the centre. On a sunny day, the light from the windows shot through the crystals and onto my bed – pink and green and blue.

Over my bed rolled a wood frame on wheels, with ropes and pulleys attached. Dr Webb hung my left leg in a sling that attached to the ropes with a hook and lifted it into the air. My mission was to pull my leg down as far as possible, let it back up, and try again. Five times only, then I could increase it by one each day. I loved the order and progress of it.

I wore a pair of shorts, navy blue, like Bannerman's and watched the left leg get pinker and thicker, the hairs standing up in goose bumps. But the treacherous right lay motionless, a dead fish on sand. Heavy. To shift it required both hands.

'Gently, gently, steady,' Dr Webb warned if I became impatient as I lugged it around on the bed. I tried to show him how I could get the tin soldier to bounce high off my psoas muscle – a new trick. Up until then, the little sergeant could only twitch and fall over. Now I could make him leap into the air. Yet just when Dr Webb was watching, he stood there, not even toppling. I was so fed up; I slapped my thigh. The pain surprised me.

'Don't do that!' Dr Webb shouted, as if defending his child against a bully. A big red blotch grew on my thigh in an ugly bloom, hand-shaped. 'Don't hate it. It's not its fault.'

'Oh, yes it is!' I was determined not to be nice. 'Stupid, bloody leg.' I growled.

He gave a sad shrug. 'It's no one's fault. Just bad luck. That's all, I'm afraid. A fleck of something nasty went into your mouth while you were swimming – where was it?'

'Lossiemouth.' The word was unbearable to my ears. 'I fell in a race with Alastair. He didn't trip me on purpose, but my knee was cut badly. Then I got a fever and terrible pains that turned out to be infantile paralysis, but no one knew till later. My left leg's getting better, but my right one's paralysed forever.'

'And you go over it and over it, in your mind, that fall?'

I nodded, then he nodded, but no one said anything. Finally, he did. 'Infantile paralysis is still a mystery, but in the United States they've had some serious epidemics, much worse than ours, and they've studied it more than we have. Even the President of the United States has what they call "polio", so you're in good company. They think it comes from contaminated water. Nowadays they're pumping raw sewage into the sea most everywhere. Some of it contains the polio virus. You probably swallowed it in Lossiemouth and it spread from your stomach to your blood, then lodged in your spine where it attacked the nerves in your back and legs. It may be that because your right leg was already weakened by your fall, it didn't recover like your left, but you'll never know. Best call it bad luck.' With that, he left, patting my shoulder, his way of saying goodbye. 'You're making good progress, lad. Keep up the good work.'

The President of the United States had polio?

* * *

Mr Obken had fuzzy ears. I'd never seen the like of them. If I had to guess what kind of animal he was, I'd say mouse, with all that fur lining his lugholes and the tips of his ears. Some women, I knew, were terrified of mice, but Mother wasn't. She waged war against the invaders. Out came the traps, with Alastair and me tossing their sweet bodies over the edge of the terrace. Mr Obken was wilier than a mouse and possibly more vicious. What was he – a ferret? A fox?

I was sitting at a card table, working on a new Meccano biplane, with floats so it could land on water. Nothing existed except this plane.

A wee spring had got caught in the end of the nose. I was doing my best to stay calm. I tried the toothpick and pipe cleaner that came with the kit. I could not get it out.

A sharp voice asked, 'What's up?' Mr Obken, for certain. I still didn't trust him. I explained the problem, banging the nose vigorously on the table surface. 'What you need is tweezers.'

'Well, I haven't got any.'

'Well, I do,' he said. 'Medical ones.' He reached inside his jacket pocket. 'Here we are, just the ticket.' Down he plopped a frightening-looking implement, long and thin and shiny. 'I often find them useful.' For what, I wondered. I took them carefully and squeezed the narrow pincers like a doctor; so exact and careful, down into the plane nose, and it worked! 'Got it!' I said, drawing out the tightly coiled spring, nasty little bugger. 'Thank you, Mr Obken.'

'No need to be so formal, my boy. Think nothing of it. Very happy to oblige. Can I see what you're working on?'

'Of course.'

I could tell he knew a lot about Meccano kits. He didn't take over, though, but watched me work, giving me a tip now and then.

A nurse brought us tea – the scones loaded with jam, the clotted cream, the grownup china – and as we watched the world outside the solarium, I asked, more to myself than him, 'What is luck, I wonder.'

'Ah,' was all he said.

'Dr Webb says it was just bad luck that made me get infantile paralysis, or as he says, "polio."'

'Poliomyelitis is correct term.'

'You've heard of it?'

'Has a fish heard of swimming?'

It took me a second to twig. 'You had it?'

'Does the King have a crown?' Yes! Right in front of me sat a kinsman, my first! 'But Graeme, those are easy questions. What luck is, that's difficult to answer. What do you think it is?'

'I don't know. My mother talks about luck all the time. Good luck, bad luck. Warding it off, bringing it on. But what is it? I can't understand how something called luck, as if it were nothing more than a breeze skittling by, can change your life.'

'That's the nature of luck, my lad. These are the imponderables of the universe. For me, luck is one of them, an accident, something no one can prepare for. Is luck God, fluttering down to bestow wealth or catastrophe? And how do we know whether a piece of luck is good or bad?'

'That's easy,' I said. 'Look at us. Wouldn't you call what happened to us the worst luck in the world? Some germ gets into our mouths and ruins our lives forever?'

'Absolutely true. But think of this. I'd probably be dead if I hadn't contracted poliomyelitis. In 1914, when the Great War started, I was eighteen. All the young men, hale and hearty, marched off to find glory. As for me, polio had wrapped its tentacles round my legs when I was sixteen. I couldn't join them in the trenches, where they found death, disfigurement. Disease. If they were lucky enough to escape those things – that word again – they saw their dear comrades die. How do you think they felt about that? Before I came here, I was in a Veteran's Hospital. Some men, without a wound on their bodies, had their minds blown through. A wounded brain is the worst; no one honours it. It's called cowardice, lily-livered, not up to scratch. I saw men shaking so badly they couldn't walk. Some screamed for hours at the sight of a broom because they thought they were about to be shot. Who was the lucky one then?'

Chapter 10

Gradually, I understood that I was becoming a long-term resident, along with Mr Obken. Morland Hall was a pleasant, clattery old hotel with unusual furnishings, where most people came and went, but not us. I decided not to get too friendly with the other boys, because sooner or later, they'd go home, leaving me sadder than ever.

I'd learned my lesson. Early on, a boy named Andrew Marin came, and we hit it off like a bomb. The day after his operation he called for a double dish of vanilla ice cream and for someone to set up his wireless. Andrew Marin was a boy to know. He was quick and clever, and he could tell good stories. Also, every day, he tuned in at 5:15 to something called *Children's Hour*, which I adored –from the music-box tune in the beginning to the final 'Goodnight children, everywhere,' at six o'clock.

Best of all was the superb Commander Stephen King-Hall, whose voice delved right into my mind, making it prickle. He talked about history, politics and current affairs. 'Is leisure bad? No. The more, the better, I say, and so would you, I imagine. Let's say, for example, that 2 million are unemployed and 10 million are employed. The unemployed are at leisure, but they need things; the employed have things, but they have no leisure. What we have is badly distributed leisure, not an unemployment problem.' If people did as he said, Andrew and I decided, the world's problems would be solved.

We also enjoyed the nature talks, though the man didn't know how lucky he was to be able walk at all. Sometimes I hated him and when I said that to Andrew, he simply nodded, which was the perfect thing to do. His silence finally paid honour to my suffering.

I was always glad to see him. Coming back from my walking lessons, I wheeled my chair faster toward the ward, knowing he'd look up from reading *Biggles* or *Just William*, look at me cross-eyed and stick out his tongue. And no matter whether I'd made no progress that day and was snarling at the nurses and drenched in sweat, I'd laugh.

But two months later? He disappeared! Ambushed once again! Some bad Indian, hiding behind a rock had shot an arrow into my heart. I missed him so, I was ashamed.

Let them go, the lot of them. Mother, Father, even Alastair, carrying on – la-de-da – without a nod toward my empty chair at the dining table. Panic – what did they do with my napkin ring? Silver, my name engraved in a scrolly script, given to me when I was christened and still bearing my teeth marks because I liked to bite it and Mother didn't mind. Did she polish it anymore on a Sunday afternoon? I imagined her calling us to dinner, standing at the foot of the staircase, where that dear, sweet smell seeped out of wooden panelling, a forest of walnut that wrapped itself round the space rising to the skylight, to welcome whatever sun Dundee could muster. Stop it, Moodie!

* * *

I did manage a new wireless out of them, by writing a long, sad letter about how much I missed hearing the programmes that taught me so much, now that the rich boy had left with his.

Surely Mother wouldn't have sold my napkin ring. Stop!

* * *

Learning to walk again was so difficult! How did babies manage it? First, I had to become vertical – for the first time in nearly a year. Dr Webb was there for the occasion, and he and the nurses laughed, saying they were raising a barn. I swung an arm around two shoulders and they lifted me from the edge of the bed. My calliper supported my right leg; the left leg trembled like a leaf.

But there I was, no longer flat. What astonished me was how much I'd grown! My eyes were so high up – taller than the nurse beside me and not far off the height of Dr Webb. I looked round the room from my new position, thrilled. 'Oh my,' was all I could say.

My walking lessons involved a frame that looked like a metal skirt. I stood inside it, wearing my calliper, with a square of bars around my waist, another much bigger square on the floor, around my feet. The skirty look came from curving bars that ballooned out from my waist to the floor. It was the strangest contraption. But it worked. The lessons left me panting like a dog and in a glorious, athletic sweat. 'Hurray for Graeme!' the nurses shouted, coaxing me on.

My family was coming to visit at the end of July. I *had* to be walking by then.

Nevertheless, despite my inch-by-inch improvements, as July wended its way through balmy nights on the balcony, it became clear I would not be walking, not even with sticks. I couldn't bear for them to see me struggling inside that iron ballgown, as one nurse called it. I resolved to stay in my wheelchair. The nurses tried to dress me in the suit Mother sent, but it was too small, so I stayed in my dressing gown.

The visit was not a success. Matron took us to the craft room, to see the sort of things we did. I enjoyed needlepoint, and on the wall, framed, was something I'd made, called 'Strawberry Thief.' I'd spent hours doing the stitches, enjoying the silky feel of the threads in rich reds and greens. I became good at darning socks. On the more boyish side, I painted a small wooden bar a glossy brown and screwed four brass hooks into it. This was a gift for Father, to hang his keys on by the front door. I didn't give it to him, though. I could tell he didn't like the look of anything in the room. 'When and where do they study?' he asked the Matron. 'You know, become educated.'

'We believe,' she answered, her voice full of patience and pity, 'that it is best for our children to learn a trade so that they may become employable in the future. We teach them to weave cloth and baskets. Basic woodworking skills are encouraged. Modest cottage industries that give satisfaction and provide a bit of income.' Father's eyes darted about; it was obvious he wanted to leave, the way he rocked on his heels, his hands behind him, sighing. 'Dear God,' he muttered to Mother as we left.

Because the weather was fine, we took tea on the wide, soft lawn, shaded by great trees overhanging us like umbrellas. We did our best to be cheerful, eating smoked salmon sandwiches and ginger cake around a white metal table. I told Father about Commander King-Hall's idea of dividing up leisure and work among the employed and the unemployed, but all he said was, 'Hmmmph. Socialist nonsense.'

He stood, brushed off invisible crumbs – a habit Mother hated.

'Come on, everybody,' he almost shouted. 'We're going for a ride.'

He didn't ask anyone on staff if it were all right, because he was a doctor friend of Mr Fairbank's. He jiggled one arm under my bottom, another behind my back under my arms and up I went, swinging my inside arm around his neck. I was used to being lifted by orderlies, but not like this, from the ancient times we both remembered perfectly. 'Ready, steady...' and together we said, 'Go.'

He set me tenderly onto the back seat. Alastair lumbered in beside me. We breathed in the air of familiar territory. Father's sweet pipe and Mother's perfumes dented the deep, leathery car-smells I'd forgotten. As he started the motor, its rumble started us too.

Our four backbones pushed hard against the seats as Father jerked us into gear and crumbling the stones beneath the tyres, we took off, our wild and happy car tearing up and down hills, past field after field of freshly mown golden hay, waiting to be gathered into bales. Father called out the sights, as he'd always done, as if we needed his help to see. It was like old times. When they drove away, my sickening friend, loneliness, crept back into my stomach.

* * *

A few days after the family left, I was called into Dr Webb's office. He held the door open as I wheeled in. Perching on the edge of his wide, paper-stacked desk, he folded his arms and looked at me closely. He looked tired, not his cheerful self. 'How are you,' and then strangely, 'dear boy?'

'All right,' I said.

'How did the visit go?'

'Fine,' I said quickly, preferring to look at the oak patterns on the floor rather than his gentle face. Thankfully, he returned to business.

'You're doing well here, you know. Polio is a difficult disease, with a long rehabilitation. Still, Mr Fairbank is pleased with your progress. You're on your way to walking and returning to a normal life. But after consulting with your parents, the decision is that you will remain here a while longer where you receive the best treatment possible. Naturally, however, they are concerned about your education. Mr Fairbank wants me to arrange a tutor for you so that you don't fall behind. What do you say to that?'

'Not much.'

'Most of our patients are here for shorter periods, you see.'

'I do see. I see it all the time.' I heard my voice falter.

'I'm sure you do,' he said sadly. Then more like his old self, he said, 'There's something else we could try. The BBC has a programme for schools, where the children listen to the wireless as part of their education. We've tried it in the past, but not on a regular basis. Most of our patients...'

'...get out sooner.'

'I'm afraid that's true. And because of that we need to pay attention to your education.'

'Whatever you say.' I was verging on rudeness, I knew, but he didn't pick up on it.

'Very well. We'll start tomorrow. A Mrs Sawyer is going to be your primary tutor and she'll also set up your wireless.' I nodded. 'Where are you going now?'

'Back to the ward, I guess.'

'Same way I'm going. I need to see a couple of patients. Mind if I go with you?'

'No.' He offered to push me the rest of the way. I didn't say no.

That night I lay in bed thinking. This life at Morland Hall would be over, later rather than sooner, but someday I would go away – where, I had no idea. What were they preparing me for? Bannerman? Cold shivers scurried through me, like rats, head to toe.

My future was not a thing to contemplate. Future was lunch tomorrow, when Mr Obken might decide which animal I was, whether I could make it to the end of the sixteen-foot aisle with bars on either side, whether I could bear my next bed companion or what Commander King-Hall might talk about on Friday.

* * *

Once again, in came the stuff of education I remembered from Bannerman – newly sharpened pencils lined up in a smooth tartan case, ink bottles, shiny pens – ready to begin their tyranny. I did my best to make them happy. I flashed my cheerful smile, but all the while, I kept a dark, sweet corner of me safe from pain and disappointment.

Mrs Sawyer came to teach me composition, reading, spelling and recitation; Mr Winter, MA, my tutor in arithmetic, started out being cold and nasty, till I won him over with my marvellous maths skills. He showed me my first report card, written on Morland Hall stationery in a fine, tall script: 'Graeme Moodie is a clever boy with quite a turn for Mathematics. He has made excellent progress in Arithmetic, and a good start in Algebra and Geometry.' Then he sealed it into an envelope and posted it to my parents.

As for *Broadcasts to Schools*, I couldn't get enough, especially Commander King-Hall's *Tracing History Backwards*, on every Tuesday at 11:30. Fascinating.

* * *

One morning I decided that I wanted to get dressed. Proper clothes, with vest and shirt, jumper and jacket, trousers, belt or braces, I didn't care which, and real socks and shoes, no more slippers.

However, no one living could imagine how difficult going to the toilet was when one was dressed and had polio. Undoing buttons and zips, balancing on both feet, letting go of one stick, and at last, taking aim and hoping. Taking a shit was easier. Everything just pulled down; sit on the seat and Bob's your uncle.

Through the autumn I slept on the balcony, waking to the smell of poplar leaves rotting on the lawn. My cheeks were the only chilly part. Everything else was cosy. I squinched the covers around my neck, waiting for breakfast sounds. Wood smoke might be in the air and from high, from the tops of pines where I'd seen them gathering the night before, I'd hear crows cawing to their friends on nearby branches.

'Good morning, young master Moodie.' Good, oh good, it was Nurse Seyl, my absolute favourite nurse. She was new to nursing and to us, so she was nervous, trying to make a fine impression. What was best, though, was how pretty she was. Her eyes were blue, particularly when the sun shone into them, and her hair was dark and curly. Little bits would come away from where she tied them up under her cap and I saw them curve about her neck, reminding me of Cousin Isla.

Washing came first. Nurse Seyl cranked the front of my bed and pulled the wheeled table across my lap. Onto this she set a metal bowl of hot water that steamed. Then with a squeezed-out facecloth, she rubbed my face with just the right pressure, softly around my eyes, and not too hard around my ears and the back of my neck. 'I put a little lavender water in the bowl,' she said the first time. 'I think it makes it nicer. Do you?'

'I think so,' I said, as if I'd given it careful thought. After that simply knowing that the smell of lavender water was coming was a reason to wake up. And of course, there was her.

* * *

13 September, 1934. I took my first steps, exactly thirteen months after I took ill. No more iron ballgown. Just two wooden sticks with curved handles. Eight steps, quite a lot for the first time, Dr Webb said. Everyone applauded. They even had a cake, my second in two weeks, because I'd also had one on the 27th of August, when I turned ten.

* * *

By November, things were looking up, as long as I kept my nose in a book, or my ears peeled to the wireless. I looked at my watch. Ten past four. Mr Obken would be in the library reading the evening paper. Maybe someone had laid a fire. There'd be tea, scones, Ovaltine.

I wheeled myself in, the rubber on the tyres creaking. Usually Mr Obken beamed at me, but not today. He was in a sweat, wiping his face with a handkerchief. 'Just the one I wanted to see. Wasn't it a beautiful day? Indian summer. What you been up to?'

'Not much.' I took out my *Hotspur* comic from the side of my wheelchair. Mr Obken went back to his *Daily Mail*, but soon muttered, 'Bloody fool.' He often swore when he read his paper. 'You got another comic there? I don't think I can stand reading these abominations anymore.' He took out his handkerchief again.

I shook my head. 'Sorry. Why do you read it, then? The newspaper, I mean.'

'Good question. I suppose I feel I should. Know the enemy and all that. But I've had enough of Mr Hitler today. My blood pressure can't take it anymore.' He folded the paper and tossed it onto the table. 'Beautiful day, wasn't it?'

'Yes. Beautiful.' I'd heard of Hitler, but I wasn't sure who he was and it was too late in the afternoon to start asking.

'Indian summer. But the weather's begun changing. Winter's coming.' I thought about the dark months ahead. Then Mr Obken said, 'You know why they call it Indian summer?'

I shook my head.

'Before the white man came to Canada, and the native people had a day like today, they said that Gitche Manitou – that was their god – was smoking his pipe. He warmed the earth, you see.'

A picture spread before me. A handsome, sleepy Indian, lean and tall, stretched on the grass beside his tepee. I could see the pale blue sky, unmarked by clouds. The soon-to-be-rotting world shivered. But Gitche Manitou, legs resting on a nearby log, warms the earth one last time, just to be kind, before the dark times came.

Chapter 11

I was deep into a jigsaw of The Flying Scotsman with Mr Obken. Five hundred pieces and I'd just found the missing piece of the smokestack. 'Hurrah for Graeme!' he said, banging the table and making some pieces bounce. 'Whoops, mustn't get too excited.'

'It must be time for tea,' I said.

Morland Hall had been my home for over two years now, as familiar as a pair of old slippers. I knew what every clatter and smell meant, yet still wondered at the sound of each New Year, this time 1936. And I always remembered, how Miss Marshall had been amazed by the sound of 1932. Uh oh. Lonely feeling coming.

Thank God for the BBC. Its *Broadcasts to School* saved my life. And though I didn't dare say it aloud, the lessons in history and current affairs of Commander King-Hall had planted a seed: one day I would be prime minister, like President Roosevelt in America.

I looked out of the solarium's ceiling-high windows onto the fresh green lawn and saw two people walking toward us, a man and a woman leaning on each other, heads down and huddled in coats, although it was mid-April. The man's familiar, jaunty walk jolted me.

And when they looked up at our building, there was no doubt.

I lurched from the table, frantic. 'You all right?' Mr Obken said.

'It's Uncle Sandy! Miss Marshall, too!' I grabbed for my sticks leaning against the table, but they crashed to the floor. I shoved the back of my chair with my bottom, with none of the patience I'd been taught for months.

'Take it easy, take it easy,' Mr Obken said.

I managed the solarium door with an easy shoulder-push and once I'd made it across that bloody gravel drive, onto the lawn, I moved faster. Step left, swing right hip. Step left, swing right hip. Tears pricked my cheeks. If I hurried any faster, I'd fall on my face.

They watched me struggle toward them. Perhaps they didn't recognise me, in the same way I didn't know them at first. I was so much taller.

But then Uncle Sandy hurried toward me, breaking into a run, then flying to me, holding out his arms. He spun me around, and – of all things – burst out crying.

When I saw his tears, I stopped mine; he wept for me, which was enough. My sticks fell and I hugged him back. This was the greeting I'd waited for, ever since the 13th of August, 1933, the day I took ill.

Miss Marshall clapped, and I, overwhelmed, did nothing.

After a bit, he put me on my feet and we calmed down. They watched me, stiff-legged, pick up my sticks. Uncle Sandy's arm reached out to help, but I said, more harshly than I meant, 'I can do it,' and he stopped. I hoped I didn't look too awkward.

'Come along,' Miss Marshall said, 'we're kidnapping you! We're taking you to lunch!'

'Oh,' I said, afraid, 'I don't think I can. I'm not allowed.'

'Of course you are! It's all been arranged behind your back. It's a surprise.'

'Oh.' I was still rather confused. 'Do my parents know?'

'They do. I had to get your father's permission, as well as that surgeon-fellow. What's his name?'

'Mr Fairbank?'

'That's the one. He made me promise a lot of nonsense about no more than a three-hour journey.'

'Well, he is a doctor.' Miss Marshall said.

'So?' He rubbed his hands, then took a silver flask from the side pocket of his coat, 'I need warming up.'

'I remember that!' I said. 'You had it at Craigisla. It's got your name on it. Can I see?'

'Absolutely. You can even have some.'

'Now Sandy...' Miss Marshall said in a friendly warning.

'Eh, I'm only teasing.' He held out the flask.

To take hold of it, I had to prop a stick against my jacket, which I managed after a few seconds.

I'd forgotten about the flask's existence, this friend from Craigisla days. How fascinated I'd been by the way 'Sandy' was written on the side in a fine, slanting script, surrounded by curving lines of leaves and vines. And how young I'd been then, how free.

I handed it back and watched him take a long drink. 'Ahhhh,' he said in a funny, drawn-out way to make us laugh, which we did. 'That's better. Shall we go?'

'We can do that?' I asked. 'Just leave?'

'Why not?' Miss Marshall put her arm around me. 'You must be getting awfully cold, never mind that silly Sandy. Let's get your coat and let them know we're spiriting you away.'

We found Matron and Nurse Seyl in the staff office, drinking mugs of tea at Dr Webb's big oak desk, piled high with files and books. 'These are my guests,' I said proudly. Matron smoothed her pinny as she stood, and Nurse Seyl pulled a few stray curls back under her cap. She looked pretty, though somehow smaller. 'Mr Cochrane and Miss Marshall – may I present Matron, and this is Nurse Seyl. She's the nurse who looks after me, mostly.'

'Lucky you,' Uncle Sandy said, removing his hat and bowing.

Matron scowled, and Miss Marshall moved in fast. 'Dr Moodie has been telling us what wonderful progress young Graeme has made; that he gets the best care in the world here.'

'We do our best,' Matron said. Nurse Seyl stepped back against the wall and looked down.

Something was going wrong. I wanted them to like each other, but my carers didn't think much of my visitors. The room grew small and tight with the differences between them. Sandy and Miss Marshall took up so much more space, moving about with their big coats and voices, smelling of perfume and whisky – the very opposites of starched aprons, caps and hospital rules.

'You'll have him back by four?' Matron asked. 'May I enquire as to where you might be going?'

'Winchester. I've booked at the Southgate Hotel. Marvellous food.'

'As far as that?'

'We'll be there in an hour. Wait till you see my new car, lad.'

Matron sighed. 'Don't let him eat liver. It disagrees with him.'

'Liver doesn't disagree with me,' I couldn't help saying. 'I hate it, that's all. That's why I puke.' Complete silence. Maybe I'd overstepped the mark. I wanted Matron to see that this was my real life. Parties and noise and loud laughter. New cars and restaurants.

Then Nurse Seyl said thoughtfully, 'I don't care for liver, myself.' Everyone looked at her. No one knew what to say.

Matron said in the same wondering tone, as if she'd just realised it, 'Nor do I.'

'I don't either,' Miss Marshall nearly whispered.

'Well, who the hell does?' Uncle said in a voice that made me shudder with the nerve of him. But then, like a miracle, everyone laughed. I'd never understand the world. Somehow this joined-up hatred of liver had made everything fine.

* * *

'There she is, my boy. What do you think?' Sandy opened Morland Hall's front door for me, and we stepped outside. 'Sleek as an otter, eh?'

Sandy was right. So long and black and close to the ground, the car was like an otter. I could just see it going after a salmon, twisting and curving through the calm dark water of Loch of Lintrathen, where we always fished when we stayed at Craigisla.

In my slow, careful way that took forever, I reached the bottom of the stairs.

'Aston Martin Mark II. Four-seater, one and a half-litre, long chassis. She'll go seventy if I let her.'

'Which you won't today,' Miss Marshall said in a hurry.

He flashed me a wink. 'Look at those wheels. See those wire spokes? They're dark red, not black. I ordered them specially. They're a bit dirty. The red stands out more when they're clean. I bet you haven't seen that before. What do you think? Beautiful, eh? Come, look at the front.' I lumbered around, pivoting slowly to aim in the opposite direction. He watched me move, with a pleasant, curious smile. 'You're pretty clever with those sticks, aren't you? What keeps your leg so stiff? Have ye a wee support there under your trouser leg?'

He bent to look. I was taken aback. No one had ever asked a question like that. Father hadn't, although he probably knew about it. But Uncle Sandy looked so normal, I didn't mind. Still, I didn't say anything.

'Well, you show me later. I'd be interested.'

'Look at that grille. Beautiful, eh?' The front end was covered with fine bars, shiny as silver. On both sides was a round headlight, poised on a curved torch. Sandy took a handkerchief from his pocket and polished each. 'This is a new breed, a cross between a touring car and a sports car. I bet your father doesn't have anything like it.'

'Sandy, Graeme's father has a wife and two children to support. And not everyone is in love with your car the way you are. Poor Graeme's getting cold.'

I hated being called 'poor Graeme,' but it was true. I was shivering, tired of standing up for so long admiring this car that was much nicer than anything my father had. I stared at the elegant grille and thought of Father's big, boxy Hillman.

Uncle Sandy winked again. 'Doreen's right, as usual. We should be off.' He took an awfully long drink from his flask, finishing with a loud and raspy 'Ah,' wiping his lips with the back of his hand.

Getting into the car was a palaver. I had to show Uncle Sandy how Father lifted me, and he managed, though for a minute I thought I might crash. Miss Marshall held the front seat, while he lowered me. 'Cream-coloured leather, the finest money can buy. Guess how much this car cost?'

'Now, Sandy, if you don't stop raving about this car...' Miss Marshall said.

'Seven hundred pounds. There. What are you going to do? Punish me?'

'Maybe.'

'I hope so. I haven't had my bottom spanked for a long time.' They were playing a game, but an odd one. And even odder, the thought of Miss Marshall spanking Uncle Sandy gave me a wiggly but good feeling that shot across the bottom of my stomach.

Miss Marshall tucked a thick tartan rug all around my legs that stretched out along the seat, because my right leg didn't bend. 'I can't get over how tall you are!' She gave my knee a pat, and we were off.

'I've got some magazines on the floor, Graeme,' Miss Marshall called to me. 'Take a look if you want.'

* * *

After a while I got used to the speed and reached for a magazine. On the cover a nasty-looking woman stared at me from under half-closed eyes. She had eyebrows so thin, they looked like fingernail clippings. I didn't like the look of her, in her man's hat and red polka dot bowtie. 'Who's this?' I asked, shouting. Miss Marshall got up on her knees to turn.

'Marlene Dietrich. She's German. She's a film star in Hollywood. She's just come out in *The Scarlet Empress*. Do you think she's pretty?' I shook my head. 'She's very famous. Her voice is frightfully low when she sings – like a man.'

'Well, I don't like her,' I said, feeling cross that someone so horrible-looking could be so famous. 'I don't like anything about her. Particularly her hat.'

'I agree. I don't like her, either,' Miss Marshall said.

'Nor do I,' Sandy said. 'I guess she's the liver of the film world.'

* * *

Lack of motion woke me. We were in Winchester, in front of what must have been the hotel. I squinted out at a red brick, fine-looking building with white columns on either side of the door. My neck ached, I was cold, starving, and worst of all, I had to go to the lavatory.

Sandy held out his hand and gently pulled me up. I got my achy legs going and managed the five stairs without much problem. I'd practiced stairs for hours at Morland Hall and I had it down pat. Give left stick to someone, in this case Uncle Sandy. Left hand on handrail. Left foot on first stair. Then right stick up, swing right leg in a sort-of circle to meet the left foot. Repeat. Left foot, right stick, right leg.

Sandy, behind me, said, 'Clever lad. A very neat way to go upstairs. I'm impressed.' Here he was again, talking about my polio. My parents never said a word.

'It took a long time to learn,' I said, grunting.

'I bet it did.'

At the top of the stairs, a man in a blue uniform and cap greeted us. Sandy held out his hand, unusual to do for a servant, but the man took it easily, as if it were normal. 'Ah, Mr Cochrane, welcome back to Southgate. We've all missed you.'

'Yes, it's been far too long. You know the fair Miss Marshall, of course. And here's our dear lad, my favourite nephew, Graeme Cochrane Moodie.'

'Mister Moodie,' he said, nodding, and holding the wide wooden door open.

'Sorry to be late,' Sandy continued. 'We made up some time, but I never went over sixty, did I Graeme?'

'How should I know?' I said, laughing. 'I couldn't see the speedometer.'

'Well, I did,' said Miss Marshall. 'And I made sure he didn't go too fast. They have laws now. You can't go over sixty.'

Sandy sighed. 'She knows everything, now that she passed her driving test. I haven't bothered to take mine yet – I know, I know – I will. Soon. Oh, Edward. Here are my keys. Stash Miss Bixie somewhere safe, will you?'

'I'll put her in our garage.'

'Splendid!' Edward took our coats and I nervously asked where the Gents was. That went fine. Like stairs, I'd mastered peeing standing up.

When I got back to the lobby, Uncle Sandy was leaning against a shiny black pillar, smart in his tweed jacket and golden corduroy trousers. I could tell he'd combed his ginger hair while I was gone; it was so smooth and perfectly parted. Miss Marshall's dress was silky and red, with a black flowy collar that tied in the front. She wasn't thin, like Mother. Miss Marshall was most definitely English, for she had, Mother said, 'Far too much bosom for a Scottish lassie.'

Edward led us through the main dining area to a small, beautiful room, just for us, with pale green walls decorated with gold ovals. Our table, the only one, stood to the left, laid with silver and glassware and pink roses in the middle. A crystal chandelier sparkled with so many pretty little lights you could never count them. A different planet from the white walls and clattering stainless steel of Morland Hall.

A sideboard stood nearby with a huge bowl of more pink roses, and on the other side, a flowery sofa and chairs snuggled near a fireplace that was bright with a sweet-smelling fire.

A waiter brought champagne cocktails in odd, funnel-shaped glasses, and a tall lemonade for me with a bending straw. And from a menu with a gold tassel we chose our food. Pea and lettuce soup to start, and I would have had sausages, but Uncle Sandy convinced me to have something called Chicken Kiev. 'Trust me. It's the best thing you ever put in your mouth.'

He was right. Somehow they had got a pat of butter inside the chicken breast and when you cut it open, the melted butter burst out like a bomb, but not so much as to make a mess.

I only made one mistake, which was to order 'assorted ice creams.' Miss Marshall had to explain to me that 'assorted' meant that they had several kinds in the kitchen, but I had to choose one. 'That's utter nonsense,' Uncle Sandy decided. 'I agree with the boy. "Assorted" means just that. Bring him a little of each.'

Then we moved to the sofa where I had hot chocolate and they had brandy and we all had small, fat chocolates with different fillings.

Everything rather melted after that – after the gramophone was brought in and I watched them dance. 'No, no, don't feel bad,' I said. 'That's silly. I'll watch. I can't dance yet, but one day I will.'

* * *

'You smell good.' I knew it was Miss Marshall touching my cheek.

'Oh, that's Vol de Nuit. I just put some on. You like it?'

Everything was quiet and dark. 'Where am I?'

'In the car, sweetheart, back at Morland Hall.'

'Oh no!' I struggled to sit up; I'd been lying across the back seat, like a baby. 'Not already.'

'I'm afraid so. Your uncle's sound asleep, too. I did the driving and made a much calmer trip of it.'

Uncle Sandy, full of whisky-smell, pulled me up. 'Don't worry, old chap. I'll bring you back to Dundee for Easter. How would that be?'

'I don't know,' I said. 'Remember Mr Fairbank.'

'How could I forget Mr Fairfuck? Pompous fool.'

'Sandy...' Miss Marshall warned.

'Well, he is. He compared Graeme to a seltzer bottle.'

'He told me exactly the same thing! "Timothy," he calls all his patients Timothy. "You must nevah travel more than three hours! Jiggling will upset your muscles, like a seltzer bottle. You don't want to explode, eh Timothy?"'

'Tosh. No one gets the best of Alexander Reid Cochrane. I'll think of something.'

Chapter 12

The 'something' Uncle Sandy thought of was to charter a private aeroplane from his old friend and flying Ace, Gordon Olley. Easy-peasy.

A week before Easter, a biplane with the splendid name of de Havilland Dragon Rapide, waited on a field near Morland Hall. Uncle Sandy lifted me into the back, beside Miss Marshall, while he sat next to Mr Olley. Everyone acted as if this were normal. I did my terrified best to copy them.

We rattled over grass, faster and faster, no stopping now and then the promised miracle – we lifted into thin, soft air and felt the earth's touch no more. Sky-bound, we rose, up and up. I dared peer out and saw the world shrink into chequerboard fields, wormy roads, puffball trees. Goodbye Morland Hall! I watched it disappear, a toy, no longer needed.

The flight to Dundee took three hours, as promised to the Mr Fairfuck – as Uncle Sandy called him. We landed in another field, just outside the city, where Collyer waited in the Daimler, and we set off for 166 Nethergate. Home.

'Aren't you coming to dinner?' I asked.

'Nay, I'll be heading straight on to Craigisla. I'm not your father's favourite person. I have too much fun.'

'That's not true.' Miss Marshall sounded worried. 'Is it?'

* * *

Two hours later I was sitting in my wheelchair, in front of the fire, Rufus beside me, having nearly killed himself with joy when he sniffed my outstretched hand. He went berserk – rolling, whining, leaping. He didn't wet himself, though; he was too grown-up for that, and Father stopped him when he tried to leap onto my lap. 'Rufus, that's enough!' he said crossly. 'Mind your manners.'

Father shook my hand and Mother, trembling, kissed my cheek. I saw what they were doing. They were pretending things were normal, that I hadn't been banished for more than two years. Alastair was the only one who wasn't acting. He punched my shoulder and covered an eye with his hand, our secret sign that our parents were idiots. We broke away, laughing, and Mother said, 'You boys just pick up where you left off, don't you?'

'Of course,' Alastair said. 'Come see, Graeme! You and I are sleeping in Father's office, just for the holiday. They wanted to bring only your bed downstairs, but I made them bring mine, too.'

'Grand,' I said. We inspected the room, with its two beds side by side, the same table between us, same lamp. We adjourned to the sitting room, Alastair pushing my wheelchair to the spot I used to sit. Five o'clock was too early for cocktails, but 'just this once,' Father said. Mother agreed.

'Welcome back, Ulysses,' Father said in a shaky voice as he raised his whisky glass. After that, things got better. They usually did, I remembered, after their drinks.

We were sipping away when Mother said, 'Graeme, there's something I want to talk to you about.'

'Not now, Ann,' Father said in quick warning.

That sparked my interest. 'What?'

'Your father says I should wait.'

'That's not fair,' I said. 'Now you've mentioned it, you have to tell me… Please,' I remembered to add.

Father took a heavy breath. 'Nothing for it. Go ahead.'

She put her hands in her lap. 'Well, you know your Father and I were concerned that you get a good education, and we're very pleased with how Mrs Sawyer and Mr Winter are teaching you.'

'And the BBC, don't forget that,' I added.

She smiled. 'Of course! Mrs Sawyer says Commander Stephen King-Hall is your favourite and that you show a penchant for history.'

'I do.'

She took a bigger breath and went on, 'And she's written about a placement agency in London that recommends schools for boys. We realised Bannerman wouldn't do, so I went and had a chat. There's a school outside Reading with a very good headmaster. They take some – uh – foreign students, boys who are recuperating from this and that. Special cases.'

'Wait a minute. Are you talking about a boarding school?'

'Don't raise your voice to your mother,' Father said, taking charge. 'It is a boarding school, but not like Bannerman. It's more enlightened.'

'What does that mean?'

'They never beat boys, for one thing, and there's more freedom in areas of study.'

I narrowed my eyes. 'What's it called?'

'A strange name,' Mother came in. 'Maiden Erlegh. Pronounced like "early." They think some nuns used to live in the area.'

'It doesn't matter if it has a strange name. I'm not going. Absolutely not. Nothing you told me about Bannerman turned out to be true.'

'We'll discuss it another time,' Father said, giving Mother a severe look.

'It's dinnertime,' she said sweetly, ignoring him. 'Alastair, would you tell Cook we're ready?'

* * *

During the next few days, the subject wasn't brought up again. The weather, though, was foul, with sleety snow, and Alastair caught a cold, so we stayed put. The good thing was Berry stopped by and made the terrific fuss over me I'd hoped for.

Father had reserved a table for Easter lunch at The Physicians' Club and declared Alastair well enough to go. We piled into the car; Father put my wheelchair in the boot – easier all around. I left my splint at the house, since it didn't bend at the knee and I didn't want to lay my legs across Alastair's lap.

Father's club we used only for the grandest of occasions. It used to be a linen merchant's house, with a huge dining room that used to be the ballroom. The waiters knew us and Alastair and I had loved wandering about, while Father chatted with friends.

The front door was at the top of steep stone stairs. 'I hadn't thought of that,' Father said, after parking the car and wheeling me up to the building. 'Damn,' he muttered. 'We'll figure this out.'

He carried me up the stairs. Alastair opened the door; Father set me on a bench, just inside. Alastair went for the wheelchair, but came back, saying he couldn't fold it, so Father fetched it. 'What a faff!' he said, as Mother smoothed his hair and dabbed his face with her handkerchief. 'Shall we proceed?' he added with a grand swoop of his arm. 'I've reserved my favourite table, overlooking the garden.'

At last reaching the dining room, bedecked in white linen and Easter flowers, Father apologised to Joseph, the maître d'hotel, for being late. We all knew him and he smiled, but seeing my chair, gave me an uneasy look. 'I'm not sure, Dr Moodie, if there's a clear passage to your table.'

The window looked a long way away, past large and small tables crowding along a snake-like path. 'We've added a few, you see, being so busy for Easter,' Joseph explained.

'Do you have anything closer?' Father asked. Beside us was an empty table.

Joseph regarded a clipboard he had tucked under his arm. 'Let's see. This one is Dr Jenkins' table.'

'Charles Jenkins?' Joseph nodded. 'Fine. He won't mind swapping.'

'Let's see now,' Joseph said, as he thought what to do. We gazed at the lovely setting, the centrepiece of tulips, the damask napkins standing in tents, the gleaming silver cutlery. He pulled out a chair for Mother.

'Hello, what's happening here? Oh, there you are, Joseph. You've abandoned your post.'

Father turned. 'Ah, Charlie, good to see you. I'm afraid we've upset the applecart a bit. We need your table. You can have ours by the window. Nicer view.'

'Is something wrong?' said a portly woman, probably Mrs Jenkins. 'Could someone explain what is going on?' Beside her stood two children, both younger than me.

'Why, hello Helen,' Father said with his most winning smile, but he was flustered. 'You see, the journey to the window table, that I requested, is precarious. Not enough room for my son's wheelchair.'

'The one with that dreadful disease? What's it called, Charles? You told me.'

'Infantile paralysis,' Dr Jenkins muttered.

'Dr Moodie, are you out of your mind, bringing him here? The boy shouldn't be spreading germs. As you see, I have two children.'

'It's not contagious, Helen,' her husband said.

'So they say. If you don't have the sense to ask them to leave, I will. The sight of him in that – wheelchair – makes me sick. No one should have to put up with it. It spoils the appetite. People like that should have the good sense to keep out of view.'

Dr Jenkins turned to Father. 'Would you mind, Alex?'

I'd seen Father angry, but never like that. His face went white, which I'd learned from some BBC programme, was a dangerous sign. Much worse than red.

'My son,' he said in a voice so calm, it terrified me, 'has spent nearly three years in a nursing home, getting well enough to come to his father's club and you ask that he leave?'

'Father, please,' I said, 'let's go home.'

'I'm not moving. This is a club for people of the medical profession who should know better than to turn away the… afflicted.'

Mrs Jenkins waved her hand as if shooing away flies. 'The hospital is for that. Take him there or leave him at home. People like that should stay hidden. There is enough misery in the world without advertising one's own.'

'You, madam,' Father said, 'are a fool.' He was breathing hard. He couldn't stay calm any longer.

'Now just a minute,' Dr Jenkins said as he advanced toward Father.

* * *

Mr Obken and I sat in the garden outside Morland Hall because the solarium was too hot by the middle of June. We scattered sunflower seeds as we chatted, a shoebox full, on the table between us. Already we had some customers. Not only blackbirds, but tits, blue ones and long-tailed. Sparrows, too.

'Are you certain about this?' he asked.

'I've never been certainer… more certain, that is.' Every memory of that Easter lunch was a fresh wound, even after two months. Father about to pummel his old friend; Mrs Jenkins' chair turning over. I tried not to think of it, but at night especially, scenes returned. I'd never put myself through that again. I would never – ever – go to that 'enlightened' boarding school with the silly name. Yet Mother persisted in asking. I had her latest letter.

'Could you read it to me?' Mr Obken asked.

'Very well. "My darling boy…" Ugh, she always calls me that.'

'That's what mothers do.'

'"I pray that you have at last recovered from that unpleasantness" – unpleasantness? Hah! A mortar attack, more likely. Anyway, "Your father has resigned from the Physicians Club and we've joined The Metropolitan, which is much nicer." Oh, Mr Obken, it's too ridiculous. Anyway, at the end, she says, "Captain Fox writes that you will lose your place if he doesn't hear from us by the end of June. I must have your answer in a week." My answer's the same – no. I will never go to another boarding school. The only reason I went to – that other place – was to be with Alastair and I never saw him. No, no, no. I'm going to stay here, just like you. A permanent resident. I understand why you never left.'

'I'm sorry to hear that.' He reached for more seeds.

'I thought you'd be happy, Mr Obken. We get along so well.'

'We do indeed. But the world is changing – much too slowly. We must help it along; give it a firm nudge.'

'Why don't you leave, then?'

'Too late for me. I'm sixty. Too set in my ways. How old are you?'

'I'll be twelve in August.'

'Exactly.'

'But I have everything I need: the BBC, Mrs Sawyer, Mr Winter, books, newspapers, you.' At my feet was a pair of sleek blackbirds, their fluffy fledglings shadowed under fragrant mock orange.

'You need the world in the flesh! Not one step removed. Look at what President Roosevelt has done in America.'

'I suppose so.'

'He can't even stand by himself. True, it's a secret how disabled he is, but people know he's had polio. That's progress. Rome wasn't built in a day.' We kept on with the feeding.

'I have a proposal,' he said at last. 'Write a contract with your parents. Say you will try it for one term. From September till Christmas. Whether you return in the New Year will be up to you.' When I laughed, he said, 'No. I'm serious.'

I contemplated his words. The birds kept pecking.

'You know,' I said, as if I'd thought of it, 'It just might work. Will you help me write it?'

'No. You must do that yourself.'

Chapter 13

Nurse Seyl helped me dress. Not that I needed help. The Maiden Erlegh uniform wasn't complicated – navy jacket, grey trousers, shirt, tie, belt. Other than the jacket colour, it could have been Bannerman's. 'But since it's for the last time,' she asked. 'You don't mind, do you?'

I shook my head, not daring to speak.

When she'd finished straightening my tie, patting this and that, she pulled back, looked me up and down. 'That's pretty,' she said, her eyes holding the crest on my breast pocket. She squinched her gaze closer to read the banner at the bottom. 'What does this say?'

'*Ad altiora tendons*. "Reach for something higher." That's what Mr. Obken says it means.'

'And you are! Think of that.'

I shrugged, and looked out on the balcony, where my bed had already been stripped of linen. I would not look at her eyes. Nor her hair. Nor her cheek.

Downstairs, Mr Obken and Dr Webb were waiting for me in the solarium. A party was being held in my honour. A fuss.

On the table in front of Mr O was a chocolate cake, glossy with swirls. 'Good Luck!' was written across the top in white icing. Happiness rose within me despite my resolve to remain like the iceberg that sunk the *Titanic*.

'I have a little something for you,' Mr Obken said. 'A going-away gift to remember me by.' He turned over a picture frame lying upside down in front of him. 'I've finally decided what animal you are.' He'd painted a sitting cat with a face that looked like mine. High tufty eyebrows, blue eyes tipping up, my smile, even the dent in my chin. 'I hope you like it. It took me nearly three years to make up my mind. But you're definitely a cat. Independent, handsome, intelligent. You like being comfortable, you're aloof, but every now and then you jump on a lap and purr like mad.'

I couldn't help laughing. 'It does look like me!'

Dr Webb said, 'It's Graeme, absolutely. I don't know how you do it, Harold. Mine's good too, though I hate to admit it. I'm an owl. I'd always fancied myself a lion.' We all laughed at that; he was such a wise, gentle man. I started on the cake, slicing it myself.

Mother's clacking heels told me she'd arrived, and in she burst, coiling her arms round me. Collyer, the Daimler chauffeur, followed. Her stupid school would be yet another banishment, just when I was getting happy at Morland Hall. Dr Webb offered them cake. Mother said no, like always, but I cut an extra big piece for Collyer.

I showed off Mr Obken's watercolour and Mother said, 'I have something for you, too.' From her bag she took a small leather box. Mappin and Webb was printed in gold on the top. I opened it. Hanging from a silver safety pin and lying on white satin was a cross, with slightly curving bars – like the Victoria one. My initials GCM were engraved at the crossing point, a 'V' above, a 'C' below.

'When I was sewing your crest onto your jacket,' she said cosily, as if she were telling a bedtime story, 'I noticed that the emblem looked like a Victoria Cross. And I thought: Graeme should have a VC of his own. He's been so very, very brave. So I had this made at Mappins – a precise miniature. No soldier ever earned it more.'

The little pin – silly, babyish – glinted at me. I was supposed to say thank you.

'That's lovely,' Nurse Seyl said for me.

'It's silver,' Mother went on, 'isn't it sweet? Shall I pin it on you?'

I jerked my shoulder away. 'No!'

'Why not?' Dr Webb said. 'What's wrong, Graeme?'

'I'm no soldier. I just endured, that's all.'

'There are many kinds of bravery,' Mr Obken said. 'Enduring is one of them.'

'Are you sure you wouldn't like some of your cake, Mrs Moodie?' asked Nurse Seyl.

'It's *my* cake,' I said. My front teeth bit together like a guard dog's. 'Not Mother's.'

'Your mother ordered it,' Nurse Seyl said. 'That's what I mean. Chocolate cake with chocolate icing. Your favourite kind.'

'Never mind,' Mother said, but I could tell she did mind. Her voice was shaking. 'We'd best be off.' Her legs sped her to the door, the way mine used to, before I was cursed, never to be a soldier who might truly earn a VC, by carrying his wounded comrade across a battlefield, dodging bullets all the while.

'It's been a strain, all this,' I heard Dr Webb say to her, putting a hand on her arm. 'He's tired. Not himself.'

We did our best, my little party. Much hoopla and happy handshakes, a few tears from the nurses and – I was surprised – from Mr Obken, who blew his nose heartily into his pocket-handkerchief. 'Don't forget your old pal,' he said.

'Never.'

The journey from Alton to Reading wasn't long, a little over an hour. Collyer drove fast, but so well, we never felt afraid, and damn it, despite my determination never to forgive Mother I got that cheerful going-somewhere-new feeling. Brown autumn farm fields rolled over the hills, making me think of our drives to Craigisla. Perhaps Mother did, too, because she gave my hand a squeeze. 'Thanks for the cake,' I said. I didn't mention the pin. It still made me sick.

'We're almost there,' Collyer said in a big voice. 'The town of Earley.' My body jerked, but Mother's hand was dry and warm, so I didn't take it away.

'Wokingham Road. That's the ticket.' We drove along a straight, treeless road alongside a railroad. The houses and shops were a dirty brick and sparsely placed in messy yards. The only big thing was a pub, called The Three Tuns. What was a tun? Something unpleasant, no doubt.

'There's Earley Station,' Mother said. 'Maiden Erlegh must be just ahead. Wait till you see it, Graeme.'

The Daimler slowed and turned into gloomy brick pillars with a matching lodge just behind. A sign read: 'Maiden Erlegh School for Boys. Private Drive.' My heart whacked against my ribs. *Iacta alea est.*

Slowing down, our car rolled up a road so wide you could fit three bloody Daimlers in a row. Immense trees made a canopy high over our heads between thickets of dark rhododendrons. 'How are you doing there, Graeme?' Mother sounded calm, but her hand was clammy now. I took mine away.

'Fine.'

At last the road broke into a thunderclap of bright blue, alarming and making me squint. A great green lawn lay beyond, an ocean of the stuff. Inch by inch we creeped along, the drive curving, till I saw what looked like a reddish mountain range with jagged peaks and towers and domes streaked white. 'This is Maiden Erlegh,' Mother said. 'I told you it was as big as Buckingham Palace.'

Which side was the front? Each side looked like a front. Wide porches, gardens, stone terraces spewed out in every direction. Columns, gables, arches and balconies stuck onto wing after wing. On one side, a dome rose halfway to the moon.

I'd be dead just trying to get from one place to another.

'What do you think, Graeme? Splendid, isn't it? You're going to enjoy yourself here. Ah, here's the headmaster,' she said as the car drew up under a roofed entrance. Standing in the open doorway, which was huge like everything else, was the man I'd heard so much about. Captain TS Waterlow Fox.

He wasn't at all what I expected. I expected a foxy fellow, lean and elegant, with gingery hair going white above the ears. This fellow was round and ordinary. Not fat exactly, but not a fox.

Everything about him was brown – his pressed hair, moustache, even his crookedy teeth when he smiled down at me and shook my hand. Mother had said he was remarkable. What a disappointment.

He introduced me to an older boy with long, skinny legs wearing big, round spectacles. 'This is Page-Roberts, one of our NCOs. He'll show you around.' What was an NCO? Had the farewell come so soon? I felt all shaky, like that little mouse I found under a flowerpot at Craigisla, sniffing for danger. And this place was beginning to smell a lot like Bannerman.

Captain Fox stood with his chest curved out, as if puffing up to look taller than Mother, but failing. 'Mrs Moodie, shall we have tea in the Palm Court? Graeme, you're welcome to join us when you're settled.'

'We'll go in the main entrance, since we're here,' Page-Roberts said. 'Under the porte cochère.' I looked round. 'That's the brick canopy thing above our heads. Handy when it's raining. Keeps people dry when they're getting out of their cars. Used to be carriages, of course.'

'Of course.'

Through a wide, heavily panelled door that bore the school crest in gleaming stained glass, we came to an immense hall with black and white squares on the floor. Page-Roberts pointed to a door on the left and then opened it. 'Lav. All marble. Handy when you need a quick piss before lunch.' He closed the door. 'But far more interesting, I thought you'd like to see this.' He led me to another door. 'What do you think it is?'

'I don't know. A classroom?'

He shook his head. 'It's my favourite.'

'The dining room?' I peered through his spectacles. Was this a trap?

Seeing I was a nervous wreck, he clapped me on the arm. 'No, but good try! Could've been the dining room! Sorry, Moodie. I was just having a bit of fun. You'll never guess.' He opened the door with a great flourish, his voice like a circus ringmaster. 'The billiard room!'

He was right. Never in a million years would I have imagined that the first room I'd see at my boarding school was the billiard room. Best not tell Mother. She didn't approve of billiards. They paved the road to ruin. Yet another happy thought flickered through me like a newly lit candle – I might learn to play! I'd lean against the table on my good leg and...

'Well?' Page-Roberts asked. 'Is it not grand?'

'Oh, yes,' was all I could say. On every surface was panelling the colour of Rufus's coat, even the ceiling and floor, in a lovely diamond pattern. The air smelled of pipe tobacco and furniture polish. On one side, floor-to-ceiling windows looked onto a paved terrace where great stone lions rested to either side of a wide staircase, quietly guarding against the world beyond.

The billiard table had the thickest, curviest legs I'd ever seen. They reminded me of Aunt Herald's, which Mother said were ugly, but here, they were gorgeous.

On one wall were stuffed animal heads, quite horrible really, particularly the one in the middle – an elk? – with the biggest antlers imaginable and bulging eyes. I hoped they were made of glass and not the real thing.

'Come on,' Page-Roberts said, putting his hand lightly on my shoulder, 'It's best not to see everything at once. Maiden Erlegh is like a museum in that way. So much to take in, one goes numb. I'll take you to your room and your roommate will take over.' Pity, I was beginning to like old Page-Roberts.

He took me back to the great hall, where a fine staircase curved up magically. 'Beautiful, isn't it? But we're not allowed to use it. Only Captain and Mrs Fox can. Even his daughter's not allowed.'

'They have a daughter?'

'Oh yes. The famous Beryl. You'll meet her in time, God help you. Here,' he said, 'we use the servants' stairs.' He took me through a door under the stairs, where a sturdy wooden staircase rose straight up without fuss. I was getting tired already and accidentally let out a sigh. 'You go at your own pace,' he said. 'I'll stand behind.'

I could have done better if I hadn't been so tired and nervous. No stranger had ever followed me like that, so close. Did I look clumsy? Nothing for it but to go on.

We reached the first floor and looked down a long corridor with doors and chests of drawers on either side. 'They've divided the big bedrooms up so it's more like a dormitory.' We walked on. 'Here,' he said, 'This is it. Number seven. Your room.'

A boy was sitting against pillows on the first of two beds side by side. He popped up and held out his hand in a formal manner. 'How do you do?' He had a foreign accent. 'You must be the new boy, Graeme Moodie. I am Paul Caspari, your roommate.' I leant my stick against the foot of the bed and we shook hands. 'I believe I am a year older than you. I was born in 1923.'

'That would be right, then,' I said. '1924, for me.' I tried to sound jolly.

'Splendid.' He clasped his hands together like an old man. 'I'll take over now, Page-Roberts. The Captain has asked me to help Moodie unpack.' My new leather valise lay on the bed beside Caspari's.

'Righty-ho,' Page-Roberts said amiably. 'See you at dinner, then.'

The early afternoon sun was summer-hot as it came through a massive window, too big for the made-smaller room. I was starting to feel sick. 'Am I allowed to take off my jacket?'

'Of course. Everywhere else, jackets are required at all times, except at tea, which is after games. I only had mine on because I was reading. I mean, I felt the cold. There's central heating in the corridors, but it's not on during the day.'

'I'm used to the cold,' I said, taking on that jolly tone again, but sitting gratefully on my bed. 'Where I came from we lived on balconies most of the time. Slept out on them every night. Even in winter.' I knew this would impress him.

He frowned, not sure he heard right. 'Where was that, may I ask?'

'Morland Hall. A tuberculosis hospital.' His eyes widened and he stepped backward. 'Don't worry, I didn't have tuberculosis. I had polio – myelitis. Poliomyelitis is the proper term, but most people just say polio. They used to say infantile paralysis.' I wished I hadn't started this talk on polio. 'I'm not contagious, anymore. I had it three years ago. I'm all better now, but my right leg's paralysed – in case you didn't notice,' I added with a silly laugh.

'I'm glad to hear it,' he said. 'I mean – about being better. I apologise. I still make mistakes in English. When I came here, three years ago, I didn't speak a word. That's why I have a funny German accent. In case you didn't notice.'

We laughed, most pleased at our wit and how we could share a joke about ourselves.

After unpacking we went down all those stairs again to find the Palm Court where Mother was having tea with Captain Fox. Caspari waved me off.

The room was big, rather like the solarium at Morland Hall, but grander. Tall plants reached toward the domed glass roof overhead, but what amazed me was the nearly naked statue of a young maiden – plop – in the middle of the room. No one paid any attention so, with difficulty, I didn't, either.

A lovely tea was set out. Captain Fox and Mother appeared to be fast friends, puffing away on cigarette holders. I helped myself to tea.

'Welcome to Maiden Erlegh, my boy,' he said, lifting his teacup in a toast. 'May your stay at Maiden Erlegh be a happy one. Just let me know what you need, and we'll do our best to accommodate you.'

* * *

Next morning, when Caspari shook me awake, I knew the shaking had been going on for some time. I opened my eyes. 'Thank God,' he said. 'I was beginning to be worried you wouldn't wake up. The maids brought our hot water ages ago. We've got to get breakfast, now! Come on.' Was he mad? It felt like the middle of the night. I wasn't moving. I tried to focus on his face. 'I'm not getting up quite yet.'

'Moodie, you can't stay in bed. Everyone gets up for breakfast. Are you ill?'

'Possibly. I don't think so. I just need more sleep.'

Sometime later a firm, low woman's voice and a firmer jerk on my shoulder brought me round. I got onto an elbow and saw a nurse, an important one judging by the size of headgear. 'I'm Matron. I understand you're under the weather. What seems to be the trouble, my boy?'

'I need to sleep; I think that's all. It's going to take me a while to settle in. That's what Captain Fox said. I'm settling in.'

'You're the boy with…'

'Polio?'

She nodded.

'That's me.'

'I'll have to speak to the Captain.'

'Good.' I grunted and turned over.

It must have been the quiet that woke me. On the bedside table my clock ticked in that hollow, disapproving way you only hear it when you're alone. A bell sounded, far away, I heard a few calls, some scruffling sounds, then quiet again.

I should have told the Captain I needed help dressing. I could dress myself, but it took three times longer. I waited some more. Surely someone would come for me.

I was getting hungry. At Morland Hall, a nurse brought a breakfast tray with a metal hat covering two eggs, sausages and fried tomatoes. A pat of butter swimming in my porridge. A rack of toast. Marmalade. A pot of tea.

Nothing for it. I'd have to dress myself if I didn't want to die of starvation.

I did have a routine for dressing. I put yesterday's clothes at the foot of my bed. When it was time for fresh clothes, Nurse Seyl would take the old ones away and replace them.

I managed to wriggle into my pants, vest and shirt. I swung my left leg and, with my hands, hoisted my right one on to the floor, so I was sitting sideways on the bed. I got my splint around my leg, the belts and buckles round the ankle, calf, lower and upper thigh. My socks, my shoes – was the built-up sole on the right one very noticeable? I managed my tie, put on the jacket, combed my hair with my fingers. Stood up with a lurch. How was I going to get downstairs? The thought of calling for help was too humiliating. My clock said 10:45.

At 10:50, a bell went again, followed by sounds of life, boys shouting, laughter, banging and clattering.

'Moodie!' Caspari stood at the door, my long-lost friend. 'Ah, you're up at last. The Captain wanted me to check on you. It's our break. We've already had three classes.'

'Really?'

'I've brought you some biscuits, but the Captain wants to see you, before lunch.'

'When's that?'

'One o'clock. You better hurry.'

'Today?'

Caspari rolled his eyes and gave my arm a yank.

* * *

Captain Fox sat behind a desk in his office, looking over his spectacles at me. His eyes weren't brown after all, but blue and sharp. He smiled. 'Matron tells me you're settling in. And so you are, my lad. So you are. I suspect it will take a month. What do you say?' I looked down at my knees, but still felt his eyes.

'Oh, not as long as that, sir.' Such a pause followed that I had to look up. 'I think it will only take two weeks. At most.'

If I had passed Captain Fox on a street, I'd never have noticed him. I wouldn't even recognise him the second time, but for his eyes. They made him, as Mother said, remarkable. Not just because they were that sharp blue in a field of wheaty brown, it was the way he leaned in, to better understand me, and his eyes wove over me in a figure of eight.

'I have your school reports from Morland Hall. Mrs Sawyer says splendid things about you.'

'Thank you, sir.'

The lunch bell jarred the air. 'I'll put you in the same classes as Caspari,' he said. 'He's one of the brighter boys, so I think you'll get along.'

* * *

It soon became clear that I'd have to manage with only one stick. I had my wheelchair tucked under the staircase if I got desperately tired, but there were stairs everywhere. I had books to carry, banisters to hold. In the beginning, Paul carried books for me, but gradually I managed more. I liked Paul's formality, which reminded me of Alastair. No extra words. One just got on. He didn't pretend I wasn't crippled, but he didn't draw attention to it either.

And like Alastair, at night, he told me about himself. He and his brother Ernest had arrived from Munich, in September 1934, when Paul was eleven and Ernest only eight. Their father had died in a car accident when Paul was seven.

'That must have been terrible.'

'Not really. He travelled so much, I never got to know him. He owned the most important art gallery in Munich. Les Galleries Caspari.'

I didn't know what to say.

'After his death, Mother took the business over. We specialise in the newest German Expressionism, as well as the Impressionists. Degas. Monet.'

I hadn't heard of them, but I did know some impressionists. 'Ever heard of Tommy Lorne?' I asked.

'I don't think so.'

'Probably because he's Scottish. He's ever so funny. My uncle is his friend. We saw him in *Jack and the Beanstalk* last year in Glasgow. Afterwards, we saw him in his dressing room. I have his autograph.'

Caspari gave me a strange look. 'I'm talking about art.'

I'd made a mistake – a big one – but since Paul seemed to think he was the one who had got a word wrong, I didn't correct him.

But if it hadn't been for him, I wouldn't have lasted a week. I didn't talk much to other people for fear of making a fool of myself. I wanted so much to fit in. I stayed in the main house, not venturing out in my wheelchair. My uniform was my camouflage; sitting down, I looked like everyone else.

The day began with English, with Miss Taylor, the only woman teacher at Maiden Erlegh. A bottle blonde, Paul said, and sometimes, a boy would drop his pencil near her feet, hoping to glance up her skirt.

Mr Piper taught French; his name was pronounced Meesyeur Pee-pair, even though he was a thin little Englishman with a pencil moustache and smooth black hair, shiny as a grand piano. He wore a suit like the other teachers, but he also wore sandals, which I'd never seen in my life.

'Does he wear them even in winter?' I asked.

'Oh yes, but with socks. He's artistic, you see, and sandals are his way of showing that. He often acts in our plays, he and Monica Taylor. I think he's in love with her.'

The other odd thing about Mr Piper was the cloud of incense that travelled with him.

A break came after French, then Mathematics with the Captain, and Geography with Mr King, who was quite young and working on his PhD.

Then lunch, an hour's library prep, followed by two hours of games for everyone but me. I told Captain Fox I listened to BBC School Programmes in my room, but really, I was so exhausted, I had to sleep.

Thank God, tea came next, served at 4:30 with scones and sandwiches, no one the wiser about my naps. The day wasn't over though: we still had Science, History and finally Latin taught by Mr Mellor, the best teacher in the school, Paul said. It may have been true, but I couldn't appreciate whatever greatness he offered. At last, dinner at eight, which I was almost too tired to eat. Roll call, prayers, lights out at 9:30, when reunited with my bed at last, I was so happy, I kissed it.

Chapter 14

I'd been at Maiden Erlegh a little over three weeks when I came to Mr Piper's French class to find him wearing a chef's hat. 'Oh good,' Paul whispered. 'This'll be good fun, Graeme. We're doing a play.'

Our desks – there were only six of us – were pushed to one side and in the middle of the room sat a round table complete with tablecloth and faded fake flowers. Mr Piper spread his arms. '*Bienvenu au restaurant La Gavroche, mes chers amis!*' The ends of his moustache were twisted in the corners like a real Frenchman.

All term we'd been learning food words – biftek, haricots verts, crème glacé – and now, he explained in French, occasionally dropping in an English word, we were going to stage a play of a family having dinner out. Caspari, whose French was good, would play the role of le maître d'hotel. From a large leather trunk covered with travel stickers Mr Piper took a cut-away jacket and white bow tie to clip round Caspari's neck.

'*Parfait.* And now for the family.' He produced a bright red, curly wig. '*Qui veut être la mère?*'

'*Moi, moi!*' said Smailes, who was famously good at sports and could do whatever he wanted. Dressing as a woman would be a lark.

'*Et le papa?*'

Several hands shot up. Everyone wanted to be the head of the household. Mr Piper looked at our band, long fingers on chin, thinking. '*Ah, je sais. Monsieur Graeme. Avec son baton, il a un air très distingué.*' First I felt pleasure – he'd chosen me – then shame – he'd mentioned my stick! No one had yet dared to, not even Paul. When I went up or down the stairs, he'd hold out his hand, saying, 'Shall I?' and I'd pass it to him.

'Aw,' some whinged. One boy, Boch, glared at me in fury, as Mr Piper hooked a false beard around my ears and I plonked on the fedora. What fun.

He cast the remaining parts. Tibbles would play the baby; he was a bit of a clown, so as soon as he tied the frilly bonnet under his chin, he walked around shaking his rattle and saying ga-ga to everyone. Poor Boch was made to be my son and scowled like the devil when Mr Piper handed him a teddy bear.

In our family strolled au restaurant, made by pushed-together tables. Paul became the snootiest waiter in the world, bowing deeply and half-closing his eyes. '*Bonsoir, monsieur*,' he said to me without the flicker of a smile. '*Pour combien?*'

'Ga-ga,' said Tibbles.

'*Quatre*,' I said, forcing my eyebrows down like Father.

'*Très bien*,' said Paul briskly. '*Suivez-moi*.' We sat at the table and studied the menus that carried our vocabulary words. Mr Piper had decorated them with a curly border.

Another bow from Paul. '*Avez-vous décidé?*'

'*Biftek*,' I announced; it was the easiest word to say.

But then, Smailes said '*Biftek*' too. And so did Boch! Tibbles, he just said, 'ga-ga.'

Mr Piper popped out from behind a cupboard door, waving his arms. '*Tragedie! Nous n'avons plus de biftek! Il faut commander d'autre chose.*'

'Aw,' Smailes said. We ordered again, choosing proper French words: Le poussin, les champignons, le jambon.

But good old Tibbles couldn't resist and just said 'Ga-ga' again.

Out Mr Piper popped, this time cross. '*C'est quoi, ce "ga-ga?" Nous n'avons pas de "ga-ga" sur le menu!*'

In the highest possible squeak, Tibbles said. 'Ga-ga, *c'est le poisson*.' That brought the house down.

Everyone roared, but Boch – who took this as an opportunity to throw his toy car at Tibbles. Smack – it landed on his forehead, and Tibbles forgot about being a baby, stood, and hurled the thing against the blackboard.

The bell rang – class was over. Mr Piper, in a terrible temper, tore his hat off his head, and said in English, to make sure we understood, 'Put the desks back before you go. And Boch, this is disgraceful behaviour! Go immediately to Captain Fox's office!' He wiped his forehead with a handkerchief and clapped his hands. '*Vite vite. Rapidement.*'

A mayhem of shoving and sliding followed in an attempt to win back Mr Piper's approval. When I tried to lend a hand, Smailes said, 'Best stand aside, Moodie, but thanks, anyway.'

But I was too late to get out of the way of Boch's desk careering toward me. Horribly, I saw it coming; and just before it slammed into my legs, I saw Boch smile. Over I went like a felled oak. Stiff in its calliper, my right leg forced my left to twist horribly, as all my weight landed on what I knew was my patella. The pain in my knee was tremendous. All I could do was moan and roll in agony.

'Get Matron. Immediately,' Mr Piper said. 'Don't move, Graeme.' He took his jacket off and put it under my head.

'Boch, you idiot,' Smailes said. 'Didn't you see Moodie?'

'Well, I'm sorry,' I heard Boch say. 'But he was in the way.'

* * *

Nothing was broken, the doctor from Earley said; the patella stayed in one piece. He'd feel better, though, if Mr Fairbank came for a look. 'You've got a badly bruised and swollen knee, lad, but it will soon be right.' After he'd given me something for the pain, he exchanged glances with Matron and frowning, sniffed the air and left.

Gradually, the pain got less and I got sleepy. One thing I'd learned at Morland Hall was the art of dozing off anywhere. As I faded away, I heard a series of sharp little sniffs, like Rufus at a badger hole.

I was halfway to dreaming of my beloved pup when Matron said sharply, 'Graeme?' which made me jerk. 'How are your baths going?'

I forced my lips to shape the word. 'Baths?'

'Baths. Yes. How often do you have them?'

Hmmm. What was the right thing to say here? 'I'm not sure.' I knew baths existed, but I saw no one taking them. Paul didn't. And it wasn't proper to ask. 'I think I was waiting for someone to fetch me and give me a bath. Whenever it was the right time. And no one's come yet.'

'Oh dear,' she said, and her uniform, stiff and noisy with starch, swished out of the room.

I was in trouble.

I sniffed. Yes, there was something there. Was it me? I hadn't paid attention. But now, as if I were tiptoeing into a new room, I lifted the sheet and sniffed. Then sniffed again. Oh dear indeed. I hadn't had a bath since I got here.

An oven of odours was cooking away under the covers. My face went hot with it. How had I not noticed these new smells, gamey and lush? From under my arms I caught a whiff of something oniony. Familiar, but not mine; these were mannish, somehow pleasant and reminded me of... what?

My head was still coming in and out of the covers when I heard Captain Fox's voice. 'Good news, I hear. Nothing broken, eh? That's a relief.' I scrambled out. He must have known what I was doing. He must have.

He pulled up a chair and sat beside my bed without a twitch. 'We just need affirmation from that London fellow, but our Dr Chapman knows his stuff. Bad luck, that. Running into a desk, or rather, a desk running into you.'

I couldn't speak, but I remembered Boch's smile.

'How are you otherwise? Anything we can help you with?' He had to be talking about bathing. This was a nightmare. I should have gone to the Captain or the Matron. Or someone. But I did nothing! Just got stinkier and stinkier. Morland Hall, here I come.

'Please sir,' I said in a wobbly voice I was certain he could hear, a foxy man like him. 'Please don't send me away.'

He looked at me in that digging way. 'Why would I do that?'

Now, I really couldn't bear it. 'Because I can't even bathe.' I slapped my hands over my face to hide my tears, my shame.

'Oh yes, I heard about that. Mix-up somewhere. This fancy doctor from London wrote in your notes, I have them here: "Boy – he doesn't even say your name – able to bathe self. Uses bath splint."'

'He showed me once at Morland Hall!' I took my hands away, outraged. 'And the nurses said it was easier to do it themselves, never bothering with the bath splint. They'd lift me from my wheelchair into the tub. I've never used the stupid thing.' I almost said bloody and he knew that, too, the way he raised an eyebrow and smiled the tiniest bit.

'We'll sort this out with the consultant, see if one of the nurses can give you a hand till you're happy with this famous contraption. Where is it hiding?'

'At the back of my cupboard. You won't send me away?'

'I jolly well won't. It takes more than a missing bath to defeat me. What you didn't know was that the boys always shower after games. Keeps them smelling sweet, after a fashion. I'm afraid we've let you down, Moodie. We trusted the doctor's notes. Must remember not to do that.' He walked to the door. 'Oh,' he added, 'and before our London guest arrives, you better have a bed bath. Me, I'm well accustomed to the smell of unwashed boy on his way to manhood, but someone so well versed in the world of back splints and their mysteries might not be. Cheerio.'

* * *

Mr Unfairbank came the next day, skating into the infirmary in his silky-smooth way. 'So, what's all this about, Timothy? I hear you've been causing trouble already, eh?'

'His name is Graeme,' Captain Fox said, behind him.

'Doesn't matter. I call all the boys Timothy, eh what? So much easier. Now – uh – headmaster…'

'Captain Waterlow Fox.' I saw that he was rocking on his heels, which Paul said he did when his temper was up, or when amused.

'Yes, yes. Well, you can go now. I'll take over.' The Captain didn't move but gave the doctor a poker-hot look, which changed into a slow, gracious nod, as if to say, what an idiot. And left.

'Now boy, yesterday I get an urgent phone call – everyone down here panicking, it seems. You'd had a fall, and no one knew what to do with you. I told your father it was a risky business, a cripple in the midst of young boys running about. Morland Hall is much better equipped to look after you.' He sighed. 'Let's take a look at you, shall we?'

He pulled back the covers. I was as clean as a whistle, having had a bed bath the day before and wearing a new nightshirt someone had fetched from my drawers. He looked at my knee, white and purple and twice the size of the other one. 'Is this what all the fuss is about? From the way that medic was talking, I was expecting to order amputation.

'Now. Turn over. I had better check your back. I trust you've been wearing your back splint?'

'Yes sir. Every day.' I hadn't used it once.

'Good.' He poked and prodded my spine. 'Wonderful things, these back splints. Otherwise, you'd be listing over like the *Lusitania*.' He rubbed his hands together, sighing. 'Much ado about nothing. Nasty bruise, but you'll be right as rain by… what day is today?'

'The first of October.'

'That's the date, Timothy. I asked for the day.'

Since I couldn't rip his throat out, through bared teeth I growled, 'Thursday.'

'Now, now, keep your pecker up, Timothy. You'll be back in your room on Sunday.' Closing his bag with a triumphant snap, he managed a creaky smile, no doubt because he was done with me. 'Pip pip. Cheerio.'

Chapter 15

Mr Unfairbank was right, the bugger. On Sunday morning, the fourth of October, Matron sent me back to my room. I was surprised how happy I was to see Caspari propped up in bed, reading.

'Moodie!' he said, springing up and shaking my hand. 'I've missed you. You need any help?' One of the staff had brought my bag.

'No, I'm fine. It's good to be back, Caspari.'

He sat on his bed, watching me unpack. 'I say, old chap. I've an idea. Seeing as we're chums, why don't we dispense with surnames? Please call me Paul, and may I call you Graeme?'

'I'd like that – Paul.'

'Graeme.' We sealed it with another handshake.

I wasn't at all sure I wanted to stay at Maiden Erlegh, but I wanted the choice to be mine. Morland Hall still felt like home. One term, that's all I agreed to – if I could last out the exhausting schedule. Christmas seemed a century away.

* * *

My bath problem was solved neatly, however. I had to give the headmaster credit for that. He'd called a meeting around my infirmary bed with Dr Chapman, Matron and a new nurse I hadn't met before. The upshot was that every Sunday and Thursday afternoon, this new one, Nurse Dickenson, would fetch me for my bath.

I'd always got on with my nurses. That was key. Nurses held all the cards, of joy or sorrow, feast or famine, cold or warmth. If they didn't like you, you were finished.

Right on time at two o'clock, Nurse Dickenson appeared with a stack of fluffy towels. I had got undressed earlier and was sitting on my bed in my scratchy tartan dressing gown, nothing on underneath. The afternoon was fine, the sun pouring through the masses of yellow leaves outside my window, but I was starting to sweat and felt uneasy. Could I trust her?

I gave her the once-over. Not fat, but strong, muscular. Not young, not old. Not what you'd call pretty. A surge of longing wended its way through my heart. I wanted Nurse Seyl. This one looked at me, arms crossed, not smiling, but calm. Beside me lay the bath splint I'd dug out of the cupboard. I didn't trust it either – nothing more than a footplate with two light rods on each side. Cloth straps wrapped round it to stop my leg giving way when I walked. So they said.

We talked a bit about the beautiful day, how quickly autumn was coming, her sitting on the bed, too. 'Shall we have a go?' she asked sensibly as she placed a hand on the bath-splint.

'Are you sure it will hold me? It looks so flimsy.'

'Only one way to find out. I'll be standing beside you, and if you fall, I'll catch you. I'm strong as an ox, I am.'

I parted my dressing gown. Some boys might be embarrassed being seen without their clothes on, but I was used to it. The only thing that bothered me was the sight of my bad leg – such pale, delicate skin stretched along the length of it. One could snap it like a wishbone. And between my bonny left leg and the bad one was my willy. But no one cared about that. It just hung there, thin and pale itself.

She set my foot on the plate and did up the buckles on the three canvas straps.

I slowly stood. She passed me my sticks, but held me under my right arm, just in case. 'There, you see? It holds. Now take a step. The struts are stronger than they look. They're made of aluminium. Very light and they won't rust in water.' Ever so cautiously I did as she said and tied my dressing gown again.

We headed out the door, slow as two snails. 'I'll get used to it,' I said. See how plucky I am? Please like me.

'Of course you will. Everything takes time.'

'My big splint was hard in the beginning.'

'I'm sure. It weighs a ton, but you're stronger now, I'll wager.'

'I am. Much.'

'You're going to be in for a treat. Wait till you see the bathroom. It was Solly Joel's own private bath.' She pointed up a short flight of stairs, very wide with heavy curving banisters on each side. 'Just up the royal stairs.'

'Who's Solly Joel?'

She stopped, her head bending down in front of my face. 'You don't know who Solly Joel was?' Her sturdy brown eyes went wide with surprise.

'I think I've heard the name,' which was what I said when I hadn't a clue. 'Who was he?'

'Ah, that's a long story.'

'Good. I like long stories. You can tell me in the bath.'

'It will have to be many baths. Your water would get cold.' We ascended the stairs. 'I used to work here, you see. I was one of Mr Joel's private nurses, and after Captain Fox purchased Maiden Erlegh, I came looking for work. I thought, a school for boys, they're bound to need extra nursing hands. All those scrapes they get into.'

She opened the door. The bathroom was larger than Alastair's and my bedroom in Dundee. The tub was like the *Queen Mary*, and against another wall stood a great, carved wooden chair, mounted on a dais as if the King were going to watch. 'That, believe it or not, is the toilet.'

'No,' I whispered.

'Solid mahogany. I'll show you after you're settled in the bath.'

Getting into the tub was a production, but already I had confidence in Nurse Dickenson. After she filled it – which took ages – I heaved my left leg in and transferred my weight. She gently lifted my right leg in and I lowered myself into the water, hands gripping tight onto the rolled sides.

The temperature was perfect.

First, she washed my hair, using a metal pitcher, and my back. I did the rest with a big, squishy sponge. Nice as the bath was, I wanted to hear about this Joel fellow.

'Very well,' she said, her face blotchy with the steamy heat. She looked around and boldly got up on the dais. 'I'm going to sit on the throne. See, it really is a toilet.' She lifted a wicker seat, then a wooden one, and after, the seat for the bum.

'Solly Joel. Now. How do I begin?'

'At the beginning!' I lifted my arms out of the water to show how simple it was.

'Right,' and in a lovely story-telling voice that takes its time, she began, 'Solly Joel was born in the poorest part of London. East End. Dismal as dismal could be. He had an uncle named Barney Barnato, who was adventurous and bright; he went off to South Africa and discovered diamonds in an area called the Rand. When his nephew, Solomon, better known as Solly, joined him, he welcomed him with open arms. The money they made was out of this world.'

'When was this?'

'Mmm. 1890s, something like that. Now. Barney was quiet and clever. Solly was noisy and clever. He was larger than life. Everyone respected him. In no time he became a multimillionaire.

'He returned to England with his wife whom he met in Johannesburg, an English woman named Nellie; she had to convert in order to marry him.'

'What does convert mean?'

'Oh, to change your religion. She became Jewish.'

'Did she mind?' I'd learned at Bannerman that a lot of people didn't like Jews.

'No, no. This wasn't Germany, where Jews are having a terrible time.'

'Why is that?' I asked. 'I don't understand it.'

'I don't either. People are stupid sometimes.' We spent a moment thinking about the world, its Jews, and how stupid people could be.

'How's your bath water?' she asked. 'Are you warm enough?'

'Oh yes, toasty warm. But tell me, what happened when Mr and Mrs Joel came to England?'

'Well, when he got to England, he bought Maiden Erlegh, and made it grander than before. And it was just his country home. He had a massive house in London, too. We had better stop. Matron will think you drowned. I'll tell you more next time.' With that, she lifted and turned a long silver cylinder between the taps that let the water out with a lazy gurgle.

* * *

Heading to the dining room the next day I thought – I may have to change my mind about my favourite part of the day. It used to be lunch; now it may be bath-time. However since I would only be having baths twice a week, lunch still could be my favourite daily activity.

There were many reasons why I liked it. After lunch, the others went to games and I could drift off to sleep in my room, listening to the wireless. Then there was the dining room, itself. I'd already seen big rooms, cosy rooms, fancy rooms, but this was the most beautiful I'd ever seen. It reminded me of the sun shining on water. When I'd got close to the walls, I saw that they were grey silk with blue velvet flowers twisting up on curving stems. And as the sun hit the wall, the shapes moved, like water rippling on a lake.

Three long tables sat us all – the Captain headed one, and Mrs Fox and Matron headed the other two. I was at Matron's. I would have preferred the

Captain's, but I knew that was just for the older boys. His daughter, the famous Beryl, was at the other end. Her fame was still a mystery, but her bosoms were enormous. Definitely not a Scottish lassie. Mrs Fox was thin and grand and I hadn't met her yet.

Every lunch there was a roast on each table – pork, beef, lamb or mutton – and the Captain made a big to-do carving his, but the other two had been already carved in the kitchen. Flash, swish went his knife and sharpener ever so grandly, then the plates were served up with things like potatoes, parsnips, carrots or sprouts. Dessert was usually some kind of pie. My favourite was apple and blackberry.

But the reason I loved lunch wasn't the room, or even the food. The reason was Captain Fox's talks afterwards. As soon as he tapped his glass the room grew quiet.

Sometimes he'd speak about what happened at school. Mention someone's good mark or an odd thing he'd noticed on a walk around the grounds. He'd talk about the lake, where he felt reminded of Sutton Courtenay, the school he had before, and then he'd get sad and happy at the same time. About a week after I arrived, when I was still settling in, he told us we had some new boys from Spain because there was a war. He asked them to stand, so we'd be sure to give them a hand if they needed it. They were older than I was, more like men.

My first day back since my fall, I was looking forward to an entertaining talk, a good joke, perhaps.

He tapped his glass with his cigarette holder and stood.

'I want each of you to think what you were doing yesterday afternoon. I was walking down by the lake with Mrs Fox. Some of you may have gone into Earley for a soda, or enjoyed a programme on the wireless. Countless possibilities. But yesterday afternoon, in London, while we were all enjoying a beautiful Sunday afternoon, a vicious fight broke out in Cable Street between Jews and fascists – something I never thought would happen in this country. A man named Oswald Mosely led his British Union of Fascists, also known as Blackshirts, into a predominantly Jewish area to cause mayhem and disorder. The Jewish people and their supporters rightly tried to stop them by barricading the streets with cars, lorries, anything they could find. "They shall not pass!" these brave souls shouted. The police and their horses did their best to stop the fighting, but to no avail. Dreadful violence broke out, scores of people were injured, arrests made on both sides. But none of this would have happened if the Blackshirts had not antagonised the innocent people living and working there.

'Let us hope that the behaviour of these dreadful fascists has shown that hatred and bigotry lead only to more hatred and bigotry, and eventually to the destruction of the world.

'That is all I have to say. Enjoy your games, play hard and be glad that you live in a country that won't put up with this nonsense.'

No one said anything. A few chairs scraped and one boy called out, 'Hear, hear!' Others joined, but the noise soon faded, and we went our separate ways. I went upstairs to my room, alone, and lay down. The room felt cold, so I pulled up the rug at the foot of my bed.

Chapter 16

Caspari was still my only real friend. The other boys, while not cruel, stayed clear. 'Don't worry,' I said, as a group ahead parted like the Red Sea, 'I'll be there by Christmas.' This – to my delight – made them laugh, so I decided to poke fun at myself whenever I could. During my afternoon rest, while they were at games, I schemed funny things to say – like, I'd decided to sell advertising space on my built-up shoe when I grew up because people stared at it so much. I'd found a career. I'd be rich.

Sometimes I came up with a joke on the spot. In English class, Miss Taylor asked for new people to join the school choir. 'How about you, Graeme?'

'I'm afraid you wouldn't want me, Miss Taylor. The only thing as bad as my leg is my voice.'

But not in Captain Fox's Maths class. I didn't dare try funny business with him. Besides, here was my chance to shine. My mental arithmetic skills were top-notch, even better than Paul's, which was something.

The Captain conducted the class in an odd fashion. Instead of standing in front of us, like teachers normally did, he sat at a beautiful desk in the library, and the boys – about eight – stood behind, looking over his shoulder. Being lame, I sat beside him. Boch, the one who ran his desk into me, complained that it gave me an unfair advantage. 'And how would that be, pray tell?' the Captain asked.

Boch threw me a nasty look. 'He might cheat.'

'Well, you let me know if he does,' and Captain Fox gave me a wink. We knew, without him saying, that Boch was jealous of my maths skills. Luckily, he stayed clear of me. 'I don't want to catch a disease,' he said under his breath. I ignored him. Best all around.

Amazingly, the Captain could draw the shapes without a compass or ruler.

He was a magician, the way his hands moved. Presto! A perfect circle. We were enthralled and his patience was infinite.

As we huddled close, whatever he used to make his hair as slick as a new car gave off a smell that nearly knocked you out. I liked it. The rest of him, however, was bristly. His moustache was clipped short, with stiff red hairs poking out. His suit, too, had tiny prickles all over that stood out against the window whenever the sun made its brief appearance in the morning light.

I was just so tired. That was the trouble.

Sometimes I was so exhausted I shook. I had trouble paying attention. Latin was the last course of the day, with Paul's favourite teacher Mr Mellor, but by then I was a rag and couldn't appreciate anything. Each afternoon, I could hardly wait to get to bed.

One afternoon, I was just beginning to settle into sleep, when the games outside rattled into my room. Irritated, I threw back the covers and from my window, watched them practise rugby on the field nearby, remembering how well I'd played with Father, years ago. The shouting and tumbling amazed me, the leaping without injury. My anger slid away, and a strange sadness crawled into my heart.

Here I was, clean and frail, with just my wireless for company, longing for the mud and sweat they wore without a thought. The difference between them and me stretched out to an uncrossable sea. I could be clever, they'd laugh at my jokes, but that was the best I could hope for. I'd never have a friend. Not even Paul. Not really. We couldn't do things together – like pals.

Silly that it should take over three years to dawn on me, a bright lad, but it did. I would be lame forever. Never run again. Nor ride a horse. Nor play rugby, cricket or football. I – so nimble and quick that I learned the foxtrot at seven – would never foxtrot again.

The knowing hit me like a train. I could no longer stand. Turning away from the clattering outside my window, I headed for bed and pulled the sheet up over my ear till the crushing weight in my chest faded into sleep.

I even named the plight: The Stone Feeling, as if my heart had become a boulder that pressed against my ribs with unbearable force. The only bright thought that stopped sadness from destroying me was Morland Hall. I longed for it with all my heart. We were in the same boat, us poor sick devils. Our friends, Nurse Seyl, Dr Webb and dear Mr Obken, understood our illnesses, limps and scars with such kindness.

* * *

My sadness showed. I got things wrong, even in Maths, and Captain Fox sent me to Matron who gave me syrup of figs. The next day, thanks to her, I spent the morning on the toilet.

I even dreaded going to my room after lunch because the Stone Feeling grew, filling every inch of me. Could this pain be polio again? Somewhere I remembered not, but doctors could be wrong. An early heart attack? I lay in bed, eyes clenched, waiting for sleep to save me. But I'd forgotten how it came!

Sleep, my dearest friend, had gone.

'I think I'm ill,' I told Nurse Dickenson as I sat in Thursday's bath.

'Yes,' she said. 'You don't look your cheery self. What are your symptoms?'

'Well,' I said, and sloshed the facecloth round in circles.

'Well?' she said.

I took a deep breath. 'Can polio come back?'

'No. Absolutely not.'

'That's what they said. But sometimes they're wrong.'

'Not about this.'

I sloshed the water some more.

'Then, what does it mean when it feels like you have a stone in your chest? Can someone my age have a heart attack?'

'Tell me more,' she said calmly, as if what I said wasn't strange.

The facecloth hung in the water, moving loosely. 'I'm sure no one feels as badly as I do.' I wrung the damn thing out. 'Not at Maiden Erlegh, anyway.' Rubbed soap on it. 'Everyone runs around, happy, laughing, strong as a horse.' Scrubbed my chest. 'I ache all over, in my bones, but mostly in my heart.' More soap. 'I can't sleep.' Keep washing my lad, keep washing.

She stood from the toilet seat that no one would know was a toilet seat. 'How about some more hot water? You look cold.' She was right. My teeth were chattering.

She let in good, steamy water, nearly to the top. 'Now,' she said, as she took her position back on Solly Joel's throne. 'I can tell you what I think.' I nodded, feeling slightly better.

'I've seen a lot of this; believe me. It feels terrible, but it's common. It's what they call homesickness.'

'But it's not my home I want.' I held the facecloth over my face. 'It's Morland Hall.' I said it fast because it sounded so silly.

'Pardon? What was that?'

'Morland Hall,' I said a little louder, but still into the facecloth.

'Oh yes, the nursing home. Tell me about it. What you miss.'

So I did. Everything I could think of. Nurse Seyl's curls, Dr Webb's quiet, sensible wisdom and the oddities of Mr Obken.

'And you liked that.'

'Yes.'

'Dear Graeme, you can't imagine how many of our boys are homesick at some time or other.' True, I couldn't. Anyone who didn't have polio should be happy. 'You should have seen the Caspari brothers when they came. Poor little Ernest was so young.'

'He didn't have polio, though.'

'No, he didn't have polio.' She thought a while. 'All I can say is, it will pass. Be patient. I promise you. Now anything else you want to know?'

'Something about Solly Joel, perhaps?' So she told me about a time he hid a rooster under a guest's bed that woke him up at the crack of dawn.

The next week, November came, and with it, early dark. I did my best to follow nurse Dickenson's instructions – be patient and wait – but I wasn't good at either. So far, the stone in my heart wasn't budging. Oh, perhaps a little, and I was glad not to be dying. That helped.

At the end of Maths class, I was making my way to the door when I heard the Captain's voice. 'I say, Moodie, could you stay behind a moment? I'd like a word.'

Bugger. What was this about? My work had been lagging, but I hoped he hadn't noticed. More the fool, me.

I turned awkwardly, like a lorry reversing into a narrow street.

His eyes canvassed me, top to bottom. 'I have a special request, my lad, if you don't mind. Mrs Fox and Miss Taylor have contrived to see this new film showing in Reading – what's it called – *Rose Marie*? That's it. I hear it's about the Royal Canadian Mounted Police, Indians, and horses. I would appreciate having another fellow along to keep me company. I was wondering if you'd care to join me.'

'Me?' I looked round. 'Me?'

He smiled and nodded. 'If you would.'

'Yes, sir,' I managed. 'I'd be pleased to, sir.'

'Splendid. We'll go this Sunday, after lunch. Have a spot of tea at Pierre's, afterwards. You look like you could do with a little feeding up. Nurse Dickenson mentioned you were below par.'

'Just a touch of grippe, sir. I'm better now.'

'Splendid.'

Why in the world would he choose me? Did he like me? Or perhaps Nurse Dickenson told him I was homesick. I hoped not. She wouldn't betray me, surely.

Oh, who cared? I was going to the cinema!

The following Sunday, after lunch, I was sitting next to Miss Taylor in the back seat of Captain Fox's car, a neat, brown affair, the colour of toffee. Mrs Fox sat in the front, which was good, because her fur coat took up the space of three people, and her long, thin neck poked up and out like a periscope. Miss Taylor wore a wool coat like a normal person. As we drove toward Reading I learned that her first name was Monica.

The Captain drove slowly, not like Uncle S, and even so, Mrs Fox told him, 'Watch out for this crossing up ahead. Here comes a lorry on your left. Do you see it?'

I was excited to be seeing a film about Canada – I'd read many stories about lumberjacks and logging camps, good Indians and bad. Miss Taylor said she had been to the Canadian Rockies once, and saw a wolf standing on a rock. Perhaps there'd be wolves in the film, real, wild ones.

We followed the Wokingham Road straight into Reading, and on the King's Road, found the theatre, the Gaumont. A big poster showed a man named Nelson Eddy, in a Mountie hat, and Jeanette MacDonald, a pretty lady leaning on his shoulder.

Captain Fox paid for us all, which was kind.

Mrs Fox told an usher we wanted to sit quite close and he led us with a torch to our seats. First, we watched the news, which was mainly about the new king, Edward VIII, and his girlfriend, Mrs Simpson. People were beginning to worry he might want to marry her, which was bad because she was divorced. What bothered me was that he wanted to marry her at all. So skinny! Who would want that? I remembered Uncle Sandy saying to Miss Marshall when she was worried about her weight. 'If I wanted a skeleton, I'd hang one in my wardrobe.' Then he'd coax her to eat a little more.

I liked *Rose Marie*, except for the singing, which was a big except. Singing like that made no sense. Here they were, barely acquainted, and they knew the words and the tune perfectly, while behind some trees a full bloody orchestra played.

I liked the Mountie, a fine fellow, steadfast and true. I could imagine being him, never afraid – of horses or anything else. The Indians were good, but their tom-tom dancing around the totem pole went on far too long.

Afterwards, tea at Pierre's was excellent, with tiers of different sandwiches and more pastries than you could count.

One thing about my mother – she taught me good table manners. 'You must be able to go anywhere, eat with George V (if he hadn't died) and not disgrace yourself by using the wrong fork.'

The result of her drilling was that whenever I ate, her voice murmured like a noisy brook. Take small bites, close your mouth, chew slowly. Use your napkin only when necessary. And never talk with your mouth full.

'And how is Mrs Moodie?' the Captain asked, as if Mother had made her presence known to him, too.

'Uh – fine. Busy with golf. Dundee is so close to St Andrews.'

'Ah, yes. I remember her saying she was a golfer. No wonder she keeps so slim. Like Mrs Simpson, eh? But,' he muttered, 'Much better look–'

'Will you be spending Christmas in Dundee,' Mrs Fox asked, but she sounded cross. Maybe she didn't like Dundee.

'Yes, but we always go to our grandmother's house for New Year.' This gave me an opportunity to let fly with tales of Craigisla, the vast estate, its billiard room, its legendary waterfall, Reekie Linn.

I plunged ahead. 'All my uncles will be there.'

'Goodness,' Mrs Fox asked. 'How many is that?'

'Three. But my favourite is my Uncle Sandy.'

'Oh, do tell us why,' asked Miss Taylor.

Where to start? How does one describe a perfect man? 'Well, he's very rich, for one.' That sounded bad. 'What I mean is, he charted a private plane to fly me home when I was at Morland Hall. That was very kind. And this year, he's going to teach me billiards at Craigisla.'

'Why, we have a splendid billiard room at Maiden Erlegh,' the Captain said. 'Have you not seen it?'

'Yes, sir, I have. But I haven't played – yet.' I didn't say I was afraid of that bloody elk looming over the table.

'I can understand that. Settling in takes a while. But you must. I'm confident you will manage beautifully.'

How could I possibly tell this kind man who looked – I realised – like Aunt Herald's Border terrier Max, that I wouldn't be returning to Maiden Erlegh? Everything was too much effort.

* * *

On Sundays, Paul wrote long letters home. No one made him, he wanted to. I wrote, too, but mine were short. Then I'd sleep, or if his scratchy pen kept me awake, I'd read a comic. *The Dandy*, a new one out of Dundee – was grand.

I used lined paper on a pad for my stationery, but Paul had cream vellum with his name engraved at the top and under it: Maiden Erlegh, nr. Reading, Berks. How splendid. I might want something like that for Christmas. But what would I put at the top?

Paul bent over his letter, his wavy hair neat as always, writing steadily.

I tried to copy him, but I could never write so fast.

Dear Mother and Father,

I hope this letter finds you well. Captain Fox draws a circle without a compass. How is Rufus? How is Alastair? Have you seen Cousin Isla?

I watched Paul zooming away. 'Did you know I have a child prodigy for a cousin?'

He lifted his head. 'I beg your pardon?'

'My cousin, Isla. She's played the piano on the wireless.'

'Indeed. That is interesting.' He went back to writing.

I did, too. *Could you please send me Isla's address for I would like to write to her?*

What else could I say? I was looking forward to Christmas gifts, but it was only mid-November. I'd already given the matter thought. A new game called Monopoly, a *Just William* book and perhaps even some Sherlock Holmes. More of those Dinky Toys from Uncle Sandy who, Mother wrote, was travelling through Italy with Miss Marshall. 'He won't have any money left at this rate,' she added. I hoped that wasn't true.

Paul's pen scratched like mad, never stopping. 'What are you writing,' I asked.

'Oh, this and that.'

'Anything about me?'

He smiled in a sad sort of way and shook his head. 'Not this time, but I have in the past.'

'Good things?'

'Of course.' He gave a friendly little laugh.

I wanted to ask him for details, but I knew that would be fishing, so instead, I said, 'Would you read me it, anyway? I need some ideas.'

'Hmm, well, I was writing about the political situation in Germany.'

'Oh.' Never had something like that occurred to me. Still, I said, casually, 'How interesting. But yes, I'd like to hear what you've written, if you don't mind.'

'Not at all, my friend. I'll have to translate, for I've written in German.' He read to me in spurts as he changed the words into English. The fellow was a genius. '*Dear Mother, I am glad to hear that the new exhibition has opened successfully. I am glad you are well. I agree that it is best if Ernest and I remain in England for the holidays this year, but I will miss seeing your dear face. The news we have in England about Hitler is not good.*

'*Captain Fox has suggested that you think of coming to live in England, also. He would find you a house on the Maiden Erlegh grounds. Would you consider that? I am quite serious. You must not be in danger.* There. That's as far as I've got.'

I was confused. With his first sentences, I was only thinking how clever Paul was to speak two languages, but then I saw that serious things were going on.

'Why should she be in danger?'

'Because Jews are not very popular at the moment in Germany, you may have heard.' He said this with the same sad smile.

'You're Jewish?' was all I could say. Except for the Reuben Brothers, who made my school jackets, I'd never met a Jewish person. Not that I knew of, anyway.

'No and yes. My family used to be Jewish. We came from Venice centuries ago, and we were always more interested in art than religion. In the 1870s my grandfather became Christian when the Jews in Germany began to be even more disliked. It was easier to get along if we switched. "Converted," I believe, is the term. I have never been in a synagogue, but because my ancestors were Jewish, that is what matters in Germany now. The pedigree. As if one were a horse or dog.'

I tried to remember when I first heard of Jewish people. Possibly when I was seven, in my first year at Bannerman, and that boy saw the label inside my jacket. He said the Reuben brothers were horrible little Jewish tailors.

Before then, I thought Jewish people only lived in Bible times, like Moses and Solomon, and wore long robes and beards.

I knew, now, of course. I was twelve. But how could anyone be against a fine fellow like Paul Caspari or his mother? Or the Reuben brothers, for that matter? 'Is your mother in danger?'

'She's not concerned for herself. Les Galleries Caspari is famous all over Europe. People stand back and bow when she comes to the opera. She sent us here because we can no longer get a good education in Germany. "This will pass," she says. "It always does. Like a fashion."'

He looked at his watch. 'Damnation,' he said. 'I told Ernest to be here at 3:00. It's quarter past. He's supposed to add his letter to the bottom of mine. Otherwise he's hopeless.'

We went back to our letters. *Paul has a younger brother named Ernest who is hopeless at writing letters. Even worse than I am.* The shadow of my hand was getting longer over the paper, making my words hard to see.

At half past three, Paul slammed his pen on the desk. 'That rapscallion!' He stood, leaving the open letter and unhooked his overcoat from the side of his wardrobe. 'He'll be with that Jimmy Black. I'd best be off to fetch him.'

I imagined Jimmy Black to be a dangerous character. Even his name was thrilling. He rented stables from the Captain and trained hackney horses. I didn't know much about Ernest, except that if there were animals about, he'd be there.

'How far away is it?' I asked.

'Why, would you like to come?'

'If I could; I don't want to hold you up, though.'

'Shall we bring your wheelchair?'

'I suppose. Just in case.' We put on our caps and coats and outdoor shoes. I had a special pair made, its built-up sole made of tough rubber, like a tractor. Wearing it made me feel tough, too, which I liked.

Outside, the air was dull and damp, with a mist collecting on the lawn. Paul pushed the empty chair for a long while, along a fine gravel path that went along the south side of the house toward the stables, where I'd never been. 'Time for the wheelchair,' I said, panting.

'By all means.' Once I was seated, we took off like a rocket. I could see how eager he'd been to get to Ernest, though he'd never said a word.

'Here we are!' Paul puffed, as we approached some low brick buildings. 'I bet the little devil's buried in manure.'

Past the stables was a big red barn; and when my chair reached its wide-open doors, a rough clutter of smells hit me, of steam, straw, manure, and horse.

I'd never ridden; large animals frightened me, particularly their massive backsides that might kick. Horses could smell fear, and I hoped that, as Paul pushed me along, they could not smell mine. 'I say, Ernest!' Paul called. 'Ernest Caspari! Are you there?'

In the dim light, I saw chestnut heads peering at us mildly over low doors. Bridles and saddles hung on walls; dark blue blankets draped over a low beam. 'Show yourself, damn it!'

'I'm here,' called a voice from further down. A stall door opened and out popped a head in a tweed cap. 'Uh-oh. Am I late?'

'Late? It's getting dark, for God's sake!'

I was amazed these two could be brothers. Two more different people you couldn't imagine. Paul was stately and proud, while Ernest was not quite tame. He was always darting here and there and had a pet rabbit he'd found when it was a baby. He fed it bits of carrot and bread, and it didn't mind if he held it.

I also knew that Ernest didn't care for schoolwork.

Paul shook his head. 'Come on. Do you want me to tell Mother you're too busy shovelling filthy muck to write to her?'

'At least Mr Black pays me!' Ernest said. He wiped his hands on his mackintosh and stamped his wellies – covered, as Paul said they would be, with manure. 'I have to finish. I'm almost done. Hold on, would you?'

He did finish quickly and, after hanging his dirty work trousers on a nail, changed into his grey flannels. With his navy overcoat he looked more like us, but the wildness was still there in his smudgy face and messy hair.

I liked him, the way he did everything, fast, with no wasted action. He took his bicycle from against the wall, an old, rusty number, and walked along with us. Around him a cloud of barn smell lingered. As we approached the house, he jumped onto his bike and said, 'See you at supper!'

'You'd better, and no tricks!'

'Who, me?' He charged away. No sooner had he started off, an enormous dog came running from the house, straight for him. I grabbed Paul's wrist that held my chair. 'What's that?' I shouted.

But it was too late. A long, thin, monster of a dog leapt up onto Ernest, its paws hitting him sideways and knocking him off his bicycle.

'Ooof!' The dog went for his throat, I was sure, but Paul rested his hand on my shoulder as if to say, don't worry; we're used to this. I watched them roll and tumble till eventually Ernest got up.

'Shadpar – you damned nuisance!' he scolded. 'Stop doing that!' The dog leapt up, his paws on his chest, and together they took to the ground in a kind of happiness that only belonged with dogs.

'You haven't met Captain Fox's Afghan hounds, I see,' Paul said. 'Shah and Shadpar. Usually they're better behaved, but they adore my brother.'

Chapter 17

Big news about the King. The King did want to marry the skinny Mrs Simpson, after all.

Paul had warned me. His mother had read in the German newspapers that the two were crazy about each other and planned to marry. I didn't think it could be true because the BBC didn't say a word about it, but bang – they suddenly announced their engagement and the BBC was never wrong.

I'd never liked this new king much. I loved the old one, and when he died last January, I even cried. Don't worry, everyone said, you'll like the new one, in time. I tried, but no luck. The fellow looked puny and tired, like a boy getting old without becoming a man. Not like good old George V. Now there was a king.

And now this Abdication Crisis. I wasn't sure what it meant. I'd come across the word in a book we were reading for English class. '"The crisis is over," Dr Ripley said, turning to the family gathered round the bed. Everyone wept for happiness.'

Miss Taylor had advised us to look up new words in our dictionary. A nuisance, but 'crisis' was important if people cried when it ended.

'Crisis: The point in the progress of a disease when a change takes place, which is decisive of recovery or death.' In this case, it meant that the hero, Jack, would recover from snakebite.

My diligence with the dictionary soon paid off when Captain Fox stood to give one of his after-lunch talks. 'Who knows what a crisis is?' he asked.

I raised my hand and said what I knew.

'Absolutely correct. Well said, Moodie. But "crisis" can also be used in the political world, when two sides disagree. They can't see the other point of view. They argue and argue until the point where something gives, some change happens, and for better or worse, one side wins. That turning point is called a crisis.

'We're in a crisis now about the Abdication. Abdication simply means "to give up." And today, we're talking about our king, whether he must give up the throne in order to marry Mrs Simpson, a foreign woman who has been twice divorced. The Church of England does not recognise second marriages. If the King and Mrs Simpson should have children, they would be considered illegitimate.

'Some people think he should give her up and just be king, because ruling Britain is more important than a woman. Others think this is old-fashioned; if he loves her, he should be allowed to marry her. Being king is arduous enough without having to do the job alone.

'Things must go one way or the other, and that, my boys, is a crisis.

'I abhor a crisis. Compromise is always the best solution. One suggestion, which I share, is to let them wed in what is called a morganic marriage, which means any children of theirs cannot inherit the throne. Elizabeth, the ten-year-old daughter of Edward's brother, Albert, would one day become queen.

'So, in your spare time, which I hope is not extensive, I ask you to think – what would you do if you were in Edward's position? Would you bid Mrs Simpson farewell and do your duty? Or would you find your duty too burdensome to carry on alone?'

I pondered this problem and decided I would have told Mrs S to bugger off. She was American, she'd been married twice, and she was skinny. Surely he could do better. I'd ask Jeanette MacDonald to marry me if I were king.

On the 11th of December, Captain Fox called us into the common room and we listened to the King give up his crown. Edward's younger brother, the Duke of York, would be King George VI, and his daughter, Elizabeth, queen when he died.

* * *

That sorted, my busy mind turned itself to going home for Christmas.

I took the train by myself, which pleased me no end. A steward did check on me, a bit too often, but otherwise, I was on my own. I had my own compartment, like the one Mother and I had when we went to Morland Hall three years ago.

I was far more excited about seeing Uncle Sandy than my parents. Perhaps this meant I loved him more. If true, I could never tell them. No, it was because of the billiards – Uncle Sandy promised to teach me when we got to Craigisla. I'd be playing a sport again.

It was still dark when the train went clackity clack over the iron bridge just before Dundee station. Lights shone from the platform outside. A few people stood, hatted and stamping their feet, their hopeful faces lifted, hoping to spot their loved ones through the window.

When I saw mine waiting on the track, my heart swelled like a little boy's. My tall, old father, a little stooped; my mother huddled against him. I banged on the window. They didn't see me.

The steward led me to the carriage door, carrying my suitcase. Steamy air rushed at me, blowing my hair and making me squint. He lifted his hand to help me down, but beside him stood Father, blinking with cold. 'Allow me,' he said to the steward, edging him away with his shoulder. 'That's my son.'

I took Father's hand, his strong rugby hand, still much bigger than mine. I tried to make a graceful descent but collapsed into his arms. He kissed the top of my head.

The steward cleared his throat in a loud harrumph. 'Oh yes,' Father said and gave him some coins. Mother stood apart, still hunched. Her face was wrong. There was no joy in it.

'What's the matter?' I asked. I looked at them, back and forth.

'We're just cold,' Father said. 'We'll talk when we get home. Let's go.'

'Is Alastair all right?'

'Yes, yes. He's fine.'

'Then where is he?'

'He's at home, sleeping.'

Mother started to cry.

'What is it?' I was frantic. 'Tell me.'

'We have to, Ann,' Father said to Mother, and she nodded.

Then I knew. 'It's Uncle Sandy, isn't it?' Somehow I knew.

'Yes,' Father said. 'He died.'

Mother fell against him. He put his arm around her. 'Let's get to the car, for God's sake.' He picked up my suitcase. 'We didn't mean it to be like this, Graeme. I'm sorry. I know you were terribly fond of him.'

I was standing in icy water, frozen, unable to move. I was aware my jaw was hanging open and closed it.

In the car, I asked, 'What happened? What made him die?'

'Pleurisy,' Father said. 'And pneumonia. But really Graeme, we'll talk at home. This is no way to talk of such things.'

The rest of the way home we were quiet, as the sun rose in a dry, blue sky.

Berry, our old nanny, was in the house. It should have delighted me, but I greeted her dully. 'Poor lad,' she said, and also kissed me on the top of my head. 'We'll have a chat later, you and I, all right? Your mother has asked me to stay and help. I'll be here a while. So that's nice, isn't it?'

I tried to smile but couldn't. She understood, I was sure.

Alastair came downstairs, and we shook hands like old men. Rufus was the only happy one. The carry-on was hilarious. 'Stand back,' Father said. 'He's about to explode.' I was glad to laugh for a bit, even though I knew it was wrong. Then, over Berry's delicious breakfast – too delicious, I thought; it wasn't right – Father told how Uncle Sandy and Miss Marshall had been in Monte Carlo, but the weather was unusually cold. He took ill and by the time they returned, pneumonia had set in. 'He died yesterday in Dundee Hospital. He was forty-two years old.'

They sent me up for a nap. I was pleased to manage both flights of stairs, though Father followed close behind. 'Quite a victory, son,' he said as he set my suitcase at the foot of my bed. 'You can unpack later. You're exhausted.'

Thoughts of death had scuttled around me for as long as I could remember. Familiar tales of old uncles and lost children told me death waited behind some distant pillar, to grab its prey – a weak child or unlucky traveller.

But Uncle Sandy? Never. If anyone was charmed, it was him. Light flowed from him in shafts. Gone?

I wanted to weep but could not. Sleep, but could not. Outside, a bright sky stared at me and I stared back. It didn't care one fig about me or the terrible things that happened on earth. By and by a train rattled by on the tracks far below our house, and that comforted me enough to sleep.

* * *

Our Christmas became a precious thing, our gifts more treasured because they belonged to us, the living – who knew enough to be glad we were not lying in a dark box waiting to be buried in Alyth churchyard. Alastair got a gramophone and recordings by Mozart, as well as the scores. I got a camera, an odd gift, but the more I thought about it, the more I liked the idea of capturing the strange things I came across.

We drove over to Craigisla the next day. Uncle Sandy's funeral would be on the 29th, 'Which took some doing,' Mother said. 'Normally, everything shuts down between Christmas and New Year, but your Granny got her way. The vicar is terrified of her.'

'Thank goodness for that,' Father said, and we laughed, which surprised us.

* * *

I'd never been to a funeral. The curious part of me was looking forward to it.

We got to beautiful Craigisla, looking the same, but changed. Inside, the servants went about their work like sad machines. They loved Uncle Sandy, too.

I was glad to see my cousins, particularly Isla. I no longer wanted to marry her, though. I just loved her. She told me she would be playing 'Abide with Me' at the service. She wasn't worried. It was an easy piece.

After dinner, Uncle Sandy would be what they called 'laid out' in Craigisla's front hall, against the big staircase, the same place where he'd played his fiddle at Hogmanay and winked at Miss Marshall. She'd be coming tomorrow, Mother said, because trains didn't run on Boxing Day.

'Poor Miss Marshall,' I said.

'Yes, we had such hopes. She was a good influence on him.'

'What do you mean, "a good influence"?'

'Oh, you know, she was helping him to take it easy. They were going to get married in the summer.' She started crying again.

After dinner, we children were sent upstairs to the playroom while the undertakers set up for the wake. Aunt Herald came and said anyone who wanted to see our Uncle Sandy should follow her downstairs in a few minutes. 'He looks quite nice, just like he's sleeping,' she said at the door, then left.

We didn't know what to say, what to do.

Tam, the oldest, went to his book. 'I'm not going. It will give me nightmares.'

'Me, too,' said Jack, who never could think for himself.

'I'd be afraid,' said Irene in her babyish voice. 'I've never seen a dead body before. It might bring me bad luck.'

'Don't be stupid,' Alastair said, 'they just look like they're sleeping. I'm not going because it's ghoulish.'

'He's not an "it,"' I said, nearly weeping. 'That's Uncle Sandy we're talking about.'

'Not anymore,' muttered Jack.

I headed for the stairs, getting out before I collapsed in tears.

The front hall had a fire going, but otherwise, was lit by candlelight. Beside the staircase lay the coffin, with Uncle Sandy in it, and resting on his chest was his violin.

I'd never seen him sleeping, but I doubted he looked like this. Yes, his eyes were closed, but the lids had sunk down like two craters on the moon. A grey smudge lay on one cheek. His red hair was combed straight back, the comb marks in wide, deep furrows. All the lively colour of his cheeks was gone. Strangest were the fingertips and nails of his hands. They were blue. But not like the sky. More like bruises.

This man wasn't sleeping. He was dead. What made him alive wasn't there.

I understood why they said 'departed.' And why people believed in heaven. It wasn't just to be fancy or make it easier. It was because Uncle Sandy had moved out and left behind this empty house that was his body. All that life and energy, all those springy flames that made him Sandy, had to be somewhere.

Still, I was glad to see him, these remnants of my uncle. He'd travelled to Morland Hall to see me; he chartered an aeroplane to bring me home. I'd thank him forever for that, wherever he was, for being so kind to me.

I wanted to believe he could hear me – my departed uncle – departed like a train from King's Cross Station.

At the funeral, my first one, I noticed how strong the Scots accents were. The church was packed to standing, with all the Alyth people who knew of Granny and her sorrows. She sat, and this was the first time I saw her, in the front row, beside her children, her back as straight as a rod. Isla played her hymn. People sang so loudly you couldn't hear her, which was a shame. I told her it was perfect.

In Alyth Cemetery, the Cochrane stone, by far the largest, had an eagle on top. Fresh snow lay on the ground, but the hole had been dug a few days before, when the ground was soft – another bit of luck, I heard Mother whisper to Father. A hand touched my shoulder, as the vicar mumbled more words and lumps of snow and earth were thrown on the coffin.

It was Miss Marshall, the first I'd seen of her, too. She looked so pitiful, we took hold of one another and cried as if we'd never stop.

* * *

Two days later, on the last day of 1936, Father drove Alastair and me back to Dundee. Mother would stay for a few days to help Granny.

We had an unusual Hogmanay, not what we expected, but pleasant. Berry had gone home to be with her sister, so Father took us to the cinema, where Father nearly had a heart attack laughing during *Mr Deeds Goes to Town*. Alastair changed his seat, he was that embarrassed, while I just laughed at Father laughing. 'Whew,' he said as we left, 'I needed that. Sorry boys.'

Berry had left a cold supper, which we ate in the sitting room on laps in front of the fire. Father even gave us a dram of whisky, as it was Hogmanay. Alastair, who was still cross with Father for drawing attention to himself, went to bed – after finishing his whisky.

Father pulled over two ottomans, one for him, one for me, and we put our feet up. I'd known these footrests, their cracked red leather and flaking gold designs, all my life. Till now, I'd only sat on them, but now we matched, our legs stretching toward the glowing coals.

'How's school?' he asked.

He caught me by surprise. I had been thinking about telling Mother and Father that I didn't want to return to Maiden Erlegh. But Uncle Sandy had taken over. I wasn't prepared for this conversation.

'It's all right,' I said, with little enthusiasm. He looked at me with eyebrows raised but ignored my tone.

'Speaking from a doctor's point of view, you're on the up and up. Your colour's better, you're definitely stronger, you've better balance.'

'I suppose. But compared to the other boys, I'm hopeless. Games are everything there. I don't fit in.'

'Hmm, well, you're getting properly educated. Games don't really matter.' But he knew that wasn't true. 'You'll need a profession.'

'I know, I know. You want me to be an accountant.'

'What's wrong with that? You don't have to move around much and your skills in mathematics are first rate.'

I didn't have an answer. He was clever, my father, cleverer than I was.

I spoke anyway. 'I don't want to be an accountant.'

'What would you like to be then?'

'If I hadn't got polio?' I watched him pick up his whisky, tip his head back and drain it.

'All right, then. Yes.'

'I think – I would want to be someone – like Uncle Sandy.' From his pocket he took his pipe. A packet of tobacco sat in a silver box beside him. He kept several about the house, to make it easy for himself.

'In what way?'

'In every way. Someone who gets on with everyone, knows famous people, who gets the best tables at restaurants and is an excellent billiard player…'

'Billiards.' Father spat out the word like a nasty taste and battled with his pipe, his hands fumbling as he lit it.

'And I'd go to concerts and have a lovely car and a big modern flat in London with four bedrooms and three servants.' The glorious picture left me breathless.

'I can see the appeal,' he said, looking away, and in a terrible dawning, I knew I'd hurt his feelings. I should have said, I wanted to be like *him*, of course! But he went on calmly. 'Sandy Cochrane was a very attractive fellow. But Graeme, you'll need an occupation. You won't inherit a fortune like he did. Money doesn't fall out of the sky.'

'I could learn to be an accountant at Morland Hall. It's much cheaper than Maiden Erlegh, you said so.'

'True, but cost isn't everything.'

'But I'm happier at Morland Hall. Doesn't that count?'

'It does, but it is my duty to see you have a proper education and take your place in the world.'

'The world doesn't want me. Morland Hall does. A nursing home is much better for people like me.'

'You cannot convince me that Morland Hall is better for you than Maiden Erlegh. Your getting polio was one of life's cruel misfortunes. Your choices are limited, it's true, but you cannot exist without an occupation.'

I was losing this battle.

A loud ring from the telephone made us jerk. Father sighed – he'd been sighing a great deal – and picked it up from the table between us. 'Dundee 60316,' he said wearily into the mouthpiece and placed the hearing part on his ear. The way his face lit up, it could only be Mother. 'We're fine, fine. How are things there?' He listened for a while, frowning. 'Yes, yes, he what?' Tremendous shock struck his face. 'How much?' He shook his head, his mouth open, as if unable to take in her words. 'I don't know what we should do. Do you want to wait till you get back?' Another long pause. 'Very well. Yes, I'll tell him.'

He hooked the earpiece back on the phone. 'That was your mother.' His voice was soft.

I waited. Another sigh. 'I have some news for you, my boy. It seems your Uncle Sandy left you some money.'

'He did?'

'Quite a sizeable sum, it turns out.'

'Did he leave Alastair money as well?'

'A little.' He poured himself another dram. The light from the fire glowed into its crystal-cut sides. Heaving his big self from the chair, how tired he looked, he took a long brass poker from its stand by the hearth and jabbed the coal. A spray of red flew up and crackled.

'Cold night,' he said. I was desperate to ask how much was a sizeable sum, but it wouldn't be right.

He turned to face me. 'I think he was concerned about your having polio. He was worried you might have trouble making ends meet. You won't anymore. He left you ten thousand pounds.'

Ten thousand pounds. I couldn't begin to imagine how much that was. I knew that Morland Hall cost fifty pounds a year. A new car – I'd read – a hundred and fifty. A whole house for five hundred. 'Properly invested, you could live off it for the rest of your life,' and he muttered afterward, 'unfortunately.'

'So I can go back to Morland Hall?'

'You need to be properly educated, damn it.'

'I was, at Morland Hall. Even Captain Fox said I was ahead for my age when I arrived. You don't believe it, but it's true.' I was gaining on him.

He turned and poked the fire some more. My moment had come.

'Father,' I said, 'I don't want to go back to Maiden Erlegh. You and Mother promised me that I only had to stick out one term, and that if I hated it I could leave. Well, I don't hate it. In fact, it's better than I thought it would be. Morland Hall suits me better, that's all. You promised. And I know you keep your agreements.'

My heart pounded. I had stood up to Father for the first time in my life. My hands were sweating. Father sat, but he didn't stretch out his legs, as I still was doing. He rested his arms on his knees and looked at the floor. His head hung almost between his knees.

'Don't you see Father,' I said as cheerfully as I dared, 'I think Uncle Sandy gave me that money so I could be like him. Enjoy the finer things of life, travel, not be an accountant all my life. He's given me my freedom.'

'So it seems.'

'Then why aren't you happy?'

Finally he sat up straight and turned toward me. 'Graeme, I'm going to break a promise, but not about Maiden Erlegh. I'm going to break a promise I made to your mother, and you must never tell her. Agreed?'

'Yes, sir.' I guessed that this moment was more important than any we'd had before, so I took my legs off the ottoman.

'When Sandy arrived back from Monte Carlo, he was already dying, but not from pleurisy, nor pneumonia. He died from drink, pure and simple. His liver had given out. He could still be charming, the life of the party, impress everyone, fool everyone. That's the way with committed alcoholics. Doreen Marshall tried her best to get him to stop. When he met her we were all so hopeful, and for a while he cut down and turned a corner. Before long, he was back to a bottle a day, not to mention the wine and brandy. A few weeks ago, she took him to a clinic in Switzerland, but after the first week, he returned to Dundee to die.

'I had to beg the coroner to change the death certificate. He was an old friend from medical school. Granny would have died, herself, knowing it was cirrhosis of the liver that killed him.

'So… I'm going to bed. I don't think I'm going to see the New Year in, if you don't mind. But I will keep my promise to you. You stuck it out, as you say, for a term. That was the agreement. It's your choice about where you go next. And I'll abide by it. Sometimes people do know what's best for them, even at your age. And you are, as we know, a clever lad. Turn the lights out, will you?' He gave me one of his winks I used to love and probably still did. His footsteps were slow on the stairs.

I looked at my watch. Fifteen minutes till midnight. Might as well wait for New Year.

Outside, exactly at twelve, the fireworks exploded. Flashes flickered from the windows. Voices cheered and laughed as they wound their way down Nethergate, happy and drunk, banging on doors for first footing. Someone knocked on our door, but I ignored it.

I'd never been left alone in the sitting room before. Some rite had been enacted, some empty space given round me, but my freedom felt like a cold wind. A great loneliness overtook me. I'd first learned to walk in this room, Mother said. And here I was, alone in the first minutes of 1937.

I had no idea where I belonged. Could I choose my home like one chose a pair of shoes?

I turned off the light on the table beside me and went to bed. Alastair was asleep.

In the middle of the night I remembered something I'd left out of the calculations.

The next morning, on my way to the bathroom, I met Father in the upstairs hall. He was already dressed – three-piece suit, gold watch chain – neat as a pin as always, and about to go downstairs for breakfast. We bid each other good morning, and he took hold of the banister.

'Father,' I said. 'I've made up my mind. I want to return to Maiden Erlegh. I'm going to give it a go.'

He started to kiss me on top of my head, but thought better, and held out his hand. 'I've been proud of you many times in these past few years, but never as proud as today.'

'Thank you. I know I've made the right choice.'

'Splendid. Oh, and happy New Year.'

'Same to you.'

We had a lovely breakfast. Berry had come early and got everything ready. I could smell the kippers as we went downstairs.

'What made you change your mind?' Father asked, as we pushed away from the table.

'I don't know,' I said. 'I just did.' I thought it best not to say that the deciding factor in choosing Maiden Erlegh was that it had a billiard table and Morland Hall did not.

Chapter 18

The next day we all came down with terrible colds – no doubt, Father said, from standing in Alyth Cemetery for so long in all that snow and wind. Mother got cross at that, as if Father was blaming poor Uncle Sandy for our colds.

Father telephoned Maiden Erlegh – and Bannerman for Alastair – to say that we'd be delayed a week and we took to our beds, even Father who never missed work. Cheery Berry popped in with meals of beef tea and custard, and plumped by fat feather cushions, I mulled over the past days, how we had planned such a pleasant holiday and had no idea what lay before us.

Stuck in bed, I was still mad keen to use my camera, the oddly named Ensign Selfix 20. I took it out of its handsome brown leather case complete with strap. Father gave me the basics. 'Look. The front pops out like an accordion. Neat, eh? These dials control the light and the shutter speed. Have a play.'

I tried this and that and by the end of the week, mostly recovered, I went about, taking my first photographs – Rufus's head poking out of a hole he'd dug in the back garden; Mother giving him a bath in the wash house; a serious Father peering over his book at me, pipe in hand.

He posted the roll with instructions to send the prints to Maiden Erlegh School for Boys – where I found myself the following Sunday.

* * *

I arrived just in time for lunch, not fresh from the overnight train. A quick wash in the front hall lav and I took my place in the dining room. But what a fine to-do. People were so glad to see me – like a long-lost brother returning home. 'Moodie, good to see you! We heard you were ill. I feared you might not come back.' On and on. It was great.

Up in our room, Paul gave me all the news. Mohammed Khali had been given his own car, 'A lovely little Aston Martin.' We didn't know Khali well, he was older, he came from Egypt and claimed to be a pasha, whatever that was.

Hearing 'Aston Martin' gave me a sharp pang. Uncle Sandy's car. I told Paul my news, but I left out the inheritance bit. Father made me promise not to say a word to anyone.

I asked him how he and Ernest had fared over Christmas at Maiden Erlegh. I felt sorry for him and the other boys left behind.

'Well, I think I had the best Christmas ever. Of course, we missed Mother, but the Captain was first-rate. He took us all to the Bertram Mills Christmas Circus at the Olympia, in London.'

'You must be joking,' I said, though I knew Paul didn't joke. The Bertram Mills Christmas Circus was famous throughout the Empire. I'd seen newsreels of the trapeze artists, the clowns, the ladies standing on horses, but Paul was the first boy I'd met who had seen it first-hand.

'As you can imagine, Ernest was over the moon about the animals.'

'How is Ernest?' I loved hearing about his escapades.

'Same little devil. Mother sent money to the Captain to buy him a gift. Ernest said he wanted a pet, so guess what Captain Fox bought?'

'A horse?'

'No, no. Too expensive. Nothing like that.'

'Tell me.' I liked guessing, but I was starting to flag and needed a nap.

'A baby ferret. He's named her Glamorous Priscilla, of all things.'

'Brilliant ! Any other news?'

'Let's see,' Paul went on, scratching his head and squinting, determined to give me a thorough accounting of the holidays, 'Hmm. This isn't so good. A rather unattractive fellow from Bulgaria has arrived. Finzi by name.'

'Unattractive how?'

'Hmm. Like a member of the Secret Police. Big muscles, short legs. To be frank, he frightens me. He and Rudy Boch have become friends.'

'Ugh,' I said. 'Well, Boch frightens me,' I said.

'Oh, he's not so bad. He came to Maiden Erlegh the year after me, in 1935. He was so timid and afraid he followed me everywhere. Spoke not a word of English.'

I showed Paul my camera, which seemed a let-down after circuses, ferrets and Secret Police, but to my surprise, his mother had sent him one, too.

'This is a wonderful set of events,' he said. 'Captain Fox is going to organise a photography club, with exhibitions and prizes and things like that.'

His camera was called an even stranger name than mine – the Agfa Karat. It was made in Germany and looked modern, sleek and curved. I hoped it wasn't better than my Ensign Selfix 20. 'We'll have a jolly time, won't we, wandering around, capturing life, things like that?'

I pictured it – us taking shots of the lion statues on the terrace, the greenhouses, the lake – but a terrific yawn engulphed me.

'Oh, I beg your pardon. I forget that you spent the night on a train. One is always kept awake by the noise and jostling, things like that. Please. You must sleep.' I smiled at Paul's newest expression. I'd be hearing 'things like that' for some time.

* * *

The following day, after Maths class, I approached the Captain's desk as the last of the boys trailed away. I wanted to ask him about learning to play billiards.

'Well, my boy. Good to see you again. I hear you had a difficult Christmas. Your father telephoned. I was sorry to hear about your – your uncle, wasn't it?'

'Yes sir.'

'And then you got ill. Rotten luck. Still, you're looking well.'

'Thank you.'

He looked up at me over his spectacles, his blue eyes bright and friendly. When I didn't say anything, he said, 'Hmm, well,' and went back to collecting his papers. I knew he was waiting for me to speak, but I couldn't form my words. He pushed his chair away and stood, not ignoring me, but just getting on with himself, as if it were normal to have a silent boy by his side. 'All done here. I'm going back to the middle common room before lunch. Care to join me?'

'Yes, sir.'

He walked at my pace as we came into the inner hall. Now was my chance. I pointed to stained-glass panels rising on the right-hand wall. The sun poured in through them, turning the white squares on the floor blue and red. 'Would that be the billiard room opposite those windows?' I asked, as nonchalantly as I could. 'Why yes, it is. Why do you ask? I do hope it's because you're interested in taking up the game.'

'As matter of fact, I am.'

'Ah, sometimes I'm a mind reader. Not always, but occasionally.'

'You see,' I went on, 'my Uncle Sandy, he's the one who died, he was a very good billiard player and he was going to give me lessons at Christmas, but…'

'I see. And now you need a billiard teacher. I'd be honoured if you'd let me have that privilege. I would wager he'd approve of your continuing. You were obviously fond of him.'

'I was.' Watch it, Moodie. You're getting wobbly.

'Tell you what. Meet me here tomorrow after lunch. Say, two o'clock? I'll give you a few lessons. Get you started, so to speak. What do you say to that?'

I nodded.

'Good.' He took his cigarette case and ivory holder out of his breast pocket and looked at his watch. 'Well-well, lunchtime already. I'll save that smoke till afterwards. Shall we go in?'

* * *

He was waiting for me by the stained-glass windows the following day, but because it was raining, the colours didn't light up the floor. 'It's a bit of a roundabout to the billiard room door. Follow me.' I did, through the short dark corridor I'd seen before. 'A private entrance,' he explained.

The air felt dank. He flicked some brass light switches gleaming dully on the wall. 'Ah, that's better.' Pulling on an ornate brass handle, he opened the thickest, most heavily carved door I'd come across. I must have seen it on my first day, but everything was so new and enormous, I hardly noticed anything. He stepped into the darkness, reaching for more switches. 'Welcome, Mr Moodie, to the world of billiards.'

Such a confusion of light and dark hit my eyes – I had trouble making sense of it. The only lights hung on chains over the table, glaring down like sun on grass. The rest fell away in shadows – half-church, half forest. To the right, were dim panels of stained glass – of what, I couldn't tell. Men in armour, possibly, holding swords. From another dark wall, a row of animal heads stared out with gleaming eyes; the one in the middle, the huge elk I'd seen my first day, looked just as terrifying. Its gigantic snout hovered over the table; its pale antlers gave off a sickly sheen.

'Quite impressive, wouldn't you say?'

'Very,' I said.

'Some of the littler boys say the billiard room is haunted. You won't have that trouble, of course. Solly Joel killed all these animals, himself. And the window there tells the story of Sir Gawain and the Green Knight, a gruesome tale, but never mind. Shall we start by getting acquainted with the equipment?'

'Certainly, sir.'

'Billiards is played with only three balls – one red, one yellow, one white.' He picked up the brilliant red one. 'Take it in your hand.'

I did, my hand sagging at the weight. It was only about two inches wide, but amazingly heavy.

'Next, the cue. Old Solly left some beauties behind. Take a look.' Under the animal heads was a wooden rack holding a dozen sticks, some light, some dark, many carved with twirling scrolls and leaves. 'Beautiful colours, aren't they? From ebony to this pale, sandy greenheart.' He took a plain one from the middle. 'This one's mine. Simple oak, but it suits me. Perfectly balanced.' He held it horizontally. 'Feel its weight,' he said and dropped it into my waiting hands. 'The tip is made of leather, so it doesn't slide off the ball, but you always apply a bit of chalk just after shooting, so it's ready for the next shot.' He looked at me top to bottom. 'Hmm. You'll need a slightly smaller cue, but I reckon you'll be taller than me one day. Which one do you fancy?'

I knew as soon as he said, 'sandy.' I put my hand on its handle. 'This one.'

'The greenheart? Good choice. Now the table.' I followed as we turned round toward the sea of green. 'There's a reason it's this colour. It's supposed to resemble grass. The French, who settled in our beastly climate after 1066, missed their lawn bowling so much they invented an indoor version. 'Billiard' means simply 'stick' in French. Only they say, bee-yar.'

In half an hour he taught me three basic shots, carefully bending me at the waist, quite low over the table, my back arm working like a piston at right angles. He moved so smoothly as he demonstrated shots, I wondered how I would manage. 'It's a lovely game,' he said. 'Relaxing and exciting at the same time. And you, you're steady as a statue.' He thought for a bit. 'I'll say something else, Moodie. That leg of yours? It just might be an advantage. Keeps you anchored.

'That's enough for today. There are a lot of fancy rules, gentlemanly behaviour and all. But you're a gentleman already, so it will come naturally.'

I wasn't sure why the Captain had formed such a high opinion of me; I hoped I wouldn't disappoint him.

We agreed on three half-hour lessons a week and I'd practice the same amount of time on my own.

* * *

My only problem was that bloody elk. I'd just be getting into position for a shot when I'd feel his eyes on me. I glanced up. Surely his eyes moved. I looked back down, and the same damned thing happened again. I could almost hear his eyes creaking downward to watch me. I snapped my head, but he was too fast. He stared out, same as before.

Now, I didn't believe in spirits. Nor did Father. But Mother did, and in that infuriating way she had of interfering with my mind, she kept dragging me back to old Scotland, those centuries of superstition and stories and songs.

Maybe she was right. It was such a subtle thing, just the tiniest flick of the eyes. The more I dismissed it, the more I believed it. Sometimes, minutes would go by with me trying to catch it red-handed.

I found reasons not to go.

'Moodie, what's wrong?' Captain Fox asked. 'You need to practise more. Is there a problem somewhere?'

'No, no. I've just been tired lately. Needing a nap.'

It was Nurse Dickenson, who still helped me with baths, who guided me over the billiard-room hurdle.

'Do you believe in ghosts?' I asked. 'Or the possibility of anything being haunted?'

'Heavens no. Do you?'

'Of course not. It's just that some boys say that the billiard room is haunted. Silly, don't you think?'

'Utter twaddle. Put any such thoughts out of your mind.'

* * *

I stood outside the billiard room in the dark antechamber gathering my courage to go in – reminding me of – yes – Bannerman – standing outside Mr Cubbage's science class, too terrified to move. For God's sake, Moodie, get a hold of yourself. Have you learned nothing in – I quickly counted – five years?

A group of older boys walked by, laughing. I saw one look at me. It was that new boy, Finzi. I opened the billiard room door. Better a haunted elk than a Bulgarian thug.

I turned on the lights. Get your cue, Moodie, get your cue. Sweat prickled at my neck. Just as I bent over the table, a slowly creating door, like a dying groan, moved through the room.

I nearly took a chunk out of the baize.

'Sorry, old chap. I didn't know anyone was here.' It was Smailes, the head boy.

I'd never spoken to him. I knew that he was king of the school – the best at tennis, swimming, rugby, rowing. 'Say,' he continued, walking over and looking at me up and down. 'Aren't you Moodie? I hear you've got a great sense of humour.'

I looked down at the table. I could feel my face getting hot, as he waited, I was sure, for me to say something hilarious.

'Sorry to interrupt. Mind if I play along?' He took off his jacket.

'That's all right. I was just leaving.' I moved toward the rack to put back my cue, feeling him watching me.

'What a shame. You sure?'

'You wouldn't want to play with me,' I said quickly, 'I'm just learning.'

'Let's play together anyway, just practice shots.' He tossed his jacket toward a bench on the dais. It landed perfectly. 'Come on.'

'Well ....'

'I could give you a few pointers. It's always tough at the beginner stage.'

I gave up resisting. Saying no to Smailes was impossible. I'd never seen anyone so handsome. Nothing was wrong with him. Even my Uncle Sandy was a little bald on top. But Smailes was a foot taller than me, and even in his shirtsleeves, his shoulders were as broad as platters. His hair was thick and blonde, and combed back perfectly. His trousers were belted high, with soft, smart pleats, so that his long legs looked even longer as he slouched against the billiard table, arms lightly crossed. 'Let's do some stringing, shall we? You go first, as if you're starting a game. I'll watch.'

Shakily, I placed my ball on the baulk line, and from the bottom cushion, hit it toward the top cushion. It bounced back and landed near, but not over, the baulk line, which was what I wanted. 'Well done,' he said. 'Don't know if I can match that!' He did, though. His ball stopped just short of the line. 'Lucky shot, that. Come on, let's play a bit, shall we?'

Nervous as I was, part of me wanted nothing more than to play billiards with Tony Smailes. I knew that if I got through this, I'd be lying in bed, smiling at the ceiling.

'I can't believe you've just started playing,' he said. 'You've picked billiards up so quickly.'

Half an hour later I was sweaty while he was still fine. He looked at his wristwatch. 'Blast. I'm due to see Claude Mellor. I'm supposed to be revising my Latin. I've got Certificate exams coming up, and he's trying to keep me on the straight and narrow. Won't work, but he can try.'

He put on his jacket, and stopped, as if thinking. 'Say, wait a minute. You're that fellow with the camera. Haven't I seen you with another lad, taking photographs?'

'Possibly.' My brain rose like a balloon. He'd noticed me with Paul! How wonderful was that!

'I've an idea. The school is starting a newspaper, the *Maiden Erlegh Chronicle*, and we've been looking for someone to take photographs of our games. You could sit on the bench and take pictures – particularly of me,' he said with a laugh, but meant it, I could tell. 'And I'll coach you at billiards. I like you, Moodie. You don't let things stop you – like – like,' and he looked awkward – just for a second – as his eyes moved toward my bad leg.

'Polio.'

'Is that what it is? One of the boys said it was a club foot.'

'No. I got polio when I was nine. I was normal till then.'

'Gosh.' He glanced at himself in a wall mirror, took out a comb and ran it through his hair. 'Well, about the photographs. Shall we meet this Saturday, half-one?' Not waiting for my answer, he clapped me on the arm. 'Good,' he said, and left.

Chapter 19

What a thrill to sit in the stands! With my Ensign Selfix 20 I had a reason to watch the boys play sports. I was their photographer. And when other school teams came, I shouted like mad when we scored a goal. Smailes called me their cheering section. His teammates did the same.

Also surprising was how much I enjoyed my camera. The Photography Club wouldn't start until next term, but I could prepare. And Paul – who knew much more than I did about taking pictures – really got me going.

Remembering his life in Munich, where his mother taught him everything about art, he revealed the fancy side of photography – line, shape and composition. 'In a way,' he said, 'photography is like a painting. You just don't do any old thing.' We took the tram into Reading one Saturday afternoon and bought magazines at a camera shop. Afterwards, we had tea at Morton's where, over scones and clotted cream, we imagined our own work appearing in them one day. We'd have exhibitions, win prizes and travel the world.

I still needed to rest some afternoons, when the strangeness of my new life hit me so hard, I felt like raw, fresh-sawn wood.

On those days, I'd do my old creep-into-bed trick, pulling the sheet over an ear, and thought mostly about photography. What would impress Paul? Shapes of leaves, bare trees against the sky? Mist, hoarfrost?

Hoarfrost. And before I knew it, Reekie Linn took hold of me. I remembered the walk through the den, higher and higher toward the great, tumbling falls that made shards of ice along every curve of holly leaf. Why hadn't someone taken a photograph so that I could hold that time forever? Uncle Sandy was there – right there – Miss Marshall, too.

How amazing photographs were. We changed every second, but a photograph caught just one and kept it forever. How powerful that would be – to capture the flash of life; and everyone would understand how important it was – that very instant when the shutter clicked.

Something wild surged through me. I must start now, *this* instant. I pushed off the covers and looked out the window, where twigs still bore traces of last night's frost. I would catch hoarfrost before it disappeared.

Outside, bundled in my long coat and cap, earflaps down, the leather strap of my camera round my neck, I heard boys running about on the field, their rugby game nearly over. I thought of heading over to them, but the frost would be gone, not by sunlight, but by them – their heat, their noise. I walked away, toward Maiden Erlegh Wood. I'd never been, but I'd find plenty of hoarfrost for sure, with no people ruining it.

I saw a path bending out of sight, into trees. Like Craigisla's den, bark chips paved the way. Never, not since polio, had I gone anywhere on my own.

High time I did. It looked safe enough. I stepped into the woods.

So silent – fog hanging in the air, quietening everything, even the uneven rhythm of my shoes on stiff, icy leaves. My camera bounced softly against my chest, my breath panted a frosty cloud of its own. Ahead was a group of pines, as tall as telegraph poles. This was an ancient wood.

Further, I found oaks growing in a tumbled wreck, some fallen long ago, rotten and crumbly, with holes half-filled with moss and matted grass. Others fought for the sun, twisting higher, with low branches in strange L-shapes. Unfallen acorns, dipped in frost, clung to branches, and near me, misshapen holly bushes struggled for light, every leaf ridge needled with hoarfrost. This was what I came for.

I steadied my legs, spacing them wide to get better balance. I leant my stick against a tree. My camera came out easily after I'd had the sense to take off my gloves. I had a new roll of twelve pictures and a spare in my pocket. Right beside me was a holly tree, its leaves lined with icy shards, perfect as soldiers. I opened the shutter, aimed it. Why bother to make something so beautiful, with only me to see? Spiderwebs stood out everywhere, the strands thick and white, drooping like skipping ropes. Don't worry. I'll remember you.

I made the adjustments, the focus, my hands steady in the cold air. Click and click again, uncertain what to shoot, there was so much. Higher, an old nest lay squished between two branches, no longer home to anyone. I caught it, too and moved on, crunching loudly on a frozen puddle, stopping to shoot anything that called to me. Graeme, don't you think I'm lovely, too? As if no one had seen it before, I was giving it meaning, so that others could have that same gasp of wonder.

'Hey!' a voice screamed.

Had I been old enough, I would have died from a heart attack.

'Hallo?' it called again. 'Anybody there?' I stood still, hardly breathing, afraid to draw attention to myself. The voice sounded young, but not nice. A young witch?

'I'm here,' I said, trying to make my voice deep.

'Billy? Is that you? Are you taking the piss?'

'I'm not Billy,' I said cautiously, getting ready to run for it, as best I could.

'Oh. Who are you then?'

I wasn't giving my name. 'Who are you?' I asked, sounding low-voiced and tough, I hoped, like a game warden with a gun.

'It's Mary Petty. Up a tree.' I didn't say anything; I was trying to absorb this information. She shouted again, 'Help me, for God's sake. I'm freezing to death.'

Mary Petty, up a tree. Not a gamekeeper with a gun, not a poacher, not even a ghost, but Mary Petty, whoever that was, up a tree.

'I'm coming.' I said. 'Where are you? Call out again, will you?'

'Here.'

I started toward her voice. 'Keep calling so I can find you.'

'Here.' She waited a few seconds. 'Here.' She called again, as I tumbled onto a fallen tree trunk.

'Agh, ow,' I said. 'Bloody hell.'

'What's happened?'

'I'm climbing over a trunk.'

'Hurry up, can't you?'

'I am.' I straddled the trunk, and with both hands, lifted my right leg, a dead branch itself. 'I'm over it,' I called.

A little trodden path moved through the prickles and tangled whips of bramble. Someone used these woods. 'Call out again, please.'

I kept asking and she kept calling, more annoyed each time.

'I see you coming,' the voice said. 'Up this oak! Straight ahead of you.'

I looked up. 'Higher! Look, I'm waving.'

I bent my neck back and, higher than I thought possible, was a girl, barelegged and partly camouflaged by a brown wool coat. I wouldn't have seen her if her legs hadn't been so white.

'What are you doing up there?'

'What does it look like? Climbing. Who are you?'

I decided it was safe. 'Graeme Moodie.'

'From the big house?'

'Maiden Erlegh?'

'Yes,' she groaned at my stupidity. 'Look. Would you climb up halfway? Help me down. I can't see my way.'

'I can't.' I said. 'I'm – lame.'

'What do you mean "lame"? Have you hurt yourself?'

'No. I'm lame. I got polio when I was nine.'

'Bugger!'

No one had ever summed it up so well. 'I'll get help. I'll go as quickly as I can.'

'How long will you be?' She sounded worried.

I looked at my watch. An hour had passed since I left the school. There and back, maybe the same amount of time. 'Probably an hour… I hope.'

'An hour? I can't wait that long. It's getting dark. My hands and feet are numb.'

'I'll be back as soon as I can.' I started off, quick for me, but slow for anyone else, dodging branches and brambles that kept catching my stick.

Wait. Alastair and I used to climb trees. Nothing like this, but if ever I got too high, he would talk me down, tell me where to step.

'I'm back,' I called up to her.

'Oh, for God's sake!'

'No, listen. I've an idea. I can see the branches below you. I'll tell you where to put your feet. You'll be fine. I'll guide you.'

'How old are you?' She was deciding if she could trust me or not.

'Almost thirteen,' I said. Not till August, but it sounded much better than twelve.

'Now. Look below you. See that branch, about two feet down? That's the one you're aiming for. Turn toward the trunk. I'll guide you.'

She let out a little wail. I didn't blame her.

'You can trust me. I've done this before.' It was not true.

'I suppose I have to. All right.' Her scrawny, scratched right leg lowered ever so slowly, the foot bobbing, trying to feel for the branch.

'A little more, a little more. You're almost there. Couple of inches. There!' She made it. Her left leg followed. 'Congratulations. Now. Ready for the next one? This one's only about a foot, it's easy.'

It wasn't easy. I guided her from branch to branch, on opposite sides of the trunk sometimes, left to right, not just up and down. She was brave, though. She had to be. She had no choice. Only when she tried to look over her shoulder, did she lose her nerve again.

'Don't do that!' Her sorry legs looked worse as they got bigger. Blue-white and scabby; I'd never seen such beat-up skin.

'You're nearly there. There's a lower branch, but I don't think you can reach it. You have to jump. Don't try and turn round.'

'Are you sure?'

'I'm sure. Jump away from the tree. Wait just a second.' I piled up some leaves to make a cushion and pulled off my coat, placing it on top. 'There. I've made a landing spot. Now. One-two-three... jump.'

Nothing. 'Well, when you're ready,' I said.

'I'm ready.'

I waited.

'I'm not usually afraid.'

'I know.'

I waited. At last, she screamed, 'Juummmp!' and landed on my coat, right in the centre of the leaf-pile.

She stayed there a while, collecting herself. I knew she wasn't happy being rescued. She wanted to stay proud and dignified. I understood.

'Well,' she said, standing, brushing off the leaves from her coat. Her hair was a mess, but she didn't seem bothered. 'I'd better be off. People will be wondering about me. This has never happened before. I know these woods perfectly.'

'I'm sure you do. You're a very good climber. Are these your paths?'

She nodded. 'Don't tell anyone, will you? I'm not supposed to be here on my own.'

'Neither should I.'

'Good thing you were,' she said, and disappeared up one of her paths.

Chapter 20

Last day of Spring Term. After lunch, we'd go home – most, anyway. Some, like Paul and Ernest, would stay at Maiden Erlegh, but Captain Fox had planned a week with them on the Isle of Wight, so they wouldn't mind so much while the rest of us larked about back home.

And I intended to lark. What a change my cousins would see in me. Walking about with just one stick, growing stronger every day.

I looked round our table of twelve, Matron at the head, Miss Taylor at the foot. I sat near her.

I like this table, I thought. Back in September, all the skin colours and accents astonished me. Now, they were just good old Kairi, Papamichael, Nisoli…

A Spanish boy, next to me, I was particularly fond of – Tomas Echeverria. Just like Uncle Sandy, he could do tricks with cards, coins, and matchbooks, which Miss Taylor allowed after the meal because she liked them too. Right before our eyes, he'd pull a coin from his breast pocket, that seconds ago we'd patted to be sure it was empty.

Echeverria was thrilled to be going home, his first time back since the civil war in Spain began. 'My father bought me tickets to travel through France, where it's safer. My town, it is just inside the border, near Bilbao. Is not important to the rebels. We are just little place. The olive trees and oleander are flowering, and I am missing all the time the sun. Tomorrow, I will be in Spain.'

'And I will be in Scotland.' Then I remembered something. 'Echeverria, you said you'd teach me how to do a trick. An easy one.'

'But of course. I show you.' He took a shilling from his pocket. 'What you must do is to fool the eye to look the other way. Watch closely.'

A loud clang sounded as Captain Fox rang his bell. We looked at each other and shrugged. 'When I return,' he whispered.

The Captain told us to enjoy our holidays. To use the time well and be sure to do our holiday work. 'Now, a word about the Coronation just two weeks after we return. Some of you will be going to London to see the parade. It will be the greatest spectacle on earth. You will never forget it, I assure you.'

I was to be one of them, for Granny Cochrane had booked rooms for us in the Grosvenor Hotel, she being such a good friend of the new queen, Elizabeth. 'Honestly,' Mother said. 'Your granny visited her once, but you'd think she was a member of the Royal Family.'

* * *

A glowing school report awaited in Dundee. Father stood by the fireplace and read it aloud. '"English Essay: Is developing a good clear style. Works carefully and intelligently. Has plenty of ideas. 94%." Good boy,' he added, as if I were Rufus.

History, Geography, and Latin came next. Good enough, although the praise could have been a bit more fulsome.

Maths from the Captain topped them all.

'"He shows decided ability. By the end of next term, he will have covered all the ground required for the School Certificate Examination."'

'Really? He said that? Gosh. Most boys who take the School Certificate Examinations are fifteen or sixteen. I'm only twelve.'

But he was frowning in that way I'd come to dread. 'What's this? "French. Twenty-nine per cent. Fair work and progress." Graeme, the average mark is fifty-four per cent.'

'Well, most of the boys already spoke French when they arrived. So naturally I'm a bit behind.'

'I'd call twenty-nine per cent more than a bit.'

'I'm only saying what Mr Piper said. Ask him.'

'I intend to. And don't be impudent. As you yourself said, you're only twelve.'

* * *

Alastair came home, the one unchangeable fixture in my life. On the outside, we'd altered. His bumpy low voice made me laugh; he saw a spot or two on my chin; and Mother declared that we looked like Charlie Chaplin, in our too-tight jackets. So the next day we taxied to Reuben Brothers, getting outfitted in garb befitting two young men on the brink of life. 'Is Dundee poorer than

before, or did I just not notice?' I asked, as I peered through the taxi window at
the city mouldering beneath The Law, the great extinct volcano that towered
over everything.

'It's worse, I'm afraid,' Mother said. 'So many shops are closing. The jute
industry is moving to India, where the labour is cheaper. I do wish your father
would move to Edinburgh.' Alastair, sitting in the front seat because he was
so tall, turned to grin at me. We'd been hearing that complaint from Mother
all our lives.

* * *

Thus equipped with new finery, we adjourned to Craigisla.

As we approached Alyth, the skies lifted miraculously, as if the clouds and
misery had belonged to Dundee and had no place here.

'Now listen, my boys, Mother said as we came up Granny's steep drive,
'You'll have to prepare yourself. The first time you go into a house after
someone's died, it can be a shock.'

She meant Uncle Sandy, of course. We'd been at his funeral, but this was
different. This was a holiday visit, when his absence would be a terrible thing.
Not hearing his voice start up like a trumpet or his mischievous face peeking
round a corner.

The cousins were a shock, too. Tam and Irene looked like adults, and kept
to themselves, thinking they were too grand to play with us. Irene got sent
away from the table for wearing rouge and Tam read in his room. Once, when
I came to see if he wanted to join our card game, his book shot under the
covers.

Jack and I didn't look at all like twins anymore – a relief to me. As if no
longer together, we'd drifted apart in appearance. Heavier with all the rugby
and cricket, he no doubt fancied himself to be better than I, since he was
stronger. But he was still thick as two planks.

Isla was Isla, playful and fun, with that upward tilt that never left the
corners of her mouth. Her blonde curls were still all over the place, but these
two little puffs sticking out of her jumper were new, the start of – go ahead,
say it Graeme – bosoms. They embarrassed her, too, and she folded her arms
and slumped, so they could hide in the little cave she made of her chest.

We did our best to get along with our new selves. We dropped some
games, started new ones. Croquet, bridge, Monopoly. Only Jack still collected
Dinky Toys.

* * *

Maiden Erlegh was a welcome sight.

I arrived in time for lunch. Papamichael stood at the door of the dining room, checking our clothes and new-shone shoes.

'New tables this term,' he added. 'You're at Mrs Fox's.' I'd been looking forward to seeing my pals at Matron's table, particularly Echeverria. Still, I took the shift as a promotion, Mrs Fox being higher up.

Her table was the longest, fifteen boys on each side. I found my spot at the far end, and whom should I find at the foot, but Smailes! I looked round for Echeverria; still no sight of him.

Smailes explained that because he was head boy, he'd asked the Captain if he could carve the joint, instead of it arriving already sliced. 'He saw the sense of it, of course,' he said. And with swashbuckling flourishes, he sharpened the knife and began carving, making rather a show of it, I thought.

Ding, ding – the Captain's pen tapped his glass, ringing thin and high. We grew quiet as he stood. He looked down at his plate. We waited.

He lifted his head and gazed nowhere. 'My young men. I am pleased to see you, cheerful, full of energy, ready to begin another term. A term that welcomes back eighty-two of you. But not eighty-three, as we expected.

'I have received the terrible news that a small town in Northern Spain near Bilbao, the home of our dear comrade – Echeverria – has been bombed by the supporters of General Franco, with the help of German aeroplanes. No one knows how many people were killed in this town, Guernica, but it appears Echeverria was one. A telegram arrived yesterday from his father, who survived because he was out on the day of the bombing, the twenty-sixth of April.'

Every mouth sucked in its breath. Echeverria.

I'd been so happy to see the flowers on the drive, and all the time Echeverria had been dead.

'So,' the Captain gave a sigh, 'instead of games this afternoon we will meet in the middle common room. I've asked St Peter's vicar, Mr Fowler, to lead the service, but if any of you wish to share a memory of Tomas Echeverria, please do.'

I didn't speak at the service. I almost did – how I'd never learn his clever card tricks – but I was afraid it might look as if that were all I cared about. So I sat, jaws tight, furious at stupid, horrible death, how it spoiled everything. Echeverria, so barely known, was gone in a flash of light and I never took his picture.

Chapter 21

Thank goodness the Photography Club started, so my mind could turn to something happy. I was eager to get to know Mr Mellor better. Paul had such a high opinion of him.

We brought our cameras to one of the smaller classrooms and sat at a rectangular table. Just me, Paul and a new German boy, Peter Basch, who'd come to Maiden Erlegh via Hollywood, where his father directed films.

Mr Mellor hadn't arrived yet, so we chatted away in English. Using one's native language was rude. I liked Basch's German-American accent, dotted with 'lemme tell ya' whenever he got stuck for a word.

In came Boch and Finzi, who sat further down the table, speaking in German. 'Good afternoon, lads,' Paul said. 'We've been discussing our cameras. What sort do you have, may I ask?'

Thuggy Finzi said, 'Boch's father order ours from Germany. Not come yet.' He turned to his pal. 'What the name?'

'Agfa Karat,' Boch answered. 'The best cameras come from Germany, as do most things.' He leaned back in his chair, his hands behind his head.

'What a coincidence,' Caspari said politely, 'Mine's an Agfa Karat. My mother sent it. Would you like to see mine?'

'I would,' Finzi said. He snatched Caspari's camera out of his hands, but Boch muttered more German, making Finzi drop the camera onto the table and shake his fingers, as if he'd touched something foul. With his forearm he shoved it back toward Paul, who grabbed it before it could tumble onto the floor.

'Lads!' Mr Mellor burst into the room, smelling of the outdoors. 'Sorry to be late. The rowboats took some tying up today. Fierce wind out there.' He was still wearing a thick white jumper with a blue V at the neck.

Shaken by Boch's and Finzi's appalling rudeness, we watched Mr Mellor brush at his sleeves and look round the table. 'Ah, a small group but a worthy one. I suppose we don't need to introduce ourselves, but let's meet our cameras. Boch, would you start?'

'Certainly, sir. As you may know, my father is second-in-command to the German Ambassador in London. He is ordering for me and Finzi the newest model of the Agfa Karat. Very superior. They have not arrived yet. He is a busy man.'

'I'm sure he is,' Mr Mellor said with slow patience. 'I've some good, second-hand ones to use in the meantime. At your level, it is best to have a good, but not the best, camera. Moodie's is a fine example, sturdy, portable. Perfect for the student photographer. Now, Basch, tell us about yours. Is that an Exakta VP I see before me?'

'Yes, sir. Latest from Kodak. From America.'

'I've heard of this beauty. It has something called a single lens reflex, am I right?'

Basch beamed. 'The first. Wanna see it?'

'Another time. No thanks to me, we started late. Best move on. Moodie, how about you?'

After making sure we knew the basics of photography, he asked us about our goals, and why we took pictures. I explained how I wanted to capture time, itself, which Mr Mellor found fascinating, he said. I could see why Caspari liked him. 'And sir,' I couldn't resist saying, 'I'm off soon to see the Coronation from the apartment my grandmother's rented. I hope to get some good shots there.'

'Excellent. We'll look forward to seeing them. Now, for next week, I want you to photograph the outdoors. The weather's been superb.'

'I'm keen on photographing faces,' Basch said.

'Oh? Interesting,' Mr Mellor said. 'Have you done much?'

'You bet,' Basch nodded. 'In Hollywood. I gonna be professional, photograph the Hollywood stars.'

Mr Mellor scratched an eyebrow. 'Lucky you. Nevertheless, we are at different stages of photography, and people are tricky, in more ways than one. We'll stay on the nature theme for a while, and Basch, you can teach us, later perhaps, about portraiture. What do you say?'

'I say ya got a deal.'

* * *

'Bloody hell,' I said to Paul, as we walked back to our room. 'They're a nasty pair, aren't they – Boch and Finzi – speaking German? And what was it Boch said about your camera? Did you catch it?'

'I did. He told Finzi not to touch the camera. Apparently, I am a "*schmuzig juden.*" A dirty Jew.'

'But Paul, we must report him! We must tell the Captain!'

'Why? Boch's not the problem. It's Hitler. He's made these words normal. No one stops him, so we get more and more Bochs. Germany is rearming, yet this government does nothing. If there's a war, Britain will lose.'

* * *

A week later, fresh from having attended the Coronation, I rushed into Paul's and my room. He was at his desk, hunched and writing in the near-dark. 'Paul!' I flipped the ceiling light on. 'Stop worrying! Hitler could never defeat Britain! Our power is bigger than the whole world's!'

I flung my suitcase on my bed. 'Just a minute. Look at this.' I pulled out the souvenir programme, a grand, silver book.

I regaled him with the parade of troops, how Father had read out the names of each one, and I did the same: United Kingdom and Indian Empire Representative Detachments, The Royal Air Force, The Indian Contingent, Officers Training Corps, The King's Own Malta Regiment. The Territorial Army, The Five Regiments of the Brigade of Guards, whatever that was. The Royal Corps of Signals and Royal Engineers.

'I tell you, Paul, the British Empire owns more countries than you can count.' I couldn't speak fast enough. 'If only you could have seen them – Father tried counting and stopped at sixty. I tell you, our power is beyond anything you can imagine. The Navy, RAF, the Army, Royal Artillery marched by for hours. Hitler could never defeat us. No one could.'

He gave me a shaky smile. 'That is comforting news, Graeme. I'll add that to my letter to Mother. And let's hope our new prime minister, that Chamberlain, will stand up to Hitler.'

* * *

I brought my Coronation photographs to Camera Club, but they were a disappointment. The prints themselves were small, and I only had one lens, so the people looked like ants. Contrast was poor, too, with the misty rain and shooting through glass.

'Don't worry,' Mr Mellor said as I slid them back into the envelope. 'That happens. Big events are hard to capture. If we had an enlarger, which we will next year, you'd see a big difference.'

'Whatcha want is a zoom lens. I coulda leant you mine, Moodie. Ask me next time.'

'Next time there's a Coronation?' Caspari asked, which made people laugh.

'Nah,' he said. 'Before den. Any old time.'

'Thanks, Basch,' I said, feeling better, 'I just might take you up on that.'

'You call yourself a photographer?' I looked across the table at Boch, who gazed at me with a tilted-up chin. 'And you only have one lens?'

'Well…'

'Dat's rich, coming from you,' said Basch. 'You don't even have a camera.'

Mr Mellor cleared his throat. 'Basch. You've brought us some of your portraits, I believe?'

But Boch would not be silenced. 'Oh, and another thing. Agfa makes colour film now.'

'As does Kodak,' Mr Mellor said, his voice patient, but strained. 'Colour would have enhanced the Coronation, true. The splendour of the robes, the jewels in the crowns.'

'That's a bit silly, don't you think? In Germany we do not require velvet and furs to show our might. The modern world respects none of those things.'

Mr Mellor spoke at last, hardly moving a muscle. 'We are not discussing the might of our countries, but what we can bring to photography. Basch, please. Could you show us your portraits? We'd be very interested in seeing them.'

Basch fetched a large leather portfolio standing against the wall.

What was our teacher doing? I'd have been bloody steaming. Sent Boch to the Captain, who'd dish out some worthy punishment.

But for Mr Mellor, it seemed that Boch no longer existed. We carried on.

Basch took his work out of the portfolio. Fine tissue paper folded over each large photograph. Some were obviously taken in a studio, with soft or dramatic lighting; others came from the street – old people, dockworkers, farmers. They were the most beautiful photographs I'd ever seen.

'Congratulations,' Mr Mellor said. 'Lads, this is what you can accomplish, not just with good equipment, but dedication, a good eye and a love of the subject. Young Basch here can teach me more than I can teach him.'

I itched with jealousy, but stronger was my delight at seeing Boch shrink to the size of a pea, like something out of Alice in Wonderland.

Chapter 22

About three weeks before the end of term, if I paused in any afternoon or evening, I could hear a conglomeration of extraordinary sounds – accordions, pianos, voices, ukuleles, banjos. These were rehearsals for the last night of term; one shouldn't listen, so that each performance would be a surprise – rather like not sneaking into the Christmas-presents cupboard.

I did know that Paul was in a play called *Vice Versa*. I helped him with his lines. He was playing a woman, there being no girls about.

The big night came, and after a splendid dinner finished off with Charbonnel chocolates because a Charbonnel was at our school, we headed to the Middle Common Room. What a transformation! Before us stood a theatre, complete with red velvet curtain. I'd brought my camera and was about to sit, when I heard a voice behind me. 'Moodie?' I did my slow turn-around.

A girl in a stiff green party-dress, hair trapped in tight, bent-up plaits, stood looking at me, not smiling. 'Mary Petty,' she said.

Dear God. I never would have known. She recognised *me*, everyone did because of my sticks. Only when I saw the scabs and bruises adorning her legs, I knew it was her. Not a pretty sight.

'Mr Grumbar's my uncle,' she said, as if this solved everything. Mr Grumbar, I knew, taught biology. Coached rugby, too.

'I'm sorry. I didn't recognise you.'

'In these stupid clothes. I know. They forced me.'

'My parents do that, too.' I tried a smile.

'They're not my parents,' she said, 'I just live with them. My parents died.' It could have been the weather she was talking about. 'In a road accident.'

'I see.' I knew what she was doing. She was showing me that she didn't care anymore, so I wouldn't feel sorry for her. I did the same thing about my lameness.

'Who was that?' Ernest asked as I sat down beside him.

I shook my head and pointed to the stage, hearing a loud applause.

First came Mrs Jones, wife of our History teacher. Bowing cheerfully, she sat at the piano and wiggled her bottom with confidence. 'Watch this,' said Ernest. 'She can play anything.'

'My cousin Isla is like that,' I said.

The Tin Band tumbled out next – an assortment of boys of vastly different heights, scraping chairs. Here were the ukuleles, guitars and saxophones I'd been hearing for weeks. The conductor, Papamichael Two, in morning suit and villainous moustache, bowed and announced: 'Ode to Joy.' He raised his baton. A single violin sang out the tune quite well, but in seconds, others launched themselves into the fray, completely wrong and off-key. If I'd been younger I might have been afraid. No longer.

This was hilarious bedlam! No one could hear Mrs Jones anymore, but her fingers kept flying and her bottom kept bouncing. The audience stood and joined in with imaginary instruments – me a violin, for Uncle Sandy. It was so ridiculous and so very awful, no one could hear anything and no one cared.

Paul's play, *Vice Versa*, was the main piece, and we settled down to be vastly entertained. And I was. Nevertheless, I saw a serious side that hit me hard.

It was about a father and son who change places – magically – because they had a stone, stolen from a maharajah who granted wishes.

The boy hates his boarding school and begs the father not to send him back.

'Nonsense,' says the father 'I wish I could take your place.' And zip! His wish comes true. They become each other. The son manages the family business, and the father goes to boarding school, where a cruel headmaster beats him, and bullies make his life miserable. Just like Bannerman.

Paul, in a blond wig and flowery dress, was excellent as the teacher, swatting the father away because he fancies her so much. Yes, we laughed, but I couldn't get over the boarding school – that such wickedness existed and no one cared. It was normal to send little boys off to be beaten and bullied and made to feel stupid.

I wished I'd had a magic stone when I was seven years old.

* * *

Back in our room, Paul was jubilant. 'Did you really think I was believable? I didn't want to overdo it, even though it *was* a farce. I do love theatre. There's something so exciting about being on stage. One feels extraordinarily alive. Do say you'll give it a go next year.'

'I'll think about it.' I took off my clothes, and undid my splint, the happiest moment of the day. I didn't realise how uncomfortable the damned thing was until it was gone. I gave my leg a good scratch and crawled into bed.

But Paul was on fire! Not only had he tasted the triumphs of theatrical success, he was going home to Munich the next day. Two weeks earlier, his mother had finally agreed to her boys returning to Germany for the summer. 'Hmm,' he said, popping up from the edge of his bed and pacing. 'Perhaps we should begin packing tonight. Get a head start.' He put his hands on his hips. 'What do you say, Graeme?'

Sleeping with that whirlwind in the room was impossible. Back on went the splint. 'Sorry, old chap,' I said, giving my leg a pat. I didn't mind. We could steal a few more winks in the morning.

We were nearly packed, suitcases jammed with stuff yanked from our chests of drawers in the corridor. Just a few things left out deliberately – soap, toothbrush, comb, clothes for tomorrow's journey. Last, I went to fetch my camera from its usual place in the top drawer. I'd nestle it safely among some soft things.

My hand reached into the drawer. Nothing. I opened it further, my fingers scuttling faster and faster along the empty corners. It wasn't there. I closed the drawer. Opened it, as if this time I'd find it. Every drawer, open-shut, open-shut, open-shut, but nothing, nothing, nothing.

'My camera's gone.' My voice was brittle and glassy.

'Surely not. You must have packed it already. Check and see.'

I gave a heavy sigh. I willed my hands to be slow and careful as I rummaged through my suitcase, but I knew I hadn't. 'It's not here.'

'Don't panic. Think. When did you last have it?'

I sat on the bed, legs shaking. 'Twenty minutes ago! I almost packed it; I had it in my hands, and thought, no. Put it in the top drawer and wait till my suitcase was full.'

'You're sure?'

'Yes, I'm not stupid! Sorry, Paul, sorry… but someone's stolen it. It can't be anything else.'

'You're right. We've got to tell the Captain. Right away. Before the morning.'

The Foxes' apartment was down the hall, through a heavily panelled door that led to their famously vast quarters. I'd never been inside. Caspari gave two sharp raps and after a few minutes the Captain appeared, putting his arms into a dressing gown. His eyes grew wider as Paul explained. I was having trouble forming words.

'You say you had it *after* the entertainment?' The Captain looked down at me.

I nodded.

His moustache twitched. 'That means your camera must be in the building. The doors were locked *before* it disappeared. I'm sounding the alarm. We're going to find that camera.'

In no time, the eight NCOs had sped along the halls, calling everyone downstairs. We'd rehearsed an 'Emergency Situation' many times.

Once again in the Middle Common Room, where we had just been having such riotous fun, we sat in chairs, still askew. The stage was dismantled, lying in a wreck; the job to be finished in the morning. We sat, confused and mussy-headed, most in pyjamas, while the Captain who had changed into a suit, stood in front of us.

'Someone has stolen Moodie's camera from his chest of drawers. We aim to find it. The doors were locked before the crime was committed. Please wait quietly while the rooms are searched.'

How long would it take the NCOs to go through forty-some rooms? Could I be wrong? Was it in a drawer after all? Had I deprived everyone of sleep?

It was Dimitriou who found it – in a tall rubbish bin in a corridor on the second floor. He held it up in victory, passing it to the Captain, who passed it to me. Some cheered, and then thought better of it. The thief had panicked and tossed it in a rubbish bin when we were called downstairs. I touched its well-known scratches, nearly crying with relief.

Only after breakfast did Ernest tell me that he saw someone toss a paper sack into the rubbish bin as he hurried down the corridor. He was almost positive it was Finzi. I might have known.

Like a shot, I tore to Captain Fox's office, the fastest I'd gone since I was nine. The door was open. I stopped short, panting.

He looked up, trying to smile. 'Do come in, Moodie.' He looked done in.

I stayed in the doorway. 'It was Finzi,' I said, hoping I sounded like Sexton Blake, hero of my favourite detective stories. 'Finzi stole my camera.'

The smile faded. 'Take a seat.'

I carefully explained what Ernest had told me. 'You're quite certain? Ernest could be mistaken.'

'No, sir. He was right behind Finzi. He saw him toss a brown bag in the rubbish bin.

'It is a large rubbish bin. There might have been more than one in it.'

I groaned. 'But it must be him. No one else would throw out rubbish in the middle of an Emergency Situation.'

He pushed back his chair. 'Don't worry, I'll see what Finzi has to say for himself, but remember that you could be wrong.'

I looked down. I wasn't wrong. I knew it.

From a wooden box on his desk he took a cigarette, tapped it. 'Oliver Cromwell said an interesting thing once about certainty. I don't agree with him on most things, but on this I do.' With great care, he twisted the cigarette into its ivory holder. 'In 1650, he went to Edinburgh to stop the General Assembly from supporting King Charles II. He wrote a famous letter, in which he quoted verses from Philippians, I believe. Most uncharacteristic because this mule-headed man was attempting to convince others not to be mule-headed. Still, his words live on, and they are these…' He swiped a match against a matchbox with a long, clean stroke, and when its flame was calm, lit his cigarette.

I leaned forward in my seat.

'"I beseech you, in the bowels of Christ, think it possible you may be mistaken."' My brain shook its head. I must have misheard.

He held up his hand. 'Let me explain. "The Bowels of Christ" is an unusual expression, but in Cromwell's time, people knew it well. It simply means deep inside one's self. A more familiar term today is "the bottom of my heart." Cromwell is entreating the Assembly to contemplate the possibility of error even when all evidence points toward one conclusion. In this case, he hoped to convince them to stop supporting the divine right kings and thereby avoid more killing.

'It didn't work, mind you. The Scottish Assembly continued to support the King. Much blood was shed. Still, they are good words. Think about them over the summer, Moodie. I do hope you have a pleasant holiday,' he stood in that brisk way he had when ending a matter.

'You are going to–'

'Saint Andrews.'

'Ah, lovely spot. Home of golf. Invented there, you know.'

'Yes.'

'You ever play?'

'No sir, never. Now it's too late.'

'You never know. You could be wrong.' I felt his gentle smile inviting me to friendship, but I was having none of it.

I was *not* mistaken. Finzi was caught red-handed! On the train back to Scotland, I imagined what I would do if I were Captain Fox. Present the evidence, walk around him, slapping a cane against my leg to frighten him. Eventually the cowardly bugger would confess. 'Be gone,' I'd say, and off he'd creep, back to Bulgaria. Would I beat him, like Mr Moffet, till blood ran down his legs? No, I'd never sink that low.

Anyway, I had my camera back. But I hoped, even in the bowels of Christ I hoped, that I would never see Finzi again.

Chapter 23

At least, my parents were shocked when I told them over dinner. 'Oh my,' Mother said. 'What luck your little Jewish friend saw the boy stealing it.'

I had to think for a moment whom she meant. 'Ernest Caspari isn't Jewish. His great- grandparents converted to Christianity back in the last century.'

'But you just said he and his brother were worried about going back to Germany.'

'They are!'

'Once a Jew always a Jew. It's a matter of blood. Anyway, keep your camera locked from now on. These things happen, even at the best of places. Pass the rolls, would you darling?'

* * *

In August we went to St Andrews. Not since Lossiemouth, had I sat by the sea, and I dreaded it – the smell of low tide's rotten air, the sound of gulls and waves splashing in the night – all those things I sniffed and heard as I lay in bed five years ago, unable to move my legs. So I wasn't exactly keen when we drove along the shore and saw the grey waves rolling and crashing onto the sand.

I'd never swim again. Mr Fairbanks had made that clear. 'Don't even try. Your splint will pull you down like a stone. And without it, a heavy wave will snap your leg like a twig.'

As if hit by a thunderbolt, my body remembered how bloody cold the North Sea was. Hallelujah! I'd never have to put a toe in the buggery bugger again.

There were other reasons to be happy. Golf suited me. I could play well. As with billiards, my splint steadied me, giving me an advantage. And in the evenings, I learned to play bridge. Alastair and I were a stellar team and often beat the parents, using the secret signals he taught me.

And Rufus simply adored the seaside; sand was much easier to dig than the heavy soil of Craigisla, while I, stretched out on a quilt, all cosy and warm, watched others scream as they creeped and shuddered into the frigid water. Alastair stayed to keep me company, but he hated the cold water, too. Then he'd give my arm a tug and we'd go further down the beach for a smoke. I still wasn't allowed, though Alastair was, and he made a shelter against the wind with his coat, lighting two Craven As and passing me one.

I told him the strange words of Oliver Cromwell. Perhaps the notion of Christ's bowels might be of interest since he planned on being a doctor. 'Christianity,' he said, dragging sand over his cigarette end with his foot, 'such an idiotic religion. Virgin birth. Sacrificial death, resurrection. "Bowels of Christ" doesn't surprise me. I reckon that his were pretty much like everyone else's – filthy, unpleasant places, one should best avoid.'

* * *

Nicky Littman stood in the Palm Court directing people to their rooms as they arrived.

'What-ho, Moodie,' he said with a cheery grin. Littman was Romanian and a beautiful tennis player, Smailes had told me. Girls swooned over his guitar playing when they had little parties at the cottage on the island.

I looked at the impossibly old teenager as he searched his clipboard for my name. 'Moodie, Moodie, you're here somewhere,' His finger traced down the list. 'Ah, yes. You're with a new boy. Charles Marshall. First floor, room six.'

'What?' It never occurred I wouldn't be with Paul. 'Where's Caspari?'

'He's around somewhere. I saw him.'

'There must be some mistake. I'm supposed to be with Caspari.' I gripped my sticks. 'Where's the Captain? I'll check with him.'

'Later. He's too busy. The list is probably right.'

'Can't it be changed?'

'Possibly. Moodie, move along. There's a queue.'

Room six was on the first floor, down a corridor that led to the back of the house. It would look south onto the terrace and rose garden, a nicer view than my old room.

I pushed the door open. Sitting on the far bed was a small, hunched back and a fair head gazing out the window. 'Marshall?' I said. His arms flung out, his body leapt, as if I'd dealt him an electric shock. 'Welcome to Maiden Erlegh.' He resumed his deathly stillness. 'I'm Graeme Moodie. This is my second year.'

Zero.

'Well, I might as well unpack. I see my trusty trunk is here.' I opened the lid. My belongings – socks, under vests, etc. – lay on a shallow tray on the top, the heavier things underneath. Marshall wouldn't budge.

This was ridiculous, So I, feeling the older, braver, wiser boy, went round and stood before him, holding out my hand. 'How do you do? You're Marshall, aren't you?'

His face was blotchy from blushing or crying. He took my hand in his freezing one. 'Y... y... Ch... ch... ch... Charles,' he exploded. 'Charles Marshall.'

Until now, I'd thought Mary Petty the most disagreeable-looking creature I'd seen. But she was Greta Garbo compared to what sat before me.

'Would you like help unpacking?' I asked. Nothing. 'Hmmm, well, I'll get on with mine then.'

I finished – it took ten minutes – and still Marshall hadn't budged.

My stomach told me dinner was at hand. I looked at my bedside clock. Half past seven, half-an-hour to go.

What to say, what to say? This fellow was helpless as a new-born babe and I was used to *being* helped, not dishing it out. Should I ignore him, pretend he hadn't sat for half-an-hour staring at a pine tree?

'I'm getting hungry,' I said. 'How about you?' Nothing.

I put my hands in my pockets and my fingers hit – ah – chocolate! 'Hello,' I said as I swaggered about in a casual style, 'this is a bit of luck. What do you like better, Chocolate Crisp or Milkybar?' I held them out.

From somewhere came an aeroplane's low buzz, probably from Woodley Aerodrome, a few miles away, where sounds of taking off and landing were no longer a novelty. As its hum grew, Marshall's head jerked up and he tore to the window, pressing his cheek against the glass. 'Don't worry,' I said, 'It's not going to land on us.'

Marshall grabbed the two fasteners at the bottom of the window, giving them an almighty tug. 'Help, would you?' Was he trying to escape Maiden Erlegh?

'Everything's all right,' I shouted. 'Stop worrying!'

'I'm not worrying.' Only he said 'wuwwying,' because he couldn't pronounce his Rs, like many English people. 'I just want to see the bloody plane.'

'Oh.'

I put the chocolate back in my pocket, and together we got the window lifted, but too late. The plane had gone. 'Don't worry,' I said. 'There will be lots of them. There's an airfield nearby.'

'There is?' For the first time he looked at me, but kept one hand over his eyes in an odd salute.

'There is. It can be quite annoying on a Saturday morning when a fellow wants to sleep.' Marshall's eyes moved everywhere, seeing our school in a new light.

'I've been on a plane,' I couldn't resist saying.

Those pale eyes again. 'You have?'

'Oh yes, last year, with Olley Air Services.'

'Gordon Olley?'

'The very same. Ace in the War, I believe.'

'He certainly was. Ten vic-towees. You saw him?'

'Oh yes. He piloted my plane from Morland Hall. My uncle Sandy chartered it. He was terribly rich, but he died.' I sighed.

'What's Morland Hall?'

'Nursing home near Alton. I stayed there when I had polio.'

'Oh.' He looked at me, top to bottom. 'Is that what's wrong with you?'

I gave him my thinnest smile. 'Yes. As a matter of fact, it is.'

We stared at each other, until in a stroke of terrible genius, I added, 'What's wrong with you? Everything?'

Like a slug when you poke it, he shrank on himself and burst into tears. 'Yes,' he sobbed in a voice I could barely understand. 'Everything. Everything's wong with me!'

Good Lord. When had I ever had such power over anyone, particularly a boy with two good legs? I was afraid. Someone might hear. The Captain might give me a telling off for being unkind to a new boy.

'Hey… hey,' I said softly. 'Come on, I was only kidding. Everything's not wrong with you, I'm sure. Please stop crying.' I waited while he wept and eventually he eased up, poor fellow.

'Marshall, look. I'm supposed to help you unpack, so what do you say, let's get you unpacked.' I passed him the Milkybar – which he took without comment. I kept the Chocolate Crisp for myself. He didn't even say thank you.

* * *

Jolly shouts clattered toward us from the front hall where the boys were gathering. What a motley crew we were – I had forgotten. After two months with the pale skins of Scotland, I was back among the colours of Africa, India, Arabia. 'We have to find our table first. I'll show you.'

We wended through a forest of heights and ages toward the notice board, standing on an easel, but we'd have to wait our turn. I knew the drill. Three rectangles represented three tables. I'd begun at Matron's, moved to Mrs Fox's and hoped for another promotion.

'Graeme Moodie, as I live and breathe.' The huge happiness I felt as I turned surprised me. Paul Caspari – my dear friend, back safe and sound. We shook hands heartily. But he looked thinner, older, wearier somehow.

'How are you old chap?' I asked, tilting my head.

'As you see, the same. How was Scotland?'

'Not much to report. Played golf. Didn't disgrace myself. Wandered around graveyards with Alastair. And you? How was Munich?'

'Ah, splendid.' He perked up. 'Mother took us to the opera. *Die Meistersinger*. Have you seen it?'

'Afraid not. Any good?'

'Oh, yes. Usually, I don't care for Wagner. So overblown, but this was deeply moving.'

As he spoke, Ernest scuttled up beside us, his face like an inkblot, dark and messy. 'Tell him what happened the day after.'

Paul looked down. 'Well, that wasn't so pleasant. These things happen.'

'Then I will. Some boys who lived a few doors away chased us down the road. They threw rocks at us, shouting "*Juden, Juden.*"'

'Shh!' Paul hissed. His face went red. 'Pipe down.'

'Why should I? They did! And we used to play football with them!'

Paul grabbed Ernest's arm. 'I'm not going to discuss it now. Let's find our tables, for God's sake. I'm hungry.' He started for the easel, but Ernest shook him away.

'And Graeme,' Ernest continued, tears starting, 'That's not the worst of it! Glamorous Priscilla's disappeared! I knew I shouldn't have left him with Harris.' Harris was the gardener.

'Surely she'll come back, now you're here.'

'I doubt it. She's probably gone wild by now. And,' he smacked his forehead, 'on top of everything, I've got the worst roommate in the world. Dudley Browne. He's fat and he calls his mother, "Ma-*mah!*"'

That made me remember Marshall, whose bleak eyes were still on the seating chart. I made the introductions, and we found our tables. Marshall and I found ourselves at Miss Taylor's, with Beryl at the other end.

I was starting to enjoy myself with tales of St Andrews when across the room, I saw Finzi at Captain Fox's table. No one else at Maiden Erlegh was that big and broad and had such a short neck. And he was sitting on the Captain's right! Sweat broke out on my chest. How could the Captain allow him to return? And sit on his treasured right.

I sank into my chair and glanced his way, and he, sensing it, looked back. Catastrophe!

After prayers, Marshall and I got ready for bed. I was bloody tired, having done so much one-sided talking. Tomorrow I would tell Ernest he wasn't the winner of the worst roommate competition. I was.

'Moodie,' Marshall said.

'Mmm?' I was nearly asleep.

'Goodnight.'

'Goodnight.' I thought I should say something more, to mark Marshall's first night at Maiden Erlegh. 'So, Marshall, what do you think of our school so far?'

'Hmmm,' he said. 'I think that Miss Bewill Fox has vewwy lahge bweasts.'

Perhaps I'd misjudged the fellow.

Chapter 24

At the start of the year, each boy had his autumn interview with Captain Fox. I was determined to be standoffish, since he'd been so foolish not to expel Finzi. Already I'd caught the Bulgarian bastard lying in wait as I came downstairs, but I walked right past him in a first-class snub.

The Captain stood in his office looking out onto the wide stone terrace. His back looked tired.

I cleared my throat.

'Ah.' He turned, fixing those eagle eyes on me. 'Have a seat, Moodie.' He gestured to the seat opposite his enormous desk, and leaning toward me, arms folded on the shiny wood, he said, 'How do you feel about having a go at School Certificate?'

What? He must have confused me with someone else. School Certificate floated on some faraway planet where older boys dwelt. Hairy boys with low voices and university plans. I was thirteen.

'You look surprised. You know what School Certificate is, then?'

'Sort of… sir.'

'Let me elaborate. To attend a university, the goal of all promising young men, of whom you are one, a student must sit that institution's examinations. The only exemption is by obtaining School Certificate beforehand. And that golden piece of paper is achieved by passing national examinations in five subjects while in school; in your case, Maiden Erlegh.' He leaned back and blew a long plume of smoke toward the ceiling. 'It's all quite complicated these days, unnecessarily so, in my opinion, but have I explained sufficiently?'

'I think so, sir.' Gosh. Only this summer did the notion take root that I – like normal, running-around people – might go to university one day. The family had discussed Alastair's plans over our holiday. He would leave

Lousy Old Hole and begin at a school called Stowe, to prepare for Medicine at Cambridge.

'You're saying that School Certificate is a good thing to have.'

'Exactly. There are five levels of success: distinction; good; pass; fair; and fail, but 'pass' is all that's required. Any that you don't pass in June, you can take the following year. And beyond that lies an even holier Grail: Higher Certificate, which is the finest polish a young man can receive. But we'll leave that discussion for another day. I suggest you take the courses to which you are most suited: Mathematics, History, and so on.'

He regarded my still-stunned face, the mouth of which had forgotten speech.

'You'll have to apply yourself, make no mistake, but do keep up a hobby, like Camera Club. Mr Mellor says you show great promise.'

'He does?'

'Indeed. And pass the word around to any boys who might be interested. He needs new members. Some, like Finzi, have left Camera Club. Playing rugby instead.'

'Oh,' I managed.

'I don't expect you to decide this minute. Sleep on it, come back tomorrow to let me know if you are willing to accept the challenge.' Captain Fox gave the desk a light smack, stood, and sat back down. 'Oh, I almost forgot. If you succeed, you will be the youngest pupil, ever, to achieve School Certificate at Maiden Erlegh.'

I left in a daze. Our headmaster had more confidence in me than I did. Yes, I was clever but not what Paul would call an intellectual; the idea of competing with those bigger boys frightened me. I preferred to show off with people my own age. Not people sixteen or seventeen – older, even, than Alastair.

I stopped halfway across the front hall as a magnificent calculation cantered into my head. Alastair was nearly sixteen. All my life I'd tried to catch up with him, but he was always two years ahead. If, by some miracle, I passed School Certificate at thirteen, we'd be at university at the same time, as if the same age. The impossible would be possible. I'd caught up.

* * *

'Excellent news, my boy,' the Captain said when I returned the following day with my decision. He leaned back in his chair, hands behind his head. 'I had hoped for that outcome.'

'Thank you, sir.

'But please, sit. I have something to ask you.' His gleeful face changed to one of concern as he lowered his voice. 'I need some advice. It's about your new roommate.'

'Marshall, sir?' I hadn't seen that coming.

'Yes. You see, the teachers and I, were wondering what might bring him out. You know, what makes him tick.'

'Tick, sir?'

'Silly expression, really.' He smiled, a little ashamed. 'My father was a watchmaker, so I enjoy using it.'

'I see. Well…' I took a deep, shuddering breath, 'I don't know. He *is* shy. I try talking, but he doesn't seem interested. He just reads magazines.'

'What kind of magazines?'

'Aeroplane ones. He orders kits and builds them. Quite good at it. They sit on the windowsill.'

'Hmm, Aeroplanes, eh? Not sure what we can do about that.' He lit a cigarette. He smoked as much as Mother. 'I wonder if you could do a little detective work for me, like that detective, Hercule Poirot. Find out more about him. I believe Marshall has had a rough time, perhaps at school, but something has damaged him. If we can discover what, we might bring him out, so to speak.'

'I'll try.'

'I'm sure you can do it. You've got a reliable face. One trusts it, somehow.'

I left, proud of the Captain's trust in me; but then I remembered I was supposed to stay angry with him.

* * *

Another autumnal event was a visit from that famous charlatan, Mr Fairbank. I dreaded his visits for many reasons. One, he was loathsome; two, he still called me 'Timothy'; and three, he always measured me for new boots. And every year, the sole of the right boot got higher.

'Two inches now,' he said after he'd done his twiddling. 'But Timothy, I have pleasant news.'

'Oh?' This was a first.

'Yes! We're going to get rid of that splint of yours.'

'Really?' I couldn't believe what I was hearing. 'I won't need it anymore?'

'Not quite. I'm going to replace it with a jointed one. I've decided you're mature enough to manage it, wot?'

If I had a gun I would have shot him.

* * *

Nevertheless, about three weeks later, I decided that a bendable splint was a pleasant thing, after all. In fact, quite terrific.

Until then, my right leg had been as stiff as a board, held between two rods that slid into rock-hard leather sleeves on either side of my boot. Whenever I sat, the leg stuck straight out and to stand again was always awkward. People stared. This new splint, however, was hinged at the knee, with a latch on the side that kept it locked. When I wanted to sit, I reached behind my knee to find a leather loop and gave it a tug. This released the hinge and the splint bent. Wonder of wonders, I could sit with a bent knee. When I wanted to stand, I leaned on my left leg for support, and pressed my hand against my right knee till I heard the hinge click into place.

Marshall talked better in the dark; he didn't hold his hand over his eyes as if the sun was in his face. We could lie in our beds – voices rising, eyes sharing the ceiling. The problem was he only talked about two things: aeroplanes and something I couldn't mention to the Captain, Beryl Fox, and in particular, her breasts. Initially I thought we might have a point of contact, but I soon realised that, while Beryl had breasts, she had little else to recommend her. Her face reminded me of mashed potatoes.

'I spoke to Miss Bewill Fox today,' he announced one night.

'Really?'

'I asked to her pass the bwussel spwouts, you know the ones we had at lunch, the ones with bacon?'

'I remember.'

'And she said, "Again?" And I said, "Yes, it's my favewat vegetable." And she said, "Be my guest." So I took this opportunity to say, "What's your favewat vegetable, Miss Fox?"' Marshall paused, waiting for comment from me. 'And do you know what she said?'

'I've no idea.'

'She said, "Mashed potatoes."'

'I'm not surprised.'

'And thinking of potatoes made me think of her bwests, big bowls of mashed ones, and I couldn't speak after that.' He waited again for comment. 'Gwa-em,' he said at last, 'I once saw a woman with no clothes on.'

It was as if Marshall had struck a match and held it sizzling and flickering above our heads. 'Go on.'

'Well, I was nine; it was soon after Mother was allowed to live with me again, and I came into her bedroom and a maid was trying on a dwess of hers, a silky one with sparkles. She was tewwified, and begged me not to tell Mother. Then she said she'd show me her bwests if I promised to keep quiet. I said, vewwy well because that sounded all wight to me. But now I'm angwy, because I didn't appweeciate it. I didn't weelise how lucky I was. Now I think about bwests all the time. It doesn't matter if they're big or small. But I can tell you, Miss Bewill Fox has the biggest ones I've ever seen.'

'Did you see the maid's bottom?'

'No, just her bwests. I've never seen a woman's bottom. Good night, Gwa-em.'

I was just drifting off to sleep when I remembered something else interesting Marshall said. 'What do you mean,' I asked, 'when you said your mother was allowed to live with you again?' But Marshall was asleep.

Rhododendrons line the route along Maiden Erlegh Drive.

Bedecked with wisteria, Maiden Erlegh School for Boys is joined by Captain and Mrs Fox in welcoming the boys back for summer term.

The Foxes relax with one of their Afghan Hounds.

Maiden Erlegh School for Boys: Going home for Summer holidays

Aged 15, Graeme Cochrane Moodie strikes a pose.

The grand staircase; no boys allowed.

*The Swimming Baths draw a crowd as mermaids
and water nymphs adorn the walls.*

The cottage on the lake.

Chapter 25

I could have whistled a tune as I strolled into Camera Club and Mr Mellor looked up and said, 'Well, if it isn't my old friend, Moodie.' Beside him sat Boch, but at least Finzi would no longer be there. I sat, and the two of them went back to bending over photographs, their pale-yellow heads both neatly combed and secured by hair oil. The others arrived – Basch, Caspari and a new fellow named Cahn – also from Germany, also escaping Nazism, Paul told me.

A rap on the desk and Mr Mellor looked round in that casual, energetic way of his, as if we were about to discuss the most interesting thing in the world. 'Today, my colleagues, both Caspari and Boch have brought colour photographs from their summer holidays in Germany. A delightful coincidence – and an opportunity to explore the pros and cons of the new medium. One disadvantage is obvious: so far, colour photos are available only in transparencies. Hence the projector.' He gestured to a slender metal box on the end of a small desk at the foot of the table. 'Shall we begin? Who'd like to go first?'

'I would,' Boch said at once.

Eyebrows raised, Mr Mellor gave a slow blink and looked at Caspari, who set down his pen with patient precision and said, 'Be my guest.'

Boch headed for the projector with his box of transparencies. After turning on the machine, which moaned as it cast a cold light onto the wall, he faced us, soldier-straight. 'This summer I and my father – number-two-man in London embassy – we returned to the Fatherland. We are very happy to be away from England and the rain. My father buy for me a new Afga Karat camera, to make colour, which we know is better than the American Kodak.

'The transparencies have just arrived from Germany. Here is the first. You will see the view from our balcony, how green the Bavarian Forest is.' But we didn't see any green, just a mass of bright blue shapes against a white sky. 'Something's wrong with the film,' he muttered. He tried a few more, but they, too, were blue.

'Hey, that's the prettiest blue I ever saw!' Basch called, while we tried not to laugh.

Mr Mellor shot him a look. 'Try the other box. Perhaps the film is defective.'

Boch took out a slide from a second batch. 'Ah yes, this will be our big house in Berlin. My parents stand in front.' There was a building, possibly with people, but everything was else was red.

Boch removed the slide quickly. 'Mr Mellor must be right. I deeply apologise, but it is not my fault. Perhaps this one...' He held up another against the light. I could see panic in his eyes as he lifted one after the other. 'Ah,' he said finally, 'This one is good.' He inserted the slide and we saw Boch standing in a uniform – in fine colour – tan shirt, loose brown tie, leather short trousers and a diagonal strap across his chest. He stood with his hands behind his back, gazing toward some unknown dream above the photographer's head.

'They have Boy Scouts in Germany, eh?' Mr Mellor said.

'That's not Boy Scouts,' Caspari said softly.

'Caspari is right. I am wearing my Hitler Youth Uniform. Is it not handsome?'

We stared. 'Yes, the exposure is perfect,' Caspari said, 'but who took it? Not you, I assume, unless you can be in two places at once.' Nervous laughs tumbled round the table.

'The shop clerk took it. But he must have been cheating me because the camera stop working after that.' He slammed the transparencies into their box and sat beside me, muttering, 'Dirty Jew,' as he scraped his chair, so Mr Mellor couldn't hear.

'I believe I know what has happened,' Caspari said in his scholarly manner, so different from Boch's barks.

'Do tell us,' Mr Mellor said. 'And please, show us your photographs, as well, would you?'

'Yes sir.' Caspari gathered his material and looked about the table with a weary smile, the taste of victory in it. 'When we see the advertisements for colour film, they make us believe that taking colour pictures is as easy as taking black-and-white. That is not true, for one reason: you must expose correctly. Either over or underexposure will make your photo turn blue or red, which is what happened to the unfortunate Boch. In black and whites, almost everything can be printed with a satisfactory result. This will never be possible with colour. Few of us can expose correctly without a meter. The shop clerk erred in not telling you to buy one. I would suggest, Boch, that the best meters are the Sixtus or Bewi; I, myself, have a Bewi, and I would be most happy to lend it to you. And now for my transparencies.'

His hand shook as he picked up a slide, but his voice was calm. 'Boch is correct in his attempts to photograph the beautiful countryside of Germany, because the best subjects for colour photography will always be nature: flowers, trees, animals and the blue sky. This is what I have attempted, but only in a city park.'

His hands stopped shaking, for he was not thinking of Boch, but of his Munich, on green lawns, with Ernest, his mother and a little dog named Trixie. The exposures were perfect. The family sat on swings and ate sandwiches on a yellow blanket. So at ease they were, I felt I was spying. One specially pulled at me – a close-up of his mother's drowsy face, lying near the blanket's edge, blades of grass casting thin shadows on her cheek, while the dog lay sleeping in the crook of her arm. I could seep into a summer afternoon – its heat, the feel of wool, the grassy smell of Mrs Caspari's cheek.

After a break of tea and biscuits, I showed my St Andrews snaps, amateurish after Caspari's, but I was proud to show Scotland and good, old Rufus to the group.

At the end, Mr Mellor said, 'It's strange not one of us brought photographs of England, except me, who was born in Rhodesia. I took a long boat along canals. That's for another day, though. I need to tell you about your next assignment – capturing autumn. And though we usually think of autumn's red and yellow leaves, this time I want everyone to work in black-and-white. Try and discover the architecture of autumn. The stark shape of branches, empty seedpods, the beauty of decay. Go into forests. See what you can find.'

As I was walking out, Boch strolled up behind me. 'Glad you joined us. I was getting outnumbered.'

'What do you mean?'

'Too many Jews. Cahn, Basch and that Caspari. Didn't his photographs make you sick? Ugh, that one of his mother, that Jewish nose. I could almost smell her. They have a different odour, you know, different from us. More like swine.' My legs began moving me away. 'Moodie, where are you going?'

'To have a bath,' I called and kept going. It was true, I was heading for Solly Joel's magnificent tub, but never had I wanted one more –as if he'd scooped muck from himself and smeared it on me, trying to make us the same.

* * *

Nurse Dickenson still perched close by my tub, on Solly Joel's mahogany toilet lid, reading a magazine while I stretched out, feet still unable to reach the end, but getting there.

I'd been bathed by women, most of them kind, all my life. At thirteen, long past the time most boys needed help, she stood by just in case – though no one said it – I slipped and fell. She didn't *do* anything; she was just there. I could relax and say any old thing without fear of being laughed at or corrected. Another of polio's gifts.

After I'd scrubbed and washed my hair – I used a metal pitcher and she checked to see I got all the soap out – we'd talk.

I thought of telling her what Boch said, but I might foul the air, so we discussed how I could carry out Captain Fox's assignment of finding out what made Marshall tick.

'Ask questions,' she said. 'That's what I do. When someone's suffering, they can't see beyond their sorrow. They need to talk about what happened but can't. One coaxes them along about this and that, and suddenly one senses a moment – it lights up the dark – when it's right to ask the question that will open a door into the sorrow and begin letting it out.'

'I see, but all he talks about are aeroplanes.' I didn't mention his other interest.

'Keep asking questions. The more you listen, the more people will think how interesting you are. The truth is, most people want to talk about themselves, no matter how happy or sad they are. But the happy ones are better at listening.'

I moved on to Camera Club and our assignment to photograph the beauty of decay, as Mr Mellor put it. 'I'm going to find mushrooms in Maiden Erlegh Wood.'

'How interesting! My father used to take us mushrooming. Look for them under birches. They're often there, as I remember. They like a little light, but not too much.'

* * *

I had just switched off my bedside light and pulled the covers around my neck. The nights were drawing in. How I loved that expression. It made me think of a big cloak getting closer and closer, preparing to wrap itself around a house, where inside was me, all safe and warm.

Time to start my detective work with Marshall. I'd ask a question to get the ball rolling. 'Who do you like better, Marshall, Tarzan or Sexton Blake?'

'L-rrr. Lrrr-ring,' he answered with great seriousness.

'I beg your pardon?'

'L-rrrrrrrrrrrrrrrrrrrrrr... I'm having speech thewapy. The Captain has engaged a lady to come fwom London to teach me how to say my "ahs." She's vewy nice and pwetty. Do you know how to make the "ah" sound?'

'I've never thought about it. I just do it.'

'It's vewy intwesting. You place the tongue on the woof of the mouth and say an L. Then you dwag it backwawd as far as you can. And just like magic, the L turns into an R, all by itself.' 'Lllllrrrr. Lllll-rrr. See? You twy, Gwam. Make an L sound and pull your tongue back toward your thwoat.'

I obliged, and the L did indeed turn into an R. 'How clever,' I said.

'I have to pwactice evwy night and morning. Will you help me? Make sure I do it?'

'Very well, I'll twy.' Sometimes my brain thought up things to say that might be insulting, but were so funny, I said them anyway and hoped for the best.

To his credit, he gave a sleepy chuckle. 'Now Gwa-em, don't be wude.' I'd leave my detective work for another time.

Chapter 26

I knew it was cold – I hadn't realised how cold – but as the sun hung just above the faraway pines, I wished I'd brought my cap and gloves. I looked back at the school. Too far to go back; I had to rough it, be an explorer; so off I went across the remaining lawn, camera-strap across my chest and my bendable splint giving me a good pace. Anyone watching from a window might think I was a hiker with his walking stick on a hearty jaunt.

I liked the way civilisation dwindled with each step – from stone terrace to lawn and empty flowerbeds, to scythe-cut grass, to a hem of younger trees before revealing the ancient canopies of Maiden Erlegh Wood.

A twisty path beckoned. I pushed through trees for at least half-an-hour without finding a single birch. A pheasant gave his rat-a-tat-tat of warning. and all at once the air grew darker. Steady, Moodie. That's just the sun dropping behind pines. Birches, where are you?

As if in answer, up ahead I saw a small clearing where yes, a few scrawny birches grew, and under them I found some small mushrooms, the kind I liked to squish with my shoe.

Oh well. Take a picture, if only to prove you were here.

I felt for the little strap through my trouser leg behind my right knee. The joint released, I eased myself to the ground; and through my Selfix 20, I studied the poor, lonely things. Focussing was tricky but as I snapped, my mushrooms took on beauty as I tried to capture them, both of us on the forest floor. I admired the pale gills underneath the slimy umbrellas, sagging here and there, about to collapse. I thought of Caspari photographing his mother.

Twigs snapped, sharp, nearby. I waited. A badger, perhaps? The approaching dark frightened me.

I stood, leaning forward, and pressed with a hard twack against my right knee, to lock the splint. No click. I tried again, but there was only a slithery slip. Stupidly, I took a step and toppled to the ground.

On a soggy mat of leaves, I assessed myself. Startled, shocked, but all right. I twisted onto my good, left leg and with it, and my hands, I lifted myself like a three-legged stool. I was upright, but the other leg was hopeless, helpless, and again, I toppled.

Bugger Mr Fairbank and his bendable splint. My fingers felt the knob that used to hold the catch, but the catch itself was gone. What good was it if it left me cold and wet, with the dark creeping in? Once more I stood, and despite knowing I couldn't, I took a step and crashed again. Sweatier, dirtier, colder.

Stay calm. Perhaps I could crawl on my elbows as I did in Lossiemouth to hear the marching band. I dragged myself along the ground, but in less than a minute I was done in, my face slick with frost and sweat. Grit scraped my teeth. I spat it out.

This was serious. No one knew where I was.

A creak and crunch moved through the trees, a person's slow trudge. Help, surely. 'Hello?' I called.

It came closer. I twisted to look back along the path and saw, filling the slit of path, making everything darker – Finzi.

If I called for help, would anyone hear?

'Have you lost something? You on the ground.' He smiled his stupid Finzi smile, jaw hanging.

'My splint is broken.'

'You cannot walk?'

'No, but someone's coming to help. Any minute.' He came toward me with his blunt flat face, small nose, boulder chin. Don't panic. Keep cheerful.

He knelt. A muffler round his neck was all he wore against the cold. He pulled his collar up with the biggest hands I ever saw, skin red-raw.

'Help,' I called feebly, like in a dream. 'Get away.' Finzi pushed one arm under my back, another under my legs and prepared to lift me. 'What do you want? My camera?' I struggled with the strap round my neck. 'Here, take it.'

He drew himself to standing and stared into the trees. What was he thinking? I could see the wheels turning. 'You saw me putting bag in rubbish bin. You think I stole your camera.'

He was cleverer than I thought. He'll have to kill me, burying me in a hole, never to be found. Years later people will tell it like a ghost story, how they never found that boy, Moodie. Lame, wasn't he? Maybe he drowned in the lake and was eaten by fish. Oh yes, his heavy splint pulled him down.

Finzi's face went dark, his little eyes wild. 'Please don't tell Captain Fox,' he said in a loud whisper. 'You tell him already?'

'No, no, of course not! It's just a rumour, anyway.'

'What mean "rumour"?'

Oh, bloody hell.

'I see you hating me at school. I know now why. You think I the monster who stole your camera.'

'No, no…'

He grabbed my arm, a twig next to his. 'You must believe me. When they ring the bell to call us downstairs, I walk down corridor. I meet another boy. "Hey Finzi," he say, "Be good chap and bin this for me. I go back for slippers. The floor is too bloody cold! He laugh, I laugh. I put bag in bin. But I not the thief. Please don't say it was me. I not do it. I not taking camera. Never take. Don't say to Captain Fox. He helps me, is kind, but will believe you and not me.' His eyes filled with tears. I almost laughed. This enormous young man with his piggy face was afraid of me. 'He will call police. They send me back to Bulgaria. You are the English, I am the stupid foreigner.'

'No, I won't. I believe you. Don't worry.'

'You believe me?'

'Yes.' I didn't know what I believed. I just wanted to get warm. My teeth chattered so, I could hardly speak; and then my poor body joined my teeth and everything shook.

'Thanks God you believes me.' Giving a shuddering sigh, he took notice of me at last. 'But Moodie, you cold!'

'Oh y-y-y-yes, please. Can you make it back t-to school and bring help? P-people to carry me, or maybe a stretcher?'

'No.'

'What?'

'You are too cold now. And the school is too far to carry. Even for me.' For the first time he smiled. 'I have idea.'

'What's that?'

'I take you to rugby coach, Mr Grumbar. He live near. I going to his house when I find you.'

He picked me up as if I were nothing and we continued along another path, me bouncing gently in his arms.

He'd been trudging five minutes when he looked down at me quizzically. 'Why you come to the forest?' He was scarcely out of breath.

I tried to sound important. 'I was looking for mushrooms to photograph.'

He laughed as if I said the funniest thing. 'You won't find mushrooms here. Only on the edge of forests. They need light and air.' We continued without speaking, but every now and then he'd chuckle.

The path became a wide track that opened to a field. By this time, sweat rolled down his cheeks; his breath became heavier, but we kept going. 'Don't worry,' he said. 'Almost there.'

Following the track that now had crates and timbers alongside it, we went round a cluster of trees. 'We are here, Woodbine Cottage.'

It was as if I'd stepped back in time. A thatched roof curved, like a hood, over a lovely little brick cottage, whose many leaded windows glinted in the fading light.

The house had a misty look, as its brick shone through old, chipped whitewash. Bent-over hollyhocks clung to one side of the door, untrained rose canes sprang from the other.

Finzi, on the verge of collapse, knocked at the door and not waiting, opened it.

A biggish room filled the front of the house. Low sofas and soft, sagging chairs had been cosily placed round around an iron stove, where coal burned behind amber glass. A woman stood before a sink on the right-hand wall and smiled when she saw Finzi and frowned when she saw me lying in his arms. 'My goodness, what's happened?'

'This is Moodie. He cripple. I no put him down. He dirty.'

'Never mind that. Goodness. Put the poor fellow there, on the sofa.' She shook her hands in the sink.

'Put me down, please. I'm not hurt,' I said in a loud voice. Somehow, I had to take charge – of the embarrassment, the fuss, the helplessness. To be called a cripple *and* dirty was more than I could bear. 'My splint broke, that's all, and I'm lame without it.'

Finzi laid me on the sofa and Mrs Grumbar took over, arranging cushions behind my head and laying a thick rug over me. 'Fetch Mr Grumbar, will you, Peter?' She knelt beside me, sharp grey eyes moving all over my face. 'Tea,' she decided, as she sprang from the floor. I liked the look of her, her strong back without any curves, her peppery hair pulled in a knot. Finzi disappeared to a room behind, pulling aside a heavy green curtain. Clearly he knew the family well.

Mrs Grumbar brought the tea. I'd never tasted anything so good.

I vaguely knew Mr Grumbar. He taught botany and biology and coached the rugby. I'd seen him piling his old truck with kit when the boys went to fixtures at other schools.

I saw his belly first; he simply followed it, moving with serenity like a steam liner coming into dock.

He pulled over a wide cane chair that creaked when he sat beside me. His hair was wild, like he'd been combing it with his fingers or just thinking. I couldn't see much of his mouth, the moustache so big, but his eyes crinkled up, making him look kind.

'How do you do, Mr Grumbar,' I said in the way my parents taught me. 'I'm Graeme Moodie, sir. Sorry to be such a bother, but my new splint has come a cropper. It's a bendable contraption, but the joint broke the first time I put it to the test. Jolly poor show.' Moodie, you're sound like a pompous twit.

'Hmm,' was all he said, as he looked at me up and down.

'My right leg's paralysed, you see. From polio when I was nine. You heard of it?'

'I have.' His voice dropped down to nothing. 'Previously known as infantile paralysis.'

'Yes.'

'Wretched disease,' he muttered bitterly, turning away, but quickly came back to himself. 'We must phone the Captain. He can stop the search party if there is one. Then I'll phone the doctor.'

'No, sir. I'm fine really. Matron can look me over at school. But could you ask the Captain to send a car?'

His eyes crinkled again. 'No need for that. I'll drive you myself.' He slowly stood. He took up a lot of space, this Mr Grumbar, even more than Finzi because he was fatter. 'Assistant!' he called to the back room in a voice that could carry across a battlefield. 'Could you finish that mount for me? Tidy up?'

'Horatio, please,' Mrs Grumbar said.

'Sorry, my dear.' He shrugged apologetically. 'I always forget.'

'I'll get her,' Finzi said and disappeared to the back room.

'I was born with this voice, June. I should have been a general.'

Mrs Grumbar laughed. 'Over an army of butterflies, perhaps.' And to me she said, 'I hope you come and visit us again, Graeme, under happier conditions. Will you?'

'If you'd like.' But I couldn't imagine why.

Minutes later, a young voice came from behind. 'I hear you're going out in the car. I want to come, too.'

I knew at once who it was, but I peered over the back of the sofa anyway. Through the parted curtains came Mary Petty-up-a-tree.

As soon as she saw me, she stopped. 'On second thought,' she said, 'I've changed my mind. I remembered something I had to do.' She disappeared, back behind the curtain.

When we got to the school, Mr Grumbar turned off the motor and looked at me.

'Do come to Woodbine Cottage when you have the chance, eh? It would please Mrs Grumbar; and me, too, for that matter.'

'I don't understand, sir.'

With his eyes looking straight ahead through the windscreen, he said, 'It's like this. He took a big breath, preparing his words. 'Two years ago our Martin died. He wasn't as lucky as you, you see. The polio paralysed his lungs, everything. He couldn't even breathe. Life must go on, but we don't know how. Having Mary here helps, but she's suffering, too. Peter Finzi finding you like that – well, it's extraordinary. You've brought a flicker of light to June's eyes. Just come when you can.'

Chapter 27

A week later, stripped to my underpants and freezing, I struggled with my new, sturdier splint while Mr Fairbank watched. I felt like a specimen, hardly human. 'It may be man-sized, but you're far from that, eh Timothy?' He shrugged when he saw I wasn't laughing. 'Here's the joint that bends. When you want to sit down – pay attention – yank this strap at the back of your knee, same as before. You won't break this one, I promise. Now off you go, across the room.'

No one should endure this.

'I say, isn't the spine straightening nicely? Turn around.' Hard fingers prodded each nodule. 'The night corset must be working. You wear it every night?'

'Of course.' I never wore the fucker ('fucker' being my current favourite swearword, thanks to Basch's time in America).

'Back toward the window please.' Loud uneven clunks banged the floor as I marched. He tsked. 'Still have that nasty lurch. No matter how much I raise the height of the sole. Can't be helped, Timothy, and it'll get worse. Your good leg's outstripping the bad. Stop growing, would you?' He ho-hoed again. 'Never mind, you'll get used to it. Who would have thought you'd become such a man about town, traipsing about, eh Timothy?'

'Yes, Mr Winterbottom.'

'I beg your pardon. My name is Mr Fairbank.'

'And mine is Graeme.'

'I know what your damned name is.' He closed his satchel with a furious snap, 'I'll send the bill to your father, telling him how nicely your spine is developing. Pity I can't say the same for your manners.'

* * *

'I think you should weport him,' Marshall said that night. 'He sounds like a howibble man.'

'It's not weport. It's re- port.'

'But I'm tired.'

'Still.'

'All wight – rrre-ight. Rrrr-eport.'

'Good. It's part of my job, you know?'

'I know. But you said that Captain said it was only an idea to help me with my Rs.'

'Ideas don't work if you don't do them.'

'Twue. Trrr-ue.'

I hadn't told Marshall that my reason for helping him was to assist in the Captain's assignment – to find out what made him tick. Marshall still kept his head down in class, but he didn't shield his eyes as he spoke. 'Well, goodnight,' I said, turning over and pulling the sheet over my ear, the habit since hospital days.

I was almost gone when he started again. 'Do you know any gossip? I love gossip.'

'You mean secrets? Bad things about people?'

'Well, gossip is usually of a sexual nature. That's the kind I pwefer.'

'For heaven's sake, Marshall,' I said, but liking the idea, began thinking. 'Well, some people say that Miss Taylor is the Captain's mistress.' I laughed because the notion was preposterous.

'Weely? Intwisting.'

'But you mustn't believe it.'

'Oh, I do. Mrs Fox isn't what I'd call attwactive. He must have maweed her because she was wich. She looks wich. And she keeps birds. Only wich people do that.'

'I'm not going to talk to you unless you speak properly.'

When he didn't answer I felt mean. 'I wonder where the money to buy Maiden Erlegh came from? Marshall?'

'What?' he muttered, sulky.

'Do watchmakers make a lot of money?'

'I shouldn't think so. That's twade. Why do you ask?'

'Captain Fox told me his father was a watchmaker.'

'Ah,' he said, like Sherlock Holmes.

'So the money must come from Mrs Fox.' How clever we were.

'And Miss Taylor is the captain's mistwess, that pwoves it.'

'Shh. That doesn't prove anything.'

'But she's much pwettier. How could he resist?'

'That's absurd.' I didn't like the way this conversation was going. It seemed disrespectful. 'Miss Taylor just happens to be pretty. I don't like you saying things like that.'

'Like what?'

'That… that the Captain does something… wicked.'

'Most people do.'

'They do not.'

'They do.' His tone softened. 'Believe me. Everyone is wicked in some way. Some are better at hiding it, that's all. Even my mother. Even she. That's been my experience.'

His voice became an invitation. 'But Marshall, what is your experience?'

'My experience?' Some time passed. 'Mine is a sowwy tale.'

I recognised the delivery, formal and flat; mine had been like that when I told my own sorry tale. Rehearsed in the mind, but not spoken of. So that when it emerges at last, there is a dullness of speech called up to survive.

* * *

Three days passed before I could report back to Captain Fox. He'd gone to London for some stupid reason. All I could think about was Marshall's 'sowwy tale'. His story grew, taking on flesh till by the time I sat across from good old Captain F, him sipping tea, me hot chocolate, Charlie's wisp of a tale had become epic.

I'd make it sound like something from Dickens. We'd been reading *David Copperfield* in Miss Taylor's class, and if I skipped the boring bits, a cracking good yarn came through.

Charlie Marshall's sowwy tale was such a story. I had to do it justice.

'Well?' the Captain said softly, after we'd gazed into the logs far too long, him waiting for me to begin. 'What can you tell me about Marshall?'

'Well, sir…' A storm of confusion spun round my brain. The start of my story had vanished. I had a sentence in mind. What was it?

'I'm not quite sure how to begin, Captain Fox. Marshall's history is complicated.'

He nodded. 'Most histories are. How about with his birth, perhaps?'

'Marshall's?'

'Why not? Something like, "To begin, Charlie Marshall was born…"' His hand circled the air.

'I've got it now, sir.' I cleared my throat. 'But before I begin with Marshall, I must start with his mother.'

'Very well.'

'Here goes. To begin with, Marshall's mother was beautiful.'

'Intriguing.'

'And French, which could explain a lot,' I added in a manly tone. Moodie, you twit, just tell poor Marshall's tale – for his sake, not yours. Stop being clever. And out of the blue, my stormy brain calmed.

'Her father was a famous chef in Paris, and after the War, he decided to open a restaurant in London. Soon he was famous there, too, not only for his food, but for his beautiful daughter, who greeted the customers and showed them to their tables.

'Now, one of the customers was a rich gambler who, once he saw Sophie – that was her name – Sophie – gave her so many jewels she married him even though he was old and fat.'

'Oh dear,' the Captain said.

'Oh dear indeed,' I echoed. 'A monumental error, but she didn't know it at the time.' We looked at one another knowingly, raised our teacups and sipped deeply.

'After Charlie was born, they moved to a big mansion near the Natural History Museum, but his father wouldn't allow Mrs Marshall to spend time with her son. Only a nanny would do, and a nasty one, at that. The poor woman was left to wander long corridors by herself, terribly lonely, while her husband was off making fortunes.

'But whenever he was gone, Mrs Marshall took Charlie to the park where he played with the toy aeroplanes she brought, both wishing they could fly away. They were, I suppose, each other's only joy.' I stopped. Tears pricked my eyes.

'Poor lad.'

'I know.'

I was stuck being sad for Marshall.

'More tea?'

'No sir, but thank you.' I recovered. 'Anyway, whenever Mr Marshall was home, he invited other gamblers to his house, but because he was so old and fat he often went to bed early.'

'Now,' and the embarrassing part began. 'One of the gamblers was very young and handsome.'

The Captain sighed. 'I can see it coming.'

'Really?'

'Of course. Why is the past a crystal pool and the future such turbulent waters? Mrs Marshall fell in love with the young, handsome gambler. Who could blame her?'

My relief was dizzying. No explanations needed. 'Yes! Married to such an old, fat pig.'

'Still, when he found out, he divorced her – like that!' I tried to snap my fingers, failed, but continued. The story held me in its sway. The Captain, too. 'The divorce was in all the newspapers and in court for ages. Everyone gossiped. Charlie, who was only five, couldn't understand where his mother had gone.

'The upshot was Sophie could see her son just once a month, for two hours on a Sunday afternoon. She waited at a street corner till the nanny brought him and off they'd go to the park to play with the toy aeroplanes she'd brought. If it rained, they'd have a lovely tea somewhere and play with the aeroplanes across the table. When it was time to go home, she put the toys back in her satchel so Mr Marshall wouldn't throw them out, the way he had the first time. At the corner there would be the nanny, waiting, looking at the watch pinned to her coat, and very cross if they were late. No wonder Charlie likes aeroplanes.'

'Ah,' he said slowly, blowing smoke at the ceiling.

'A year later Charlie was shipped to boarding school and Sophie couldn't see him at all! Mr Marshall didn't love Charlie, you see. All he wanted was to make Sophie suffer.

'And then – and this is the most extraordinary thing – when Charlie was eight, Mr Marshall dropped down dead! Mrs Marshall got her son back, and enough money to look after him. A happy ending, eh?'

'One would think.'

'But he'd been hit so often at boarding school, he held his hand up to ward off blows. He couldn't talk properly, he'd stutter sometimes. He'd even forgotten how to smile.'

'I see. So not a happy ending after all.'

'No. He'd been ruined. She tried a day-school, but it was too late.' A shiver rose up my back like a snowy hand. And to my horror, tears for Charlie Marshall burned in my eyes. 'Oh sir, I'm sorry.' I raised a hand to hide them but I could not. I groped in my pockets for a handkerchief, but I didn't even have that.

'Here,' he said, 'Take mine.' From his breast pocket he pulled a perfectly folded square, gave it a soft shake and passed it.

Through cloth and spread-out fingers I tried to explain. 'You see, it wasn't just bad luck, as my polio was. It was *people* who harmed him and they meant to. And he never did anything wrong.'

'I understand. I knew Marshall had troubles in school, but I didn't know why.'

'Probably Mrs Marshall didn't want to tell you.'

'I think you're right. This is strictly between us, mind you.'

'Yes sir. I wouldn't want him to think I've been gossiping about him.'

'What I've heard is not gossip, but compassion.' He stood. 'Thank you for coming.'

I held the soggy handkerchief halfway out. 'What should I do with… this? I usually have my own.'

'I'm sure you do. Pass it over, Moodie,' he smiled, and put it in his pocket. 'A gentleman should always carry a handkerchief – in case he should cry, and that is a good thing. It is our tears for one another that will save us in the end.'

Marshall didn't talk much that night as we got ready for bed. I was worried he might know I'd spilled the beans. We turned on our side lamps and read. 'I've got *With Wolfe in Canada*,' I said with cosy relish. 'I love the Henty books, don't you?'

Nothing.

'Have you read it?'

'No.'

'Oh. Well, you should. I'll lend it to you when I've finished. The hero, Jim Walsham, gets caught with a gang of smugglers and is pressed into the Navy. He gets sent to Canada where he joins Wolfe against the Americans.'

'Do you mind, Moodie, shutting up?'

'Me? Not at all. What are you reading? A magazine it looks like.'

'Something I sent away for.'

'What's it called?'

'*Passion in Paris*. Now be quiet, please.' Pretty soon, he turned out his light and turned toward the window.

'Goodnight,' I said. 'You mind if I carry on reading?'

'Not at all.'

I'd read to the bottom of the page when I heard whimpers and snuffling from Marshall's bed.

'Marshall? Are you all right?'

'Shhh.'

'What are you doing there?'

'What do you think?'

'I have no idea.'

So I learned about what he called 'greeting', a strange, happy term for what must be the pleasantest thing in the world, and I knew I'd thank Charlie Marshall for the lesson forever.

Chapter 28

Thus blessed with Mr Winterbottom's man-sized splint, I went to Woodbine Cottage whenever I could. Finzi accompanied me, or I him. Which was which wasn't certain.

Every day after lunch, he waited outside the dining room to see if I'd be going. Lucky him, he *had* to be there, for the Captain had arranged for Finzi to help the Grumbars with heavy lifting and Finzi needed the money. What he didn't know was that Mary Petty's arms would have managed most jobs.

'Not today,' I'd say with a sigh, when I couldn't avoid the English essay one more second. School Certificate loomed like the ghost of Hamlet's father. Stop messing about at Woodbine Cottage. Get on with your studies, you lazy lout. But each day, I'd say: tomorrow will do. There's still plenty of time.

Why I loved that place so much, I didn't know. Having spent the better part of three years in hospital, I knew the outdoors only from balconies, where the trillion scents of flowers and seeds wafted over us, bringing healing goodness. But at Woodbine, I was in the thick of it! A thorn snagged my coat as I marched by Finzi's side. Mud slid over my shoes. I was becoming a ruffian.

As for Finzi, he became handy mounting butterflies with pins, a surprise given his big paws. I tried, but it was too fiddly, and I lacked patience. Best leave them to it, tinkering away in the back room, while Mrs G and I chatted.

I enjoyed explaining things to her, and every now and then, she stopped peeling just to listen. Sometimes I did prep at the kitchen table with a cup of tea, and she'd joined me with hers. One day – why I didn't know – she spoke of her son, Martin, the one who died from polio when he was thirteen. I wondered how she felt about me being there, still alive. But as Mr Grumbar said, she liked me.

* * *

I'd just slipped into my place at table before the Captain rang his silver bell, the signal to say grace. As I closed my eyes, I noticed that Ernest hadn't arrived yet. His chair opposite was empty. He'd have to apologise to the Captain for being late.

On my left sat Dudley Browne, Ernest's roommate. He drove us mad with his talk of Fortnum and Mason, and 'Mamah' this and 'Mamah' that. Captain Fox said everyone had something to recommend him, but only words like 'numptie' and 'dunderhead' sprang to mind when I considered Browne. It would have been easier if he'd been the pitiful type, but not him. No matter what one did, he'd done something better.

At least Smailes was at my table.

'Good evening,' Miss Taylor said to Ernest Caspari as he took his seat. 'What have you been up to? You look a bit breathless. But first, go and say you're sorry to the Captain. Late once more and you'll have to skip a meal.'

'Yes, Miss Taylor.' I watched him, ruddy-cheeked, hair uncombed and jacket littered with straw, stand to attention before the Captain.

Only slightly subdued, Ernest took his seat. 'Guess what, everyone!' Before we could say a word, he announced as if it were the biggest news to hit the street since the Abdication, 'Glamorous Priscilla is back!'

'Who in heavens name is that?' asked Dudley Browne.

'Sshh, his pet ferret,' hissed Smailes.

'What a stupid name,' Browne sneered.

I couldn't have that. 'It's not. It's – glamorous!' Everyone laughed.

'Now boys,' said Miss Taylor. 'Let's hear from Ernest.' She continued spooning out mountains of cabbage and apple, beside pork slices gleaming with crackle. 'Where was she?'

'Well.' Ernest took a big breath; he didn't usually have centre stage. 'She's been gone the entire summer. When Paul and I went to Munich, Harris the gardener said he'd take care of her. But he didn't, because she disappeared!'

'Who cares about a ferret?' Browne gazed toward the ceiling, eyes rolling, both chins wobbling.

'Stop interrupting,' Miss T said with a fearsome stare. 'Go on, Ernest, please.'

'It was horrible. Every day I called for her. It turns out she set up house in Mrs Fox's aviary, living off the rats who were living off the birdseed. But it's been so cold lately, she decided to make friends with humans. Only she chose the wrong person.'

Miss Taylor's eyes went wide. 'I can see it coming. This is too good to be true. Go on.'

'Well. According to Harris, Mrs Fox was in her aviary putting out seed, cooing over her parrots and cockatiels and such, when up pops Glamorous, doing her ferret dance, leaping and rolling around – trying to look adorable. But Mrs Fox, thinking an enormous rat had gone mad, leaps onto a stool and starts screaming! Harris comes running, but by now, Priscilla is terrified, too – puffing up and hissing like a snake. Even Harris is afraid to go in the cage. He tells some boys to find me, which they do, at the stables, and I head there as fast as I can, and hear Mrs Fox shouting for Harris to shoot the thing.'

'Oh, oh,' Miss Taylor said, tears running down, 'I can just see her – perched on her stool. That's the funniest thing I ever heard.' She tried her best to stop laughing. 'Poor Jane,' she said gravely. It didn't help. Off she went again.

'What about Priscilla?' Ernest said. 'At least she was fat and sleek from feasting on rats all summer. I promised Mrs Fox I'd keep her on her harness; otherwise she'll have him shot.'

'Pass the potatoes, would you Moodie?' Paul Caspari muttered at my right elbow. I turned and saw he didn't find his brother's story funny. His head was down. 'After you.'

I took two big spoonfuls, for the crumbly white lumps looked irresistible – butter melting, parsley sliding. But when I passed the bowl toward Paul, he was staring, in another world. 'Paul? You all right? What's wrong?'

His mouth twisted in a bitter smile. 'The matter is not fit for the dinner table.'

'Please. Tell me.'

He looked round the table and leaned into me, as Ernest was regaling them with his imitations of a ferret's cry. 'I got a letter from my uncle. He said someone's opened an exhibition in Munich called Ewige Juden.' He dropped his voice. '"The Eternal Jew." He's sent me the programme. Revolting beyond words. On the cover is a cartoon drawing of a bent-over Jew in a robe and long beard, the usual thing, hooked nose. In his hand are coins and under his arm, a slab of stone with the hammer and sickle on it. Designed to stir up hate.'

'But your mother is safe, isn't she? She's famous, you said.'

'Not anymore. They are calling Les Galleries Caspari degenerate. Some thugs even stole several paintings for their exhibition! Graeme, the entire country is going insane.'

'Oh, Paul. I'm sure that can't be true. A whole country cannot go insane. My father says the Germans will come to their senses and see how foolish the Nazis are. Most Germans are kind, intelligent, artistic. Like you,' I added, hoping for a smile that didn't come.

Chapter 29

A Christmas holiday had never seemed so long. We were supposed to go to Craigisla, but Granny had flu so we'd been stuck at home, the parents banging on about my term marks not being good enough. '"Must try to be tidier," Father read as soon as they arrived, '"must take more care over details... his work in French is consistent but marred by elementary mistakes." But son, you're supposed to be preparing for Certificate!'

'I am, but that's not till the end of June!'

How could I ever have been happy in Dundee? No wonder Mother wanted to move. She was right – the house was just a shoebox on end. Dundee was a backwater, its dismal dirty buildings squashed on narrow streets. Even the docks were off limits, because of another tuberculosis outbreak.

'I can't wait to get back to school,' I said and pounded my fist on the card table where we were working on yet another jigsaw.

Father lifted his head and fixed his eyes, mild and terrifying, on mine, and a judder of fear shot through my heart. I'd overstepped the mark.

'Oh come on,' I said, hoping for a laugh, 'We might as well face it. This Christmas has been a dud.' I laughed but, like Christmas, my joke was a dud.

'That's not very kind,' Father said almost in a whisper.

I backtracked like mad. 'No, that's not what I meant. We've had a splendid Christmas really. It's just that ... Well, I'm very much looking forward to getting going on the *Maiden Erlegh Chronicle*. Did I tell you? Tony Smailes is reviving the school newspaper and I'm the sports photographer. I'm going to write for it, too.'

'*Another* outside activity? What in God's name are you thinking of?'

'Aren't we having tea sometime, Father?' Alastair said with a wink.

'Tea?'

'Yes. *Tea.*' He widened his eyes, as if tea had become terribly important.

'Yes of course!' Father said. 'Tea. What a good idea.'

Mother started to get up from the card table, but Father put his hand on her shoulder. 'Oh no, my dear, I'll get it. I insist.'

'Oh that would be lovely. There are biscuits…'

'On top of the icebox, I know.'

'And if you'd carve a little of that ham in the larder.'

'Certainly, my love. Boys, don't finish the puzzle before I come back.'

'Little chance of that,' I said.

Mother and I worked away, while Alastair popped up and began pacing. Odd.

'Well done,' I said to Mother when she fitted part of the 'S' into the lettering.

'Thanks. I'd been looking for that curved bit for ages.' We smiled at each other. All well again.

'What's happened to Father,' Alastair said. 'I better go check.'

'Sit down,' I said. 'You're distracting me.'

'Good God!' we heard Father call from the kitchen.

Alastair popped up, alarmed. 'Something's wrong.'

'Give him a hand, Alastair, would you? He probably can't find something.'

'You better come too, Mother. I don't – uh – understand the kitchen.'

'Ann?' Father called again. 'Come. Quickly.'

'You come, too, Graeme,' Alastair said.

As we headed for the kitchen, Alastair nudged me, whispering, 'This'll be rich. Just play along.'

Our kitchen was square with thick wooden counters, always waxed to a shine. Father stood in front of one, arms crossed. He looked very serious. 'Now don't be alarmed, Ann.'

'What is it?'

'We have a problem with mice again.'

He stood aside. On the counter were hundreds of tiny black specks.

'Oh dear God!' Mother put her hands on both cheeks.

'Wait,' Father said. He held up a finger. 'Only one way to be sure.' We watched him press his finger onto a little pile of specks and popped it in his mouth. 'Oh yes. Mouse droppings, most definitely.' He licked his finger.

'Are you sure?' Alastair asked, joining him.

Mother couldn't grab his arm in time; stunned, she watched him copy Father, down to the solemn finger licking. 'Not bad,' he said.

I'd been as terrified as Mother, but then I twigged, remembering Alastair's poke in the ribs.

Mother, though, was frantic. 'Are you mad?' she shrieked. 'Rinse your mouth, both of you! Immediately! Graeme, call the doctor.'

'I am the doctor,' Father said and took from his jacket pocket a pink confectionary bag of what we knew to be chocolate sprinkles. We'd tasted them often when cook made a cake.

Then the great hee-haws began.

Like twins, Alastair and Father took out their handkerchiefs to mop their faces. There they were, like two comedians on a stage in Glasgow, stomping a foot and holding on to one another. They could hardly stand.

Mother's mouth was wide open for ages (she wouldn't want to know for how long) but then it closed into a tight line with the corners curling up, as she tried not to smile. 'You – you – devil! You dev-*ils*!' She ran over to Father and he put his long arm round her and she collapsed in laughter against him. The way he held her was almost embarrassing. 'I'll get you,' she said, trying to give him a spank. 'Just you wait.'

'Promise?'

* * *

Two weeks later my taxi tottered up Maiden Erlegh Drive and deposited me under the porte cochère. In no time I was settling in with good old Marshall, him raving about an airfield he'd visited with his mother, outside London. He'd grown over the Christmas holidays, I told him. 'And,' I added, 'your "R" problem has vanished.'

'Weally?'

'Well, nearly.'

He crinkled his eyes. 'Ah, you're right. Just a minute.' He frowned and did his magic trick of turning an L into an R.

'Bravo.'

Across the hall, a new boy had settled into a huge room which, before Christmas, had been shared by three boys. I smelled the fellow before I met him, as delicious odours of foreign food curled out of his vast space into our much smaller room.

We knocked on his door. 'My name is Barbu Calinescu,' he said grandly. 'The son of the Romanian prime minister.' He clicked his heels and bowed, and with a great sweep of his arms, stepped back and grinned. 'Come in, my friends, come in.'

Showing us around, he explained how, each week, a hamper of Romanian delicacies would be delivered, to keep him healthy and ease homesickness. 'Come after dinner. You eat real food. Here no taste to nothing.'

That night we sampled his Romanian wonders, which after a few seconds of shocking our tastebuds, we adored everything – the fat-speckled sausages and long, dark loaves he sliced as thinly as onions, with a long, carving knife on a splendid carving board. Mother would have had a fit. The garlic! The peppers! The spices! 'I tell to send bigger next time.' His English was bad, but we knew that by summer, he'd be fine.

Often in the mornings we heard Romanian music from his gramophone, which stood in a tall mahogany console with big speakers and a powerful radio. He even had his own telephone, speaking to his family in what I guessed was Romanian. Native tongues were taboo at school, but none of us had a telephone with a line to Bucharest, so it was all a bit peculiar, even for Maiden Erlegh.

* * *

Eight of us sat round a long oak table in the senior common room for the inaugural meeting of the *Maiden Erlegh Chronicle*. AA Smailes, editor, stood at the head, tall and blond, quite perfect. His deputy, Dimitriou, an amusing Greek fellow, small and dark, was at Smailes' right. Then a couple of older boys, friends of Smailes I knew vaguely. Caspari, me, and – of all people, right beside me – Dudley Browne. His presence must have been the Captain's work.

Smailes tapped on a half-filled water glass, just like the Captain, waiting for all eyes to fix on him. 'Having a bit of leisure time over the Christmas holidays, I wrote the first editorial. It goes like this.' He proudly read it aloud, thanking Captain Fox, 'A keen and enthusiastic supporter of our all-too-venturous project, which we begin, we trust, with equal portions of modesty and ambition.'

We applauded. 'And now, dear lads, what do we put in the damned thing?' Everyone grinned. 'The world is our oyster, other than for Miss Taylor, who wants each issue to include the best essay, her choice.'

Many suggestions followed. Sports events, news from our clubs: photography, the Scouts, Dramatic Society, chess.

'How about something like a real magazine, like film and theatre reviews?' Caspari asked. 'I'd be interested in that.' He often went to London with Miss Taylor, at the Captain's expense I guessed. His money from Germany had dwindled.

'An excellent notion,' said Smailes. 'Of course.'

'Uh, excuse me. I'd like to do that one, sir,' Browne said. 'Mamah takes me regularly to London to see all the latest shows.'

I looked at him with fascination, the way his porky neck swelled out of his collar.

'I rather think not,' Smailes said.

'And why not, may I awsk?' He spoke in that gargling way, which Smailes proceeded to imitate.

'Becawse I ahm the editawww.' We laughed. 'And I say Caspari will do it.'

'Well, I'm going to tell Captain Waterlow Fox.'

'Please do.'

'He told me to join your silly newspaper. Write about something I like. Which is going to theatah and cinemah.'

'And eating.' My mouth said ahead of my brain. When the laughter had died down, Caspari stepped in. 'Seriously, gents, perhaps we can have two writers. There are certainly enough plays and films to go around.'

'Possibly,' Smailes allowed. 'I'll think about it. That's enough for today. But Moodie, could you stay behind?'

When they'd left, Smailes held his arms out as if to embrace me. 'Moods, that was hilarious. Wish I'd said that. What a loathsome twit. Now listen here, I've got a special assignment. The Captain wants us to write something on the history of the Old Boys, you know, from his earlier school on the Thames? Courtenay Lodge, something like that. What do you say?'

'Well...'

'Don't look so disgruntled. I know it sounds boring, but I heard Captain moved the school because one of his boys drowned in the Thames. There was an inquest where nothing was proved. See what you can find out. It might be interesting; a little dirt never goes amiss.'

'Why?'

'It might come in handy someday.'

* * *

But how dark the Captain's sitting room was! Having heard so much about its grandness, I was looking forward to being bowled over by the gilt, the marble, the very size of everything. Instead, a dim coal faintly glowed from the dark opening of the fireplace. I couldn't see much else. No lights were on.

He'd told me to come at five o'clock, Sunday, and after knocking softly on the partially open door, I entered.

The back of a tall leather chair was angled so that I could make out some shiny shoes as they rested on the ottoman. 'Hello?' I said more firmly, but good lord, an explosion of arms and legs sprang from all directions.

'Who's that?' Feet dropped to the floor and what looked like Captain Fox peered from a wing of the chair.

'Moodie, sir. I'm here for the interview.'

'Eh?' I'd caught him napping. I didn't expect to find him so confused. He stood, one hand on to the back of the chair and jiggled his head. 'Courtenay Lodge. Yes, yes, of course you are. Come in, come in. I must have dozed off. Jane's away. I mean Mrs Fox. I'm a poor bachelor this weekend, as you see.' We shook hands.

I felt I should leave. A dark inch of whisky stood in a tumbler and beside it was a half-full decanter, the stopper off.

'Would you rather me come another time, sir?'

'No, no not at all. I could use some company. Take a seat.' He tried to smooth the parting in his hair, which for once had gone crooked. 'Goodness, it's like a tomb in here. And cold. What time is it?' His shoulders shivered as he walked to the fire. 'More coal, more coal.' Kneeling, he gave the scuttle a stab with its short black shovel. He turned to me. 'Goodness, let's throw some light on the subject, shall we? Could you turn on some lamps? Over there, and there, on the tables. Whatever you find.'

I walked about, pulling brass chains under silk shades. With each new light, the grandeur grew. As if I were a magician, I summoned the gleaming wood on tabletops, their curved legs carved in deep swirls. One table bore red and blue flowers against a snowy-white surface. I bent for a closer look and saw that the thing was made of tiny squares.

'They call that "mosaic work,"' the Captain said. 'It's Roman, from the time of Christ, they say.' He stood near some fat sofas and chairs gathered round the fireplace which, thanks to the Captain's stoking, was getting brighter, warmer.

'Nearly done the lamps,' I said cheerfully. 'Just that part over there.'

Against the last dark wall stood a tall desk, whose front had been pulled down to make a writing surface with neat little drawers at the back. I turned on a floor-lamp and saw a stack of papers. The top sheet grabbed my eye. Taking up the page was a silhouette of two hands, each holding half of a broken rifle.

'Never mind that.' The Captain's voice was sharp and strong, making me jump. In one fell swoop he scooped the papers, lurching sideways. I steadied his arm, but he pulled away. stiffening. 'Not to worry,' he said. He gave a blustery laugh, more like himself, and finished gathering the papers, which he straightened with quick taps on the desk. 'Just some old work I was going through.' He placed them into a drawer which he then locked. 'Not to worry. Shall we begin the interview?'

He returned to his leather chair, sighing. 'Ah, have a seat. Here, beside me. In Mrs Fox's place.' He took a long, slow sip of whisky.

I sank into a wide-armed chair, feeling lost in its fleshy padding and loose covers gone looser – the piping frayed at the seams.

'Now you're the journalist. What would you like to know? Fire away.'

I had prepared a list of questions on a pad of paper, but they seemed silly to me now. Get yourself together, Moodie. 'What was the name of the school you had before Maiden Erlegh?'

'Courtenay Lodge. In the charming little village of Sutton Courtenay. Would you like me to spell it? It's a tough one.'

'Yes, please.' I wrote it down.

'Well, my lad, you will be surprised to know that the precursor of our dear Maiden Erlegh was founded thirty-three years ago, in 1905, just after Mrs Waterlow Fox and I were married. We started in a fine old Queen Anne house. In those days the majority of our boys were being prepared for the army and thus to Sandhurst.

'The first addition to the school building was Courtenay Cottage. A little later came River Cottage with its beautiful garden going down to the edge of the backwater. Enthusiasm for rowing began to grow and we were competing with success in the regattas at Reading, Marlow and Henley.' I wondered if that was related to what Smailes wanted to know. Perhaps someone drowned in a rowing accident.

But he went on, smooth as cream. 'From the beginning there was an interest in sport. Very soon there were enough boys to run a creditable cricket and soccer team and a tradition of keen sportsmanship was established. And true sportsmen they were – men who were to play on a different field soon after leaving school – to fall fighting for their King and Country.' He stopped; gazed into the fire. 'Sorry. I lost my train of thought. Where were we?'

'"Falling for King and country," I… think, sir.'

'Ah yes,' he mumbled, 'The Great War.' He put his lips together and blew softly, a sighing whistle.

Then, like a train chugging out of the station, he started up again. 'I was sent to India and Afghanistan, where I took an interest in the Afghan Hound.'

He continued happily, telling me more than I wanted to know about the different breeds, colours and origins.

My eyes drooped. 'But what happened to the school? Did it keep going?'

'Yes, yes. Well. With the outbreak of the War, Courtenay Lodge would have come to an end but for the wonderful way Mrs Waterlow Fox took control. With untiring energy she carried on, supported only by a new and strange staff. Most of the teachers were ladies; very efficient, too. Few can realise the strain of such an undertaking, but those who do can never forget it.' He went quiet again.

I looked at my watch. 'Well, sir, thank you. That's a very interesting history. So long ago.'

I was half-standing when his voice lurched. 'No.'

I sat back down. 'History is alive. A story still being told, and we are all contributors.'

I felt something new was coming. I waited and at last he spoke.

'No one can tell the history of a school as well as the Old Boys, but unfortunately they cannot be summoned to the task. One by one, I saw them go.' He paused. 'Calvert at Flanders. Pincher Bailey – who passed the Sandhurst examination at the top of the list. Served in the Royal Field Artillery through the greater part of the War. I thought he'd made it, but he died of pneumonia just after Armistice.'

I didn't dare speak.

'Two hundred and sixty-three of them. Gone. We brushed their coats. Groomed them like lambs to the slaughter.'

I wondered if he still knew I was there.

'Our very first pupil was Fred King. He passed London Matriculation and went onto Sandhurst. In 1914, as his battalion passed through Culham Station on their way to France, he threw an apple on to the platform to which he attached a farewell letter to his old school, telling them where he was going and wishing them goodbye. Within a week he was killed, close up to the German wire, the bullet passing through a cigarette case, his farewell gift from the school. I have them both, the letter and the cigarette case. Would you like to see them?'

'Yes, sir. Of course.'

I followed him to a wall of bookshelves protected with glass doors. Most held books, but some bore strange things: a piece of wood like a log with layers of paint; an army canteen, faded telegrams. 'Here it is. I keep it polished. Do it myself to remind me.' He handed me a flattish shape, but with a deep crater tearing into it. I could see my palm on the other side. 'A lovely lad. I presented it to him at the departing ceremony.'

'That's nice.'

'His mother signed him up, the very first on our list. She lived in one of the big houses down the road and had heard about our new school. She was a widow and insisted Fred be a boarder for she felt he lacked male company. He was twelve.'

'Like me,' I said. 'I'm thirteen now, of course.'

'Of course. He left at eighteen for Sandhurst. He and about ten others. It was our tradition to give them a gift from the school on leaving and because Jane and I were feeling a bit skint, the boiler in the Lodge needed replacing, when we went to Mappin and Webb we decided to hold back a bit on the gifts. We bought the boys this and that, the usual letter opener, leather billfold, that sort of thing. But because Fred had been our first pupil I wanted to give him something a bit more... special. He'd often admired my silver cigarette case and when I saw one on display, I settled on it. I was so very fond of him, you see? But Jane said it was too expensive, which it was, and the jeweller showed us one that was a little lighter, thinner, so we went for that. He'd never know the difference.' He considered this and burst into tears.

I should not be here. I stepped back, preparing to flee.

'I'm sorry, my boy,' he said, coughing into a hand, fumbling for his handkerchief with the other. He mopped and blew, coughed again. 'Most unfortunate, my boy. My fault, entirely. You've caught me off-guard, it seems. Jane gone, the problems in Germany, memories.' He risked a glance my way and pulled away the crumpled cloth. A string of snot hung from one nostril. I had to get out of there.

'Yes, well... best be off,' I said in a cheery, awful way.

'Indeed.'

I made for my chair where I'd left my notes. 'Thank you, sir.'

When I opened the door, he said in a bigger voice, the voice I knew, 'Oh, and Moodie, I almost forgot. Your parents are not happy with your report, and I agree. You can do better than that. Even a bright lad like you must poke his nose in a book now and then, eh? You're confined to quarters every afternoon for two weeks. No more idylls at the Grumbars.'

'No sir.'

'Don't disappoint me.'

'No sir.'

But he'd disappointed *me*. This was Captain TS Waterlow Fox, not some *boy* – who shouldn't be crying anyway. But a man – never! What could I do for a grown man in tears, who then has the nerve to punish me!

Chapter 30

I told the chaps it was my own decision to work in my room every afternoon. Still, Finzi waited for me after lunch in case I changed my mind. He'd walk me to my room and bid me a sad farewell, before going to Woodbine Cottage or rugby alone. He was becoming a star on the pitch, people said. He'd let his hair grow, with a neat parting to the side, so he no longer looked like one of the secret police. How had I ever been so afraid of him? He was quite timid, deep down.

Banished, furious, I spent every afternoon in my room for two whole weeks. When I first came to Maiden Erlegh I sought solace there, but no longer. I was a man of action, Marvellous Me, almost. I stared out of the window, watching the boys chatting below. No footsteps echoed down the corridor. Marshall was building model aeroplanes in the workshop. Everyone was busy with things that mattered, not stupid Latin and French.

What were they doing at Woodbine Cottage? Over and over I thought of them, Mrs Grumbar sitting on a stool, alone, peeling vegetables. Did she miss me? Patient Mr Grumbar doing chores with Finzi and – the only fly in the ointment, Mary Petty – more boy than girl, which I preferred. I needed to get back, lest they forget me.

The Captain must have regretted his cruelty, because in an after-lunch talk, he said, 'That Moodie is one to watch. He's clever, yes, but he's a worker. One day he will earn a thousand pounds a year. Mark my words.' I was pleased, but my eyes remained firmly on my plate, scraped clean of apple-blackberry pie. No smiles for him.

I felt none the better for my incarceration. But as I set off for the Grumbars on Saturday morning, I noticed the deep dark of winter was lifting. I started to go the longer, safer way, along the road, but then decided to take the woodland shortcut.

Smoke hung in the cold, still air. I heard every crunch of my feet on rimy, half-rotted leaves. I rounded the arc of oaks where valiant Finzi had carried me when my splint-strap broke, a whole year ago. How much more assured, more athletic, I had become.

The sight of Woodbine Cottage startled me. I sucked in air, as if afraid, but I wasn't. I was happy. Its front still bore that misty look of brick through worn-away whitewash, like in a dreamt of place, but this was large and real.

* * *

Much was made of me. I told no one I'd be coming, not even Finzi, who ploughed through the curtain when he heard the commotion of happy shouts. Mr Grumbar, in his stained lab coat, clapped me on the shoulder. Finzi just stood back, beaming.

Mrs Grumbar's hands flew up to check her hair for loose pins and wayward strands, a habit when she was pleased. 'You've grown taller,' she said. 'But thin. I don't like that.'

'What do you expect?' I said. 'No one makes cakes like you. I've missed them terribly. Scottish cooking is boring, I've discovered. My mother thinks that anything that tastes of anything must be foreign and therefore bad.'

'We haven't seen you since before Christmas,' Mr Grumbar said, taking my coat and hanging it on a hook by the door. 'I was wondering if you'd outgrown us. Got too grand or something. What have you been doing?'

'I heard you were being punished.' This came from Mary Petty, who must have slid in from the science room. She leaned against the kitchen table, arms folded, one corner of her mouth lifted in a suspicious smirk.

'Who told you that?'

'Peter.'

'Who's Peter?'

'She means me,' Finzi said. He threw his arms out. 'I hear that from… somebody.'

'Well, it's not true. Not really. Here's what happened…'

'Come sit,' Mrs Grumbar said. 'It's almost ten-thirty. We can pretend it's eleven and have some tea, and you can tell us everything. I've got the lemon drizzle I baked last night.'

We sat down, chairs scraping, napkins passed round, as we watched Mr G perform the precarious task of lifting hefty slices of cake onto plates almost too small. 'So please tell us,' he said, looking at me, 'What kept you away so long?'

'Yes, well, you see… Captain Fox told me that even with my superior brain, I'd have to poke my head in a book every now and then. He made a joke of it. He says I have what is called a photographic memory. It's like my head takes a picture of what I see, but I have to actually take the picture, that is, open a book, in order to learn. That's why I learn so quickly. I can't help it, it seems.' I shrugged, looking innocent, I hoped.

'Bully for you,' Mary said, stabbing her fork into her cake.

'Mary,' Mrs G said.

I smiled as if I hadn't heard her. 'Anyway, Latin and French I can't see the point of. No alive person speaks Latin anymore, and French sounds like gargling.'

That brought a laugh from Mr Grumbar. 'I agree with you there, but don't tell the Captain. There are people who speak Latin, nowadays, but they mostly live in monasteries and abbeys. And the pope, he speaks Latin to his cardinals.'

'Well, I'm not planning to be pope.'

'I don't know,' Mr Grumbar went on, 'the pope is considered infallible. You might enjoy that.' That confused me. Was he laughing at me?

'Anyway, I've promised to be a good lad and study. I'm also writing for the new school newspaper. The *Maiden Erlegh Chronicle*. I had a private audience with the Captain.'

'Bully for you,' said Mary again. No one corrected her.

* * *

'Just the man I was looking for.' Smailes clippety-clopped down the stairs behind me on the way to dinner. 'How'd you make out with the Captain?' He assumed my slower gait. 'Find out anything interesting? Any tales of drowning boys?'

'No, only about how so many students died in the war. There was something rather sad about the first student who was given a silver cigarette case when he enlisted, but he died in the first week. The bullet went right through the case.'

'Hmm. Unlucky sod. But no scandal?'

'No.'

'Disappointing.'

We reached the bottom of the stairs and he took off ahead.

'Wait!' I said, and because I didn't want to disappoint him, I offered more. 'There's one thing.'

He lifted his eyebrows.

I lowered my voice and leaned in. 'He cried when he told me.'

'No.' He spread the word out long, impressed.

'Yes! Luckily he had a handkerchief, like any proper gentleman.'

'Gentlemen don't cry. Gentlemen carry handkerchiefs to pass to the weaker sex. Not for themselves!'

'What if they sneeze?' He didn't laugh.

'How extraordinary. We certainly can't put that in the *Chronicle*.'

'I know.'

'Disgraceful, don't you think?'

I didn't know what I thought, so I said, 'Rather,' which fitted for most things. At least I hadn't spilled the beans about the Captain being three sheets to the wind.

* * *

I found chocolate sprinkles at Cullen's, the posher shop, on the Wokingham Road. I'd had a brilliant idea of playing the mouse droppings trick on Mrs Grumbar, like Father had with Mother. Mrs G would scream in horror, then realise the truth, and everyone would laugh. Even Mary Petty would be impressed, that tough meat thing with her red knuckles and cracked lips. Mrs G would make a cake and invite me back to a chocolate sprinkle feast in a day or two.

The usual enthusiasm greeted me but, now I was a regular, Mrs G went back to the sink and Mary tugged Finzi to the lab, as if she couldn't wait to be alone with him. Surprisingly her hair was combed. 'Come on,' she said. 'Those slides can't wait.'

Settling against the plump cushions, I picked up *The Times* from the floor, and tucked the bag of sprinkles under the sofa. 'Mind if I do the crossword?' I called to Mrs Grumbar.

'Feel free.' She looked out the window. 'It's getting cloudy. I'm going to take some soup to Mrs Daniels, who's been poorly. I'll be back soon.'

'Don't worry about me,' I said, looking over the newspaper.

As soon as she was gone, I took my bag to the sink. Just as Father had, I scattered a few sprinkles on the counter, around some canisters.

She took forever. I was just about to sit again when I heard her quick step coming up the brick path.

'Whew,' she said, shivering and stamping her feet. 'The wind's picked up. We might get some snow.' She hung her shawl on a hook by the door, swapping it for her apron. 'I could use some tea. Mary,' she called to the back room, 'I'm putting the kettle on. Could you lend a hand?' She pressed her hands on her ruddy cheeks.

'Dear me,' I said. 'What's this?'

'Eh?' She walked toward me, tying her apron strings.

I bent toward the thick wooden counter. 'Mrs Grumbar, it appears as though you need a cat. You've got mice. Look.'

As she came closer, Finzi and Mary P came through the curtain.

'That's not possible.' Her voice was small and low.

'See for yourself. At least they look like mouse droppings. Only one way to be sure.' I pressed my finger repeatedly on a few and popped them into mouth. 'Oh, yes, mouse droppings, definitely. You're not as good a housekeeper as you thought.'

Something sucked all that ruddiness out of her face. 'See?' I kept waiting for her to twig, like Mother. I tasted some again. 'Mmm, could be rats, these are so big.' I tried to look stern and solemn like Father. I hoped she could see my mischievous adorable face. 'Want some? They're rather good, actually.'

'I think you'd better leave,' she said, her face stricken, not at all what I wanted.

She turned and left the house, just like that, into the cold. Without her shawl or anything.

'What were you thinking of?' Mary stood in front of me, furious. 'Get out of here, you horrible thing. I'd hit you except that you're a cripple!'

'Mary,' Finzi said, putting a hand on her arm. 'Don't say that.'

She shook him away. 'And why not? Why would he do something so cruel? Did he think Mother would be fooled by his stupid joke?' She gathered up a fingertip-full of the sprinkles. 'Yes,' she mocked, 'mouse droppings, for sure. You bloody sod! Did you think she'd find it funny when she blames herself every day for William's death? Just because that evil doctor told her a dirty house caused polio. Hers wasn't clean enough and that's why he died.'

'Gosh, it was only a joke. That doctor was wrong. Only ignorant people believe that.'

'Oh, so now you're calling her ignorant. Just leave, will you?'

'What's wrong with you people?' Terrible bangs thudded everywhere through me. This cannot be my fault. I made for the door.

'And don't forget your mouse shit!' She slammed the wrinkled bag into my arms. 'Oh, and when you get back to your palace, stuff it up your arse and then try eating some. I hope you die.'

My legs took me out of there. They had the sense to remind me to take my coat.

I didn't remember much of the long walk back. I'd been a complete fool. I could never go there again.

But how was I to know what the stupid doctor told them? And how could they believe such nonsense? It wasn't my fault, but theirs for not knowing better.

Marshall and I ate the chocolate sprinkles, all of them. I didn't risk playing the joke on him, but I did tell him about Father's trick on Mother. He, at least, found it hilarious.

Chapter 31

Spring came, but I spent little time outdoors. With no chance of seeing Woodbine Cottage again, I wanted nothing to do with swelling blossoms or trees wrapped in pale green gauze.

I tried to work. Caspari and I met each afternoon in the middle common room – at the Captain's suggestion to find a study pal, but Caspari took his School Certificate far more seriously than I. He was a year older and a true scholar. Down went his head over his books while I stared at my knuckles, playing again that tragic scene at Woodbine Cottage.

Why hadn't I apologised right away – writing on my best stationery, explaining that Father had played the trick on Mother, who found it vastly amusing, and thus, thusly? – I hoped she would, too. But a month had passed. Too late now.

But surely any letter is better than none. I began in my notebook, scratching out every second word. Before I knew it, Caspari had closed his books and said, 'Ah, time for dinner, which we can enjoy with a clear conscience, now that we've done our prep for Certificate.'

* * *

Thank heaven for Marshall. If not for him I would have had a nervous breakdown.

'I've written a letter,' I said, pulling it from under my mattress, 'but it sounds rather thin. I'm worried I'll just be bringing up the whole mess again. Could you have a listen?'

When I finished reading the dreadful thing, he said, 'Hmm, I see your dilemma. Sometimes it's best to forget things one can't change. Let's think,' he said, a signal for us to lie on our beds, seeking inspiration from the ceiling. 'I've got it!' He sat bolt upright. 'What you need is a change of scene.'

'Come on, Marshall. How am I going to leave school?'

'Who's talking of leaving? I'm talking about the swimming baths. You'll love them.'

I sat up, too, to give him a hard stare. 'Marshall. That is the most idiotic idea I've ever heard. You know I can't swim! Mr Fairbank put the fear of God into me. "You'll sink like a stone, Timothy, splint or no splint." Arsehole.'

'Who's talking about swimming? I'm talking about the sights! You've never seen so many naked women. The walls are plastered with them! With plaster! Well, fresco is the technical term. Like Michelangelo's Sistine Chapel, only better. I'm telling you, Moodie, breasts are all over the place. And little flimsy scarves covering their you-know-whats. But some are mermaids so they don't have any you-know-whats.'

Hope sprung into my chest. 'But what's my excuse for being there? I can't arrive in boots and jacket and tie saying, "Hello chaps, I'm here to see the naked ladies."'

'But that's the reason we're all there. Well, it is mine. Hate swimming myself. But you're right. Some are keen swimmers, and race. Smailes, for instance. He's a big-time champion.'

'Smailes? Wait! I can bring my camera, be the official photographer, like on the sports field. I'll take pictures for the *Maiden Erlegh Chronicle*.'

'Perfect notion, Moodie. There's even a gallery on one end where you'd get a good view – of the swimmers, I mean.'

* * *

One would think residing in a palace twenty-four hours a day would make one unimpressed by luxury. But no, this was more than luxury. This was flesh – pink and gloriously sinful – flesh. Painted flesh, true, but the closest I'd get to the real thing.

How to do it justice? Well, the entire room was made of creamy marble, with honeyed swirls imported from Italy at the cost of thirty thousand pounds. Thick pillars, also marble, supported a lovely arching ceiling, painted sky-blue and dappled with golden stars, where one could gaze up and dream of what lay on the walls. Beneath the ceiling, below vast windows decorated with gold mosaic swags lay, as Mr Piper would say: *les pièces de résistance*. Mermaids lounged on big scallop shells, but also normal women enjoyed the sands with their legs sweetly – maddeningly – crossed to keep their privates private. I counted seventeen. A golden sun rose on the east wall, a rosy-pink one set on the west. Marshall was right. It was quite educational.

I also learned that Solly Joel used to have parties, more like Roman orgies, with film stars and such. Once he invited dancers from a London show for the weekend.

'Come have a swim, girls,' he had said.

'Thank you, Mr Joel, but we can't. We haven't brought swimming costumes.'

'No matter! I've been given several, made of a new material from America. You must try them and tell me what you think. The manufacturer would be ever so grateful.'

They agreed, but the fabric dissolved on hitting the water! 'But they didn't mind,' said Marshall. 'Americans are used to that sort of thing.'

At first I sat in the gallery, taking off my jacket in the hot, steamy air and attempted to capture them mid-stroke or mid-air as they dived off the high-board. I needed to get closer, but I was worried the floor might be slippery. After cautious testing, holding on to Smailes's arm, I found its tiny mosaic tiles safe. So, wiping off the soles of my boots with a spare towel, I entered the realm of swimmers. White lawn chairs, poolside, allowed me to sit when I wanted; I could lean forward and snap away.

My photographs got better and better. Little Ernest Caspari became a fine diver, springing into the water like a salmon. Smailes's speciality was the front crawl; his lithe, muscled arms slicing the water, big bubbly drops frozen in the air forevermore. I even managed to get a strange, dark shot of the fat Egyptian, Sharaha, performing his speciality, called 'the Plunge' which was nothing more than an underwater torpedo shooting from one side to the other.

* * *

Before I knew it, March had gone.

A kind of wildness grabbed me by the hair that spring term, hurled me this way and that; it shook me like Rufus shook a rat. I wanted – everything. The light was brighter, sharper, clearer. From the moment I woke up, the day carried me, as if I were high up in a dinghy. I could not stop to breathe a slow, sensible breath. And at night, after Marshall's and my imagined lewd tales were told across our beds, with mumbled g'nights, we turned and travelled away, to our own starry conquests, spilling our panting selves into sleep.

Pretty soon, both Woodbine Cottage, and my studies, became nothing more than bothersome insects that needed swatting away whenever thoughts of them got near.

* * *

It was a Sunday, the eleventh of April, three days before the end of term. I was watching the boys laughing and splashing about in the swimming baths. Some were men now, with hairy chests and big willies hanging in their knitted swimming costumes. I was standing near the deep end, trying to get a shot of the bottom of the pool, where Solly Joel's coat of arms lay shining through the water. *Ad Altiora Tendons*, it read, which meant, we all knew, 'reach for something higher.'

Some of the boys were getting raucous, pushing each other into the pool, banging the water with the butt of their hands. I moved away to avoid getting soaked or slipping. Smailes stepped in. 'Here, lads, don't go overboard. Watch out for Moodie.'

'Sorry, chum,' said Rogers. 'I'll fetch a towel.'

It was strange – as if my lameness had power over them. An idea bloomed, and in a voice like some prissy teacher from Bannerman, said, 'Now, now, boys. Don't misbehave.' With a strong thrust of my stick, I pushed one of the hairiest and swarthiest – Papamichael – straight into the water. He fell back with a great splash. I pushed another. And another. Rogers took a step toward me, but paused. He couldn't fight back because of my lameness. I did the same to him – wham – and backwards he fell. Wild and powerful, with a new weapon in my hand, I'd become unconquerable.

'Now Moodie,' Smailes said, stepping forward, his voice gentle and firm as he took hold of my stick. 'Don't take advantage.'

'What d'ya mean?' I tried a laugh. Where was my warrior-self? Surely not gone already? Still brave and hopeful, I grinned at Smailes.

'You know. Of your situation.' He nodded at my stick, which he still held, too polite to say my lameness. He let go and I pulled the stick back to its obedient position beside me. 'No gentleman can fight back. It wouldn't be fair. And you must not take advantage of that. It would not be fair of you.' Embarrassed and confused, I looked at the others standing by.

'I know you know that. But you forgot, in the excitement of the moment. Never mind, it's mended now.'

* * *

Some blocks of learning lock into place with a clunk of understanding. Smailes' words were like that.

For the rest of the day, I thought of what he said, part by part, word by word. I must not take advantage of my lameness. No decent fellow would fight me, unless by my taking advantage of him, I made him no longer decent. And we both would become less than ourselves, because we could get away with it.

We could have hurt each other but didn't.

These boys could do all sorts of murderous things to me, but they did not. And I could not do to them what they had forbidden themselves to do. We made an agreement which could not be abused. This was how the Captain succeeded at Maiden Erlegh. He guided us, without our knowing, not to take advantage.

* * *

I burst into Marshall and my bedroom just before dinner. As if I had discovered electricity, gravity, the circulation of the blood. 'I've solved a mystery!'

He was in the middle of gluing little red stripes onto the wing of his plane. 'Shh. Ticklish moment here. Give me a second.'

Right, I thought. Don't take advantage. I sat on the side of my bed, watching, being patient. Let him finish the bloody plane.

After endless seconds, he set it down, folded his hands and gazed at me. 'I'm all yours. Do tell. I love mysteries. Have you discovered that Miss Taylor and the Captain truly are lovers?'

'Mmm, no. Something more important. More serious.'

He slumped. 'Never mind. I'm listening.'

I leaned in. 'Here it is. I know why we all get along here while the rest of the world doesn't. It's not because the Captain treats us all the same, as Caspari says, or I used to think, because he treats us all differently. It's because we don't take advantage of one another. It's the one rule, spoken or unspoken, that the Captain has. It's the key to everything.'

He stared. 'And? Go on.'

'That's it.' I tried to tell him about the scene at the pool, my embarrassment and enlightenment. I might as well have told him that it was the apple and blackberry pie that made things work.

The dinner bell rang and we went downstairs, both of us thinking the other was a having an off-day.

* * *

I spent much of the next morning wondering how I could thank Smailes for his priceless lesson. Free swim couldn't come soon enough.

When I got to the pool, Smailes was doing his laps and I had to wait. I knew it might be better not to go overboard, but thank him casually, Smailes-style.

I sat in my usual chair and took out *The Times*, nodding 'hello' at Marshall lying on a towel nearby. We three were the only ones there.

The day after tomorrow we'd be going home, where I'd have to sit in the trenches with my books, but today the sun shone through the windows in such great shafts, nothing could spoil my happiness. I was on the brink of life, of success.

I began the crossword. After a while, I took off my jacket; the heat of the sun had made the room unpleasantly close. My undervest stuck to my chest, my white shirt, to it. I loosened my tie.

'What-ho, chappies.'

Those words could only have come from Dudley Browne. No one else said 'chappies' in that silly, pompous way.

He placed a towel over the arm of the lawn chair beside me and sat with a satisfied 'Ah.' Don't let him spoil this, I told myself. He has a right to be here, but why couldn't he have just stayed away? He applied some kind of cream on his body. Ugh. I kept my eyes on the crossword.

'I say, Moodie, where's your bathing costume? Aren't you swimming?'

'No.'

'Then why are you here?'

'Moodie's the sports photographer,' Marshall said.

'How splendid for him.' Browne went back to creaming his pale, fat, hairless legs. 'I say, Moodie, you're very brave. Trying to do the things other people do. As if you didn't mind being a cripple. He's a fine fellow, don't you think, Marshall?'

I couldn't speak. I managed to give my open newspaper a thunderous shake; I put my head deep into it, hiding from him, his words, my anger.

And there was Smailes, dripping wet beside us. 'Why don't you shut up, Brownie boy?' He snatched the towel from the arm of Browne's chair and dried his arms.

'I say,' Browne said, 'that's my towel.'

Smailes stopped. 'Is it? A towel's a towel.'

'Mine has my initials on it.'

Smailes held it out by two corners. 'Well, so it does. "DMB." What's the M for, pray tell?' Browne didn't answer.

'Eh? I didn't hear.'

'Mergatroid.'

'Ah. Mergatroid.' He drew the syllables out, savouring their ridiculousness. 'Perfect. And did your mother embroider this herself?'

'Of course not. She had it done at Fortnum & Mason.'

'How splendid for you. He's a fine fellow, eh lads? Pretending he doesn't mind being a slug.' With exaggerated care, Smailes replaced the towel on the arm of Browne's chair.

Marshall got up from the floor and held out a towel to Smailes. 'Here, take mine, Smailes. I've an extra.'

'Why, thank you, Marshall. Nice that some people have manners.' He put the towel around his neck and sat away, on the edge of the pool. No one said anything. Browne lay back in his chair and closed his eyes. Smailes sloshed his legs with slow force through the water, a menacing sound. I attempted to do the crossword. Only Marshall gazed peacefully at the sights, perhaps counting every nipple he could see, as he said he'd do the night before.

'Time for a dip,' Browne said. He stood, his stomach wobbling, its surface a series of shadowy dimples. I watched him lower himself down the ladder, splash water over his head, and cautiously ease into a backstroke, his windmill arms chopping the water. After two laps he bounced up and down doing leaps of some kind.

Smailes joined us. He took the towel from Browne's chair and tossed it on the floor a few feet away, stretching his long, perfect body along the chair where Browne had been sitting.

Browne climbed up the ladder and fetched his bathrobe from against the wall where it hung on one of Solly Joel's beautiful hangers with the school crest burnt into the wood.

He padded over to us, 'I beg your pardon, Smailes. That was my chair.'

'Oh,' Smailes sat up. 'Does it have your initials on it, too?' He pretended to examine its wide, flat arms.

'Don't be stupid. Everyone knows I was sitting there, wasn't I, chaps?' He looked at me, then Marshall, expecting us to back him up, but we didn't.

'Come on, Browne,' Marshall said, 'be a sport. You can lie on that one.' He pointed to the towel on the floor.

* * *

Browne backed away, picked up his towel and walked several yards before lying on his towel, face up. He closed his eyes.

With the silence of a cat, as graceful as Browne was clumsy, Smailes lifted himself from the chair and put a finger to his lips.

He went to the wall to fetch one of those gleaming hangers, and with it, parted Browne's bathrobe. 'Don't move,' he said kindly, his voice soft as feathers. 'Don't open your eyes. I have a nice surprise. That's a good boy.'

The robe lay open. After glancing at us – we did nothing – he knelt beside Browne and with both hands took hold of his saggy baggy swimming costume and pulled. 'Lift your bottom would you, Browne? Don't move. Just your bottom. There's a good chappie.'

Browne did, and the costume slid off. Smailes tossed it aside. 'Now, what have we here? A little worm. Poor thing. Let's see if we can make a man of you.' He took hold of one wooden corner and stroked Browne's willy with the other. It flopped over, like a dying thing, and grew. Browne twitched and whimpered. 'Don't worry,' Smailes said. 'Everything is lovely.'

'Stop. Please,' Browne said.

'No. You don't really want me to stop, do you? Trust me, you'll like it.'

Browne's pale face took on a deep colour. 'Oh, stop.'

But Smailes would not, he kept on, faster and harder, till Browne's small thing grew tall and pitifully spurted over and down its sides.

* * *

We didn't speak of it, Marshall and I, not even that night as we went to sleep. We were witnesses to a terrible, quiet violence, and we would keep quiet, too. Bad things happened, I told myself, and this was one of them.

The next morning, someone knocked on the door. Dimitriou, second in command after Smailes, stepped in. 'The Captain wants to see you both after breakfast. In his study.'

Eating breakfast was difficult. I looked round the room and saw that both Smailes' and Browne's chairs were empty.

Outside the Captain's office, I found Marshall already sitting miserably on a bench. 'He wants to see you first,' he told me.

The Captain barely looked up from the blotter splattered with the ink of countless letters. He shifted the ornate inkstand, the paper knife, the scissors. 'Something serious has happened. Something to which you were a witness. Tell me what you saw… at the swimming baths.' My heart threw itself against my ribs. 'It's all right. Just tell me what you saw.'

As best as I could, I did. I wanted to say how horrible Browne had been, that he had driven Smailes beyond endurance, that he got what he deserved, that everyone hated him and part of us were cheering for Smailes, but I said as little as I could, and even these few words were excruciating.

'Thank you,' he said with no emotion. 'Send Marshall in as you leave.'

* * *

The morning classes went on as usual and for seconds at a time I forgot about Browne and Smailes. I'd be going home tomorrow and somehow had to study nearly a whole year's work in three weeks. School Certificate would begin soon after our return. I felt sick.

We had spinach and watercress soup, my favourite, and I had two bowls. But the meal ended – as usual – and Captain Fox stood – as usual – for his announcements.

'Before anything else, I have to tell you something that you may already have learned. Anthony Smailes, by his actions, has decided to leave us. By choosing not to adhere to the code and principles of Maiden Erlegh School for Boys. I regret his decision, but it is irrevocable. He was one of our finest and most promising students and I am sure we will all miss him. I regret to inform you of another departure, that of Dudley Browne, a lad who was showing promise in many areas. However his mother has decided he would be better suited to another school.

'I wish you all a pleasant holiday, but do not forget the tasks at hand. For those about to take School Certificate, do not spend all the time studying, for the work you have put in so far this year will hold you in good stead when you begin the heavy campaign of those two weeks of difficult examinations. Good luck.

'And now, a parting word to keep you smiling: A few years ago a farmer and his wife went to a fair. The farmer was fascinated by the aeroplanes and asked a pilot how much a ride would cost. "Ten pounds for three minutes," replied the pilot. "That's too much," said the farmer. The pilot thought for a second and then said, "I'll make you an offer. If you and your wife ride for three minutes without uttering a sound, the ride will be free. But if you make a sound, you'll have to pay ten pounds." The farmer and his wife agreed and went for a wild ride. After they landed, the pilot said to the farmer, "I want to congratulate you for not making a sound. You are a brave man." "Maybe so," said the farmer, "But I must confess I almost screamed when my wife fell out."'

Chapter 32

Just gone midnight. Still no sleep. I lay in my little railway bed, sleepless, writhing with regret. I should have stopped Smailes from ruin.

Over and over, every detail lined up in sharp precision: Browne's pale flesh on the monogrammed towel; hanger-hook parting his robe, the sliding, the spurting, the stupidity. Smailes should have known better! He broke the rule he'd taught me. Don't take advantage of another's weakness. But he had.

I turned on the reading light; regretted that, too. Three a.m. Bloody hell.

The lights of Edinburgh were browning the sky when a nightmare-thought exploded into being. School Certificate begins in eight weeks! Two full terms gone and I'd scarcely opened a book.

More regret, more agony.

An hour later we pulled into Dundee where, through the dirt and rain-speckled window, I saw Mother waiting on the platform amid clouds of steam and sleety rain. I descended the awkward little steps on aching legs. For a while she hugged me, which for once I didn't mind, but then she pulled back, giving me the onceover. 'You look *terrible*.'

'I am terrible. I couldn't sleep all night.'

'Oh, I hate it when that happens. Come, let's get your suitcase. Pay attention, it's slippery.' We walked into the busy station where, under the big clock, porters waited to pair up luggage with their owners. 'I thought you'd be too young for insomnia. That's an old person's ailment,' she said.

'Not anymore.' I was already thinking of my school report, soon to arrive, and the inevitable storm that would accompany it.

The plan for the holiday was to disappear so that our maid, Fiona, could do a spring clean. We'd go to Craigisla for two weeks and golf at a nearby course. Normally, I'd be thrilled, but all I could think of was my report that, any day now, would arrive. And two terms' revision to make up for.

* * *

The post usually came around 9:30. I was in the window seat in the sitting room, waiting. My scheme was to intercept the bloody thing as it came through the letterbox. If the parents imagined it to be lost in the post, I'd be back to school before they requested another – if they remembered.

I had the French book open, doing my best with *Les Lettres de Mon Moulin*.

Alastair was in the schoolroom, studying. Mother was on the phone. I could hear she was in a flap. 'But what am I to do?' she wailed. 'Everything is all planned! You can't leave me in the lurch.' Bang went the phone. Clickety-click went her heels.

'Graeme, are you there?'

'Yes, Mother, in the sitting room, working away. Why?'

'Never mind. Just wondering.' She wanted to tell me what had happened, I suspected, but Father had told her not to disturb my studies.

Half an hour later, Mother came into the sitting room wearing a hat and coat. Good. I wanted her gone. The postman was already late; he might come at any minute.

'Phew,' she said. 'Crisis avoided. What a bother servants are. That fool Fiona just telephoned. "Me back's gone," she said. "Gone where?" I said. "On holiday?" Honestly. Anyway, she won't be able to clean and I won't find anyone suitable at the last moment.'

'But you have?'

'Yes! Remember the little poem I taught you? "For every ailment under the sun, there be a remedy or there be none. If there be one, try and find it; if there be none, then never mind it."'

Oh for God's sake.

'Guess who I thought of?'

'I can't imagine. Do tell. Please.'

'Berry!'

'Our Berry?'

'What other Berry is there? Isn't it grand I kept up with her? She'd be happy to help, she says. She'll be coming by tomorrow to discuss everything. Please be here. She's so fond of you.'

'Oh, I will be – revising, as always.'

'Good lad. Well, I'll toddle off. Has the post come?'

'Not yet.'

'Hmm. Late today. Don't work too hard. Take a walk, perhaps. It's fine out.'

'Goodbye, Mother.'

A couple of minutes later I heard the postman. I knew it was him; he always whistled 'Auprès de ma blonde' as he trotted up the six stairs to our house. 'I wonder,' Father had said, 'if he sings that confounded tune through his whole route or has a collection that never varies; so that when he comes to "Auprès de ma blonde" he's at 166 Nethergate. One of life's unanswerable questions.'

The pile of letters landed on the floor as I got to the door. I scooped them up. Flip, flip, 'No, no, no… ah!' I recognised the Captain's distinctive handwriting, round and leaning to the left. I slid it into the inside pocket of my jacket and headed for the downstairs toilet. I locked the door.

With my heart in a gallop, I tore open the envelope, unfolded the foolscap and read:

English: He deserves credit for the way in which he has kept up with the class in spite of not doing regular preparation.

Geography: He must improve his English style and handwriting. A general amelioration in maturity is required, but his sketch maps are good.

History: He writes in a plain style, and has plenty of ideas. If he can write enough in the time, he may secure a Credit.

Others were pretty much the same. Lukewarm was putting it mildly. I exhaled heavily. Better than I deserved. Shame blew through me. I had let everyone down: Captain Fox, my parents, myself. Much had been given to me – a good brain, humour, a friendly nature – yet I breezed along, taking advantage of all those things, not to mention my 'situation.'

Lazy, cocky, selfish pillock. Think, Moodie. What can you do? I held onto the top of my head with both hands, thinking, thinking. Was there a remedy for me?

A loud pull of the knob shook the door. 'That you, Graeme?' It was Alastair.

'Yes, yes, I'll be out soon.' A few seconds later, after tucking away the report into my inside pocket, I opened the door. 'Ah,' I said, pretending to do up my trousers.

'I'm off for a walk. Join me?'

'I'd better not.'

'Oh come on. You're pale as a ghost. Doctor's orders.'

I couldn't resist. 'I'll fetch us jumpers.'

'Roger. Meet you in the hall.'

I took the stairs, two at a time, to the second floor. The schoolroom was still laid out the old way. I grabbed a couple of jumpers from our chests of drawers, and not knowing what to do with the evidence of my shame, I lifted my mattress and shoved the school report underneath.

Sometime during the night, I found the 'remedy' for my problem.

* * *

At breakfast next morning, I announced in my best, most reasonable, adult voice, 'You see, I need to prepare for School Certificate. If I succeed in passing all five examinations, I will be the school's youngest person ever, at Maiden Erlegh, to achieve Certificate. Thirteen years and ten months old. I have therefore decided not to take a holiday but to remain at 166 with Berry to give myself the best chance of success.'

Mother dismissed me with a shocked, 'That's nonsense! You can't not come!'

'Hold on a moment,' Father said. 'I like the idea. If he wants to study, let him. Berry would look after him very nicely.'

'He's studied enough! He needs to get out and enjoy the fresh air. Look at his colour.' All heads turned to me.

'I've had a few colds over winter, that's all. Nothing serious, Mother.' Another brilliant idea: I took out my handkerchief and dabbed my nose. 'In fact, I think I might be coming down with one now.'

'That settles it,' Father said. 'I'm the doctor and I say Graeme is not going to be standing around on a golf course getting a chill. Who knows what the weather will be like at this time of year?'

Mother lit another cigarette. 'Well, we'll have to ask Berry to spend the night. I won't have him sleeping alone.'

'I'm sure she won't mind. She and Graeme are the best of friends.'

Victory. The snuffling was laying it on a bit thick, but I had to study. It was the only way of redeeming myself.

* * *

Good old Berry – wonderful to see her again. She looked the same, just a little greyer, whereas I, nearly a man, had changed completely.

Father had wanted to set off just after lunch, but Mother went through her instructions with Berry a second time. 'Don't rush me,' she said. 'Haste makes waste.'

After about 300 trips back and forth in a drizzle to the new Vauxhall, filling its boot with golf clubs, rugs and hampers. When the drizzle worsened, Berry and I stood in the doorway with Rufus, waving the golfers off on their two-week holiday. I wouldn't wish rain for them every day, but I was glad to see a little.

After they drove away, Berry said, 'I don't know about you, but I need a cup of tea. Interested?'

'Oh yes, please.' We sat in the kitchen, sipping tea and munching on scones, just like old times. Afterwards, I showed her the daily work schedule I'd made.

'My goodness, this is splendid. I've one of my own, of sorts, but not so fine. Mrs Moodie told me what needs doing, and I've written it down. I like how you've divided the day up. I might copy out your plan for myself. Is that all right?'

'Of course.'

'Could we talk about meals and such? The sort of thing you like? I remember a lot, but people change.'

We combined ideas and an hour later, we came up with:

7:00 –	wake up; wash; breakfast; Rufus in garden
9:00 –	revise in schoolroom
11:00 –	break (don't leave schoolroom) apple, sweet biscuit, hot chocolate, brought by B.
11:15 –	back to revision
1:00 –	lunch in kitchen with B, soup, biscuits and cheese; (if fine, walk with Rufus) (if rain, crossword)
2:00 –	revision again (in schoolroom)
4:00 –	break: tea, etc. Read newspaper and talk with B (if she has time)
4:45 –	G revises, again; Rufus again
6:30 –	Dinner with B (cottage pie, roast chicken, lamb chops, no parsnips)
7:30 –	Evening activities, (sitting room) such as cards (pairs, gin, etc.) jigsaws, Monopoly.

It was a strange two weeks. In some ways, familiar: like chatting with Berry or teaching myself, all alone, as I had at Morland Hall. But in other ways, a revelation; I *chose* to study. I could have said, bugger this, I'm off to Craigisla and golf, but I saw a future that demanded work, and I said yes.

Berry whizzed and clattered about the house, the changing odours declaring her tasks. With tins and tins of Mansion wax she polished the oak panelling that wrapped round the staircases. The inside side of windows she washed with vinegar, while a man did the outsides, with Berry only paying him when no smudges were left. On her hands and knees, she spread a lovely, peppermint-smelling wax onto the floors, and polished them with our new electric polisher. 'Sorry about the frightful racket,' she said later. 'This machine may be easier, but the job's not as good.'

At the end of each day, we'd show each other what we did. I admired her work: the luminous wood; mounds of cutlery, polished to a silvery-blue, our christening cups, the heavy tea service with its weighty tray. And she admired mine: the maps I drew, maths problems solved, pages read, memorised lists of kings and prime ministers.

Evenings were spent in the sitting room, reading, playing cards, doing puzzles. What I couldn't understand was her wizardry at jigsaws. I was almost cross. She surveyed a mess of jumbled pieces and always picked exactly the one she wanted.

'I don't know how you do it. If you were a man, you'd be an aeroplane designer, like my roommate, Marshall.'

She looked at me, turning pink, head tilted, 'Why do you say that?'

'Because you remember the shape of things, how they fit.'

'I always thought it a useless skill.'

'Not at all. Remember the way you spotted four-leafed-clovers?'

'Yes, I do.'

* * *

On the third of May, Mother drove me to the train station; as we said goodbye on the platform, she handed me an envelope. I knew at once it contained my school report – I'd left it under my mattress! Sickening horror filled me as Mother turned and walked away. The whistle blew. Nothing to be done but climb those tricky steps and find my little room.

When I finally got the courage to open the dreadful thing, I found a letter inside:

My dear son,

I am glad that your cold did not turn out to be anything serious and that you spent a profitable time at home. I have been most impressed by your new maturity as demonstrated by your commitment to your studies. So much so, that I am returning your most recent report from school. Berry said that you left it behind. I have decided not to show it to your father.

Love as always,

Mother

Chapter 33

Every second day, with every window open to high summer's rose perfumes, we sat in the Middle Common Room – one examination in the morning, one in the afternoon. School Certificate was in full bloom.

The weather outside was the most perfect I'd known, the air never more beguiling. But as the Reverend Harold Hewitson Nash, vicar at St Peter's Church and our adjudicator, said, 'Sweeping zephyrs must not distract.'

I was proud, sitting among the bigger, smellier bodies. Thank goodness I twigged the colossal importance of School Certificate, though French and Latin were probably still beyond me.

Visiting Woodbine Cottage was impossible, for I never sent that letter of apology. Sometimes, faithful Finzi appeared outside the dining room, but I said, 'Sorry. Can't. I must revise. Make up for lost time.'

'But we miss you,' he said, so forlorn I wished I could have relented. 'Mrs Grumbar most of all.'

'I don't think that's likely, Finzi. I'm not wanted.'

My first examination, on the 28th of June, was in one of my best subjects – Geography. Still, as I walked into the Middle Common Room my heart clobbered bruises against my ribs. Everyone stood behind their desks, staring ahead like soldiers; and staring back was the Very Reverend and very thin Mr Nash. He surveyed the field and after glancing at his pocket-watch, pointed to a boy in the back. 'Close the door, please. The rest of you, be seated.' Chairs scraped the floor.

'Take out your equipment.' From breast pockets clattered pencils, pens and rulers. 'No one may begin until I give the signal. To do so may invite disqualification.' We waited an eternity.

'Open your examinations and begin.'

My trembling hands struggled to open the booklet and when I looked down, the words were incomprehensible. I looked round and saw hunched backs tented over their work. What if I get behind? Is my life ruined already?

My eyes scurried through the hopeless tangle of letters. Miraculously, 'sketch map' appeared, and grabbing hold of the words, I yanked my way back toward sanity.

Just before noon and several questions later, I finished. Mr Nash pushed back his chair, stood, and at 12:00 exactly, shouted, 'Stop!' with a loud 'p'. Shoulders jerked, then hunkered for more writing, but he was firm. 'Anyone caught writing from here on in will be disqualified.'

Afternoon brought Geography II. It was during this spell that Reverend Nash vacated himself to the Land of Nod. Slow rumbles accompanied us with occasional, outraged snorts that jolted him awake. Satisfied as to his whereabouts, he happily fell asleep again.

French, two days later – disaster. I knew the words, but not what they meant together.

With English Literature, I was on firmer ground. 'Show the importance of the quarrel between the Montagues and the Capulets.' Excellent! We'd focussed on *Romeo and Juliet* in class, where I'd been struck by how stupid the families were. Why didn't they just get along? Inspiration reigned as I poured forth my ideas on not taking advantage and how cruel twists of fate change everything: the letter arrived too late. The lovers died.

I left the Middle Common Room, my brain abuzz with the pleasure of working hard and knowing I'd done well.

The buzzing brain continued Monday with History, as we described the meaning of a political cartoon. Another spot of luck, for they fascinated me, the way a drawing can say so much.

Maths was another success, but for the last – Latin – woe betide me. Not only was my brain empty, I'd never filled it in the first place.

* * *

On the 8th of July, that was it. Over and done with. Nothing to be done but wait till late summer when we'd hear the results.

Classes continued, but we certificators were spent. A nervous emptiness hung about our shoulders for days. I knew I'd made a dog's breakfast of French and Latin, but the die was cast. *Alea iacta est.*

* * *

It was time for something else, but what? The first issue of the *ME Chronicle*
would come out in October; I should have looked over the school history
I wrote ages ago. I knew it was uninspired. The new editor, Dimitriou –
successor to disgraced AA Smailes – was having a meeting on Monday. But I
couldn't bear to set my mind to another piece of paper. My motor had stopped
and I couldn't crank it up again.

Other boys cranked theirs by boating on the Lodden or riding to hounds.
They played tennis and cricket. A few sunned themselves on the roof, and
in the evenings, older boys coaxed young ladies to the cottage on the lake. A
door key was hidden somewhere, its location only known to them.

I sat on the edge of my bed, after lunch, summoning the energy to rewrite
that bloody history. I hadn't looked at it in six months, not since the horrible
Smailes business. And now I couldn't remember one dull sentence.

Not a sound came from the corridor, everyone outside, enjoying sports. I
opened the window, allowing a rush of rose scent to hit me. I had to join it.

Walking along the flaking stone terrace, a sunny expanse – too hot, really
– I sought refuge inside the Indian prayer temple, shaded by oaks.

I'd not been there before. It seemed a girlish thing to do, to step inside such
a delicate structure. But how lovely it was. The encircling walls and domed
roof were entirely of metal filigree leaves and berries, so fine, it seemed
impossible that such a thing existed. I pressed my head against the fragile
ironwork, at the manly world beyond. Loneliness hit hard. Was there no way
out of this pain I knew so well, this woeful chain toward weeping over loss?

I thought of the Captain, who wept for the young men he'd raised for
better things than lying underground, where no sun could warm them,
as I am warmed now. If I sat here, weeping for my loss, would that help?
Do something you *can* do, Moodie. You, today, feel the sun. Those soldiers
cannot, ever. Tell their story, because you live, and they don't.

I went back to my room and wrote. It was all there. I let the boys speak. It
wasn't hard. They told the story and I was just the pen.

Now if I could just write to Mrs Grumbar. Not today though.

Chapter 34

Ernest held a bit of yellow cheese above Glamorous Priscilla's head. The ferret stood on its hind legs and with princess delicacy removed it with tiny teeth and fled into the shrubbery.

'She likes to eat in privacy,' Ernest explained.

'Aren't you afraid she'll run off?' I asked. 'You don't want Mrs Fox finding her in her aviary again.'

'Not when I'm around, silly. She'll be right back.'

We were sitting under the gigantic holm oak on the front lawn, Ernest, Paul and I enjoying the shade of its dark canopy.

'Ernest,' Paul asked in a threatening tone, 'Where'd you get that cheese? Don't tell me you've robbed the dining table again.'

'What do you expect me to do? Let poor Priscilla starve? Anyway, Mrs Fox was too busy scarfing her Victoria sponge to notice.' Disgusted, Paul shook his head. 'Don't worry,' Ernest said, 'In two more weeks, we'll both be rich.'

'Hardly,' said Paul gazing up into the oak's motionless leaves.

Ernest couldn't afford to feed his ferret? 'What's going on? Would someone please enlighten me?'

'How to explain,' Paul sighed. 'With the slump of the art market in Munich, Mother is going to Paris for the summer. The French don't have Germany's recent aversion to Expressionism.'

'I see.' I tried to be calm, like him, but I knew this was bad: first, some of Mrs Caspari's paintings seized for that atrocious exhibition against the Jews; and now her money was running out. 'Will you two be joining her in Paris, then?'

'No, we'll stay here for the summer,' and he sat up, cheered. 'But here's the good part. With all the uncertainty in Europe, everyone is feeling the pinch. Even the Captain is in difficulty.'

'So he's decided to hold house parties!' Ernest announced joyfully.

'Let me tell it, Ernest, for goodness' sake. Moodie will think we've gone mad. Captain Fox has come up with a clever solution. During the summer break, he's making Maiden Erlegh available to the gentry for weekend parties, during Ascot and so on. At a considerable cost.'

'And guess what?' Ernest exploded, 'He's hired Paul and me to help! We're being paid!'

'Very true, very true. Ernest and I will be assisting the Captain – I with the bookkeeping, et cetera, and Ernest will be carrying luggage, running errands.'

'The tips will be good,' Ernest added. 'The Captain says I just need to be friendly. And not annoy Mrs Fox.'

* * *

Following lunch in the dining room the next day, the Captain announced his plan to offer up Maiden Erlegh for summer house parties. 'However, as a trial run, as it were, a group of important people have expressed an interest in coming for a meeting that could not wait. And as the grounds are looking their best, I couldn't refuse. We try to keep the fees as low as possible, especially for those whose links with their mother country are not as firm as one would like. So, during their stay of three days, I ask you to politely ignore them. They shouldn't get in your way – they'll be staying in Solly Joel's guest wing. If you should happen on one of these fine men, or ladies, I expect you to be courteous, of course; but do not draw attention to yourselves. They have important matters to discuss.'

* * *

I stood outside Maiden Erlegh's front door, curious to see this party of important people. Politicians, I imagined, perhaps Neville Chamberlain.

The Captain had prepared Ernest well. He'd supplied a list of names, each with a room number. Ernest's job was to unload everything from the back of the coach and match each piece with the right name and take them up the back stairs.

'Can I see the list?' I asked. Ernest passed it over.

Such a strange assortment of names, many foreign. Hagbard Jonassen, Arthur Ponsonby, Bart de Ligt, George Lansbury, Muriel Lester – more than a dozen.

I had an idea. 'Ernest, how about you put the luggage in alphabetical order? It'll be easier to match with the names.'

'What are you talking about?'

'Well, as you unload each one, tell me the surname, and I'll tell you where it goes in an alphabetical line.'

'But I get all the tip money,' he said.

'Naturally.'

At last the coach came lumbering up the drive. We stepped aside as the Captain strode up, looking eager to greet the guests.

A tumble of men in hats – and even a few women in hats – came down the coach steps. Some shook the Captain's hand, with both hands as if good friends. One fellow, bent and thin, handed him a leather folder, which the Captain stowed under his arm. 'Esteemed guests,' he said in a splendid voice, 'do come in. I trust you will find Maiden Erlegh accommodating. If you please, I shall guide you to your rooms.'

As soon as they'd followed the Captain like little ducks, we set to work. Ernest called the names, laughing over ones he couldn't pronounce, and I pointed to the spot on the drive where I'd imagined each one to go. Some people had more than one bag, and we spread them out further.

Ernest began cheerfully, announcing his tips each time he returned, but he was a wreck by the time he got to the last one, Arthur Ponsonby, whose suitcase and overstuffed briefcase he carried back downstairs. 'Bugger, bugger, bugger. There isn't any bloody room twelve.'

'Are you positive?' I asked.

'I think so,' He was panting, sweat rolling down his face. 'I'd better check again.'

'Let me carry the briefcase anyway.' He was going slower than I was.

But he was right. The numbers stopped at eleven. Nothing for it but to go back down.

'Bloody hell,' said Ernest, 'I'm going to kill Mr Ponsonby when I find him.' He wiped his sleeve across his forehead. 'Hey, I've an idea! Let's go down the main staircase. I'm sick of those dark backstairs.'

I looked around. We weren't supposed to use them, but they looked so wide and welcoming. 'Why not?' I said, 'But let me take the suitcase. You're all in. You take the briefcase.'

'Are you sure?'

'Absolutely.' I passed him Ponsonby's briefcase, a stuffed, battered old thing. One step at a time, Moodie. Just hold that great curving bugger of a banister and breathe.

But it was Ernest who took the tumble – a terrible thing to see – all the way down, limbs floundering, till he hit the marble floor with a colossal whack.

An explosion of papers erupted from the briefcase and slid across the floor. Ernest didn't move. I took the stairs as fast as I dared.

Don't let him be dead. Don't let him be dead.

His head lifted. 'I'm all right,' he called, as if from the bottom of a well. I put my hand on his shoulder. 'Don't touch me. Let me get up by myself.' Little by little he managed to roll over and sit. He tested this and that; he was just bleary-eyed and stunned. He looked at the strewn papers. 'What's that?'

'The briefcase opened, that's all. You stay here.' I walked over to the furthest-away papers and began picking them up. Many pages bore a jagged, black design at the top. I looked closer as recognition stabbed my chest. Two hands held a broken rifle. I'd seen that before. Where?

'Good God, what's all this?' The Captain's voice came toward us from behind, speeding to the rescue.

'We're all right, sir,' I called, straightening. 'Caspari Two's taken a tumble, that's all.' The Captain pressed him here and there and looked into his eyes, like a commanding officer on a battlefield. Ah, yes. That was where I'd seen the broken rifle – in the Captain's study, when he'd wept over Fred King's too-thin cigarette case.

I began gathering the papers again. 'We can't find Mr Ponsonby's room, though.'

'I know,' he groaned. 'I'm terribly sorry. I was on my way to find you.' He shook his head as he helped Ernest to his feet. 'I meant to tell you – I've put him across from my quarters He's an old friend, you see, and that's the twelfth room.'

He helped me with the remaining papers, flustered. 'This is all my fault,' he repeated. 'Here, boys. Let me take the luggage.'

'Please, sir,' Ernest said, 'I can do it.'

The Captain and I looked at each other, understanding that he didn't want to lose the tip.

'Tell you what,' said Captain Fox, 'I'll take the lot upstairs as my punishment for being such a fool, and you do the rest. I insist. Fair is fair.'

Ernest gave a limp nod.

At the top of the stairs – I was amazed, an old fellow like the Captain, clipping up as if the bags weighed nothing – he set them down. 'All yours, gents,' he said, his cheeriness returned. He pointed to a door opposite his quarters. 'There's his room,' and back he trotted downstairs.

Ernest's fist was poised to give his jaunty knock, when a wild snort blasted from behind the door. Ernest's hand sprang back.

'Bloody hell,' he whispered. 'What's that?'

'I think I know,' I said. Nothing came for some time, and I wondered if I were wrong. Then a barrage of desperate snorts rattled the air.

'He's snoring,' I laughed. 'The kind Father does. He holds his breath for ages, then lets fly. It terrifies Mother. She thinks he's died.'

'Well, I'm not having it. I want my tip!' Rapping led to pounding and finally to thunderous shouts through the door. 'Mr Ponsonby. I say, Mr Pon-son-by!'

'Eh?' a high-pitched sound flew out. I laughed again. I couldn't help it.

'The bugger's not going to win this one. Your luggage sir!' his yell was as loud as humanly possible. My hands flew to my ears.

Like a wee creature emerging from its hole after six months hibernation, the bent little gentleman I'd seen talking to the Captain earlier, opened the door a crack and peeked out. A few alert hairs stuck up from his head. I thought about counting them. Splurts of laughter collected in my throat. Come on Moodie; get a hold of yourself.

'Your luggage sir,' Ernest said, giving me a kick. 'I'm sorry for the delay. A problem with room numbers.'

A few squints and blinks were all Mr P could manage.

'May I come in?' Ernest asked.

'If you wish.'

'I do wish. Wait here, Moodie,' Ernest hissed. He saw I was jerking about with unmanaged mirth, and disappeared into the room, closing the door. I waited.

Had the old boy keeled over?

At last Ernest emerged, his face purple. 'That was the biggest waste of time I've ever spent in my whole, entire life.'

'Right. No tip, then.'

* * *

Now Mrs Fox had never thought much of Ernest Caspari since being marooned on a stool as Glamorous Priscilla danced round her feet in the aviary. Ernest returned the disregard, as she had ordered Harris shoot his beloved pet. I guessed the Captain hoped that putting them at the same dinner table might make each realise the other wasn't as dreadful as the other thought. So far, they'd managed a fragile peace by ignoring one another.

I was surprised, therefore, when Ernest piped up to Mrs Fox as she was dishing out mashed potatoes. 'I say, Mrs Fox.' His voice was all hoity-toity. 'Have you had the pleashaw of meeting Mr Pon-son-by yet?'

'And why,' she asked with disdainful eyebrows, 'do you ask?'

'Well, I had the pleashaw of delivering Mr Pon-son-by's luggage to his room, across from your apartment.'

She was quiet for some time, gathering her words into a barrage of something splendid, and at last satisfied, she placed her spoon ever-so-gently into the mashed potato bowl. 'And why, pray tell, are you bringing up a name that you can't even pronounce, other than to display your ignorance? It's not Pon-son-by. It's Punsbeh, and furthermore – you fool,' (these two words she said in a near-whisper because she knew her husband would be shocked if he heard them) 'it's not Mister. It's Lord. Lord Punsbeh.'

Ernest didn't pause. 'Punsbeh! Of course. Ha-ha! Punsbeh! Oh, Mrs Fox, I beg your pardoon.' His hands went together in a prayer. 'I beg your pardoon!'

Now why he said 'pardoon' instead of 'pardon', I had no idea, but I found it utterly hilarious. I stared at my plate and began shaking. I thought of Jesus on the cross, but to no avail.

But Ernest hadn't finished. 'I may be a fool at pronouncing his name, but I do know he snores like Big Bertha, and... he's the biggest cheapskate on earth.'

Well, that finished me off, and the entire table, as well.

Mrs Fox expanded like a toad. 'Leave the table at once, young man, and wait for the Captain outside his office. You as well, Mr Moodie. I did not expect such poor manners from you. You've been keeping very poor company.'

* * *

The Captain wasn't much bothered, it turned out. A mountain of papers lay on his desk. He looked tired. 'Hmm,' he said, sighing and leaning sideways, his elbow on the chair-arm, his thumb propping his chin. 'I'm afraid Mrs Fox cares about these things sometimes more than she ought, poor lady; she's been working full tilt, you see, preparing for our guests. I would like each of you to write a letter of apology to her. She deserves that, don't you think?' He turned to Ernest with a look of such tenderness, I was sure he understood every wee thing about him. 'You must be exhausted, my boy. The best place for you is bed. But Moodie, would you stay behind a minute? I'd like a word.'

After Ernest had gone, the Captain took a cigarette from the box on his desk and twisted it gently into his ivory holder. Something of length was coming. I should have behaved better, I knew.

He pushed the chair back with his feet, leant back and exhaled toward the ceiling. He regarded me quizzically. The hollow clonk of the grandfather clock's pendulum thudded in the silence.

'I liked what you wrote, my boy, about the old school. Well done.'

'Oh.' Cold relief streamed through me.

'It's quite a remarkable piece. Do you know that? Particularly what you wrote about Fred King. I'd like to read this bit to you. May I?'

I nodded.

'"The first pupil was named Fred King. He went to Sandhurst, and later served in the West Indian Regiment. In 1914, as his battalion passed through Culham Station on their way to France, he threw a letter wrapped around an apple onto the platform, saying where he was going and farewell to his old school. A week later he was killed. The bullet passed through a cigarette case that was the farewell gift from Courtenay Lodge. No one knowing that this was his final farewell.

'"Though Fred King died, the cigarette case survived and lies in a glass cabinet in Captain Fox's study, a small but noble monument to the sacrifices of the old boys who are not here to tell their story for themselves. Thus, it is us who remember and tell the tale as best we can.""

He coughed. 'Thank you for not mentioning my tears, though I am not ashamed of them. The day we cannot weep for one another we are indeed lost. In your piece on King, you hint at the horrors of war, without demeaning the sacrifice of our lads. It's a fine line to tread. Perhaps because you have suffered your own war, you've had to find new roads, yourself. I don't know how to describe it, but I know it when I see it.

'Twice, now – by accident, if accidents exist – you have seen the symbol of the broken rifle. First, that night in my study and today, strewn across the hallway floor. I'd best explain, rather than leave a bright boy guessing.' His teeth scraped his lower lip.

'What you saw is the symbol of War Resisters' International. Many of its founders had resisted the First World War and were labelled cowards and traitors. As an army man, I shared that view until I saw, one by one, my boys blown up into the sky. Oh, some survived, but their injuries, seen and unseen, were unspeakable. Gradually, my friend, I came to realise that these men told a terrible truth. War is a sin against God, of which I and everyone who coaxes a man so fervently to death, is guilty.'

He looked down, ashamed, and covered his eyes with one hand. 'I didn't know what to do with my life. I was a Captain, after all; there was a school to maintain. What saved me, amazingly enough, was meeting Arthur Ponsonby on a London train. It was 1929. What time is it?' We looked at the clock, its steady beat reassuring us somehow.

'I want to know, sir. Please go on.' I sensed I was being trusted with a secret; not a bad one, but a special one. Always, the War had festered in the past like an enormous darkness that no one talked about. Now someone was.

He looked at me with the smallest smile. 'Well, we got talking, the way one does on a train, revealing more than the usual, because the encounter was unlikely to be repeated. I had heard vaguely of this man, but the slender, soft-spoken fellow was not like the firebrand I read about, who had been attacked in the street for his traitorous views. Little by little, lowering our voices, I found we were cut from the same cloth. He gave me a copy of his new book, *Falsehood in War-time*. I slipped it into my briefcase; we exchanged cards. I went home, read the book, how both sides in the War exaggerated the other's wickedness, so that killing each other became easier.

'It was an epiphany. Everything changed and soon I made the pledge all War Resisters make: "War is a crime against humanity. I am therefore determined not to support any kind of war and to strive for the removal of all causes of war."'

'The broken rifle.'

'Precisely. Anyway, that's why Arthur and all the others are here, for a meeting of War Resisters' International. I put Arthur in the room opposite because we've become great friends, you see, and we like talking into the night. Later this month, the WRI will be holding a desperately important meeting in Holland, at Bilthoven. We fear that darkness is coming again, you see, with Hitler and that complicated mess in the Sudetenland.

'I myself refuse to believe that Hitler is as bad as some say. Germans are not the monsters portrayed in the War. They are a civilised people. We must address them as such, not punish them like disgraced dogs. If you treat people badly, they act badly.' The clock chimed. 'Ten o'clock. Mrs Fox'll have my skin!' He stood and opened a side drawer of his desk. 'I'd like to give you a copy of Arthur's book. Take a look at it over the summer but keep it to yourself. People think we're traitors.'

'Why?'

He turned out the light on his desk and shook his head. 'God only knows.'

Chapter 35

'You've got spots,' Mother said.

I'd been happily reading *Anthony Adverse* in our sitting room when she started in on me. 'No one in our family has spots; we've got dry skin. I won't have it.'

Just keep reading, just keep reading.

'You must dab your face with your first urine of the day. If we had a baby you could wipe your face with its wet nappy. That's best.'

'Mother, for God's sake, I just got home! Leave me alone!'

'Now, now, none of that,' Father said.' He turned on a nearby floor lamp and took hold of my chin, moving it about in the light.

'Nothing fresh air and sunshine can't cure. Good thing we're off to Craigisla tomorrow. I prescribe taking your breakfast on Granny's veranda every morning and spending as much time in the sun as you can.'

* * *

Father was right. Gradually Craigisla cast its airy spell over me – a concoction of creamy milk, fresh vegetables and pleasant walks. Dutifully, I took breakfast on Granny's veranda, but nothing could get my conversation with the Captain out of my head.

The safest time to dig into *Falsehoods in War-time* was at night, when Alastair and I sat up in bed, reading. I grew more and more outraged that such things could happen in our modern age, how people could be so idiotic. I wanted Alastair to read it; he had such a low opinion of people; this might appeal to him.

As we were changing for dinner (Granny expected that; white shirt and tie, smart tweed jacket) I began casually, 'As you know, I'm getting frightfully

interested in history and politics. You might enjoy this book Captain Fox
gave me. It's about the dreadful lies and deceptions put out by both sides
during the Great War.' I tossed the thin, green volume on his bed, where he
sat, fixated on doing his tie.

Next night, we were both reading in bed, him my green book, me a funny
Wooster and Jeeves tale, when Alastair let out a guffaw, 'Sorry,' he said, and
went on for a few seconds when he did it again.

'Oh,' I said, remembering, 'Are you reading the bit about the two country-
house families spying on each other? It shows just how foolish war is. I found
that funny, too.'

'No, no. I read that long ago. A bit facile, I thought. No,' and he chortled
again.

'I'm reading The Belgian Baby with No Hands. It's hilarious.'

'Is it?'

'Yes! Listen! "Not only did the Belgian baby whose hands had been cut off
by the Germans travel through the towns and villages of Great Britain, but
went through Western Europe and America, even into the Far West. No one
paused to ask how long a baby would live were its hands cut off unless expert
surgical aid were at hand to tie up the arteries – the answer being, a very few
minutes. Everyone wanted to believe the story, and many went so far as to
say they had seen the baby. It was loudly spoken of in buses and other public
places, had been seen in a hospital, was now in the next parish, etc., and it was
paraded, not as an isolated instance of an atrocity, but as a typical instance of
a common practice."'

My heart sank into the mud. 'I guess it is absurd.'

'Ah Graeme, you do make me laugh.'

'Do I?'

'Yes! Aren't people ridiculously stupid?'

'I suppose so, but they start wars.'

'True.'

'Aren't you worried about Hitler?'

'Well yes, but what can I do about it? Nothing. People are no bloody
good, that's all. Wars are won and lost but nothing changes. Life goes on. Art
remains. Music remains. I'll get upset when they stop.'

'But you're going to be a doctor. You must care about people if you want
to make them better.'

'I'm interested in fighting disease in a laboratory. I'm not all that keen on
touching people. But thanks for the book.' He pushed it over to my side of the
bedside table. 'Amusing read.'

* * *

'Ah,' said Granny, plunking her small, ample self onto a wicker chair that stuttered with her weight. 'September is the best time of year, don't you think?'

'Indeed.' I hadn't seen her coming; my eyes were on an astonishing headline *in The Times*: PREMIER TO SEE HITLER Flying to Berchtesgaden This Morning LAST MINUTE PEACE EFFORT.

Since early September, the papers had been frantic with reports on Germany's demand that Czechoslovakia return the Sudetenland. It had been taken away when they lost the War, but Germany now wanted it back. Naturally Czechoslovakia refused and was ready to go to war. That would bring in France, who had pledged to help them. Great Britain hadn't pledged anything, but Chamberlain was trying to find a solution to the mess. His flight to Germany was wonderful news!

Still, I lowered the newspaper. Though dying to learn more, I'd be dead for sure if I didn't give Granny my full attention.

She sniffed the air with sumptuous zeal. 'Don't you love it? The air, sweet with barley and apples, the golden light? It's as if the world is saying, remember this day, for the cold, dark nights be coming soon.' She rang a little silver bell sitting on the bumpy wicker table. 'Hot chocolate?'

'Yes, please.' When Robert appeared she ordered the same, as well as a plate of scones. 'After all,' she said, 'we need more padding, with winter coming.'

We sipped a while in silence, but the newspaper's 'PREMIER TO SEE HITLER' kept pulling at my eyes from where it lay by my cup.

A series of clinks made me jump. She'd caught me peeking and was tapping her fingernail on her saucer. 'What is so fascinating, pray tell? Am I reading "Hitler" upside down?'

'Uh, yes, I'm afraid so, Granny.'

'I'm sick unto death of him.' She took a bite of scone piled with clotted cream.

'But this is good news, Granny. Just listen.'

'Very well. But make it short. I'm a busy woman.'

'I know you are, Granny. Here we go.' I read to her about Mr Chamberlain flying to see Herr Hitler, who was "very ready" to meet the British Prime Minister at Berchtesgaden, the Fuehrer's summer home. 'Incidentally, it is believed that this will be the Premier's first journey by air.

'So you see, Granny, instead of hurling accusations back and forth, the two leaders are going to meet and talk it over, like gentlemen, face to face.'

'That man is no gentleman. I've heard Hitler on the wireless. He barks like a mad dog. And that moustache is beyond understanding. Imagine our fine prime minister going all the way over there to meet with a sewer rat.'

'Now Granny, we don't know that he's a sewer rat. That's why it's good if the PM meets him face to face.'

'Pft! And make him feel he's just as important as Mr Chamberlain?' She stood. 'If those poor soldiers were alive today, they'd be turning in their graves.'

* * *

On the 23 September, a Friday, I'd reached the Lodge at the entrance to Maiden Erlegh. Harris, the gardener, was shuffling across the drive, pushing his broom toward a pile of brown leaves. He lifted his head as the taxi stopped and, resting a hand on the end of his stick, lifted his prickly tweed cap.

I tapped on the window between the taxi driver and me. 'I'll get out here and walk the rest of the way. But take my suitcase up to the door, if you would. How much do I owe?'

A taxi would be faster, but my legs needed to stretch, and I felt like having a chat with the old fellow. I was keen to hear the latest on the prime minister's second trip to Germany.

I calculated the driver's tip, adding a little extra for the luggage. How grown up I was.

'First leaves falling,' Harris said, arching his back into a stretch. 'Welcome back, Mr Moodie.'

'Thank you, Harris. It's good to be back. What's the news?'

'Well, Shadpar's got a new litter. It's cheered the Captain. Eight of 'em. He's been in London. Meetings. Very tired, he is. Good thing term's starting up again.'

'Yes. I'm sure he must be greatly relieved.'

'You're right there. Last time half her pups were stillborn.'

'No, I mean about the crisis in Czechoslovakia.'

'Oh, I can't be following that. Too complicated.' He aimed his broom to where he'd left off sweeping.

'It isn't really. And besides, everything's all right now. Would you like me to explain it to you?'

'No. If everything's settled, why do I need to know about it anymore?' He gave me a sly look. 'Eh?' His arm swung round to include the vastness of all Maiden Erlegh's dominions. 'Oceans of them leaves coming. The grass'll need rakin' and that's even harder. I'll be dealing with 'em till Christmas.'

Perhaps he saw I was disappointed. Perhaps he was pleased I wanted to spend time with him, that I found him teachable; or perhaps he simply wanted a respite, but he said cheerfully, 'Time for my break, just about now, give or take.' He sat on the low brick wall that stretched from the entrance pillars. He patted the space beside him, which I took. 'Go on, then.' He pushed his cap toward the back of his head, and leaning to one side, drew a wrinkled wad of tea-coloured cloth from a trouser pocket and blew with an alarming honk. He completed the deed with a series of vigorous wipes that must have hurt his long, purplish nose.

With pedagogic fervour I began. 'A few days ago, Mr Chamberlain travelled to Germany because everything was such a mess over the Sudetenland.'

'Never heard of it.'

'Don't worry. I hadn't either. It used to be part of Germany before the Great War.'

Harris's eyes moved longingly to his more important pile of leaves. I was losing him already. 'A bit of background: when the Great War ended, the winning side – that's us of course – divided up Germany. We gave a bit to Poland, some to Hungary and the biggest part – known as the Sudetenland – to a new country called Czechoslovakia. And because the Sudetenland used to be part of Germany, most of the people spoke German.'

'What else would they speak, Chinese?'

We laughed. At least he was listening enough to make a joke.

'But recently, Hitler's been claiming that the Czechs were attacking the German-speakers, beating them up and wrecking their homes. It was time, he said, for the Sudetenland people to vote if they want to be returned to Germany or stay in Czechoslovakia.'

'Sounds reasonable.'

'One would think. But both countries want it because the land is rich in resources and industries. It's the golden apple of the country.'

'Riiight,' he said. 'That could be a problem.' I still had him.

'Now, the prime minister of Czechoslovakia, a man named Beneš, said absolutely no to a vote; he'd rather go to war than hand over that land. France promised to back them, and that might mean Great Britain would have to join, and another Great War would break out.'

He pressed his hands on his ears. 'I'm not hearing this.'

'But wait! This is the amazing part: About a week ago, Chamberlain flew in an aeroplane to Germany to talk, face to face, with Herr Hitler.'

'You don't say. That was very brave of him.'

'Yes! And they had agreed that the Sudetenland would go back to Germany, and that would be the end of it. No more demands in Europe. Chamberlain even said, in his address to Parliament, that Hitler seemed a reasonable man who could be trusted.'

'I hope so,' Harris said slowly. 'That War. It were a terrible time.'

'I know. Well, I don't know, but so I've heard.' I thought of the Captain, his tears, his meetings in Norway. I could hardly wait to see him. He must be overjoyed – a solution.

'They still need to seal the deal, of course.'

'What d'ya mean?'

'The terms of the transfer need to be put in writing and signed by both. As I left Dundee, Chamberlain was on another aeroplane to Germany.'

'Again?'

'Just to confirm everything. It must be done and dusted now. Anyway, best be off. Thank you, Harris, for putting up with my lecture.'

I looked at my watch. Just in time for lunch. The noon sky was warm and still, but already the sun sagged toward the northern hemisphere. Because the angle was different, Alastair said, the sun made a softer light and cast longer shadows. 'One's not imagining it. It's actually true.'

I continued past the widely spaced cottages where our teachers lived, past the stables and storage sheds, and there stood my beloved collection of gables, towers and wings. I'd have a good year, I knew.

There was only one – well, two – flies in the ointment. I'd have to re-sit Latin and French Examinations in December. The Captain sent a letter. But I'd passed the other three – English, Maths and Geography – which was still good for my age. Besides, I'd be working with the Captain, one to one, in Latin; French would be with Mr Piper, and he was good fun.

Inside, I checked the board to find I'd be rooming with Marshall again – hooray! I raced upstairs, but he wasn't there. His belongings were, though. Glossy aeroplanes, beautifully painted by his meticulous hand, hung over his bed by thread-like wires screwed to the ceiling. A row of books stood on a shelf below his bedside table, a wind-up clock on top. His dresser bore, in soldierly fashion, his toothbrush, toothpaste (rolled up tight), clothes brush, hairbrush and razor. Razor? I looked closer. Little yellow whiskers were stuck to the blade. I didn't even own one.

'I say, Moodie, just the man I was looking for.' It could only be Calinescu, accompanied, as always, by the delicious spices of Romania. 'Come, my friend! Come see my new wireless! I call it The Beast!' I followed him to his massive room where, encased in a shining, expensive cabinet, was The Beast.

'Could we turn it on?'

'Of course. You want to hear some jazz?'

'Do you mind if we check the news? I want to hear the outcome of Chamberlain's visit to Germany.'

'I can tell you that,' he said cheerfully. 'Everything's stalled. Something went wrong, but we don't know what. Listen!'

He turned on the radio, and a fine, resonant voice told us that the talks had broken down and all telephone lines from Germany were jammed.

Nothing to do but unpack my things and head down to lunch. The dining room was abuzz, but not with the usual exuberance. Perhaps the Captain would give us any new developments after we'd eaten.

But no. 'I had hoped,' he said, 'to be able to offer a prayer of thanksgiving today, that the agreement between Herr Hitler and Prime Minister Chamberlain had been signed, but some disagreement has held the matter up. As nothing definite has been released, we will continue as normal. For the new boys I will say that we do not discuss politics at mealtime. They are not conducive to healthy digestion and lasting friendships. You will find your schedule of classes in your rooms, as well as sports activities in which you expressed an interest last term. The various clubs are also available. Classes will begin on Monday. Spend the weekend well.'

Chapter 36

Marshall didn't get back till past ten that night. I'd tried to stay awake, but sleep kept dragging me off. Next thing I knew, my bed was bouncing up and down, Marshall so excited he could hardly get his words out. He was a changed man. Why?

Because of all things on this earth – an earth I was sure God didn't create because he wouldn't have made such a bloody mess of it – my own friend and roommate Charlie Marshall was in love.

How had this happened? By a string of lucky accidents no one could have imagined back in July when we said goodbye to one another, pretty much the same, but now a sea apart.

'Let me explain,' Marshall gulped. 'At the end of August, Mother decided to go to Paris. She telephoned the Captain and asked if I could come to Maiden Erlegh – early, as it were. I wasn't too happy about it at first, but how wong I was!'

I was about to say, 'not wong, wrong,' but he kept going.

'When I got here, I met a new boy from Spain, whose parents had been killed in their civil war. He and his sister were left with the grandparents, but they were too old to look after them, so the grandfather asked the Captain if he would take them both.'

'But that's ridiculous! We're a boy's school!'

'I know! But they begged and begged because the children were desperate not to be separated.'

'But a girl, here? That's an invasion.'

'Just listen. So the Captain thought and thought; you know how he is.'

'I do.'

'And guess what? He found a way! She could live at one of the teacher's houses on Maiden Erlegh Drive and go to Earley School. Breakfast and dinner she'd have with us and she'd sit at Beryl's table, who would take her under her wing.

'Anyway, when I got here, the Captain put me at Beryl's table next to Joy. That's her name. Joy. "Look after her, would you," he said. "She's a bit lonely and shy." And guess what?' No chance of that. 'Beryl invited me to take tea in her room. And guess who was there?'

'Hmmm, that's a tough one. Joy?'

'Yes! I was nervous as anything and...'

'Listen, old chap, can we talk about this tomorrow? I didn't sleep much on the train, and I've got the *Maiden Erlegh Chronicle* meeting first thing.' Turning, I pulled my sheet up over my ear.

'But there's more.'

'In the morning,' I mumbled.

'Two minutes. That's all I ask.'

I groaned. 'Very well.' I faced my friend again, transformed by love. I'd do my best to rejoice with him, but jealousy niggled at my gut.

'This involves you,' he said.

'Eh?'

'Just now, I found a note from Beryl in my mailbox, asking me to go to the pictures with her and Joy, tomorrow night, and to bring a friend.'

'Oh no. Not me!'

'Who else? The ABC in Reading is showing *Having a Wonderful Time*, with Ginger Rogers and Douglas Fairbanks, Jr. It's supposed to be hilarious. And we'll have a – wonderful time!'

'Marshall, it will not be a wonderful time. I'd rather have all my teeth extracted.'

He pursed his lips over to one side. 'See how you feel in the morning.'

'The only thing on my mind right now is the fate of the talks between Herr Hitler and Chamberlain. The future of the world depends on it.'

* * *

Next morning, without taking breakfast, I hotfooted it down Maiden Erlegh Drive to the newsagents. Past many heads deep in papers, I grabbed the *Manchester Guardian*, as it had the biggest headline: 'ANXIOUS HOURS AT GODESBERG.'

The story that struggled up from the tiny print took ages to sort out. Yesterday morning, following an unexplained hitch in the very early hours of the previous night, Mr Chamberlain (instead of resuming talks as planned) had stayed in his hotel room, composing a letter to Hitler, which was sent at 10:30 a.m. Hitler's reply reached Chamberlain at 3:30 p.m. Once again, the prime minister made his way across the Rhine to Hitler's hotel at 10:30 p.m. And there the report stopped. The newspaper's deadline must have been reached.

Under the porte cochère, I whipped through the article again. Maybe I'd missed something, a glimmer of hope pointing toward peace. I read it again, and feeling dizzy, I realised I was starving. Moodie! Get a hold of yourself. The meeting for *Maiden Erlegh Chronicle* was the thing at hand. You're not going to survive this world if you can't remember to eat.

The maids were clearing the dining room when I came in and grabbed a couple of congealed sausages before heading for the meeting.

Someone must have newer news.

Apparently not. Around a table, sat our small *Maiden Erlegh Chronicle* committee, serious and waiting. I wondered if the Godesberg meeting looked like this. Only Caspari looked as nervous as I felt.

After Dimitriou finished his hearty welcome, he became solemn. 'Now lads, we were delayed once, by events of last year...' he was referring to the disgraced Smailes, '... but we will not allow the events of today to delay us further. We will publish our first edition, Volume 1, Number 1, of the *Maiden Erlegh Chronicle*, on the 13th of October. I realise that far greater matters than ours hang in the balance, but the Captain told me this morning that we must not allow our goals to be impeded by machinations of others abroad. He has, by the way, been called to London on a private matter. Mr Mellor will be acting Headmaster in his place.

'I have revamped Smailes's opening and made it shorter. It reads as follows:

'"October the thirteenth will from now on symbolise two birthdays, of which ours is by far the less important. There was never a more auspicious day for Maiden Erlegh than its headmaster's birthday. We are indeed delighted to be able to dedicate to Captain Fox our first number, with our most sincere and hearty greetings."'

Many 'hear-hears' resounded, accompanied by manly raps on the table's glowing surface.

'Graeme Moodie has written a superb history of the old school, Courtney Lodge, and it forms a perfect link with the Old Boys; many, as you know, paid the ultimate sacrifice in the Great War.'

'And now the whole bloody thing is going to happen all over again!' This came, astonishingly, from Caspari, who slammed the table with his fist, pushing his chair so far backward, it fell.

'Paul, please!' I called, but too late. He'd gone.

Dimitriou closed the door and resumed his place at the table. 'Poor fellow. He's been trying all summer to get his mother out of Munich, and now it looks like war. My parents left Greece last year, thank God.

'As I was about to say, Moodie's piece will go on the front cover.

'I was about to mention the many contributions of Caspari, who is unfortunately unable to hear our gratitude. He's written a history of table tennis, a feature on colour photography and a list of books that would appeal to many of our students. Despite his personal concerns, he has managed to contribute more than anyone else.

'There's just one thing more we need – a film review. I understand *Having a Wonderful Time* is playing in Reading. Any volunteers? It must be quick, though. We go to press on the 29th.' Sounds of shifting chairs and throat-clearing filled the room. 'Moodie, what do you say? Any spare time to help our fledgling journalistic endeavours?'

I couldn't think fast enough to supply an excuse. Chaperoning Marshall on his romantic expedition, was meant to be.

* * *

There was still no news of an agreement by lunchtime. Mr Mellor, acting in the Captain's place (whom I imagined was on a peace mission of some sort), made the announcements. After the routine school business, he said, 'The prime minister will be flying back to London later this afternoon. If possible, I suggest you listen on your wirelesses. The BBC will be at Heston Aerodrome to meet him. Let's hope we'll get some positive news at that time. Meanwhile, carry on as normal throughout the weekend. Busy yourselves with organising your books, your sports activities and don't forget to visit the new Scout Troop Room, located in the former hackney stables.'

* * *

On Saturday evening, before Marshall and I embarked on our wonderful time, a group of us gathered round Calinescu's wireless, munching on pickled eggs and dried salami, to hear Chamberlain's return by air on the BBC.

Once again, Richard Dimbleby described the scene – the sound of the aeroplane, its doors opening, Chamberlain making his way through the crowds up to the microphones. 'And here is Mr Chamberlain.'

We stopped chewing to hear about our futures. 'My first duty now I have come back is to report to the British and French governments the result of my mission. And until I have done that it would be difficult for me to say anything about it.'

That was it? No more news till tomorrow? Going to the pictures seemed like a good idea.

* * *

Marshall and I met the ladies in the front hall in clean shirts, polished shoes, our hair washed and Brylcreemed, our nails scrubbed and trimmed. Marshall insisted on shaving what he called my peach fuzz, but I drew the line at his Imperial Leather aftershave.

They were waiting downstairs in their coats and holding little hats and handbags. Suddenly terrified, I commanded my knees not to shake as we descended the staircase. Marshall thought it would be fun to use the grand one and not the everyday, normal stairs.

Joy Brabyn, if a peach, was a small and shy one. I was taller than Miss BWF, but she must have weighed twice as much. Her hair undulated over her ears in waves not found in nature. Luckily the tram into Reading came soon.

'Ooh, I do like the pictures,' Beryl said, wriggling her bottom as she settled, like a chicken on a nest, into her cinema seat. 'Ooh, I am warm,' she said, breathing deeply and unbuttoning her coat. She spread it carefully behind her before resuming her broody pose. This must have been for my benefit, so I wouldn't miss her celebrated assets, which I was determined not to appreciate.

'You know, Graeme, people have often remarked that I look just like Mae West. Do you agree?'

'I'm not familiar with her. All I know is that she's not Scottish.'

'Of course not, silly. She's American! You should see her in *I'm No Angel*. Even I see the resemblance, if I do say so myself.'

* * *

We watched the Pathé news, now old, about Chamberlain's taking off on his second trip to Germany.

'Look at the aeroplane, look!' Marshall's voice shot out in a frenzy. 'It's a super-Lockheed 14 airliner. Last week it established a civil aviation record when it was flown from London to Stockholm and back in a day.'

'Shh!' A man in front turned round and glared.

But Marshall was unstoppable; so convinced of the value of his words he addressed the man directly, leaning forward in a chummy manner. 'This machine has a higher cruising speed than the liner in which Mr Chamberlain flew to Munich the first time.' The man, convinced of the lad's insanity, refused commenting; but *sotto voce*, Marshall called across to us in our seats. 'So they decided to use it for Mr Chamberlain's second trip. The pilots are the same, however.'

'Please stop,' said Beryl. 'Politics bores me.'

'This isn't politics,' Marshall came back at her. 'This is aviation science.'

'What's wrong with politics?' I asked.

'Bloody hell, shut it, would you?' someone else turned and shouted. 'Have some manners.'

'Have some yourself,' Beryl blared back. 'Using language like that!'

* * *

The film was the stupidest I'd ever seen. Unbelievable, when the fate of Europe was being decided, I was watching Ginger Rogers and Douglas Fairbanks Jr prance about like fools.

Safely back in our room, except for Marshall's hands shaking my neck. 'I could have killed you!' he said. 'Mae West, indeed.'

'I know,' I said. 'I do apologise. Now be a good fellow and let me go.' We readied for bed. 'I like your Miss Brabyn, however.'

'Oh good. She is a peach, isn't she?'

'I suppose so.'

We got into our beds. 'Don't you love the way her smile turns up on one side more than the other?'

I pulled back the covers, shaking my head. 'You've got it bad. You and that Joy Brabyn.'

He was about to put out the lamp on the table between our beds when he said, 'Don't worry, Graeme, you'll have a girlfriend one day.'

'Who cares about that? I only hope that tomorrow we'll find that they've patched things up in Germany.'

'Oh, you and that Germany.'

Chapter 37

At some point, as I lay waiting for my old pal, Sleep, to cart me off, I realised something extraordinary. Tomorrow was Sunday! The day the Captain ordered newspapers for the Senior Common Room, where the fourteen-and-ups could 'read about the day's triumphs and tragedies,' as he put it. I'd been waiting for the privilege for two years. And what a Sunday to begin when the fate of Europe hung in the balance. I barely slept after that.

At 8 a.m. I dressed as silently as I could, leaving Marshall to his dreams. Surely, the papers would have figured out why the talks had broken down.

The SCR had just opened and with a crook of a manly finger, beckoned me into the privileges of being fourteen-plus and allowed to breathe in the scent of bacon, sweet pastries and coffee.

Caspari was already seated in an armchair, his head in *The Times*. I went straight to him. 'Greetings,' I said in a church-like whisper. He jerked and looked up, frantic.

'Hitler has thrown the previous agreement out the window and handed Chamberlain a Memorandum with new demands. He swept his arm across a pile of newspapers on a nearby footstool. 'Even the journalists are flummoxed. I thought my English was good enough, but this defeats me.'

'Your English is perfect, but I'll try.'

He touched my arm. 'But I forget myself. Please get some breakfast first. You'll need it.' Good old Paul, always the gentleman.

Having fortified myself with five pieces of bacon, and three buttered teacakes slathered with marmalade, I eased into a winged armchair, as a pecking on my brain told me: this is what grown men do. They sit with their friends at their club reading the papers. I began with the *Manchester Guardian*:

THE LAST MEETING AT GODESBERG
A NIGHT OF DRAMA

THE HOTEL ON THE HILL

TENSE WATCHERS WAIT FOR PREMIER

From Our Special Correspondent

BAD GODESBERG, Saturday

The last hours at Bad Godesberg last night and early this morning were a thrilling experience for the band of journalists of all nations, who waited eagerly for news.

At 2 a.m. this morning a high official of the German Foreign Office entered the Press hotel and read the German communique to the journalists, who copied it down and then stormed the telephones. Most men had become so dizzy from thinking about the unknown for the past twelve hours that the full significance of the communique was not immediately apparent to all.

But what were Hitler's new demands?

'Well?' Caspari asked. 'Has the peace plan failed? Here, *The Times* has a later report. Try that. I'm too nervous to understand.' I gave the paper an eager shake and smoothed it onto my knees, as another boy, Cweitzer from Czechoslovakia, approached.

'Join us if you like. Moodie's going to explain what's happened. Is that all right, Graeme?'

'Of course.' I rather liked this. Graeme Moodie, political analyst, would reveal all.

But as I searched the pages, my swagger turned to a rising in my throat. Nothing about the Memorandum, but there was news of German military preparation, light anti-aircraft guns and the constant noise of aircraft engines cruising over the German capital.

As I read, I was dimly aware of murmurs, heels clicking, dishes clattering, chairs dragged. When I looked up there were about eight or so lads, standing or sitting a bit away from me. I had an audience.

'I hope you don't mind,' Caspari said. 'I told them you'd explain everything. You've done so much reading on the subject.' I regarded my listeners, much older than I. There was the swarthy, enormous Egyptian, Shahara; the blond Brabyn, Joy's brother; Ogier, known to be, but never called, a simpleton; Papamichael, another Greek who fled his country last year.

I got to my feet, still dizzy, and held the wing of the chair. 'I'm sorry, lads, but I still can't find the Memorandum. Suffice it to say, something has gone wrong. Mr Hitler has replaced his acceptance of the Anglo-French Plan, as agreed at the first visit, with a series of new demands set down in a Memorandum to the Czech people, which he has charged our prime minister to deliver. And until we know the contents of that Memorandum, I am in the dark as much as you. There's a hint from this journal, who says "Hitler's new demands illustrate the proverb, 'Der Deutsche …'"

'I know that saying very well,' Caspari interrupted with a bitter shake of the head. '"Der Deutsche wird immer teurer, nie billiger." The Germans grow dear and dearer, never cheaper." Chamberlain's plan has failed. Thank God.'

'Thank God?'

'Yes. War is the only answer.'

'Oh Paul.' I couldn't believe what I was hearing. 'Let's wait for a later edition. We'll know more then.'

'But I thought everything was all right,' whined Ogier.

'Nothing's all right with the Nazis,' Paul said. 'Hitler must be stopped *now*. We must fight together – the Czechs, France, the Soviets, Great Britain – before he kills us all. He's already started with the Jews. People like you will be next.' He pointed to my leg, 'The cripples, the feeble-minded.'

'Oh, come on!' I said.

* * *

Monday morning, I was desperate for my first private Latin class with the Captain; I needed him to reassure me that all would be well.

But when I came to the classroom where he sat behind an old desk, all he said was, 'Good to see you my boy, looking so well. Shall we begin? Pull up a chair.'

He looked the same, but shrunken, like a half-deflated balloon, gone wrinkly and soft.

'Before we start, I must say I was pleased with your Certificate results. Too bad about the Latin and French, but you made some careless mistakes.

Still, I look forward to preparing you.' He picked up two copies of a book and handed me one. 'And Moodie,' he said, 'We will use the hour only for Latin, nothing more.'

'Yes, sir.'

* * *

Only after lunch were the demands of Hitler's Memorandum made horribly clear. 'In four days,' *The Times* latest edition read, 'on the first of October, German troops will enter the Sudetenland and take over the country. If, by the 28th of September, the Czechs agree, the takeover will be peaceful. If not, the Germans will take the area by force. Also, Hitler demands that the lands ceded to Hungary and Poland after the Great War be returned.'

How could this be? Hitler couldn't just change his mind like that, like some petulant child. These were adult politicians, for God's sake, with advisors and journalists following every move. We count on them to solve problems. I could do better than that.

My nerves couldn't take any more. All I could think of doing was to sleep, and my legs led me to bed. I pulled the sheet up over my ear and sank into blessed oblivion.

* * *

Shattering bangs battered the door. Calinescu. 'Quick! Come! BBC make important announcement at six o'clock! In five minutes. Come!' And on he went to bang the next door.

Our group of ten, properly sitting in a semicircle round Calinescu's wireless, heard:

'Orders were issued this afternoon, calling up officers and men of the anti-aircraft unit of the territorial army and of the Coast Defence Units.' The calm, steady voice droned on, as if he were reading a rather long and boring weather report. 'The distribution of gas masks began tonight in all areas... Moreover, the Home Office is distributing a handbook of ARP advice for every house in the country, with information and illustrations about the choice of refuge rooms, precautions against fire, the operation of the air raid warning system, including even what to do during actual air raids.'

My face went hard; my chest pounded. Where would my parents' refuge room be? The cellar? Who would dig them out if they were bombed?

'The Archbishop of York has issued a call for prayer in which he asks clergy to appoint times in their churches when united prayer will be offered every day.'

We sat silent – for how long I didn't know.

'I guess we'll get our gas masks tomorrow,' said Marshall. 'Does someone deliver them?'

'I have no idea,' I said. 'Father told me that I'd have to return to Dundee if war broke out.'

'But what will happen to the German boys?' Caspari asked, his mind no longer on the need to destroy Hitler as soon as possible. 'Where will we go? Will the school close?'

* * *

Somehow, the day passed in a mechanical marching. If we kept doing what we did before, nothing would change.

But change it did. Just before ten, we gathered round Calinescu's wireless for yet another announcement, this time from the prime minister. His voice was in shreds but he laboured on. 'Tomorrow Parliament is going to meet. I shall be making a full statement as to the events which have led up to the present anxious and critical situation.

'How horrible, fantastic, incredible it is that we should be digging trenches and trying on gas masks here, because of a quarrel in a faraway country, between people of whom we know nothing.

'Herr Hitler told me privately, and last night he repeated publicly, that after this German-Sudeten question is settled, that is the end of Germany's territorial claims in Europe. After my first visit to Berchtesgaden, I did get the assent of the Czech government that the proposals that gave the substance of what Herr Hitler wanted, and I was taken completely by surprise, when I got back to Germany and found that he insisted that the territories should be handed over to him immediately, and immediately occupied by German troops, without previous arrangements for safeguarding the people within the territory, who were not German or who did not want to join the German Reich. I must say that I find this attitude unreasonable. I would not hesitate to pay even a third visit to Germany if I thought it would do any good, but I can say at this moment I see nothing further I can usefully do in the way of mediation.'

* * *

A few seconds of my breathing normally greeted the next day, the 28th of September, until dread and ruination swelled through my body, making me gasp and cover my head with my arms.

Throughout the day, we waited for news of Chamberlain's afternoon address to Parliament. Leaves fell, clouds passed, jaws moved, to eat, to talk of the sports day. No one dared shout or laugh or cry for fear of disturbing the breath that held itself.

After lunch, the Captain told us, 'As long as war has not begun, there is always hope that it may be prevented.' But the softness in his face was gone. A hard mask had replaced it, like in photographs I'd seen of men in the trenches, their leader setting an example for his troops, which were us.

* * *

Incredibly, Parliament was still in session at dinnertime. And still, no news.

As if we each had keys in our backs to guide our bodies because our minds were numb, we got ready for bed. Removing my splint was no longer burdensome. Legs out of trousers, put on nightshirt, splash water on face, pat dry with towel. I picked up my toothbrush but then thought: Why brush my teeth when I might get bombed?

The clever people had not managed it.

Again, a stunning barrage of banging slammed on the door. *Again*, Calinescu! 'Everyone, come to my room! Chamberlain's flying to Germany one more time!' He moved on down the hall, banging his message upon each door. *Again*, we gathered round the wireless.

'In a dramatic statement to the House of Commons, Mr Chamberlain announced that he was to fly to Munich tomorrow where he will meet Herr Hitler, M. Daladier and Signor Mussolini. The German Government, in reply to representations from Great Britain and Italy, has postponed for twenty-four hours the decision to mobilise the army. Relief is felt in Paris and Rome at the calling of the Four-Power Conference. In Rome it is thought that the crisis has entered a new phase.'

'What's going on here?' Dimitriou, the NCO on our floor came in.

'Listen, listen!' we all said, nearly at once. 'Chamberlain's flying to Germany!'

'I've heard,' he said. 'It's promising, but the Captain has given orders for everyone to go to bed as usual. That means lights out at 10:30 – that's in ten minutes, lads. And he's in no mood for disobedience.'

* * *

Somehow, we got through the following day, the keys in our backs slowly running down.

* * *

The 30th September was bright, with the first chill in the air; and from our window, I saw a haze of frost over the grass terrace beyond the stone lions.

Marshall and I took our time dressing, afraid to go downstairs and hear what had happened. He sighed. 'Maybe it will be good news.'

'Shall we find out?'

'Maybe.'

'Not knowing is worse. I'm going down.'

He followed and, as we went through the hall, toward the dining room, there was a murmuring, then odd shouts, then a rolling sea of voices becoming wild hurrahs and applause. Boys hugged and danced, I felt my face opening – my mouth, eyes, ears, then every part of me as I read *The Times*'s enormous headline:

'AGREEMENT REACHED AT MUNICH TO-DAY
PLAN FOR TRANSFER OF TERRITORIES
LONG SESSIONS END AFTER MIDNIGHT

The Captain's speech after lunch, seemed infused with holy light. If ever I'd believed in the bearded eejit, Alastair's name for God, it was now.

'It would be easier for me, my boys, my men, if I were addressing members of the British Legion, those not-so-hardened veterans who would have been able to realise the significance of this moment. They would have been able to picture what another war would mean to everyone living on this earth. They had experienced the slaughter of the Great War in all its evil glory; saw the blood flow from so many dear and innocent bodies.

'Nowadays, it is the general and cynical belief that miracles do not happen, but we must realise that a miracle *has* happened. Only God could have drawn us from the abyss. He and only He could have brought us back to our senses. Yes, a great miracle has happened: Something – I know not what – changed the minds of those men in Munich as they prepared to wage another apocalypse.

'And to help you realise it – to have it sink into your souls and forever be glad – I will create a little miracle myself; that is, to give you the rest of the day off. No classes, just general rejoicing. A holiday, indeed, to mark the word in its original meaning – for this is indeed a holy day.

'I urge you to gather round your wirelesses when Mr Chamberlain's plane returns this evening. About five. Then we will celebrate tonight at dinner with a rather hastily assembled, but no less celebratory, feast.'

* * *

Richard Dimbleby's voice shook as he introduced the prime minister to the waiting crowd and to the many millions gathered around their wirelesses. 'This morning I had another talk with the German Chancellor Herr Hitler, and here is the paper which bears his name on it as well as mine. Some of you will have already heard as to what it contains. But I would just like to read it to you:

"We, the German Führer and Chancellor and the British Prime Minister have had another meeting today and are agreed in recognising that the question of Anglo-German relations is of the first import for the two countries and for Europe. We concur that the agreement signed last night is symbolic of the desire of our two peoples never to go to war with one another again."'

When the huge cheers stopped, he continued. '"We are resolved that the method of consultation shall be the method adopted to deal with any other questions that may concern our two countries and we are determined to remove other sources of difference and thus to contribute to ensure the peace of Europe."'

I'd been a witness to humanity at its best.

Chapter 38

A new boy from Germany sat at my table, with a sweet lost expression and wide sad eyes. We were all just back from Christmas holidays and Caspari sat beside him, helping him. 'Meet David Kirk, from Monchengladbach. He's just changed his name from Heinz Kirchheimer. His family is leaving Germany permanently so he's been given a name that's easier to pronounce.'

People smiled as Kirk turned his head back and forth, happy, flushed and confused. Paul went on: 'David, you see, is his middle name, and because it's the same in both languages, it won't seem quite so strange to him.'

'Kirk,' I said. 'That's a Scottish word. It means "church."'

'And "Kirche" is "church" in German. Extraordinary!' Paul was delighted and did his best to explain to Kirk, in a mixture of English and German, our astonishment.

'What does the other bit mean?' I asked, 'the Heim?'

'Heimer?' Paul said. 'Means someone who comes from a town. A 'heim' is a town. So Kircheheimer is a man from a town where there's a church. I guess the full translation would be "churchtown."'

'Like Churchill!'

'Perhaps. Many of these European names were invented for the Jews when they came from Judea. And now, they're getting new names a second time.' We turned back to Kirk, who had somehow been forgotten in our foray into the origins of names.

After lunch, Caspari and I stood by the back staircase. 'Well, so long,' I said, and as I turned, Caspari touched my arm. 'You should know, Graeme, David Kirk had a direct experience of Kristallnacht in Monchengladbach. Lucky for him, an aunt in London sent money for him to come. He's had a terrible time.'

'Poor devil. He did look a little shellshocked.'

'He's not a devil.'

'Of course not. Sorry. It's just an expression.'

'I know that, as well.' He breathed out heavily. 'I'm sorry, too. Let's not argue. Off you go.'

I'd heard about Kristallnacht, this horror that happened a week after the Munich Agreement. A young Jewish Pole, distraught by the homeless state of his parents in Poland, strode into the German Embassy in Paris and shot the first man he saw, a minor official at a desk. Days later the man died; and it was like someone had dropped a lit match onto kerosene. Drunken thugs broke into Jewish homes, stealing, wrecking, attacking. They torched synagogues and ran through streets, smashing Jewish shop windows. Broken glass was everywhere – hence 'Kristallnacht', the night of broken glass. The words made me think of cold, starry nights, something lovely.

'Only the Nazis could come up with something so malevolent,' Paul said with a bitter smile. 'For them, it's a play on words, a joke.'

Still, I didn't want to believe it was as bad as Paul claimed. As Ponsonby said, newspapers exaggerated stories. Maybe that was the case here.

In a few days we heard nothing more of Kristallnacht. The Captain had stressed that I should let nothing distract from revising French and Latin, in preparation for the School Certificate exams in mid-December.

* * *

I was still in Dundee in early January, when *The Times* printed the results: GC Moodie, distinction in both. I'd found them surprisingly easy. Amazing what happens when one applies oneself.

* * *

I still shared a room with old Marsh, who had spent the Christmas break with his mother in Paris, but on returning, found the fair Joy Brabyn had jilted him. Over the holidays she hooked the impossibly handsome Nicky Littman – a champion tennis player and an alluring singer-guitarist, known to invite young ladies to the cabin on the island in fine or foul weather.

I thought he'd be a wreck and I'd have to comfort him and build him up again, but he soon recovered. 'Never mind. It never amounted to much, anyway. She was too old for me, really. I'm still only fourteen. Life goes on.' His display of wisdom impressed me. If a girl had decided she liked someone better than me, even if it had been Clark Gable, I would have been heartbroken for weeks, months, years; no, probably not years – months, certainly.

Already, the walls above his bed were stripped of Joy Brabyn photos, and bore pictures of new designs for fighter planes. He'd received a splendid new bicycle for Christmas, so he could ride out to Woodley Airfield four miles away where it was rumoured new aeroplanes were tested. Marshall's plan was nothing less than designing planes himself. 'I know I shouldn't, Moods, but I'm hoping there will be war, but not just yet. I want to make the best bombers in the world.'

* * *

Inside my pigeonhole mailbox was a thick, small envelope – expensive quality, I knew. Sure enough, there was a folded card, the outside bearing a gold embossed square reading BF in letters so fancy it took a while to decipher. An invitation. Could it be?

Please join me for tea on Friday, 20 January at 4.00.

There was a smaller envelope with card inside:

R.S.V.P Miss Beryl Fox
Name:................
I will..........be able to attend
I will not..........be able to attend.

I had arrived.

* * *

On the assigned date and time, there I was, freshly bathed and clothed in a new Harris tweed jacket, hair combed and Brylcreemed, tapping her door, which was slightly ajar.

'Come in,' a thin song of a voice called, making me think of spiders and parlours. I pushed the door, closing it behind me. It was like being in a woman's bedroom, not that I'd had much experience in that department. Everything was pink and green; fat, flowered cushions plopped on chintz sofas, slipcovers slipping lazily. Against a wall stood a table with widely curved legs and a pink marble top adorned with a bowl of faded silk flowers. The ceiling was high, as they all were, its ornate surface like the top of a frosted cake. 'Hello?'

From another room sashayed Miss BWF, cheeks aglow and wearing a black knitted cardigan, whose every button was done up, making the jumper stretch dangerously between each one to reveal a flash of bright white linen. 'Have a seat.' Her hand swept across a sofa with a ruffly skirt.

I'd never been in such a place, so full of flounce, with a non-Scottish hussy. As I walked by her, I noticed a scent from the cinema. How could I have forgotten its cloying strands? I moved through it in a breaststroke to the sofa, losing my dignity and collapsing into its low and saggy depths.

Bam-bam-bam came a knock and in walked that new fellow, David Kirk. I struggled to stand as he strode to Miss Fox, bumbling and jerky, but with his friendly enthusiasm. I could see he was nervous, though.

'Hello,' he said, 'I hope I'm not late.'

When I shook Kirk's hand, I was surprised how much taller I was. He must have been shorter than Marshall whom I knew to be five foot five inches, but there was no mistaking the manliness. He shaved clearly, he was strongly and neatly built, and he had a pleasing shyness and energy.

'I bring a book,' Kirk said, holding up a thin volume. 'My English is not good, I know, and my aunt in London give me this to help with my English. Poetry is a good way to learn, she say.'

'Oh, yes, I love poetry!' Beryl said, though I doubted this was the case.

She sat on the sofa and patted next to her. 'Now you sit here, next to me.' He did, and I, quite forgotten, sat in the chair at right angles and watched. She took the book from him. 'AE Housman. I love him.' I couldn't imagine Miss Fox reading poetry, but I was continually learning just how strange the world was. 'Could you read one to me? How about this one: "When I was One-and-Twenty?"'

Kirk looked terrified. 'Please, you first.'

'Oh very well, then you must try.' She showily recited the poem.

When I was one-and-twenty
I heard a wise man say,
"Give crowns and pounds and guineas
But not your heart away;
Give pearls away and rubies
But keep your fancy free."
But I was one-and-twenty,
No use to talk to me.

When I was one-and-twenty
I heard him say again,
"The heart out of the bosom
Was never given in vain;
'Tis paid with sighs a plenty
And sold for endless rue."
And I am two-and-twenty,
And oh 'tis true, 'tis true

When the B-word, 'bosom' popped out, I looked for a hole in the floor, but, finding none, stared across the room and stifled a laugh. I thought about how sad it was that Uncle Sandy died.

'Guess how old I am?' She cocked her head and drew back, delivering a simpering smile.

'Eh?' Poor Kirk was confused, but I wasn't. Having been to the cinema with Miss B, I knew she had a knack for turning any subject to herself.

'I… I do not know.'

'Well, guess!'

Poor sod. I wondered what each would say. I had it on good authority from Caspari (who was never wrong about numbers) that she was twenty-seven.

'Seventeen?' he gasped feebly. At least he had the good sense to guess low.

'No, silly! I have been told I look like a young girl, but in fact I am the same age as the person in the poem. I am two-and-twenty. Now, you read it. I'll help.'

They cuddled while he laboured over words, and she gave him lessons in what to do with his lips. 'Watch mine.' Would they notice if I ran away?

Beryl poured tea. We pretended to be adults, as we sipped and used our dainty little napkins too often. I thanked Mother for her lessons in good manners as Kirk watched me closely, attempting to copy the old British rituals.

'How long have you been in England?' Beryl asked, setting down her cup and lounging backward into the sofa.

'In England, one month.'

I piped in, 'I'm so glad you are here, Kirk. You have come to a place of refuge. The Captain welcomes people from all over the world. You have an aunt in London?'

'Yes. In London, I am lucky to say.'

'Well,' said Beryl, piping back. 'I think it was brilliant of your aunt to suggest *A Shropshire Lad*. You must come and read me some more and I can give you more English lessons.'

'That would be very kind.'

Somehow I tumbled out of there, that place of hilarity, something to laugh at later, when I was two-and-twenty and not the bumbling idiot I knew myself to be.

* * *

At breakfast next morning, David Kirk sat across from Caspari and me, looking worried. He muttered in German but was reproached by Paul's lifted finger. 'English, only, my friend. English only. Right Moodie?'

'It's the only way,' I said, shrugging and giving him, I hoped, a sympathetic smile. 'But yours is better than you think.'

'Quite right. You're far more fluent than I was.' Paul laughed. 'I couldn't speak a single word. Now I have no accent at all.' I let that pass. 'So, shall we begin again?'

Kirk gazed at the ceiling in a sweat. 'I am afraid I left my book of poetry in the room of Miss Fox. I must get it back because it is the book of my aunt.'

'Hmm…' I said, 'Let me think. Ah, I have it! Write her a note and leave it in her mailbox. You know, where we get our letters?'

Kirk nodded. 'I am receiving invitation from her there.'

'Right. Well, ask her to put it in your mailbox. It's a small book and should fit. If not, make other arrangements to collect it.'

'Would you help me to write it?'

'Of course.'

He had brought a notebook and pen and after several misfires – writing to Miss BWF was trickier than I thought – it was done.

'Thank you, my friends. Now I take back and copy onto good paper.'

* * *

Ah, Sunday morning breakfast in the Senior Common Room. And after that, another pleasure – Mr Mellor was taking our small seminar group to the National Gallery.

I joined Caspari, who sat alone, reading *The Times*. Politely, he folded it and gestured elegantly to the chair opposite him. Between us was a lovely rack of toast and a plate piled with scones and little pots of butter and marmalade, all of which I fell upon.

We were munching, when up came Boch, making the air nervous and skitterish. He and Caspari usually avoided each other. May I sit down?'

'You can,' I said politely.

Caspari picked up his newspaper and flicked it open, hiding his face.

'So,' Boch asked, helping himself to toast, 'what do you have planned for today? I'm thinking of going to the pictures.'

Caspari peered over his newspaper. 'All that's playing is *Snow White and the Seven Dwarves*.'

Boch ignored him. 'Moodie, would you like to join me? It's an old tale from the Brothers Grimm. It's called *Sneewittchen*, in German.'

'I'm sure the Disney version has ruined it,' Caspari came back immediately.

'I'm not asking you,' Boch said, not looking at him. 'And don't be such a *hochmutigemann*.'

'We don't speak German here,' said Caspari. 'So I will not reply. Too bad you don't know the English word for a conceited fellow, since it describes you so perfectly.'

'Men! My friends!' Standing by our little circle was Kirk, eyes wide with joy or horror, I couldn't tell.

'Sit down, sit down,' Caspari said.

Kirk flopped into a chair, almost missing it, and grabbed his hair with both hands, then smacked them onto his cheeks, clearly beside himself.

He found more words, 'Gentlemen. I have had a remarkable adventure.'

'Well, well, take it easy there, fellow. Calm down and tell us, for goodness' sake.'

Kirk took a huge breath while we waited, the three of us agog, united for once.

'I went to get my book. From Miss Fox. She had left a note for me, in my mailbox, saying to come before breakfast. So I go. I stand outside her door – which is open a little, this much,' he made a space of about three inches with his thumb and index finger. 'I give a little knock. No answer, I knock again, this time harder, and the door moves a bit more open. Like,' and his fingers measure something more like four or five inches.

'"Is that Mr Kirk?" I hear her say. "Yes, Miss Fox, it's David Kirk." "Don't come in," she says. "I am getting dressed. I will give you your book in a minute."

'I wait. I stand at the door; the door is open a crack.' Boch, Caspari and I stare at his fingers. 'I can see on the wall just inside the door, a mirror, a big one. And in the mirror I see Miss Fox.'

Kirk looked around and lowered his voice. We moved in closer. 'She's not wearing the clothes. She is there with her... with her *brust*.' His arms made a shape on his chest of what needed no translation.

Caspari nodded. 'Go on. And then?'

'I jump back, but I can see her – looking in mirror! She holds out her – uh – white...' His hands moved wildly, 'her *bustenhalter*...'

'Brassiere.' Caspari, diligent translator, muttered.

This was too much. Two b-words in a row shot blood into my face in a torrent. 'She bend over. The *brust* hanging like *puddingform*.

'Pudding basins,' Caspari whispered.

'Oh God,' I said.

'Shh, shh,' Caspari said, his face as red as mine. But I flushed again, just contemplating the noble Caspari knowing about breasts, like pudding basins, slowly lowered into a brassiere.

'She does the hooking so I see her back. She walk away. I stay there, afraid to move. I am waiting for my AE Housman. I am waiting forever, but she opens the door and hands me the book. I am lying against the wall, fainting.'

'She smiles and says, "Sorry to keep you waiting." So calm she is. Like this happen every day. I walk away. I hear her close door.

'Gentlemen. I never see this. Ever. In my life. You understand I have no sisters. And for me – yes. A remarkable adventure.'

'Ah, there you are, Moodie.' Stunned beyond words, I looked up at Mr Mellor. 'Time to go now. The car is waiting outside. All set? Cheerio lads. Glad we've got a fine day.'

* * *

I returned about eight-thirty that night, doubtful that I could describe any of the paintings on display. Instead, I had only visions of pudding basins. I checked my mailbox by the stairs and found a note from Paul Caspari: Urgent. Come at once.

'A catastrophe has occurred,' he announced as I came into his room. He had been lying on his bed, clothed, but scrambled to his feet the moment he saw me, his face pale, his jaw hanging open.

'Tell me, for God's sake!'

He sat back down on the bed, and I joined him. 'You cannot believe it. I cannot believe it, though I saw the note.'

'What note?'

'Boch's.'

'Tell me!'

'Well, listen then! I'm sorry, Moodie, but it's so very awful. After you left I said to Kirk – in German, to be absolutely clear he understood me – to say no more about Miss Fox to anyone. He's a clever fellow and understood that this story must not get about.'

'Of course. The Captain…'

'… must never know. Anyway, as I'm speaking to him, I see Boch writing on a bit of paper. He folds it and passes it to Kirk, like it was a laundry note, and walks calmly out the door.' Caspari covered his face with those elegant, long-fingered hands.

'What did it say?'

'Kirk looks at me as if he'd seen the devil himself, which I guess he had. "There are Nazis at this school?" he asks me in German, before handing me the paper. What I read was this – written in German: "Jewish swine. One more word about Aryan women and you will be dead."

'Kirk is in a panic, breathing so fast, he cannot speak. I tell him, "This is terrible, but we will do something!" But there are others there, eating their Sunday breakfasts so I have to whisper. But he runs from the room, just like that!'

'Did you find him?'

'No! I had to bike to Slough for my job this morning, so I couldn't track Kirk down. It never occurred to me that he'd actually leave the school!'

'At tea, the Captain asked to see me. I went to his office, where he told me, not too bothered, that Kirk had gone to London to visit his aunt. She'd taken ill suddenly. "Kirk had to leave in a hurry," the Captain said, "and only left a note. Did he say anything to you?"

'Graeme, I lied to him. I just said, "No."'

A week later, the Captain called Caspari and me into his office to tell us that Kirk's aunt in London had written to say that Kirk was not returning to Maiden Erlegh. 'I must say I am surprised. He was fitting in nicely. Did either of you see anything that may have made him change his mind?'

We lied. Both Caspari and I had been silenced, gagged.

Chapter 39

Over the next days I plotted how to annihilate the monster, Boch. I must have had a hundred imaginary conversations with the Captain, but each time was stopped by the horror of what Beryl had done, a story that travelled into filthy and forbidden territory.

Suppose I only broached Boch's murderous note to Kirk, what then? The bloody Nazi would say he was merely defending Beryl's honour against the slanderous imaginings of a Jew. Would he say 'Jew'? Probably not. He was too wily.

What if, deep in his heart of hearts, the Captain knew the story was true? Had this happened before? Oh, probably. Anything was possible these days. What then? Could the story get out in the open? Captain Fox would die of it, surely. The school would close, or maybe it would stay open and Mr Mellor would take over.

Who was the greater monster, Boch or Beryl? Did it matter when the outcome was the same? Kirk was gone, a sweet, innocent fellow, who came to Maiden Erlegh full of hope after Kristallnacht, only to find himself forced out by another Nazi. And I, knowing the facts, sat mildly by, a witness to two evils, one after the other, hideously entwined. I had to do something.

* * *

'Hello, Moodie,' the Captain looked up kindly from his desk. 'How good to see you. Have a seat, do.'

I sat in the chair opposite. He looked so content, so sure of himself, as he leaned back and lit a cigarette. 'You first.' He waited. I waited. I hated to ruin his happiness, but how could I not? The pendulum swung loudly in the grandfather clock. He cocked his head sideways and raised his brows. 'Well?'

'It's about Boch.'

A perceptible dimming. 'And?'

'He insulted the new boy, David Kirk, and that's why the poor fellow left. He was afraid.'

'What did he say, do you know?'

I faffed about, a mistake. 'Oh, something about calling Kirk a Jew.'

'Were you there?'

'No. But Boch should be expelled.'

To my astonishment, the Captain looked out the window and said, 'Possibly. But Graeme, trust me here. I have met his father. I hope never to see him again. Boch needs to know someone cares about him. I could be the only one.'

'But sir, I'm also certain he was the one who stole my camera. He passed the bag it was in to Finzi, saying it was rubbish and would he put it in the bin.'

The Captain must not have heard me for he said, as if repeating a creed: 'My goal, dear Moodie, is to save young men from a cruel, predetermined future. It's relentless love that works, not punishment. A fierce and sturdy love that says: "Over my dead body will I let you go."

'So that is why I will not expel Boch. He was a sweet, kind boy when he came here in 1934. It is my fervent belief that he is still there.'

* * *

Luckily or not, a distraction came: I finally got my hands on the book making its way secretly around the senior boys – *Lady Chatterley's Lover*, a volume much soiled and greasy, opening easily to the smutty parts. I knew the gist. A woman has a wild affair with her gardener, and they meet in a little shed where they name his willy John Thomas.

What I didn't know, or had forgotten, was that her husband, whom she hates and is revolted by, is paralysed.

True, he was paralysed in both legs, but that hardly mattered. Any woman, when she saw my white worm of a right leg – if I ever got that far – would be disgusted.

I could hardly bear the pain of reading it. I was like Clifford! Perhaps at first, I could attract a girl with my mental excitement, as Connie, Lady Chatterley, called it, but the physical aversion would make anything under the covers impossible. I closed the book.

I'd been fooling myself that I was as good as anyone else, that my brains and winning personality would make people forget that one-quarter of me didn't work, that Marvellous Me was making a comeback. I sat up from my bed and did the only thing that made any sense, that had helped me out at Morland Hall. From the bookcase near my bed, I grabbed *Hulton's Adventure Stories, The Best Annual for Boys*, whose cover bore a man frantically swimming from a huge, open-mouthed shark.

* * *

Sometimes in my life I believed that someone was looking after me. Not the bearded eejit, for I only believed in planets and stars and molecules, but it was so, so strange: Marshall appeared – just at that moment. Wordless, he sat on his bed, and seeing me reading the *Hulton* while *Lady C* lay on the little table between us, he said, 'How are you getting on with *Lady Chatterley*? You are taking a long time. Aren't you enjoying it?'

'No. Not really. It's rather got me worried, in fact.'

'In what way? Do tell.'

'That I'm like Clifford, that's Lady Chatterley's husband. He's paralysed from the waist down.'

'Don't give away the plot!'

'I'm not. It happens right in the beginning. Almost, anyway.'

'Very well. So?'

'I'll be like him, for God's sake. Can't you see? You know, not able to – do it.'

'You can! I hear you – frequently! And you seem to enjoy it. As do I, I must say,' he said, giving a quick, ecstatic glance toward the ceiling.

'Not the same thing! Would I be able to, you know, do it, the – act? With, you know, a woman.'

'Oh for heaven's sake. Of course you will. Don't be silly.' He came and sat beside me.

'But my leg will put her off. Without the splint, I have to lift it everywhere. And I can't wear it when…' I let out a wail. 'Oh Marshall, I didn't know there'd be a paralysed man in it!'

'Moodie, look at me.'

Marshall put a gentle hand on my shoulder. 'You worry too much. You'll find a way when the time comes. Let's face it. We're both fourteen. Lots could happen before we find ourselves ready to bonk. You'll find a solution. Perseverance is the key to success. That's what the Captain says. Although I doubt he had bonking in mind.'

* * *

I proceeded with *Lady C*, and as spring arrived in the novel, its miraculous awakenings coincided with Maiden Erlegh's. I saw what it saw. Mists of blackthorn, swelling buds on trees greening. Now on safer ground, I read on – about flowers pushing through winter's snow, followed by trillium, aconite and bluebells surrounding their hut, where everything unknown and wonderful happened. Lovemaking became part of that – as something kind and tender, wild and delicious, and as natural as their view from the hut window. I loved this book, keeping faith, thanks to Marshall, in a future I could not see.

But – fly in ointment: it all made me think of Woodbine Cottage and its mysterious woodland I'd not seen in a year. Great knocking pangs swept across my belly, the feeling I knew was homesickness.

For perhaps the fiftieth time, and a year later, I began again.

Dear Mrs. Grumbar,

So much time has passed that I wonder if you even remember me, though I know you do, for I was the silly fool who made such a stupid joke in your home (that I miss greatly). I have not written, not because you have not been on my mind. On the contrary, I think of you often, and of how badly I returned your many kindnesses to me.

I am writing because I remember your kindness, and though I do not expect you to forgive or forget, I wanted you to know that I may be a very stupid fellow, but I am not, I dare to hope, cruel. In my family we play tricks on one another as a way of showing that we like each other, because we could never find the words to say things like that. Nevertheless, I will say that I treasure my times at Woodbine Cottage. I would be grateful if you would allow me to visit you, apologise in person and I hope, let bygones be bygones.

Yours truly,

Graeme C. Moodie

She's probably forgotten that I existed. Or she'd think: vile, stupid child. Makes a joke about my housekeeping when they said it had killed my son? One never recovers from something like that. Never.

I put it in the envelope.

I was out of stamps and I knew I had to march to Culham's right away, put the bloody 1p stamp on it and post it there, or the letter would end in the bin again. I'd catch the shop just before it closed and make the 6 p.m. pickup, the last one of the day.

Though it was no longer dark at quarter to five, the road was dark enough and I wished I'd brought my torch.

Every time the door opened at Culham's a bell shook. I knew about it, but this time I jumped when I heard its brittle chirp.

The shop was empty, lit by a metal cone hanging from the ceiling. 'Hello?' I called.

'Hold your horses. I'll be there in a tick,' a voice called from the storeroom behind the counter.

'Stamps, is it? What kind would you…' My mouth dropped. We stared at one another. Her.

'You,' Mary Petty said.

I blinked. 'Where's Mrs Culham?'

'I haven't done her in if that's what you mean. She's not here. I work here Tuesdays and Thursday afternoons. Started last week. How many do you want?'

'Oh. Ten. You're on your own here?'

'Why do you ask? You planning on robbing the shop?'

'No. I only meant…' I looked down, unable to take her on.

'Mrs Culham trusts me, though obviously you don't. How many did you say?' I'd never spoken to anyone so rude, but I would not let her win.

'Ten. First class letter, please,' I said, politely.

'Of course, sir.' She opened a drawer under the counter, took the dried blood-coloured strips, now featuring the new king in profile. I watched her hands, much cleaner, but still freckled. 'You want me to post that letter?'

'Oh, ah, no. Not now. I just remembered I need to change something.' She mustn't see my letter was for Mrs Grumbar.

'Suit yourself.'

'I will.'

I found myself outside, panting, and began the dark walk back to school, cursing myself for forgetting the Chocolate Crisp I'd intended to buy.

When I got back into the school's warm hall, I swiped the stamp with the tip of my tongue, banged my fist to make it stick, tossed it into the basket that sat on the oak chest near the door and scuttled it around so it wouldn't lie exposed. At least, there being so many letters in the basket meant I'd made the last post.

* * *

I could have imagined more pleasant ways to spend a Saturday afternoon – a visit from Mr Fairbank or Mother explaining every shot of her golf game – but here I was, sitting high in the stands, in a leaky mackintosh and hood that made me look like a medieval archer. My mission? To cover a rugby game between us and the Old Redingensians.

Dimitriou, august editor of the famed *ME Chronicle*, asked me to take snapshots of the game, but then Caspari, who was supposed to write it up, got ill, so I was doing both tasks. In the current deluge, my camera daren't see the light of day, but nothing, nothing stopped a rugby game. The muddier the better.

I knew the rules, having once imagined a future in rugby. I still enjoyed watching, but this was excruciating. Not only was it freezing and pouring with rain, but sitting three benches ahead of me were Mrs Grumbar and the barely mentionable Mary Petty. Mrs G had never even bothered to answer my letter. The one I'd dashed down in a fit of true repentance. That was three weeks ago.

Naturally, Mr Grumbar was there; he was the rugby coach, but not those two. I could only hope that in my current get-up, I'd be unrecognisable. I watched him pace in his old, knotty jumper, rubbing his hands and stamping his feet. Even he was cold.

The men took their places. I knew the names of all fifteen; my old pal Finzi was the star. Dimitriou had said a scout from London would be there, but in this weather, he might have given it a miss. I would have.

What's this? Could that be Boch taking position next to Finzi, scurrying on the line like a nervous rat? The Captain's doing, no doubt, in another effort to save him.

The referee flipped the coin, and I began writing manically. At first, the other team was outclassing us, but just before half time, Finzi got the ball and ran half the length of the field, and scored with a yodel. Kick succeeded. 5-0. Wonderful!

What a star! I hoped the scout was there, taking note. I stood – creakily – and looked down at the bench rows for a likely, scout-type candidate, maybe with a clipboard like me. Finzi shone through the mud-soaked field as everyone – except him – was slipping and sliding all over, Boch especially.

As we waited for half time to be over, Mary Petty turned and we locked eyes. She knew it was me, the way she froze dead and jerked her head back around. I picked up my clipboard and studied it with every fibre of my being.

In the second half, the score was equal until, right in the last seconds, Finzi scored the winning goal!

A frenzy of mad cheers erupted as Finzi, wet and muddy, was lifted high and bounced on the shoulders of his teammates. Good for him! I was looking forward to congratulating him. Standing, I swiped away the rivers that flooded the trenches of my mack. I collected my camera, still in its leather case because of the rain. My notepaper was sodden and beginning to tear.

'Graeme,' I heard a dull voice say. Mary's. I ignored it. 'Is that you?' Louder and sharper.

I turned, all scowly and harassed at the interruption. 'Oh, Mary Petty. Oh. Is that you?'

'Yes, but I've changed my name to Grumbar.'

'Oh,' I muttered as if I couldn't care less.

'My mother wants to know if you want to join us... at the house... for tea.'

'Oh.' I gave a pitying smile. 'I'm reporting on the game. For our newspaper.' I tapped the clipboard held close to my chest. 'Due tomorrow. Sorry.' I swung my camera strap over my neck.

'Fine, I'll tell her... but wasn't... didn't you think... Peter was wonderful?' The switch in tone – from a humdrum dislike of me to a welling, crushing, rearing-up of love – hit my chest, pushing me backward so that I grabbed the bench.

'You mean Finzi? Oh yes. Smashing. A scout might be here, you know, looking for promising talent.'

The old voice returned. 'I know that,' she said scornfully, as if she knew everything about him. 'From London.'

* * *

I got to my room as quickly as I could, writing the article before my sodden notes turned to mush.

Now, Moodie, just because you can't have something doesn't mean you can't be happy for others who get it. Good for them. But you never should have written that letter to Mrs Grumbar. Why didn't you just leave it, instead of reminding her what a twit you were, expecting to be invited into that cosy place, trees all around, its lovely brick, the homemade brown bread – the everything?

Chapter 40

Mr Mellor's verse play of Cinderella – himself in the title role – had just finished and we leapt to our feet for the standing ovation that always marked the *grand finale* of the term's entertainment – the Staff Play.

Eight of these extravaganzas I'd witnessed since I first shyly sat in 1936, planning never to return. A bit prim and sheltered, I'd been shocked by the wild conglomeration of teachers, cooks and cleaners, joining in a play where women played men and men played women.

By 1939, I adored it. There was Miss Taylor as the prince, in gorgeous green tights and a furry moustache that kept falling off so she handed it to Cinderella (Mr Mellor with fire-engine lips and yellow wig). And when he couldn't make the moustache stick, he stuffed it in his already-stuffed bosom! The crowning glory, however, was Mr Piper as the Fairy Godmother, doing his best to fly about in lavender tulle waving a silver wand. We laughed till our limbs were without bone or muscle.

When all was over, Mr Mellor came forward, stripping off his wig, and thanked the necessary people – Mrs Waterlow Fox for taking so much trouble to provide the magnificent banquet, Jake the joiner for erecting the stage and Tom the chauffeur for providing its excellent lighting effects.

All that was left was the Captain's farewell speech.

How much older, more appreciative, I felt; part of me not quite in it, but observing it like an old codger, looking backward: how I came to be there – the small chance, seven years ago, that put me in the sea that day to catch polio – and how it happened that the Great War had wounded Captain Fox's soul so profoundly that he would never prepare boys for war again, but rather, resolved to create a school that excluded no one.

Now one of the tall lads, I sat in the back, scanning the familiar crowd. My eyes fell on Mrs Grumbar as she stood and stretched. I glanced to the floor. Some heartache I didn't understand pushed into my chest. No no no no. Ignore. Ignore. She never even wrote me back, when I'd had courage to apologise. Too bad for her. Too late now. Since that dire rugby game, I'd scarcely thought of the whole stupid lot of them. The world of the mind was where I belonged. I'd done well. Next term I'd be in an advanced seminar called 'Is Peace Possible?'

A hand parted the red velvet curtain and then the rest of Captain Fox emerged, but his face was troubled. We got quieter. He put his arms up high and we got quieter still. Something was wrong.

'I have an announcement to make, my friends. We in our great country have weathered many storms in my long life, but none have troubled me more than the one confronting us.' A terrible silence pressed on us.

'We cannot ignore the madness that is taking over the entire world. Even His Majesty has become involved, and indeed his wife.'

Perhaps he saw the open jaws, eyes stretched wide with fear, because he rocked ever so slightly on his heels – the sure sign a joke was coming. Reaching his hands round to rub his bottom clinched it. 'I am speaking, of course, of the terrible menace of The Lambeth Walk.' Happy moans and groans ensued.

The curtain parted again – this time for Miss Beryl Fox, her bosom protruding like an overhanging cliff. 'That's enough, Father, dear,' she said, giving him a hefty push. 'Step aside. Let the younger generation take over.'

'Gladly.' He exited. I shook my head. Amazing. He, who saw so much in us, saw so little in his daughter.

'Many of you may know what my father is so afraid of, but he has nothing to fear. Everyone's doing The Lambeth Walk! And for those poor souls who have quitted planet Earth for the past several months, I'll demonstrate. But first, let's clear the room! Could you pick up your chairs and line them against the wall? Everyone can do The Lambeth Walk.'

Well, hoo-hah and hooray.

It was true – one couldn't escape the bloody thing. I'd heard it on the wireless, even seen the King and Queen doing it on the Pathé News. The Lambeth Walk had its evil birth in a film, *Me and My Girl*, about a cockney lad who makes a pile of money, but never forgot his roots, which unfortunately included The Lambeth Walk – a so-called dance that mimicked how cockneys walked in Lambeth, strutting along, elbows lifted. That was it, except for the climax – smacking one's bottom, then one's knees and shouting, 'Oi!'

I tried it in my room, thinking, if it's so easy – maybe, just maybe – I could. Disaster. I could never manage the jaunty steps, the quick turns. It was a stupid dance, anyway; and my mind headed back to my glory days, foxtrotting with Miss Marshall. Even then, I sense the language of love, the key to living happily ever after; and if you couldn't do it, well, you might as well shoot yourself and everyone would understand.

Before I could say Jack Robinson, the chairs were pushed against the walls. I dragged mine over and sat, determined not to move, as Miss BF circled the room, choosing a partner, as a praying mantis chose her mate. Her evil eyes fell on Noel Burrows, a skinny, unlikely candidate, and off they went.

The Captain and Mrs Fox had taken pride-of-place seats below centre stage. He continued to beam, unaware that his daughter, every now and then, ate young men for breakfast.

Caspari sat next to me, too dignified, I hoped, to carry on in that manner, but then the music captivated him too. He tapped his foot and when his brother tried to drag him to the floor, off he went, after a quizzical look to me as if to ask permission. I waved him away with the back of my hand. Of course, go. Enjoy yourself.

I examined my fingernails, the three-inch sole of my right shoe, my food-spotted trousers Mother would get cleaned over the holidays. Or she might throw them out and buy new ones. The cuffs were getting short. Can't have that.

Pretty soon, everyone was shouting the words, particularly the 'Oi!' part, and I couldn't hear the music, just people screaming with delight at the unbridled merriment of it all.

Something kicked my shoe. Then again. A girl-type shoe. I looked up.

Bloody Mary Petty.

I narrowed every part of my face at her. 'I'm not going to dance. Don't ask me to dance...'

'I'm not going to,' she said, as if she'd never heard anything so preposterous. Without asking, she plopped herself down next to me.

'Caspari was sitting there,' I said.

'Not any longer.'

'So I see.'

'Don't worry, Graeme. I won't bother you for long.' She gave a big, body-heaving sigh. 'I have something for you.' She was holding a white envelope that looked rather battered. 'From my mother.'

'What?' I was confused; her mother and father were dead, weren't they?

'Mrs Grumbar to you. I call her Mother now.' She shuddered a breath again. 'Ages ago you wrote my – my mother – a letter apologising... .'

But the din was overwhelming. 'Mary, I'm having trouble hearing you. Let's step outside.'

We walked down the corridor toward the wide front hall with its grand staircase. A clear spring sky shone through windows that reached from floor to ceiling.

'Whew,' I said. 'That's better.'

'Right,' she said, all matter of fact now. 'I've got to say this now or never. Remember when you wrote that letter about that trick you played?'

'Yes,' I said slowly. 'Don't remind me. So stupid of me.'

'Be quiet and listen. When Mother got it, she wrote you back and asked me to post the letter. She read it to me and in it she asked you to come for tea after the rugby game, you know, that one in the rain.'

'I remember.'

'Well, I never posted it.'

'What?'

'I ripped it up. And then when we saw you at the game – which I didn't expect – she told me to go and ask you if you were coming to Woodbine Cottage afterwards. Which I did, but you said no.'

'But that was the first I'd heard of it. I thought she was ignoring me.'

'I know; and she thought you were ignoring us. That you were too grand to visit.'

I tried to sift through the hurt, the misunderstandings, the damage, the things hidden and not said. 'But, but… why didn't you just post the letter?'

'I don't know,' she almost wailed. 'I guess because she forgave you, but I hadn't. I was still angry.'

'I see,' I said, but I didn't. All I wanted to do was get back to my room. Read *The Rise and Fall of the Roman Empire*. Anything. 'Why don't you go back in there and dance? Like everyone else?'

'Where'd that come from? Why would I want to do that?'

'Because you can! You can dance. I would if I could. Not that stupid Lambeth thing. That's not dancing.'

'Who cares about dancing?'

'I do! Everybody does! I could do the foxtrot when I was seven years old! Before this!' I gave my leg an almighty whop – which hurt more than I had meant. I felt tears coming. 'We used to have big parties. I remember one Hogmanay when I danced with Miss Marshall in the middle of the night in Uncle Sandy's room. They were so impressed. "How does he do it? The foxtrot's hard." "Oh no it's not," I said, "The foxtrot's easy." They all laughed, but I wasn't sure why.'

I could not add what I knew to be true, for every time I thought of that moment, cast in amber – the whirling, the fireplace glowing, our feet one perfect machine, and I'd never be that happy again.

Mary gave me a dull blank look. 'I don't know what you're on about, but could you come and visit Mother next term when you're back? I think she'd like that.'

'Why?' I gave her the same look back.

'Because she likes you, though God knows why. Why else?'

'She feels sorry for me, I suspect.'

'Bollocks! Why should anyone feel sorry for you? Because you can't dance? Is that what you mean? Because you used to do some bloody dance when you were how old?'

'Seven.'

'Oh give it over. The foxtrot's easy. Learning to walk – a second time – that's hard.' She shook her head. 'You're such a pillock.' With that, she left to find her new parents.

Chapter 41

'Is there anything particular you wanted to discuss with me?' Captain Fox asked as I sat in his office, opposite him, ready for my start-of-term talk.

He pushed away some of his familiar desk paraphernalia: the heavy, brass pen and ink stand, as if making space for my mind, my soul.

'Not really, Captain Fox. Things seem good.'

'I'm glad to hear it.'

'It's just that, well – I don't know what to do with my life.'

'Is that all?' I could see his lower lids rising in a smile, but he suppressed them. 'Must you decide now?'

'No, but back in Dundee Father asked if I'd chosen my career yet. He caught me off guard, and I rather stumbled about, I'm afraid; and he said that I was floundering.' I didn't tell the Captain the prime minister bit, nor how the word 'floundering' terrified me. People floundered in water before drowning.

'Hmm,' said Captain Fox. 'Interesting word, "floundering." One hears it frequently regarding young men on the threshold of life. If you want my opinion, I would say this: you're not floundering, Graeme. You're exploring.'

Exploring. The word had eased a comforting pillow behind my back.

'You might try this exercise. Some find it useful. What are the things you keep wondering about – that bring you back again and again – full of curiosity, pleasure – or even anger, strangely. Best of all, in some entwining combination.' He looked at me, waiting.

'You mean, you want me to think – now?' I stretched the corners of my mouth in a grimace, hoping he'd laugh, but no.

'Why not? For just a minute or two. It might prove interesting.' He lit a cigarette, always the same, steady procedure; the startling scratch of the match, the deep inhale. 'Take your time. Close your eyes, if you wish.'

I did, and as seconds passed, I felt that empty space on the desk widen and grow warm, full of possibility. Trusting the darkness, I stayed there, with his delving questions – for how long, I had no idea. Eventually I opened my eyes and blinked. The room looked the same, but different. 'The thing I keep wondering about, as you say, curious… sometimes I think I find the answer and then I realise it's not enough.'

'That's all right. Complex matters require repeated attention.'

'All right. Here it is. How do people get along with one another? Why is it that we get along at Maiden Erlegh while the rest of the world can't? Caspari says it's because you treat us all the same. I say it's because you treat us differently.'

'Ah, you've brought up the question of our age, young man. Claude Mellor often asks me what my teaching philosophy is, and to his frustration, I don't really have one. But you and Caspari are both right. We're all different; we're all the same. Take one away and we fail. Both are needed.'

'At one time I was convinced the answer was something Smailes said.'

The Captain rubbed his eyes with slow, deliberate force. 'Such a tragic waste.'

'Yes. Sorry, Sir, to bring him up.'

'No, no. I'm sorry. Go on.'

'He told me, "Don't take advantage, of either one's strength or weakness." Like I used to think it was a lark to push boys into the swimming baths with my stick because they daren't fight back.'

'But now you don't.'

'Well, no, I wouldn't dream of it. I have Smailes to thank for that.'

'I'm glad.' He lit another cigarette. 'Now, what about anger? Anything there?'

'There certainly is! I'm angry that grown people, who should know better, are so stupid.'

'Well put. And the third thing? Pleasure?'

'Oh, that goes without saying. Just being here is pleasant. Maybe I could be a teacher here someday.'

'A fine, rewarding profession.' He kept looking at me.

'The problem is, sir,' the words came unbidden, 'I can't decide whether to go to Woodbine Cottage or not!'

His eyes widened. My face grew hot. 'It's like this. Mrs Grumbar's son died of polio, and perhaps I remind her of him. Anyway, she likes having me there. She's ever so kind. More like a mother than my mother, I guess.'

'And you don't want to go there?'

'Not exactly, Sir, but quite honestly, I should spend my time on more important things, only I'm not sure what they are. I loved being there when I was younger.'

'What did you love about it?'

'Hmm, I'm not sure. The hominess, I suppose. There's something about the brick. Once the cottage had coats of whitewash, but it's half-blown off because it faces the wind. The whole cottage looks frosted. And on a sunny afternoon, the brick stands out, glowing like stained glass. And then the colour is more important than the frost. Both things I love: the frost and the burnt sunshine. If either were taken away, the house would be ordinary. Oh, I can't explain it.'

'You just have.'

'And inside, it's all higgledy-piggledy, cups hanging from beams, bunches of herbs, the sofa covers baggy and frayed. Mrs Grumbar usually has a soup simmering, a soup mother would call peasant muck, using up scraps.'

'I understand. You feel drawn there without knowing why. People can like many things for many reasons, and it's good they do.

'Perhaps, it's the uncertainty. When you study a subject like Maths, you know what is going to happen. Or with Geography, there are maps and drawings, and you'll learn all about them; and with a good teacher, the absorption of knowledge is easy.

'But in life, it's more precarious. Different people, different ideas. The mind opens in a new way. When that happens, life can turn in another direction. At Woodbine Cottage, you don't know what's going to happen. You have parents who have lost a son, and a girl who has lost her parents.'

'Mary Petty.'

'Is there a problem about that?'

'No, no. It's just, I don't think Mary Petty likes me much. And Finzi has been there, helping the Grumbars with chores. He and Mary collect insects and spend hours with butterflies and such in the back room. In fact, they've become sweethearts.'

'Have they now?'

'Well, no one's said so, but it's obvious. I've seen them after rugby games. You know the way people act.' I hoped I sounded chum-to-chum, when really, I hadn't a clue how sweethearts behaved. 'Anyway… I must think about my future, and frankly,' I knew he'd appreciate this, 'I'm too busy.'

'Too busy to be kind?'

'No... it's not that. it's risky. I might neglect my studies, like last year. Nothing's more important than getting into Oxford someday.'

'My dear Moodie, being kind is never a waste of time. Sometimes we don't know why we do things or why we like them. If the Grumbars like having you there and you like being there, go.'

'But what if...'

'One can "what if" forever. Just go.'

He gave the armrests of his chair a pat, signalling that it was time to leave. I leaned forward to stand.

'Oh, here's something for you to get your teeth into,' the Captain said. 'At the end of term we're going to have a photographic competition, our first. We'll have an exhibition in the Palm Court. Anyone can take part. Do you like competitions?'

'I don't know. I tried once, when the prize was a cruise, but I didn't win.'

* * *

The light and the birds woke me early. I lay in bed waiting for my alarm as Marshall slept. Somehow, I still hadn't made it to the Grumbars; today, the idea of winning a photographic competition was more appealing, easier to consider. I stared upward planning my day.

I'd taken snaps of this and that – trees, the stone lions on the terrace, miles of wisteria in great swags over the windows, but nothing great. I wanted to say something, not just make pretty pictures, which I knew someone like Caspari or the hotshot portrait photographer, Basch, could do better.

I looked at Marshall, twitching in a dream. I imagined his day unfolding, differently from mine, yet bearing an element of sameness. A warmth soared through me. I had it! My photos would tell a story of a day in the life of our school – through many lives – getting along together. Like a magic trick one sees but can't figure out how it's done.

I dressed. Rain blew about outside and my nose felt cold, a sign of poor weather. Never mind. It was a day for indoor photos, certainly not for a visit to Woodbine Cottage.

A groan blasted from Marshall's bed. Good, I had company. He kicked his covers off and stretched, moaning at some length. 'Ah, delicious dream. Wait till you hear this, Moodie.'

'Do I have a choice?'

'Shh. I don't want to lose it. Yes, I was at the cinema and the woman next to me put her hand on my knee. I wasn't sure if it was a mistake or not.'

'What kind of a mistake?'

'I don't know. That she thought I was her boyfriend.'

'How could she get that mixed up? She must have been pretty stupid.'

'This is a dream, Moodie, not realism. Don't ruin it. Anyway, I decided not to say anything, and then she said, "Oh, I beg your pardon, I thought you were someone else." We looked at each other. "Never mind," she said. "You look quite nice, too." "Thank you," I answered, ever so politely. So we went out together in a taxi and kissed like mad in the back seat.'

'Stop!' I said. 'Don't move. I want to take your picture.' While he'd been telling me his silly dream, I'd a second rush of inspiration. 'The Day in the Life of Maiden Erlegh' would begin with Marshall. He'd be the dawn! Then I'd go through the day, showing all the odd and beautiful varieties that made Maiden Erlegh, Maiden Erlegh.

'In pyjamas?'

'Why not? Put your arms in the air, like you were earlier, stretching. Don't get under the covers.'

'My foot is bare. Shouldn't I hide it?'

'No, you have a very nice foot. Besides, I'm going for realism, not some arty rubbish.'

'Can I get up now?' Marshall said. 'I've got things to do.' He sat up and saw the rain sliding helter-skelter down the panes. 'Too bad. No Woodley Airfield today.'

'Marshall, I'm heading down for breakfast, if you don't mind.' Usually, I would have waited, but I was keen to take photos of the breakfast table.

My hand was on the doorknob when he said, 'Wait! I need to ask something.'

I turned back. 'Surely, my friend. Fire away.'

'Are you ever going to make a play for that girl?'

'What?' I said, glad to able to lean on the door.

'Don't play the fool with me. The one you're always with.'

'I'm not always with her. Not anymore. I'm too busy.'

'Take it easy. I saw her at Culham's, that's all. She works there.'

'Still? I thought she'd be fired, she's so rude.'

'Anyway, she asked after you.'

'She did? What did she say?'

'Let's see. I was buying a little something to ward off night starvation. I thought you and I would fancy something more exotic – like Black Magic.' He said it in a fast whisper, like a magician and pulled it from under the bed. 'Was I right?'

'Yes, yes. But go on.'

'She must have noticed my school jacket, because she said, "You must be one of the Fox Cubs."'

'And?'

'I said yes.'

'And?'

'She asked if I knew Graeme Moodie. "Know him," I said. "He's my best friend." You don't mind if I said that, do you?'

'No! Just get on with it.'

'Take it easy. So she said, "You're the one who makes the planes."'

'And I said, "That's right!" It felt like we already knew each other. Then she said her mother missed you coming round. I'd say she's keen on you.'

'That's impossible.'

'Why's it impossible?'

'Just is. And anyway, I'm not keen on her.'

'You're sure? I wanted to check. You see, I fancy her, myself. Do you mind if I – ask her to a film or something?'

'Be my guest. I couldn't care less.'

Chapter 42

Next day, I stood knocking at the Gurmbars' door. I'd bathed, but I was sweating and hoped I didn't smell off.

'Why, it's Graeme,' Mrs Grumbar said, quietly, gently. 'Come in.' She watched me take my coat off, knowing not to help. I hung it on a wooden peg by the door. 'I was just folding laundry,' she said as she walked back to the kitchen table where a big basket full of clothes lay. 'Sheets.'

'I'm good at that.' I smiled, remembering how Berry and I folded them. 'Want a hand?'

'Certainly.' And that was that. I followed her, doing what Berry had called 'the folding dance,' smiling and bowing when we met in the middle.

'Mary?' she called to the back room. 'How about some tea in a quarter of an hour or so? Graeme's dropped by.'

A slight pause. 'Be there soon. Just need to finish this... tricky little – there. Done.'

She came out, followed by Finzi, both a bit pink in the face.

We caught up with this and that. I told them about the photography competition, how I'd been discovering nooks and crannies in Maiden Erlegh. And Finzi and Mary showed me the new butterflies and tiny moths they'd collected from a nearby field. 'It's sad seeing them dead,' Mary said, 'but we only take the one.'

We went about our business quietly, no sudden moves, like birdwatchers. Only we were both the birds and the watchers. If you take no notice of me, I'll take no notice of you.

The things I'd missed seemed precious and dear – pouring tea through a battered strainer, fresh scones wafting their gorgeous perfume, foamy butter trickling down their edges.

That was that. No palaver. No fuss. As I left, I promised to come back on Saturday, and they waved goodbye as they stood in the doorway.

Congratulations, Moodie. You bloody did it. You've earned that Victoria Cross.

By the time I got back to school, my face ached with glee.

* * *

'Where've you *been*?' Marshall asked as I came through our door. 'Look!' He sat propped up in bed, an aeroplane magazine on his knees. 'Look what I've ordered from America! Quick!' He'd been designing a larger model and was desperate to find an engine powerful enough to fly it. He stabbed at a page. 'The Baby Cyclone. Is it not beautiful?'

I had expected some spiralling machine, like... well, a cyclone. This contraption looked like a tin of soup, lying sideways, a stack of disks behind, more something Alastair and I made from bits and bobs in Granny's garage.

For the next half-hour I heard about every inch of the Baby Cyclone. 'Instead of the side-port induction seen on most engines, this uses a crankshaft rotary valve – pay attention, Moodie – but with the venturi on the bottom. Look at those oversized mounting lugs – virtually crack-proof!'

'Aren't lugs ears?' He closed his eyes, overwhelmed at my stupidity. 'They are in Scotland.'

'Anyway, I've ordered it airmail, so it should arrive in a couple of weeks.'

* * *

On Saturday, as promised, I was back at Woodbine Cottage, bringing a slew of photographs. I laid them out on the pine table – Marshall waking up, boys at the tuckshop, practising a fire drill. 'You see, I'm going to show that, while we're all different, we're all the same!'

'Nice,' Mary said. She and Finzi went back to their biology; I went back to the sofa, vowing not to mention my project again.

I never went outside with them. I knew they wanted to be alone. Sometimes, I'd come to the back room where they worked, arm against arm, or fingers entwined as one held paper, the other, pins. I had no skill for fine work with tweezers and glue, though Finzi and his paddle hands managed beautifully. I imagined them kissing, but didn't like thinking that, so I went back to reading. Much easier to be with Mrs Grumbar who liked me, and Mary did not.

Occasionally they asked me to join them, but I'd say, 'Oh I'm feeling mouldy today,' or 'I need to read the editorials; the Captain and I talk politics, you see.'

'I can't think of anything worse.' Mary wrinkled her nose.

The days grew warmer and the rain washed away the last of the winter dust, when one day, after returning from a foray in Maiden Erlegh Wood, Mary took off her sky-blue cardigan and laid it behind me on the sofa. And from it came a delicious smell of sunshine and of all the tiny flowers that grew among the blades of grass. It was a world of sweet air, and one I wanted. Not *her*, all scabs and tangled hair, but the outdoor smell encircling her, like fresh laundry flapping in the wind. A longing heaved through me, like a blow.

My self-willed legs took me to the back room. 'I think I'll join you next time,' I said, making my voice jaunty and firm. 'If you don't mind?'

'Do we mind, Peter?' Mary turned to him.

'No, not me. I would welcome.'

'It's the air,' I said. 'It's drawn me out.'

'I'm glad something has,' she said, going back to her microscope.

* * *

Bit by bit, we ventured a little further on each expedition, Finzi always at hand in case – though no one said it – I fell. I learnt that Woodbine Cottage was not so far from Maiden Erlegh, if one knew the way. I learnt the names of tracks – Cutbush, Beech Lane, and Gypsy Lane, which made me nervous. I'd never met a real gypsy, but I'd heard bad things about them. 'Are there – er – gypsies hereabouts?'

'Nah. There used to be – the sewage farm is just down here,' and she pointed to a thin track off to the right. 'That's the only place gypsies were allowed to live. The stench was horrible, so even they left, but the name stayed. Watch out! There's a ditch this side. You can't see it, with the grass so high. Mind you don't get a wet one!'

'A wet what?'

'Your foot, silly. We'll collect frogspawn on the way back.' She punched my arm and pointed toward a dusty light emerging from behind thick tree trunks. We'd come upon a field, where little colts, paired with their mothers, feasted on grass.

A mare and her colt trotted over to us. 'They know me,' Mary explained. 'Look, I've brought carrots. Hold one out, over the fence. That's right.'

* * *

Such an unfortunate coincidence that Marshall's airplane engine and Calinescu's automobile should arrive from America on the same day; nothing could overshadow the sight of Calinescu's Supercharged Cabriolet 812 Cord.

Even the Captain was excited. 'I've heard much about this American vehicle called the Cord,' he said in his lunchtime talk. 'The term "all-new" is often applied to automobiles and it is always an exaggeration. In the case of the Cord it is true. Calinescu will be arriving in it after four. Be ready to greet him.' He started to sit.

'Oh, I nearly forgot. Would Marshall please come to my office to collect another miracle of design – the Baby Cyclone – destined for one of his future aeroplanes. One day we will be saying we knew him when he was a lad at school. Any questions?'

'What time did you say the Cord was coming?' one boy asked, raising his hand.

* * *

Just before four, someone dashed down the corridor. 'Cord in view! Cord in view!' A thunderous gallop sounded, faster than for any fire drill, onto the gravel drive.

I was prepared to be disappointed. But then the most beautiful, long, smooth shape of bright buttery yellow appeared, gliding impossibly close to the ground. Everything sloped back, as if sculpted by the wind, as it drove into the air.

And behind the steering wheel – on the left side – was Calinescu, a calm sheen on his hair and a wide, gappy grin on his face.

No one moved. No one breathed. Only the Captain broke the silence with slow, respectful applause, which we echoed. No words, until Calinescu hoisted out of the seat and hurled his driving cap into the air, shouting 'Yahoo!'

Over the next days we learned about the retractable headlights operated by a crank; the front-wheel drive allowed the car to be close to the ground, making running boards unnecessary; wraparound louvred shutters replaced a radiator grille; the long nose was described as 'coffin shaped,' an unlucky image, I thought.

Out of respect for Marshall I tried to minimise my enthusiasm, but even he spent one afternoon going over it, particularly under the bonnet, for there were many similarities, he said, between cars and planes. He might learn something about the Cord's wind-inviting 'aerodynamic' shape.

Insects came and went; butterflies and moths lived their short lives. I learned from Finzi how Mary was known for her fearless exploits. It was she who had found the rare male Purple Emperor. Had purely by accident found a skylark's nest under a tussock, and put it back, undisturbed. She had a rule about birds' eggs. Just take one, and only if there were more than three. Birds could count to three, and if they found one missing, they never returned.

I'd never paid attention to trees and flowers. But here, they just grew, all by themselves! They had Latin and common names and Mary knew them all. If she and Finzi saw something unusual, they plopped down, head to head, to dissect a flower with tweezers, his big gentle hands working like a surgeon's. Daisies, cornflowers, poppies and geraniums. 'How do you know this?' I asked on one of our picnics of Mrs G's brown bread and Mr G's honey.

'It's easy, especially the common names. Cranesbill looks like a crane's bill. And so on.'

'What if one doesn't know what a crane's bill looks like?'

'Then one's an idiot.'

* * *

'Well, you're getting an education,' Marshall said. His head hung inches above the drawing pad on his desk.

'But pretty useless. How's your plane coming?'

'I've been biking to Woodley Airfield to sketch their new designs. I'm not much good, though.'

'I wish I could come with you – take photos. But I can't manage a bike.'

'Is three miles too far to walk?'

'I think so.' He kept on drawing, rubbing out, cursing.

Then genius struck. 'Marshall, do you think Calinescu might drive us there? In his Cord?'

I had to push him away when he tried to kiss me.

* * *

The following Saturday afternoon we set off. The Cord's top was up because of a drizzle, while Marshall sat in front so he could see the instrument panel. I sat in the back while the two of them drooled over engine-turned fascia, fan-shaped gauges and round radio dial.

The chaps at Woodley were used to Marshall, but when they saw the Cord, everything stopped. From the hangars and sheds men in greasy one-piece overalls, and dirty hands, stood round with the usual reverence the car commanded. 'Those Americans,' one said, 'they don't half know how to create a motorcar.'

While I took photographs, Calinescu gave the men rides, provided they removed their work clothes. He even put the top down.

By one o'clock I was getting faint with hunger, so we headed for The Hop Leaf, as the mechanics recommended. Calinescu ordered a round of beer, which we wouldn't dare have tried in Earley. At one point, Marshall nipped out to check the Cord. 'We don't want any curious onlookers scratching the car.'

'Let me go,' I said. 'You haven't finished eating.'

'No, that's all right,' he said quickly. 'I need the WC, anyway.'

'All's well,' he said when he returned. 'But cars are slowing down to look. Best get rolling home.' Calinescu insisted on paying the bill.

He put in the key, turned. A faint chug gurgled. He tried again. And again, this time longer.

'Careful. Mind you don't flood it,' Marshall said.

Calinescu swore in Romanian. He pounded the steering wheel, smacked the dashboard.

'Take it easy' Marshall said. 'That won't help. Here, let's look under the bonnet. I know a bit about motors.'

The three of us looked at the gleaming mass, incomprehensible to me. 'Everything looks right,' Marshall said. He checked this and that. 'It has petrol; everything is connected. Wait! I think I may see the problem. I say, old chap, your rotary valve's missing. Good thing I always carry a spare. It might fit yours.'

From his pocket he took a black, Bakelite cylinder. 'I always carry an extra. You never know when it might come in handy.' He bent over the bonnet and twisted the cap easily into its place. 'Try it now.'

'You stupid bloody car, you better start, or I'll take a hammer to you.' Steaming, frowning, Calinescu gave the key an almighty twist.

Purring softly, sweetly, contentedly, the Cord started. Marshall was doing his best to hide a grin.

Gradually the penny dropped – on me first, then Calinescu – that Charlie Marshall, on his trip outside, had removed a crucial ingredient to the Cord, and simply put it back again.

Calinescu's great furry eyebrows lowered like a gangster's. He got out of the car. His long arms and short legs stiffened, his crazily wide shoulders stretched wider and lower.

Marshall kept smiling. 'The Captain taught me how to disable a car,' he said, as if that made it all right. 'It's a good joke to play on a friend. Like you! I just took this little bit off. Did it for fun.'

'Fun!' Calinescu roared, his face white. I was frightened; Calinescu could kill him if he wanted. He stood still, thinking and translating. No one moved. Then, like a motor starting, he laughed. He staggered, his face redder and redder as he slapped the car, slapped Marshall's back, nearly knocking him over. 'You take the piss! I understand! You take this thing off. It no work. You put it back. It work.' Calinescu took off again in spluttering Romanian. He leaned against the car for support, playing the scene repeatedly. He reminded me of Father as he wiped away his tears. 'Ah', he said as he hugged Marshall excruciatingly. 'I have friend at last.'

As we came up to Maiden Erlegh's garages, we saw Boch polishing his car, a putty-grey Opel Olympia. It looked like a shineless whale, but then, the day was grey. Calinescu sped up and beeped his horn in a friendly, two-punch beep. Boch looked up with prepared disdain. We got out. Marshall and Calinescu walked off, arm in arm.

Some part of me felt sorry for Boch. 'You're working up a good shine there,' I said, which wasn't true. 'You'll never guess what happened, Boch. Calinescu's wondrous Cord broke down!'

'Oh?'

'Luckily, Marshall put things right. I'll wager your Olympia's never broken down. Such a sturdy car.'

He looked at me strangely, as if not certain why I was being friendly. Neither was I, possibly I remembered the Captain saying he'd once been a nice lad.

'You're right about that. Germany invented the car, and they are the best. Wait till you see the new ones coming out, like the Volkswagen, a car for everyone, once everything is over.'

'What's everything?'

'Don't be stupid, Moodie. The war.' He went back to polishing.

Chapter 43

It was getting toward the solstice, nearly three weeks since my first forays into Maiden Erlegh Wood, when Mary and Finzi decided I was ready for 'their' field. They'd been talking about its wonders for some time.

First, we had to pass through an area called the Muddy Patch. 'Why's the ground like this, all of a sudden?' I said, furious at its impudence. 'Stupid thing!' I hissed, as I nearly slipped and fell.

'May I take your elbow?' Finzi murmured. He looked so kind, I didn't mind locking my arm through his. Accept the help, Moodie, you pompous twit.

'I will explain,' he said as we soldiered on. 'Many underground streams join here, under our feet.' We looked down. 'That's why it's muddy.'

'Come on, laggards!' Mary called from ahead.

But it got worse, as I wobbled along boards that stretched across grassy puddles, Finzi holding my hand – bloody embarrassing – as he sloshed blithely through the water in his wellies.

'Look, there's our field!' Mary called again. 'Just over that rise.'

I didn't appreciate its wonders at first. It was, yes, a field; a wide, mostly flat stretch, no trees, different height grasses, small dots of flowers and a lot of insects zooming and hovering. It all looked itchy to me. The odd bird poking about.

But I learned.

Finzi and Mary were avid teachers, so our outings became a great game. She brought a newly published book called *The Countryside Companion* with pictures and information about every living thing in Great Britain. I was stunned at what I didn't know.

'Silly, that's a thrush! They're nothing like a skylark. See, it doesn't have the little crest on its head. And thrushes are fatter and yellow-breasted.' She'd take out a little notebook and, like a patient teacher, sketch a flower or a bird. Sometimes I pretended not to know, to see Mary's ginger eyebrows glinting in the sun as she lowered them in a scowl.

'Don't worry,' Finzi said, his hand on my shoulder. 'You will learn. It's a question of noticing.'

I held my interest in world affairs, which they appreciated and tolerated, for I was on a different plane, one of politics and government. I kept private my wish to be prime minister. To voice it would be bad luck, or worse, I'd be mocked. Even old Marvellous Me saw that. But I knew it was possible, at times a certainty, that I would lead the nation one day, when everyone would have forgotten about Hitler. This was just a temporary storm, like the General Strike and all those news stories that caused a terrific fuss and were never heard of again.

My photographs, also, were continuing apace. So far, I'd taken 150 shots. Some rubbish, some good, but I kept going, studying contact sheets with a magnifying glass and enlarging only the masterpieces – like Nicky Littman's tennis ball caught mid-air as he served; Caspari and Mr Mellor poring over a book; Ernest, grinning as he skipped rope, also mid-air.

* * *

I became taken with a tiny little moth about an inch long and as beautiful as a butterfly – a deep shimmery green, with flashes of pink or yellow, like oil in the sun. '"Iridescence" is the word you're looking for, and it's called the Burnet moth.' Mary said.

She popped up from the quilt, and with astonishing delicacy, caught one with her net. 'Look,' she said, cupping it in her hand. 'They have spots of red on their wings, either five or six. There's debate as to whether they're a different species.'

'People debate that?'

'Yes.'

'Like a parliamentary debate about the future of Europe?'

'Why not? They're important, too, but poisonous. The caterpillars eat bird's-foot trefoil, which has cyan in it, as in cyanide, which gives them a yellow colour, so birds and spiders know not to eat them.'

'What clever things!'

'I know, and the moths can fly in the daytime because their red spots warn away predators.'

'How did they know to do that?'

'They didn't. It's natural selection. Oh, and bird's-foot trefoil is also known as granny's toenails. You know, thick and yellow?'

'No,' I said faintly. How she loved making me squirm.

* * *

Caspari caught me in the hall after dinner. 'A good thing's happened,' he said, 'I've heard from Kirk.'

'Who?'

'David Kirk. Don't tell me you've forgotten him.' It took me a moment to remember. Of course – the German lad frightened off by Rudy Boch. 'I do, I do, Paul. Tell me, please.'

He sighed. 'Anyway, he's fine. He's at another school, in Letchworth. St Christophers, run by Quakers.'

'I am glad to hear it.'

Caspari growled. 'It's disgusting – how Boch got away with writing that foul note!'

I lowered my voice. 'But what could we do? We couldn't tell the Captain what his daughter did.'

'So we brushed it under the carpet! Like the so-called *good* Germans did after Kristallnacht.'

'Shh, Paul. That's an exaggeration, don't you think?'

'Why? The Germans knew what happened at Kristallnacht, yet they did nothing. You and I knew what happened here – yet we shrug our shoulders. Shame on us. And it *is* a shame. An unspeakable shame on all of us.'

* * *

Not talking much, Finzi and I were sitting on a quilt in the middle of their field. I stretched my legs out, leaning back on bent wrists. I will remember this, I thought. A haze of insects hovered in the afternoon sun, still high. Mary, however, was restless and fidgety, walking with a jar in hand, toward the stream, which I had yet to see. With a jerk she stopped, crouched and hunkered onto her heels to study the grass. 'Yes!' she hissed excitedly.

'Here,' she said, walking toward me. 'I've brought you something. Your own Burnet moth – to hatch out.' She held the jar under my face. A yellowish, leathery cocoon hung on a stiff stem of grass, like an upended hammock.

'This one's got about a week left, I'd say. Put it, not in the bright sun, but not the dark.'

'Do I feed it?'

She fixed me with a hard stare. 'You can't feed a cocoon.'

'I know that.' I hoped I sounded just as withering. 'After it hatches.'

'No. Bring it back to the field. If it's too late in the day, add a few drops of water to a leaf, so it won't dry out overnight.'

I set the cocoon between Marshall's and my beds. 'Shall we give it a name?' he asked.

'We don't know if it's a girl or boy.'

'Maybe we could find a name that suits for both. Like Leslie or Jocelyn.'

'Or Beverley.'

'That's it. "Beverley Burnet." Sounds like a film star.'

* * *

Days later I had a shock when the Captain made his announcements. 'Good news about our Finzi: a rugby scout from London has observed this admirable young man. They've selected him as a recruit. He's still a student with the school, but he will be in London most of each week for training. They can't see, barring injury, why he wouldn't have a professional career. They'll be writing to the foreign office for permission for indefinite leave. Very good news indeed.' Finzi was made to stand and he grew purple as we sang, 'For He's a Jolly Good Fellow' and gave three cheers.

How could I continue my excursions without Finzi as my bodyguard? Mary certainly wouldn't want me tagging after her and I would hate staying in the cottage all the time on the sofa. I'd rather not go.

'Why so glum, Moodie?' Marshall asked as he studied the cocoon, so far unchanged. 'What's the matter?'

I explained how Finzi's gain was my loss. Returning Beverley to the field would probably be my last visit. 'She'll be sorry she gave me a moth. She'll have to see me again when I return it to the field.'

'Are you sure? Maybe she wants to see you. What if she gave you the jar so that you *would* come back?'

'I highly doubt it, but thanks.'

In a few days, Beverley's cocoon grew dark brown and we stared, rapt, for a good half hour, urging it on as it struggled and twisted in its prison, finally breaking free. It stretched its small thin wings. We saw the green. The iridescence, the spots.

I pulled a leaf from the lime tree outside our window, sprinkled it with water, and placed it standing in the jar against the glass. 'Tomorrow, I take it to the field.' I sighed heavily. 'Please, Marshall, come with me.'

'No. This is something you must do on your own.'

The next morning, I set off, accompanied by a small moth named Beverley Burnet, sex unknown. 'Don't worry,' I told it. 'You won't die on my account.'

The way was familiar, a route that had once seemed so daring, the dark avenue of trees announcing the start of Gypsy Lane, I smiled at the memory as I passed the tender mares and colts who approached, hoping for a carrot. 'Nothing today. Sorry.'

'Almost there,' I said to my moth friend as we took on the Muddy Patch, which wasn't all that muddy this time. And as the ground slowly lifted, the field lay golden before me, but with something else, a patch of blue and faded red, which took about a half-second to realise it was the Grumbars' ancient quilt of faded squares and upon it was the slender, straight back that could only belong to Mary P, now G. And she was wearing that blue cardigan that matched the sky.

She must have heard me crunching and swishing through the tall grass, but she did not turn till I was at her side, and then only slightly, looking down.

'It's hatched,' I said.

She pulled a wayward strand of hair that had found its way to her mouth. 'When?'

'Last night. I gave it water, as you said.'

'It looks pretty chipper.' She kept her eyes on the jar, where the little thing sat on the bottom of the glass on short, bent legs. 'Shall we do it? Let it go?' I waited for her to invite me to sit. Hoping.

She put a hand flat on the quilt to push herself up, but she stopped mid-action. Perhaps she was tired, too. Anyway, she changed her mind and neatly sat and looked up at me. The sun shone on her eyebrows in that way I liked. It made me feel close to her because it was something I could see and know about, and she had no idea.

She patted the quilt matter-of-factly and I teetered down in my odd way, which she had seen many times when Finzi had been there, but now it was just us two.

She directed me to unscrew the lid. 'Will it know what to do?'

'Oh yes. They're born knowing. No one need teach them.'

* * *

'So, mission accomplished?' Marshall asked.

'Mission accomplished.'

'Come on. Details, details.'

'Later. I'm worn out,' I said, and stretched out on my bed. I didn't want to talk. Words wouldn't do.

Marshall smacked his fist against the other palm. 'What I find completely unfair is that it knows how to fly, right off the bat! Someone has already figured out the perfect configuration of weight and wing length and position on the body.'

'Still no luck getting the Baby Cyclone off the ground?'

'No, goddamn it. I must have tried 850 configurations. I'm driving my team crazy.' Marshall had conscripted a group to accompany him to the hockey field, which was encircled by an iron fence. The boys' job was to hold up old sailing canvasses to protect the plane from crashing into the railings. 'But I think I might have it the next time. I have a new plan.' He rubbed his hands. 'Why don't you watch? Tomorrow, around four o'clock? The wind's down then.'

I'd arranged to meet Mary in the field, but if I'd cut it short, I'd still have time to see Marshall's plane take off at four. 'It's a deal,' I said. 'And, if you succeed, I'll write it up for the *Maiden Erlegh Chronicle*. They're looking for compelling stories.'

He gave that lovely new smile of his. 'Then, I'll just have to succeed, won't I?'

* * *

'Mmmm,' Mary said, as we strolled. 'You can smell the mint. It grows in the stream up ahead.'

'I've not been there.'

'No? Well, high time I took you. It's wonderful. Can't you smell it?' I gave two short, sharp sniffs. 'Not like that, silly. My father taught me how to truly smell something. You close your eyes, open your mouth.' She demonstrated. 'Just a little.' Oh my God, her mouth. Had I never noticed? 'Breathe in, using both your nose and mouth at the same time.' She continued the demonstration. 'That way your throat smells too.'

Blood rushed to my head; my face went hot. 'You're so bossy,' I said, recovering my sangfroid. 'Can't I even smell the way I want to?'

'But you don't know anything. Just try, you'll see.'

'No.'

'You won't regret it.'

'All right,' I groaned, feeling an idiot, but oh, the scent of mint flooded my head. 'I hate to say this, but I smell mint. You're right. I was wrong.'

'I don't believe it. On July 3, 1939,' she looked at her watch, 'at three-twenty-two in the afternoon, Graeme Moodie admitted he was wrong.'

'What time is it?' I stretched my arm out to read my watch. 'Good God! I've got to go.'

'Where? We just got here.'

I explained about Marshall's plane and my promise to join him in the hockey field.

'I'll meet you right here, tomorrow, two o'clock.'

'Promise?'

'Promise.'

* * *

True to my word and full of happiness, I returned, bearing the article I wrote the night before. Marshall's plane had flown, and I knew the piece was good. I read it aloud to her, with all the drama I could muster.

The Pioneer

Amidst an admiring cortege of admirers, our Charlie Marshall begins the long trek down to the hockey field with four pounds of model aeroplane under his arm. He is about to find out if eighteen months of hard work has been worth the effort.

The wings are attached to the fuselage and the Baby Cyclone adjusted until it has reached the acme of perfection. Harken! Marshall has started the motor. Its sullen roar pervades the stillness of the countryside. But not for long... it splutters and stops! Imperturbably, Marshall proceeds to plunge into the innermost recesses of the motor and is rewarded by an asthmatic sound of great vehemence.

After a long period of revving-up, during which the canvas-bearers sink into a coma, the plane runs over the hockey field for nearly half a minute.

Another interval for revving-up. The audience is exhibiting signs of unrest, when they see the great red form of the plane flash far above their heads in the direction of the potato patch. And, after reaching a ceiling of something like seventy-five feet it goes high over the dangerous railings, gliding gracefully to earth, the only damage a torn-off wheel! A great shout goes up from a dozen throats, the owners of which forthwith rush up to the school for a cup of tea to steady their nerves.

But Marshall is deaf to this demonstration of enthusiasm. He stands there, examining with an anguished eye the shattered remains of his wheel. GCM. Those are my initials.'

'But that's excellent!' she said.

'You sound surprised.'

'I am. You've been hiding your light under a bushel. I didn't know you could write so well.'

I had to clench my teeth to not grin like a Cheshire Cat.

* * *

On my way back to the school, I passed the big yard, all in brick, at the far east side of the house. It was here a funny old soldier-friend of the Captain's exercised the boys in marching and drilling – left, right, at ease, that kind of thing. I'd not seen it before; soldiering was not my area, and wondered why TS Waterlow Fox, so opposed, though secretly, to war, would have such a thing. I decided it must be camouflage.

I stopped for a few minutes to watch Sergeant Eyres ordering them right and left in their shirtsleeves and ties. About a dozen of them. He stood with his long moustaches and barrel-belly protruding from his ramrod back, the bright buttons following the curve. 'Hey, new recruit! Fall out. Left means left, not right! Don't you know the difference?'

'Sorry, sir.'

'And stand straight.'

I squinted at the recruit. Surely not… Caspari? But it was his distinctive profile: big forehead sloping back, thick wavy hair. We hadn't seen much of each other lately. I knew he often rode his bike to Slough, where he had an accounting job, but I didn't know about this.

'That's it for today men,' said the Sergeant. 'At ease.'

I decided to wait for Paul and as we walked back, I asked him why he joined the drilling exercises.

'I had to do *something*. War's coming. If I must choose between the Nazis and the Communists, I'll go for the commies any day. I've joined a Workers' party in Slough. It's inspiring. I'm afraid England's finished. No one will fight for it.'

'Fighting never solved anything. It is us who must teach others. Set the example, as we do here. If people behave decently, others will, as well.'

'Oh yes, there are lessons to be learned here, but no one is listening.'

* * *

Mary had brought a picnic to eat by the stream. She spread the quilt over a large rock because the ground was damp.

She pulled out our ham sandwiches and a jar of Colman's Mustard, which she slathered all over the insides of hers, daring me to do the same, which she knew I wouldn't. Her coaxing became a game we both enjoyed.

We could hear the water going over rocks, steady and cheerful.

'It's strange to feel happy, isn't it?' she said. 'I mean, really happy.'

'Yes.'

'I thought I'd never be happy again, after…'

'I know. I felt the same when I got polio. But here we are, happy.' We saw the water move over rocks, the mint growing through the streambed. 'Do you wish you could change it? To be back the way it was?'

'Of course,' she said. 'I'd give anything to see their dear faces again. But I can't. I would never choose the Grumbars over my parents. That's unthinkable, but my life turned out the way it did and the Grumbars are here and my parents are not. And no matter how angry or sad I got, that wouldn't change.'

She was quiet for a while. 'When you first met me, I'd made up my mind never to be happy or glad again, because of what happened.'

'What did happen?' I asked softly, the first time either of us had talked about our sorrows.

I thought she wasn't going to answer, but then, 'My parents were killed in their car because a man didn't want to hit a fox crossing the road in the near dark, so he ended up killing them instead. The Grumbars kindly took me on; I knew they'd lost a son. But neither they nor I could change anything.

'To be happy seemed disrespectful, as if I didn't care their lives were taken away, made to rot in the ground and I'd never ever see them again. All because of a fox.

'Some time ago I started to be happy. I'm beginning to be happy. Like now. But I'm not sure I should. It seems wrong. Do you think I have a right to be happy, to lead a happy life, to do things I love and enjoy, even though they're not here? It's not disrespectful?'

She looked at her lap and her shoulders heaved, slowly at first. Her body rocked and her cries came like coughs or barks. I didn't know what to do, so I did the only logical thing – I gave her my handkerchief, which she grabbed and blew her nose into, a honking, comic sound. She gave a choky laugh. 'Sorry.'

It never occurred to me that she'd been suffering so very much. I wondered if I'd be so sad about my own parents, that maybe I ought to care about them more.

Sure enough, she said, 'You're lucky. You have parents.'

'I suppose I am… I suppose we only notice things we don't have. That's the way I felt at Morland Hall. All that cheerfulness made me sick, but gradually I started getting happy because everyone understood me and was kind. I wanted to stay there, the radio, making things, reading, chatting, watching patients come and go.

'Then my mother made me come here. I was furious and frightened, but little by little I've given up being miserable. Of course I wish I could run and play sports. But then I'd still be at Bannerman. I shudder to think how I'd have turned out.'

'How lovely it is,' she whispered. 'And look up at the butterflies. So many, so many. Do you know any?'

'I see a red admiral, I think.'

'You're right!'

'But what are these others?'

'Well, there's the tortoiseshell, the comma. Talking of butterflies, there's somewhere else I want to show you, where I found a White Admiral. Very rare. It's called the charcoal den. But it's best in the evening, so one can see the charcoal glowing. There won't be a white admiral, though.'

Chapter 44

I told Mrs Fox that I'd be joining the Grumbars for dinner – which was mostly true. The only difference was there was no 's' at the end of the name.

The next day I was in last year's beige summer jacket; it was too small, but after much deliberation with Marshall, we decided if I didn't button it, it would do. My uniform wasn't right for a picnic, Marshall insisted. But the palaver made me late.

Mary was sitting on the folded quilt, on top of our streamside rock, looking crossly at her watch.

'Hello,' I called. When she turned, her mouth, her whole face opened into happiness.

'About time,' she said, more like herself. She hopped off the rock. 'Let's go. Take the basket, will you?'

We headed along a vague path that disappeared into what she called Oldpond Copse, a crowded, dark collection of ancient trees – bent, but full of pale green leaves, like any young sapling. 'I love that colour,' I said. 'Primavera. Italian for "first green." You know, like in the painting.' I'd heard Alastair say this, and thought I'd try it on her.

'No. No idea.' She pushed on, holding back a long shrubby branch so I could pass.

Bugger. She thought me a show-off and she was right.

Through many tangles of twigs, bushes and honeysuckle we slogged until, after several hundred yards we came upon a wide, open glade, spreading out before us. She had said it was lovely, but never had I seen loveliness like this. Pink foxgloves grew in profusion and heavy-scented honeysuckle climbed through brambles, making golden hills. Behind them, columns of trees made the light dim, and in the middle of it all, in a large grassy area, were the charcoal kilns – great metal cylinders, about six of them, glowing softly, with smoke rising from tall chimneys mounted on their sides.

'I told you,' she said.

'You were right.'

'Don't worry about the kilns. They'll just perk along, glowing and smoking all night, it's so calm and sheltered here. Mr Valentine will check them in the morning.'

'Do the Grumbars – do your parents – know we're here?'

'Oh yes. They know I'm safe with you.' Couldn't they have considered the possibility that I might be a dangerous sort?

'I'm glad you like it here,' she said, spinning slowly, arms outstretched as if embracing the perfection around us. 'I was worried I'd raved too much and you'd be disappointed. The butterflies are sleeping, but soon the fireflies will come out. And we might hear a nightingale.'

'I don't even know what one sounds like.'

'You will. Come on; let's get the picnic out. I'm starving.'

We spread the quilt and took out food, our hands bumping as they reached into the basket. 'Sorry,' she said. 'I'll hand you things. But wait! Look how different our hands are. Hold yours out, next to mine.'

I already knew her hands: small and brown, lightly freckled, with slim, fine fingers, but I did as she said, glad that Mother always said I had good hands.

Mine were massive beside hers, her fingertips ending halfway up my fingers. It seemed such a cosy, friendly thing to do. But I felt my stomach swirl. Her nails were tinted brown as if the soil of the earth had become part of her. 'I did wash them,' she said, 'but they're always like that.'

'Mine are clean because I don't do much with them. The only work I do is writing. I've got a writer's bump on my middle finger. Look.' I touched it with my thumb. 'Feel, here.'

'Oh, yes. So you do.' She ran a finger over it, and my hand – my body – the universe – surged with pleasure.

'That's nothing. I have a chopper's finger, here, see all the little lines from cutting carrots and such?'

All I could do was nod. At least I remembered to close my mouth.

My eyes caught hers. We looked down.

'Crikey, I'm hungry,' she said, and I remembered the thing called food.

We ate the cheese and blackberry-jam sandwiches, drank the lemonade. I tasted nothing.

'That was delicious. Thank Mrs G for me.'

'I will. We'll have to come here in the daytime. When there are the butterflies.'

'Yes.'

'When are you going back? To Scotland, I mean.'

'The twenty-ninth.'

'Of July?'

I nodded.

'Of course, July. Silly me.'

The light was fading, but replaced by a warm orange glow from the kilns and the setting sun behind the trees. I felt shy, as if in church, but no church was like this.

'Graeme?'

'Yes?'

'Over the past couple of weeks, I've been wondering, I mean, we've spent so much time together and – I enjoy – teaching you, since Finzi's been gone.'

'Right,' I sighed. 'Good old Finzi. How is he?'

'I haven't heard, actually. He's written to Father. Anyway, you and I have spent a lot of time together these past couple of weeks.'

'You must miss Finzi. But don't worry, he's just been busy.'

'Why are you on about him? Anyway, what I'm wondering is – that is, for me, over the past couple of weeks – my feelings, er, for you, have changed, and I find myself, er, liking you more than just as a friend and I'm wondering whether you might be beginning to feel perhaps the same way.'

I stared at her. 'But what about Finzi?'

'What about him?'

'But aren't you…?'

'What?'

'Sweethearts.'

One would have thought I had just performed the funniest Groucho Marx sketch ever.

'Moodie, you – are – crazy!' she laughed, drawing the words out. You may be as clever as Albert bloody Einstein – but you don't know anything about people.'

'That's not true.'

'Well, you don't know about Peter Finzi.'

'Perhaps not.'

She drew in a huge breath and let it out. 'If Peter Finzi is sweet on anyone, it's you. Peter Finzi is a pouf!' When I didn't speak, she added, 'You know, a fairy, a…'

'I know what a pouf is!'

'He knew it was hopeless because you weren't made like that. All he did was talk about you. How fair you are with everyone, but not vain, how the other boys think highly of you, ask your opinion on the world situation; how brave you are, on and on.'

'That can't be true. Yes, I like people to think highly of me, but I never dreamed they actually did. If they said something nice, they were just feeling sorry for me, or I'd tricked them. I'm nothing special, deep down.'

'We don't have to be special. Being ourselves is enough.'

'But I have polio. Had.'

'Er, I think I've noticed. And so? It made you who you are. It's part of you. Like being an orphan is part of me. But it's not who I am. You're not a leg, I'm not an orphan. Bad things happen, but we're always us. But what I want to know is...'

'Yes. The answer's yes. To what you asked.'

'And what did I ask?'

'You know.'

'So you do like me – more than just as a friend.'

'Yes.' I could hear her swallowing. I waited. Had I said something wrong again?

'What are you thinking?' I asked.

'I'm thinking it's time you kissed me.'

How easy it was – astonishingly easy. We were born knowing.

Chapter 45

Marshall helped me make my final choice of photos. The limit was twenty, so I had to take away four. I spread them on my bed with captions below, cut into neat strips.

Marshall, however, had other things on his mind. 'Has his majesty finally decided it's time to spill the beans?' He was furious I'd refused to say a word the night before, following my moonlight visit to the charcoal den. But I couldn't. Talking might jinx it. 'Come on, tell me just a little: a bean or two. Did you kiss?'

'What do you think?' I tried to look serious.

'Judging by the look on your face – the cat that got the cream – I'd say yes.'

'And you'd be right.'

'Hurray!' He jiggled his fists in the air. 'What was it like? Tell me, tell me. Was it difficult? How did you know what to do?'

'I just did. Particularly by the third kiss.'

'You're killing me, you know. Details, please.'

'Well… one takes hints from the other. Little wordless clues… like in… bridge.'

'Bridge?' He screwed up his face. 'Come on.'

'Sorry, Marshall, but there are no words.'

'Well, you can't say "bridge." Hmmm. Something more poetic. Crikey! I never even dared kiss Joy Brabyn.'

'She wasn't the one for you, that's why.'

'No. I see that now. I couldn't compete with Nicky Littman's guitar. But she broke my heart. For a couple of days I considered killing myself.'

'Good God! You hid it well, I must say.'

'Of course. We're British. Now,' he said, clapping once, 'Back to the photographs. Does the first one have to be me in my pyjamas?'

'Yes! You start the day. It's crucial!'

Every shot had life coursing through its veins – I hoped. Caspari, poring over his notebook amid a stack of books; boys sunbathing on the roof; flames sizzling at a Boy Scout campfire, the muscular twist of Littman's back after whacking a cricket ball; the Captain in my doorway, about to inspect my room. The light and composition weren't perfect, as they were in Caspari's photos, but mine told a story of variety, learning and comradeship, that made Maiden Erlegh, Maiden Erlegh.

Cutting out four was excruciating, but Marshall and I were ruthless. Also, I'd told Mary I'd meet her by the stream at four.

* * *

'Come here. Just here,' Mary said. She took my hand and led me through a young-tree thicket, where birches grew. The branches soared above our heads; even mine, which was getting higher all the time. Mr Fairbank would be at my boot again. Shh, Moodie. Shh.

I pulled her closer and leant against the smooth bark of a tree I now knew to be a sycamore. She lifted her face, the sun dappling her freckled cheeks and the light touching her brows and lashes with copper, the first pretty thing I had noticed about her.

She might have kissed me first, it wasn't clear, for there were many. So much lost time to make up for and only a week of school left.

* * *

We met most days. She still brought *Countryside Companion*, more to reassure Mrs Grumbar, but she did quiz me now and then. I even told her about Franklin Roosevelt, who became president of the United States, even though he had polio. She smiled, understanding the logical conclusion. 'Your future awaits you, Prime Minister Moodie.'

One afternoon she said, as we lounged on the quilt in the charcoal glade, 'There's one place I've never been.'

'Where's that?'

'The cottage on Maiden Erlegh Lake. I've been to the island many times, but not inside the cottage. It's always locked.'

'Yes, I know. There's a key, hidden nearby.'

'Do you know where?'

'Oh yes. Under a sculpture of Pan.'

She rolled onto her knees. 'What are we waiting for? Let's go.'

'No, no. I can't.' My terror of drowning rose in a panic.

'Why? What's wrong?'

'I don't dare. I blame the horrible Mr Fairbank. He warned me never to try to swim. I'd sink immediately. Like a stone. The words were always "Like a stone." Never anything else.'

'Hello, did I mention swimming? We'd go in the rowboat!'

'Still no. Maybe if Finzi were here. He'd be strong enough to drag me out if we tipped over.'

'We're not going to tip over. There's no wind! It's a perfect day. Let's take a wee peek, as you would say.'

I'd never seen the lake up close, partly because of my fear, but also, the lake house seemed a forbidden place, for older boys, the nearly-men. I imagined it to be dark and shadowy.

* * *

What I saw from the water's edge was completely different. The cottage on the island was white, not dark, with half-timbered beams radiating above the front door. An A-shaped thatched roof hung over a wide porch, where lawn chairs glowed in the late afternoon sun.

And as if by magic, the structure appeared to hover twelve feet above the ground.

I couldn't believe my eyes. 'It can't be floating.'

'No.' She laughed. 'It's built on stilts – to guard against flooding. Not very glamorous, but it looks like a miracle. You can just see the staircase leading up, behind the shrubbery.'

'Yes, I see now. Amazing.'

'I'm dying to see the inside. You won't say no, will you?'

'No.' Disappointing her was impossible.

'Thank you, Mr Moodie!' She kissed me chummily on the cheek. 'And here's the *Queen Mary*.' She pointed to a green rowboat, lying a little away from us upside down. With no effort, she flipped it over.

'Let me give you a demonstration of my nautical abilities.' She scrambled neatly onto the boat, balancing herself with a hand on each side. Sitting on the middle span, she saluted me, pushed away with an oar, and took off, dividing the water with terrific force.

'And if, *if,* she said, on her return, 'you did fall in, I could pull you through the water, no problem. People don't weigh much, you know, in water.'

'I never thought of that.'

She pulled the boat up sideways to the shore. 'Come on, Moodie,' she drew the words out, coaxing, 'Trust me.'

With the boat up close, I saw that the manoeuvre wouldn't be that different from Solly Joel's bathtub, of which I was a master. This was lower and wider, but I would use the same technique.

'Very well. If you insist.' I knew I could do it.

She watched from a respectful distance as I swung one leg, then the other. 'Sit on the floor, in the middle. Safest place. Ballast.' Once I was settled, she gave the boat a big heave-to, jumped in like a spider scurrying and took the oars; off we went, steadily, the rhythm sure.

But the key wasn't under the statue of Pan. 'Strange,' I said. 'Maybe someone's moved it.' We searched the shrubbery, under clay pots, a small boulder, but nothing.

'Under the front stoop?' Mary said. 'That's where we keep our extra one.'

'Isn't that too obvious?'

'Maybe, but nothing's dangerous around here.' She peered under the steep, tall stairs and shook her head. 'Bloody hell. We came all the way here and we can't go inside.'

'I know, it's a bugger. Hey, let's sit in the chairs. The porch is so high, we'll still be in the sun.'

'You get cleverer all the time. Let's go.'

She went first; I followed; and her bottom looked so fine as it moved, step by step, I was almost glad we couldn't get into the cabin. I might forget I was just fourteen.

When she got to the top, she turned, and I saw those eyes, that face, smiling again because of me. She took my hand, put her arms around my neck.

Kissing Mary was everything wonderful. Always different, always the same. So many lovely and different ways to kiss her lips, her mouth; and – another miracle – she felt the same.

We sat on the stretched-out chairs. 'This is the life,' I said, but the happy remark trailed away. 'But not for long.'

'You'll go home in a week.'

'I know.' I reached out for her hand. It felt chilly. 'My parents are taking us on a cruise through Norway.'

'Sounds nice.'

'Sounds horrible to me. All those fiords. Claustrophobic, cold.'

'Better than working at Culham's. When are you back?'

'The end of September. The twentieth. We'll write, shall we?'

'Every day,' she said.

'I don't know about that. My parents will get suspicious. Maybe change your handwriting on the envelope. I can say you're different pals.'

'What a good idea. And I'll use different envelopes. We've got all sorts around the house.'

It took a few seconds for me to realise I was hearing music. Something I knew well.

We looked at one another, alert, muscles flexed. We kept listening. One of Alastair's favourites.

'It's coming from inside,' Mary whispered. 'Someone's there.'

'What should we do?'

Behind us, a loud creaking, slow and long. A door opening. Mary jerked. I scuffled to stand. In the doorway was someone in uniform. A bright red armband with its black swastika shone. Rudy Boch, with a small smile carved on his face. Mary stood, too.

'This is a surprise,' he said.

'Indeed,' I said.

'What are you doing here, as if I have to ask. I come here to think and dream. To play my Schubert, but you wouldn't have heard of him.'

'I have. That's his *Trout Quintet.*' Thank you, Alastair.

He raised his eyebrows. 'Well, well. You're full of surprises, Moodie. Please be polite enough to introduce me to your – what's the word – crumpet?'

'Fuck off,' Mary said.

Boch laughed. 'A young lady of good breeding, I see.'

'How did you get here? Where's your boat?' I asked.

He laughed again. 'You're remarkably thick, Moodie, for someone who's going to make a thousand a year someday. There's another rowing boat on the other side of the lake. I used that one. Well, I'll be off.' He looked down at himself and patted the black swastika on his arm. 'I just need to change.'

He started for the cottage door but turned back. 'I feel sorry for you, Moodie. You're a decent enough fellow, but you'll never survive the invasion. You'll be put down like a lame horse. No good to anyone.'

I couldn't hit him, I didn't dare. He might throw me down the stairs. He was strong and I was weak. He could do whatever he liked.

'Oh. Would you like the key? Just put it back under Pan when you leave.'

'No,' I said. 'We're leaving now.'

'Yes,' Mary added, 'You've polluted the place.'

'Pol… pol… What is the word? I do not know it.'

'It means you've spread shit everywhere. The place stinks.'

The smile stopped as his jaw went hard. 'You better be off before I forget my manners.'

He went inside, thank God, and closed the door. We heard the key turn the lock.

My legs shook as we went down the stairs and headed to the shore, where the boat lay.

'People like him don't deserve to live,' Mary said, setting the oars in place.

I climbed in. 'That's what he thinks about people like me.'

'Stop being so fair! You think I give a pig's arse about him?'

She pushed us off, and after a few strokes, stopped. 'I can't tell you how much my legs were shaking as we went down the stairs. I wish I'd been as calm and brave as you were.'

Chapter 46

With Mr Mellor's assistance, I hung my photo-boards in the Palm Court. 'A two-man job,' he said.

When we'd finished – him on a stepladder, attaching wires, me hammering the lower-down nails – he asked, 'May I look?'

'Of course.' I tried to sound off-hand, but my heart lurched. My precious darlings, about to be scrutinised by the world. 'They tell a story, sir, so you must start here.' I pointed to the first photo on the left-hand board. 'Read the words underneath.'

'Sounds intriguing.' I knew he'd do his best to be kind, but one could always tell the difference between true enthusiasm and just being polite.

He read aloud as he walked. 'At Maiden Erlegh School' (my excellent shot of the front door, gleaming letter-box, stained-glass coat of arms) 'we sleep a lot' (good old Marshall in pyjamas, stretching) 'we eat a lot' (the Captain's table; boys' backs straight, perfect manners) 'but the staff eat more' (Miss Taylor and Mr Humphreys, hunched over plates, open-mouthed, forks poised to shove in huge amounts of food; I couldn't resist!).

'Close to the wind, Moodie, close to the wind, but hilarious!'

'Do you think Miss Taylor will mind?'

'Let's hope not.' He laughed. 'But no. She has a good sense of humour.'

He moved on, past the sports photos, the Scouts, Calinescu's Cord, the fire drill, the Captain standing in my doorway, about to inspect my room.

I could tell he liked my work: the way his face lit up as he examined details. When he got to the last, he gave me a crafty smile. 'I was wondering when you'd get to me.' The photo showed him sitting at a desk piled with books, with Caspari at his side. '"Strange to say, we even do some work." Bravo! The assignment was "Life at Maiden Erlegh" and you've certainly done that, with some mischief and humour, too. Well done.'

* * *

Three days to wait. Every boy could vote for two, with the Captain, Mr Mellor and head boy, Saywell, having the final say. Normally, we didn't have competitions within the school; the excitement and tension were strange, unsettling. The Captain tried to make light of it in his lunchtime talks. 'Never since the great election of 1854, has so much hung on a result. The uncertainty is agonising.' Everyone laughed, but then he put up his hands. 'Seriously, lads. This is not life and death. Everyone who submitted is a winner.'

I inspected the competition. Seventeen entries hung on the circular walls of the Palm Court and as I walked by them, each drawing either pleasure at my superiority, or fear that some photographs were better than mine

Calinescu's photographs worried me. They were in colour, which might impress the ignorant. Also, he'd placed them in a big, red leather album – a note on the table explained – because the delicate colours might fade. Delicate, hah! All of them were oversaturated, the reds too red, the blues too blue. I hoped people would see that.

The last entry on my tour round the room was Caspari's. He'd only submitted three, but they were so perfect, so lovely, I couldn't move.

He'd name them Water, followed by One; Two; and Three. First was Djalal's white Arabian horse, muscular and gleaming with sweat, as a sponge washed him down; then, a sailboat, its triangular mainsail, dark against a setting sun. But the third stopped my breath. It was Solly Joel's cottage on the island, which I vowed never to see again. But here it was, hovering weightless above low bushes, the scene repeating in the ridged lake water coming toward me, before Boch ruined it.

I felt sick. Its beauty mocked me. You'll never take a photograph as beautiful as I am, it whispered. My photographs were rubbish, boyish jokes and silly captions. For an instant I hated Caspari for his artful skill. Mine were lame, no good to anyone. I walked out onto the terrace.

Where could I go? The sun was cruel, too bright. My room, too small. Woodbine Cottage, too far.

I walked alongside the house to where the stone terrace ended; under a canopy of trees stood the prayer temple, where I'd been inspired to write up the Captain's account of the school's history. Unchanged, its slender pillars rose to the dome, made of brass from India. The rule was, if we saw someone there, let him be.

Someone was sitting there now, looking out over the rose gardens, with a long cigarette holder. The Captain. I stopped abruptly. He turned and raised a hand. 'Graeme,' he called. My first name. 'Come.'

'I'm not disturbing you?'

'No. Please, have a seat.' He rolled his shoulders and stretched his neck, side-to-side. 'I was miles away. What have you been up to?'

'I've been to see the other entries at the Palm Court.'

'Ah, yes, the photographic competition. What do you think about it? Good idea?'

'I'm not sure. I walked around, looking at the other entries, feeling either better or worse. I didn't behave very well, in my head.'

'That's the trouble with competitions. I wish I hadn't agreed to hold the damned thing, but there seemed a kind of doldrums at the school, everyone exhausted from thinking the unthinkable.'

I felt badly for the Captain. I'd not seen him so low since before the Munich Agreement. 'Well,' I said, cheerily, 'I'm looking forward to coming back, preparing for Oxford.'

'I'm glad.'

'That will be so exciting.'

'Yes.' The man of many words scarcely had any. He was thinking of Hitler. I knew the news was bad these days, but I couldn't bear the papers. All I wanted was Mary.

'Sir,' I said, in almost a whisper, 'We won't go to war – will we?'

'I hope not. That's why you find me here, praying.' He gestured to the brass tendrils overhead. 'Nothing more I can do. Poland may be next, I'm afraid, and that will be the end. The fellow with the silly moustache may be a monster, after all.'

'We can't go to war!' I wanted to put my hands over my ears. 'My parents say I can't come back if there's a war. The Germans will be bombing London. Surely that won't happen, will it?' I sounded childish.

'The problem is, Moodie, we don't know the future. We must wait for the history books. Meanwhile we can only use our best, deepest judgment with what we know. And one thing I do know is that war is a crime. Atrocities may make one more powerful for a time, but they don't solve the most fundamental question on earth, which you mentioned before: how do we get along with one another? And if we can't do that, everything else falls to pieces.'

We looked at the rose garden below, already past its best. Petals littered the ground.

'Selfishly,' he went on, 'if there is a war, Maiden Erlegh will suffer. No one will want to travel through London to get here.'

* * *

The tap on the water glass sounded. Captain Fox stood, his old self again. 'Gentlemen, never, when the idea of a photography competition was raised, did I imagine it would turn into a matter of world importance. The prime minister rang me yesterday, hoping to get the results. I told him he had to wait like everyone else.'

Thunderous laughter, shouts, hear-hears.

'The decision has been made. *Alea iacta est.* The die is cast. We shall adjourn to the Palm Court, where you will find ribbons on the three winners. I shall lead you, like some silly sergeant to battle.' He reached to the floor to lift – not a rifle – but a tennis racket, and slung it over his shoulder, army-style. 'Fall in behind me, two by two! Left-right, left-right, left-right.'

The boys were confused at first, but I saw precisely what he was doing. By his silliness he punctured the competition's overblown importance. Soon, eighty of us rolled along on a wave of absurdity. Some skipped; some whistled 'Rule Britannia', others just marched, left right, left right. What a genius the Captain was, to transform the competition into just a bit of fun.

Marshall and I fell in together toward the end of the queue. As we approached, wild shouts came from inside the Court's open doors. I thought I heard my name. Don't be silly, pillock, but then, when they saw me, it was like the parting of the Red Sea. They stepped back, shooting their fists up in the air. Someone shouted, 'Three cheers for Moodie,' then came the usual answer of 'hip-hip-hooray' – but never had it come for me. I'd won. First Prize. Caspari, Second. Calinescu, Third.

I knew the Captain was right. Yes, yes, none of this should be taken seriously. It was just a bit of fun.

Nevertheless, I couldn't have been happier than if I'd been elected prime minister.

Chapter 47

'**M**oodie! Mr Champion, First Class!'
I was glad to see old Calinescu. After all the hoopla, my room felt empty and lonely. Marshall had gone to Woodley Airfield, mad keen to see some aeroplane called the Hurricane. But I wanted more hoopla, festivities, praise.

'Listen to this!' Calinescu commanded. 'I have an idea you cannot refuse.'

'Shall I save time and just say yes, then?'

'Ah, you are a funny man, Moodie!' He grabbed my shoulders and grinned like a jack-o'-lantern. 'You, me, Caspari celebrate our victory at The Three Tuns. After dinner. I buy.'

I backed away. 'Nice idea but perhaps not. The Captain doesn't approve of us going there.'

'Ah, but there you are wrong, my fellow. I ask Caspari. He ask the Captain. The Captain say yes! If we back by eleven.'

I'd never been to a pub without adults. Calinescu was right. I couldn't refuse.

* * *

Also, I was worried about Caspari. He didn't behave like himself – as if a Caspari-doll had usurped the real one and only I could see it. He was still courtly and patient; he said the proper things, but if I could look inside his chest, I'd find that a motor had replaced his heart. There was no light in his eyes. Even when he won second place in the photography competition, only a faint energy glowed, then disappeared. I remembered being like that when I took ill. Enduring was the best one could do.

I would write to him from our family's cruise through Norway's fiords; and when I came back, when the Hitler business had faded, the real Caspari – who loved art, music and theatre – would return.

We agreed to meet in the front hall after dinner, having changed into our civvies. The Captain didn't want us advertising Maiden Erlegh School in pubs. Calinescu shook our hands, as if we'd achieved more than a photography competition, and off we strolled, into the summer evening. The light, already a month past solstice, was fading.

The Three Tuns sat back from the Wokingham Road, looking like a haunch of raw beef against the bright lamps beside the door. The old pub had been knocked down a few years ago when the road was widened. A peaked-roof centre section had wings stretching in either direction, a separate door in each. 'We go in here.' Calinescu pointed to the middle bit. 'I come here many times. The publican expects us.'

As Calinescu opened the heavy oak door, an explosion of light, noise and smells assailed us. Hunched backs of men in caps lined the bar, which seemed a live, chugging thing, as the servers pulled the brass-knobs mounted on the ends of white china handles. On the wall behind, thick shelves held glasses, bottles and towers of cigarettes. A sign warned 'no betting' and a wall clock boasted 'no tick.'

Spotting us from behind the bar was a ruddy-faced man, king of all he surveyed. His white shirt was sharply pressed, his braces tight. 'Mr Broodbank,' Calinescu told us. 'The publican.'

The man nodded and came round. 'Good evening, Mr Calinescu. This way. I've put you in a cosier room. Ruby will come round to take your orders.'

Calinescu grinned at us as we followed. 'I look twenty-one,' he whispered. 'You don't. He hide us away somewhere safe.'

After we'd sat in our snug, little room, Ruby arrived. 'What'll it be gents?' When had I ever been called a gent?

I couldn't take my eyes off her. She wore a splendidly tight jumper and her hair was a shade of blond I'd never seen, more like pink. 'Three pints of your India Pale Ale,' Calinescu said. 'Only the best for my friends.'

My mouth watered as she placed the frothy, golden nectar before us. We talked about this and that – other entries in the Competition; our cameras; the *Maiden Erlegh Chronicle* coming out at the end of the month. Summer plans would normally be next, but I knew Paul wasn't going anywhere. Mentioning my Norway cruise would be unkind.

'How happy I'll be to be home in Romania!' Calinescu said. 'Father says it is safer these days, more soldiers protect our house. What will you do, Caspari?'

'Ernest and I are staying here, helping the Captain with summer parties.'

'You no go home?'

'No,' was all he said.

'You a Jew?'

'Evidently so.'

'Oh. That's all right. I don't mind. You stay here for the summer. You safe. You lucky.'

The muscles in Caspari's jaw throbbed. 'Perhaps. But I have a mother who is not so lucky. She can't leave Germany.'

'Oh. Well. Down with the Nazis! Need war now! Hitler will stop at nothing. He kill the Jews. He even kill good Christians in Romania!'

I could bear no more. 'Listen, Calinescu.' I felt I was talking to a five-year-old. 'How about we have the same rule we have at school – we don't talk politics at table. As the Captain says, it takes away the appetite.'

'Moodie's right,' Caspari said in the same explaining tone. 'He and I never discuss the world situation. We've agreed to disagree and that's the end of it. He thinks Hitler can be reasoned with, while I know he can't. He's not human.'

'I see,' Calinescu said, humbled. 'I thick sometimes. My apologies.'

A hulk appeared in the doorway, darkening the room.

'Finzi!' I scrambled to my feet. We shook hands heartily. 'What a surprise!' I hadn't seen him since he'd gone to train with the Harlequins. His chest, in a navy jumper, swelled from within a too-small woollen jacket. His face glowed with a sheen of sweat.

'I found you!' he said, overjoyed. 'Captain Waterlow Fox said you'd be here.'

'Sit down, sit down. Another round!' Calinescu cried. 'What would you like, Finzi me lad? I'm buying. The Best Ale for everyone.'

'Just lemonade. I'm not allowed alcohol. I would like something to eat, though.'

'Leave it to me, I find. The publican and I are friends. You no drink, Caspari?'

'I'm fine for the moment.' Caspari placed his palm over his glass.

'Just a half for me,' I said.

'Righty-ho,' and Calinescu was off again. Finzi took off his jacket and sat, a picture of flowering health. His torso looked sculpted, all traces of boyish flesh pared away. Even the planes of his face were sharper. Inside, he was what I remembered, flustered and cheerful, but he'd discovered words! He told us about his training, the weightlifting, the slow and fast running. Best, he said, was the food. 'So much meat and eggs! I never see so many vegetables! Mountains of everything!' He stopped and turned red. 'I forget myself! Tell me about you, Moodie.'

'I'm fine. I'll be back in the autumn, preparing for Oxford.'

He smiled. 'And how's Mary?'

'She's very well.'

'She wrote me about your... your... romance.' This time I went red. 'I knew she loved you, but you did not see it.'

We laughed. 'I know,' I said. 'It took a long time, but eventually we managed, Mary and I.'

Calinescu slid in bearing drinks, followed by Ruby, with a platter of cheese and bread. 'Who's Mary,' he asked, plopping the drinks on the table.

'Moodie's sweetheart,' Finzi said – and no one was surprised. Moodie's sweetheart. I let the words flow over me.

'So,' said Calinescu, taking over the conversation once again, 'you play for the Harlequins, eh?'

'In the autumn I will.'

'How I love that team. Their jerseys are beautiful, the four quarters of different colours.'

Finzi looked round to make sure no others could see. 'Like this?' he said, pulling up his jumper. Underneath were the Harlequin squares of maroon, blue and grey. I thought Calinescu would faint. He flopped back in his chair, arms limp.

But he revived quickly. 'Listen!' he said, 'I have a Cord automobile. You know the Cord?'

'No.'

'Oh! Just you wait. It's the most beautiful car in the world, isn't it, lads? And such a funny thing...' and off Calinescu flew, recounting the tale of Marshall disabling the Cord. 'I nearly kill him but I see the funny side of his trick. Will you be here tomorrow? I take you for a drive. Excuse me. I go for piss.'

'Piss away,' Caspari said.

When he returned, he moved in close, beckoning us nearer. 'Guess who is out there, playing darts?' We looked up. 'Rudy Boch.' Caspari jerked as if a prod had hit his shoulders. 'I hear he's a Nazi.'

'You hear correctly,' Caspari said.

'Well, well, who have we here?' In the doorway stood Boch, his measly frame so different from Finzi's. 'The winners of the Photographic Competition if I'm not mistaken. And Finzi, too!' He leaned against the doorjamb, giving him the onceover. 'You have done well for yourself, haven't you? I say, anyone for darts? I warn you, though, I'm good. Who dares play against me?'

Caspari was already preparing to stand. 'I, for one.'

'Shall we all play?' I said cheerfully. There might be safety in numbers.

Caspari put a hand on my arm. 'I prefer to play him alone.'

I knew what an excellent dart-player Caspari was. He often played with Ernest at the stables and taught me the basic rules. 'Moodie will keep score,' Caspari said. 'Keep us honest, eh, Boch?' I got up; my mouth dry.

This might have been fun, just an ordinary game. 'Finzi and I stay here,' Calinescu said. 'He hungry and I want to hear more about the Harlequins. You speak Romanian?'

'No.'

'Never mind. I try speak Bulgarian. Our countries neighbours.'

'Let us speak in English, yes?' Finzi said. 'We live here.'

'Very well. Did you know my father is…'

* * *

The dartboard room, on the other side of the bar, was much colder. A chalkboard hung on a wall beside the outside door. 'Shall we play 301 or 501?' Caspari asked. He dusted off his hands and smoothed his lapels.

'It won't take long to slaughter you. Let's make it 301.' He paced, keen to begin battle.

'Very well.' A couple of men at a small table watched, heads lifted, dull eyes glazed.

I wrote their names at the top of both columns, reviewing the rules in my head. Both players began with a score of 301; the aim was to reduce one's score to exactly zero, by landing darts in different sections, each having a number stamped on it. For the players, and the scorer, the tricky part was keeping the subtractions correct; not an easy feat, when one is under the influence. I'd had a pint and a half but knew I should manage.

To begin, one had to land on a tiny section marked '20,' which earned double points, before advancing any further.

Boch went first. 'Watch this,' he said, standing behind a black line on the floor, called 'the oche marker.' Threw. Missed.

'Aw, too bad,' Caspari said. 'You must be out of practice.' He landed a perfect 'double' the first time. 'Hmm, a lucky shot.' He smiled as he elegantly stepped aside.

Ten minutes later, Boch had only just scored his 'double'; but Caspari was down to 167.

In another ten, Boch saw the situation. He was getting slaughtered. He blamed me. 'That's not right, Moodie, you idiot! My score should be lower! You're cheating. I shot a triple last time.'

'No, you didn't,' one of the geezers said, all dullness gone from their faces; they sensed the tension and were watching like hawks. 'It were a double, warn't it?' he said to his pal.

'It were.'

'Well, then, you're a lying bastard, Caspari. You're an expert and never said.'

'Was I obliged to?' He spoke with icy sweetness.

'You dirty Jew. I don't know why I even play against you. Just wait! You'll see what's going to happen. Britain doesn't stand a chance. Our Luftwaffe will destroy your cities. London will be in ruins!'

'I very much doubt it.'

'You do, eh? Here's more! Your Jewish whore-of-a-mother will be gassed like all the other *Judenswein* and fed to pigs. My father told me the Fuhrer's secret plans. *Endiosung Judenfrage.* There won't be a Jew left in all Europe. We won't stop till you all are dead.'

Caspari's face went white. Boch switched to German, his hand piercing the air in fury, like his hero did in cinema newsreels.

From my friend came a long, inhuman cry like those I imagined soldiers made as they climbed over their trench into no man's land, but Caspari was no soldier. He flailed at Boch's chest, like a child, getting nowhere. He stopped, and the two faced each other, inches away. Boch stepped back, twisting, gathering his mouth strangely, and spat a generous wad of saliva in Caspari's face.

Wild beyond thought, Caspari leapt on him, his heavier weight falling upon the fiend. As they fell, I saw Caspari's hands tighten around Boch's neck, squeezing, squeezing. I knew he would not let go.

Boch's arms groped the air, useless, as they rolled on the floor, then Boch went still and reached a hand down his leg, feeling for something. I heard a heavy in-breath; a slower outbreath. Boch spun from the motionless Caspari and stood.

But my brain could not make sense of what I saw. Boch had something grey in his hand. Parts were dark and dripped thick spots on the floor. Only when the knife fell, making a clattering sound, did I understand.

Boch ran at me, aiming for the door that led outside, as my arm – uncommanded – held out my stick as he passed. It caught his ankle, bending it sideways as he fell, hard, onto the floor. '*Scheisse!*' he shouted, yet instantly rose, beyond pain. Limping, he made for the door and was gone.

'Help!' I shouted, 'Someone help! My friend's been stabbed!' The two geezers just stared. 'For God's sake, get the publican!' I ran to Caspari.

A faint groan trickled from his open mouth. His hands fumbled over the wound on his stomach, trying to staunch the blood that oozed between his fingers.

'What's happened? Christ almighty,' Mr Broodbank shouted hoarsely. He knelt beside Paul. 'Don't you worry, lad. You're going to be all right. We'll look after you.' He took his handkerchief, gave it to me. 'Press,' he said, 'as hard as you can. I'll phone for an ambulance. Keep talking to him.'

'Won't that take too long?' I asked, desperate, shaking. 'Can't someone drive him?'

'Mind you keep pressing. No, Berkshire Hospital's very good. They're nearby. Don't worry, lad. Leave this to me.' I did as he said, thankful for his calm. He must have been a soldier in the War.

Finzi knelt beside me. 'Tell me what to do.' Calinescu stood nearby, saying nothing. 'What should we do, Graeme?' Finzi said again.

I blew out a plume of air. Steady on, Moodie, I told myself. I willed my shoulders down and thought of Boch, who was now running away. The ambulance was coming for Caspari. My duty was to stop Boch. I pictured him staggering up Maiden Erlegh Drive, but remembered that shorter paths cut through the woods. Did he know them? Which way would he go? Yes, once at the school, he'd get his car and drive to London, to the German Embassy. He'd have diplomatic immunity. He'd be free.

I stared at the floor, making a stillness inside me, once again. In less than a minute, a plan took shape.

'Calinescu, here!' I took out my handkerchief and instructed him in the way Mr Broodbank had shown me with his, now sodden with blood. I tore a sheet of paper from my diary and with my fountain pen wrote a note as neatly as I could, using the diary's cover as a table.

I folded the paper and said to Finzi, who was still kneeling beside me. 'I want you to run up Maiden Erlegh Drive as fast as you've ever run in your life. You know where Captain Fox's quarters are?'

'I do not.'

'Right,' I gasped, thinking, thinking. 'Top of the big staircase, turn around and go back to the rear of the house. Door on the left. Fox as a doorknocker. Give this note to the Captain. You understand?'

'I understand. I go.'

I knelt by Caspari, talking to him. His eyes were open, but unseeing and by the time the ambulance came, he was unconscious, making no protest as they lifted him and carried him away.

The walk with Calinescu back to school had never seemed longer, yet my gait had never been faster. 'You can go ahead if you want,' I said to Calinescu.

'Never. I stay with you.' He aimed his torch on the ground ahead of us. I wondered what we'd find when we arrived. Boch's fate would have been decided. The Captain would have acted or not. There was nothing more I could do.

We rounded the tree-lined curve toward the house. I saw lights, a promising sign, then more lights spilling out onto the lawn, the drive, the small car park. We got closer. Under the porte cochère stood Captain Fox in his dressing gown, next to a big black car that looked like a London Taxi, but for a lit-up sign saying 'Police' on the roof. 'Keep going,' I said to Calinescu. 'I need to find Boch's Opel.' We found it in the parking area, dimly lit by a tall lamp. I touched the bonnet. It was cold.

Seeing me walking back toward the police car, the Captain beckoned. I was afraid to approach. Everything was still unclear.

In the pale light, his face was grey, leaden. 'Congratulations, Moodie,' he said grimly. The police arrived just as he was attempting to start his car – the car I disabled, thanks to your note. I obeyed your orders, though I loathed carrying them out. If I hadn't, Boch would have driven to the German Embassy, and he'd be free as a lark – a grave injustice.'

'Tom!' I heard a woman cry. It was Mrs Fox, in a near gallop, her hair streaming behind a fur-collared dressing gown. 'The hospital's phoned. Paul is about to have surgery, but he should recover. None of his vital organs are affected.' The Captain held her tightly. I was pretty sure they were crying. I wanted to but couldn't.

After she'd gone back to the house to make up hot toddies for medicinal purposes, the Captain asked me to walk back with him. 'Why couldn't I cure him, Moodie?' he asked me.

'I don't know, sir.'

'We gave him every advantage, every benefit of the doubt. He abused every gift.' We walked on.

'Thank you sir, for disabling the car. I know it went against your principles.'

'It had to be done, didn't it?'

'It had to be done.'

'Still, I failed him. I failed him.'

Chapter 48

Mary saw me off at Earley Station. I had my long, overnight journey ahead, once so difficult, now as easy as breathing.

Speaking was harder. We stood on the platform, each looking away, afraid to look at each other.

'I don't want to say good-bye,' was all she could manage, her voice all on one tone.

'Let's not then. I'll see you in two months.'

'That seems too long.' She turned to me, laying her forehead on my chest. I put my arms around her, but she pulled back. 'I hate feeling like this. My protection's gone. Like a crab that's moulted.'

I laughed. I couldn't help it. Then she did, too. 'You're right. We should think about the autumn.'

'Good idea. In September – I'll be fifteen – at last! I'll be studying for Oxford. Seminars with Captain Fox and Mr Mellor. Independent study.'

'I'll be preparing for Reading University, reading biology and entomology. Oh! I wanted to tell you, I've already looked at trains. There's a direct train from Oxford to Reading. Guess how long it takes?'

'Does it go through London?'

'No.'

'An hour?'

'Twenty-five minutes.'

'That's all?' I asked.

She nodded. 'No stops.'

The train shuddered in earnest. More smoke gathered round the wheels.

'Enjoy Norway.'

'Enjoy Culham's.'

'I'll send you flowers from the field. Oxeye daisies, starflowers, poppies.'

'Maybe not poppies. They're bad luck.'

Her brow furrowed then unfurrowed. 'Yes, I suppose you're right.'

'Let's forget bad luck,' I said. 'Send lots of flowers. Send poppies! Who cares?'

A loud, spitting whistle blew, reminding me of the long journey ahead as I travelled up the country, past all the cities, fields and farms that lay between her spot on earth and mine.

We kissed quickly, awkwardly, too embarrassed to do more, with people around. I mounted the iron stairs and located my little room. She walked along the train till we found each other through the window. I absorbed each detail, memorising her face, the way a photograph did.

The train moved. She ran a few steps to keep up. I pressed my cheek on the window to see her for as long as I could, until the train pulled away and her face slipped out of sight.

The End